Pam EVANS

Lamplight on the Thames

HEADLINE

First published in 1990 by
HEADLINE BOOK PUBLISHING PLC

First published in this paperback edition in 2016 by
HEADLINE PUBLISHING GROUP

1

Cataloguing in Publication Data is available from the British Library

ISBN 978 1 4722 4364 5

Typeset in 12/14.25 pt Bembo by Jouve (UK) Milton Keynes

Printed and bound in Great Britain by CPI Group (UK) Ltd, Croydon, CR0 4YY

MIX
Paper from
responsible sources
FSC® C104740

Headline's policy is to use papers that are natural, renewable and recyclable
products and made from wood grown in well-managed forests and other
controlled sources. The logging and manufacturing processes are expected
to conform to the environmental regulations of the country of origin.

HEADLINE PUBLISHING GROUP
An Hachette UK Company
Carmelite House
50 Victoria Embankment
London EC4Y 0DZ

www.headline.co.uk
www.hachette.co.uk

To my husband Fred,
with love and gratitude
for understanding my compulsion to write
and for his practical help with research.

Chapter One

Saturday tea-time was Bella Brown's favourite time of the week. Its special blend of homeliness and holiday pervaded the parlour in a warm, enveloping tide which imbued her with a sense of belonging at number nine Napley Road, Fulworth-on-Thames, West London.

Such was the case one Saturday in July 1944 when she was seated at the tea-table with her sister Pearl, their cousins Trevor and Donald, and the boys' parents, Violet and Wilfred Brown, with whom Bella and Pearl had lived since their mother's death four years ago.

Insinuating rays of sunlight crept patchily across the worn wallpaper and the semi-circular wireless set resting on top of the mahogany sideboard, and beamed a pale light on to the cluttered mantelpiece. There was a round oak clock, a china crinoline lady, a Toby jug, some framed photographs, two brass ashtrays and an opened packet of Players Weights, all coated with a film of debris dust which clung persistently in times of enemy activity. An ageing mirror hung over the unlit hearth and on the window sill sat Tiddles, the tabby cat, his huge yellow eyes fixed on the family in a mixture of hope and disdain.

1

Their lively conversation was halted only by the appearance of one of Vi's special Saturday teas: tinned pilchards, salad and bread and butter, with rock cakes to follow, was no small treat after the weekday regime of bread and dripping.

Thoughts of the evening ahead lapped pleasantly over Bella. They might listen to the wireless, or play a game of cards, or perhaps even go to the cinema with Auntie Vi while Uncle Wilf went to the pub or to ARP duty. And later would come the highlight of the week – chips in newspaper, if they could find a fish shop that was frying. And the proceedings were further enhanced by the blissful anticipation of another holiday tomorrow, though Sunday, dimmed by the shadow of workaday Monday, never held quite the same magic.

All of this was with Mr Hitler permitting, of course, though the doodlebugs didn't seem to cause quite the same disruption as the air raids earlier in the war. Mainly because the alert was in force so often many people only dived for cover if in immediate danger and ignored it otherwise. Auntie Vi said that the war would soon be over now that there had been a breakthrough from the Normandy beachhead.

'Do yer want that last bit of tomater, Bel?' asked twelve-year-old Donald, his blue eyes glinting hopefully in his freckled face. ''Cos if yer don't, bags I first claim.'

Bella was jolted back to the present. Anyone slow to finish invited persuasion, bribery or even robbery, especially when a few rare slivers of tomato graced the plate. She looked uncertainly at her cousin who was smiling seraphically, his normally wild ginger hair combed into place in deference to the mealtime. He was a natural extrovert, his many pranks a source of amusement to the whole family. 'Oh, orlright then, you can 'ave it,' she said.

2

But Auntie, a staunch upholder of justice, intervened firmly. 'No, Bella luv, you eat it. 'E's 'ad 'is.'

The girl's conscience was nudged, however, by the memory of Donald's recent generosity with some aniseed balls, and she decided on a compromise. ''Ere yer are then, you can 'ave arf.' And she sliced the coveted morsel in two and slipped half on to his plate. The light caught her profile, the thirteen-year-old's indeterminate features beginning to firm with incipient womanhood, long dark lashes fringing rich brown eyes just a shade or two lighter than the raven hair tumbling wavily to her shoulders.

'Yer a greedy pig, Donald,' taunted her cousin Trevor who was the same age as Bella. An angry flush suffused his thin face. 'Yer oughta be ashamed of yerself takin' the food from someone's plate.' He was the serious one and had a slightly authoritarian attitude towards his brother.

'It was only a bloomin' bit of tomater, mate, not 'er rations for the week,' said Donald, grinning wickedly and showing no signs of remorse.

'Just the same yer shouldn't . . .' Trevor began.

'Boys!' Auntie's voice cracked through the room like a whip, producing immediate silence. 'If Bella wants to give 'er food away that's up to 'er but I won't 'ave bickerin' at the table. Pack it in or you'll be up those stairs and into bed so fast yer feet won't touch the ground! And the gels can 'ave your share of the rock cakes.'

A death threat couldn't have been more effective, and with order restored Auntie collected the plates and took them to the kitchen. The boys' banter and subsequent admonishment were an integral part of family dialogue and by the time she returned, a few minutes later, all was outwardly calm. But it

3

was at that moment that Bella detected subtle undertones in the atmosphere which, on reflection, had been present all day. There was nothing she could put her finger on, but she felt darkness lurking beyond the levity.

She studied her aunt for a clue, since something must have created the sensation of foreboding. But Auntie seemed to be quite normal and was pouring tea from a large brown pot whilst keeping a shrewd eye on the rock cakes which were disappearing faster than butter on crumpets.

She was a stout woman with wild ginger hair which she made ineffectual attempts to control with kirby grips. Lively blue eyes dominated her round, freckled face which wore a permanently pleasant expression by virtue of the fact that her wide mouth turned up slightly at the corners. Her short-sleeved cotton dress was topped by a wraparound floral apron and displayed strong freckled arms. A forthright person, she never bore grudges and was not a creature of moods. As a girl she had been in service as a kitchen maid but was now employed by the school meals service as a cook, something for which she was eminently suited since she was never happier than when at the oven, even in these times of desperate shortages. Bella thought she was about thirty-two, which was six years younger than Uncle Wilf. To Bella she represented integrity and stability and the girl loved her dearly.

'Gawd, Vi, is this washin' up water?' asked Uncle Wilf, making a face and setting his tea cup down on the saucer. 'It's 'orrible.'

'You'd 'ave cause to complain if it was, mate,' snorted Vi, her snub nose twitching slightly. 'We're low on tea, so drink it and look 'appy – there's thousands worse orf.' Her unusually abrasive tone confirmed Bella's premonition. Auntie had something on her mind and it wasn't good news.

The bombshell came when everyone had finished eating and the spirit of Saturday was destroyed forever, or so it seemed to Bella at the time: the children were to be evacuated to the country because of the proximity of the flying bomb attacks. They were to catch the train to Dorset in the morning. It was all organised. Auntie had arranged it with a friend from work and had said nothing until it was absolutely necessary so as not to spoil their day.

Some children might have loved the idea, but the Browns had had a miserable evacuation in 1940 so the news was greeted with gloom and accusations.

'You said we'd never 'ave to go again, after last time,' reproached Trevor, his greasy brown hair flopping limply on to his brow.

'Yeah, you promised,' agreed Donald, this unwanted development uniting him with his brother against their parents.

'Mebbe I did, but now we've got no choice but to send yer. It won't be for long and you'll enjoy it once yer get there.' A strawberry flush suffused Vi's face and neck and her voice wobbled slightly.

'I ain't goin',' announced Donald, rebellion gleaming in his eyes. 'I don't wanna live with people we don't know in some 'orrible country place.'

But now his father intervened. 'You'll do as yer told, me lad.' His pale factory complexion was smudged with a dark shaving shadow. A stockily built man, he had thinning hair and grey eyes set in a square face whose abundant hollows and lines produced an appearance of toughness. He wore blue serge trousers fastened to braces which stretched over a white shirt from which the collar had been removed. He was not a hard man despite his normally brusque manner, but the emotion of the moment lent an even gruffer edge to his tone. 'We're doing what's best for yer, so no more of yer lip.'

Bella had turned pale during all this and twelve-year-old Pearl had burst into tears. 'I don't wanna go away, Bel,' she sobbed, staring miserably at her sister with wet blue eyes.

Acutely aware of her powerlessness over the situation and her duty to her sister to remain strong, Bella rested her slender hand on Pearl's arm in a comforting gesture. 'We'll be orlright, now don't you make a fuss or you'll upset Auntie,' she said.

Auntie Vi lit a cigarette and inhaled deeply. 'Gawd Almighty, you're goin' to the country, not to the bloomin' front line.' She drained her teacup and Bella noticed that her hand was trembling. The young girl heard the pain in her aunt's voice as she said, with forced firmness, 'You've gotta go, kids, so make the best of it and 'elp me by packin' yer things.' Into the sad, resigned silence her next words seemed to imprint themselves indelibly on Bella's memory: 'And chin up, troops, you're Browns remember, and we don't let things get us down.'

Upstairs in the girls' shared bedroom, Pearl's tears had turned to tantrums, which was usual when things weren't going her way.

'If Dad was 'ere, he wouldn't send us away. I 'ate Auntie Vi,' she said, sitting mournfully on the edge of her bed with her head in her hands.

Bella sighed. Pearl could be very tiring. 'You shouldn't say that about 'er. She's been good to us. And it ain't 'er fault. The government is tellin' people to send children away. I 'eard it on the wireless.'

But Pearl's self-pity was fathomless when she was in this mood. She threw herself dramatically on the bed face downward and punched the pillow. 'And what'll 'appen to us if this 'ouse is bombed with them in it, like what 'appened to Mum? They'll put us in an 'ome then 'til Dad gets back,' came her muffled lament.

Fear shot through Bella in electric waves. 'Don't even think about it,' she snapped, blocking the dreadful memories from her mind. 'That won't 'appen again.'

''Ow do yer know?'

'I've got faith that it won't,' she said firmly.

But no matter how brave Bella managed to sound to Pearl, she herself felt sick with worry. Not about going to the country, but about what might happen while they were away.

She glanced around the room with the nostalgia born of imminent departure. It was situated at the back of the little Victorian house overlooking rows of narrow gardens and the rear of another tightly packed terrace. Each house in Napley Road had a parlour, a best room and kitchen downstairs, and three small bedrooms upstairs. The residents were more fortunate than many in the surrounding streets of this shabby part of Fulworth in that they had the benefit of a bathroom.

The room was sparsely furnished but spotlessly clean. Two single beds, covered with well-used pink and white damask bedspreads, stood on a polished linoleum floor along with a light oak utility wardrobe and chest of drawers. Diagonally set across the latter was a lace cover on which stood two mother-of-pearl brush and comb sets which had been given to the girls by their mother before the war.

'Better start packing,' suggested Bella, removing some clothes from a drawer and laying them on her bed.

'I ain't doin' mine yet, there's plenty o' time,' said Pearl, sitting up now and looking gloomily at Bella. From the next room came the sound of the boys' sparring – the thud and slither of their bodies against the wall as they wrestled, accompanied by roars of laughter. High spirits never deserted them for long. 'Sounds like they're 'avin' fun in there, I'm gonna see what they're doin'.'

Because Pearl needed regular reminders not to be selfish, Bella said, 'Well, don't leave yer packin' to me or Auntie. You must do it yerself.' The year that separated Bella and her sister often felt like a generation, since Pearl was young for her years and Bella surprisingly mature. Most of the time Bella took the supervisory role she had inherited from their mother in her stride, but occasionally it was a burden for one so young.

'I *am* gonna do it meself,' said Pearl, flushing.

Bella winced guiltily since she was fond of Pearl, in spite of everything, and knew that she needed her elder sister right now. The light from the window fell across Pearl's small, thin body and Bella was reminded that although her sister might not be bright, she was certainly pretty. Her cornflower-blue eyes were set in a doll-like face with a dear little nose, lips so pink and shapely they might have been painted on, and golden curls framing it.

'Just make sure yer do,' said Bella severely, then added in a softer tone, 'Go on then, orf yer go.'

Watching her depart, her scrawny shape clad in a white blouse that Auntie had made from an old bedsheet and a dirndl skirt that had once been a summer dress of Bella's, the older girl sensed that her sister's combination of petulance and prettiness somehow made her vulnerable, though she didn't know why. Within minutes of her going, shrieks of laughter erupted from the next room. Auntie was right: the Browns might not be rich but they were certainly resilient.

Welcoming the rare solitude Bella sat on her bed and closed

her eyes, resting her fingers against her temples in an attempt to erase the feeling of *déjà vu* that engulfed her. But the situation felt identical to that other time in 1940. She was filled with trepidation but admonished herself firmly. If she was to be able to reassure Pearl, she must maintain her own confidence.

But the room was suddenly so dear it brought tears to her eyes. She registered as though for the last time the fresh scent of starched cotton sheets and floor polish, the whiff of carbolic soap drifting from the bathroom. Anger eliminated sentiment. Why did people have to die and families be separated just because those in power couldn't get things right?

She crossed the narrow landing to the bathroom and washed her hands and face, her skin smarting from the harshness of the soap. It was a small room with brown stains on the yellowing white bath, a cracked handbasin and a toilet with a long chain with a ball on the end. Floorboards peeped though the brown linoleum and a tarnished mirror hung over the sink. Dipping her toothbrush into the tin of toothpowder she brushed her teeth in front of the mirror. Large luminous eyes stared back at her from an olive-skinned, heart-shaped face. After rinsing her mouth she studied its shape which was wider than Pearl's, with a deep bow in the upper lip. Like her mother her nose was straight and finely cut; Bella was proud to have inherited her dark good looks.

The door handle rattled. 'Who's in there?' called her uncle.

'It's me, Bella.'

''Urry up, duck, I'm desperate.'

'I'll just be a minute,' she said, aware of a recent, but increasingly familiar, longing for privacy.

Back in the bedroom she could hear the distant sound of

Auntie and Uncle talking above the drone of the wireless, and the boisterous cries of Pearl and the boys sliding down the banisters. Thuds and bumps and excited squeals echoed through the house, filling Bella with a curious sense of exclusion. She felt neither child nor woman, increasingly at the mercy of curious and conflicting emotions. There was the passionate longing for escape from the family, whilst loving them and wanting the security of home, too. There were, shamefully, dark, bitter-sweet sensations which seemed wrong in a decent girl like herself. There had been tears, too, and she'd never been a weeper. Strange to think that this time next year she would be working and paying her own way. But right now she needed to get out of the house for a while, to breathe freely, get her thoughts in order and prepare herself for the parting.

'I'm just going round the corner to say ta-ta to my friend Joan, Auntie,' she announced a few minutes later. 'I'll finish me packin' when I get back. Shan't be long.'

'Orlright, luv, but if the siren goes makes sure you take cover.'

'Yes, Auntie. Ta-ta.'

'Ta-ta, luv.'

Violet Brown stood anxiously by the window, watching Bella hurry down the street. She had to be careful not to be over-protective towards the children during these dangerous times. She sent them to school and let them go out because life had to go on, but she wouldn't have a moment's peace until Bella was safely home again. Still, Bella was growing up, she needed a degree of independence now. This time tomorrow they'd all be in the safety of the country, Vi thought, but drew little consolation from the thought.

How callous they must think her to send them away again. But what choice did she and Wilf have? It wasn't right to leave their young lives at risk. And it surely wouldn't be so bad for them again. Last time their homesickness had been made all the more acute by an insensitive foster mother, blind to the extent of their suffering. Their premature return, immediately the raids began to ease off, had been precipitated by a letter from the aforementioned lady complaining about the children's *disgusting* habits, not least the fact that Donald had become an eight-year-old bedwetter. Never again, Violet had vowed in the emotion of their homecoming. Sorry kids, she thought to herself now.

Conscious of the fact that the girls would, quite naturally, be questioning their future security, Violet's thoughts turned to their mother, Phyllis, the late wife of Wilf's younger brother Bob. Drawn together by the brothers' closeness, Violet and Phyllis had become firm friends. The two couples had lived in close proximity to each other, and as the children had been born within a short time span they had always been more like sisters and brothers than cousins.

When, back in the thirties, Bob had lost his job in vehicle maintenance at the docks and joined the dole queue, Violet and Wilf had put their fireside and food at his and his family's disposal, for Violet had personal experience of hardship and she knew of its demoralising effect. The daughter of an unskilled dockworker, she had been raised in the East End in abject poverty. When she had met Wilf, at a dance at the Hammersmith Palais, and later married him, it had been a blessed relief to move across London to his slightly more genteel patch.

With the outbreak of war, Bob's mechanical skills had once more been in demand and he'd found employment at a small car repair workshop in Fulworth High Street, repairing and servicing essential vehicles. Wilf, who was a welder, had gone on to factory war work, Violet had put her culinary talents to good use at the school, and Phyllis had taken a job as a domestic assistant at the hospital. Apart from missing the evacuated children dreadfully, life had been tolerable for them all until one night in September 1940 when Bob had arrived at Violet's door, ashen-faced and inconsolable. His home, with his wife in it, had received a direct hit while he had been out on ARP duty. Even now Violet couldn't remember that night without wanting to break into sobs as Bob had done then. Nor could she recall him breaking the news to the girls without the same thing happening.

She had gone to Somerset with Bob to give him moral support. Pearl had succumbed to immediate hysterics on hearing the news, whilst Bella had turned scarlet, then chalk white, and had busied herself in calming her sister. She still hadn't found relief in tears when Violet and Bob had returned to London. But several weeks later Trevor had mentioned, in a letter, that Bella had been in trouble with their foster mother for crying for a whole day.

Shortly after that they had all come home to number nine where Violet loved the girls as if they were her own. When their father had eventually been called up into the REME, Violet had thanked God that Wilf's age and pierced ear drum would keep him at home to support her in her task of maintaining a stable family life.

Outwardly Violet favoured neither girl, but in her heart she had an especially soft spot for Bella. Whilst Pearl sought favour through her cherubic looks, Bella, whose dark nascent beauty was not yet fully apparent, earned her aunt's affection through her strength of character which was quite astonishing for one so young. Soon she would blossom into a stunningly beautiful woman like her mother, but right now the poor child was beset by the agonies of adolescence.

Watching her turn the corner and pass out of sight, Violet's heart lurched. Bella might very well be going to her friend's house, just around the corner, but after that she might be tempted to head for the river which she had loved passionately since she was a small child. Out of concern for her aunt's peace of mind she would not mention this when leaving the house for raids in that direction had been increasingly frequent lately.

Violet's glance scanned the street scene on this summer afternoon. Front doors were open and women stood gossiping on their paths. Groups of men chatted in the smutty street, while the few unevacuated children played hopscotch and hide-and-seek as exuberantly as ever. People looked shabby and run down. It had been a long war. She turned away and breathed deeply to quell her fears. Bella was a sensible girl, she'd not expose herself to danger unnecessarily.

Bella's aunt was right. After briefly visiting her friend, Joan Willis, the girl continued through the narrow streets past endless reddish-brown brick terraces with slate-grey roofs, separated from the pavement by gardens measuring no more than two yards in depth. Small, dusty shops broke the monotony – a newsagent's, a shoe mender's, a chemist's, a butcher's with an empty window – between gaps in the landscape accommodating only piles of rubble. Many of the houses had blown-out windows covered by sacking or board.

Skirting the allotments she went under the railway bridge displaying a poster which warned: DON'T TAKE THE SQUANDER BUG WHEN YOU GO SHOPPING. Bella's throat was dry from the soot in the air, but she scarcely noticed it in her haste to reach the river. She was so used to the characteristic street smells of industrial Fulworth she barely noticed the lingering scent of yeast from the bakery, steam from the laundry, acidic chemicals from the print works and the ever pungent smell of hops from the brewery.

She crossed the High Street, a wide shopping promenade with cinemas, pubs, dance halls and a variety theatre. As she took a side turning the street scene changed, war-torn still but becoming noticeably more salubrious. Luxuriant trees overhung lamp posts in the wider avenues of Upper Fulworth where laburnum-gardened semis and detached houses replaced the terraces. There were graceful Georgian squares with lawns and chestnut trees, playing fields with cricket pitches and tennis courts, and Fulworth Green with its glorious oaks and duckpond. Excitement speeded Bella's step as the earthy smell of the river grew stronger. She took a narrow lane and there lay the Thames, gleaming in the sunlight. Distantly downstream lay Chiswick and the city, upstream was pretty Strand-on-the-Green nestling below Kew Bridge.

Situated north of the river as it was, Fulworth was an area of many different faces. Passing through the elegant residential area, Bella now found herself in a thriving commercial stretch of the river. Men were unloading barges at the wharf on the opposite bank where angular factory buildings rose darkly to the sky, whilst boat repairs were in progress at the boatyard this side. Grimy tug boats hauled loaded lighters up and down stream, billowing clouds of steam from their funnels, and a police launch chugged by on its regular patrol. Wartime meant working weekends for many people.

Continuing along the river's edge past the ancient Seagull Inn, Bella came to one of the most beautiful riverside promenades for miles. Here, abundant willows and silver birches, lilac trees and banks of wild flowers, overhung the river wall. Backing on to the promenade were large gracious residences with names like Riverview and Tides Reach. Bella remembered a time before the war when the lamp posts along here had touched the dark waters with gold at night. That had been in another, simpler life when she and Pearl might come here some summer evenings for a stroll with their parents before pausing at one of the quaint pubs where their father would buy them lemonade to drink in the gardens.

Pausing by her favourite of all these houses, Bella stood and stared. Ivy House was a three-storey redbrick property with balconies to the upper rooms. The eponymous ivy covered much of its walls, and stone steps led up to an oak door with a large brass doorknocker. It was one of those houses that induced curiosity. Who lived there? What was it like inside? Different to anything she had ever seen, that was certain.

She turned back to the river and stared at its dark waters, rippling with compulsive life force. To Bella the river was much more than just a strip of water on which to transport goods, or to paddle in. It was a living thing with its own personality and sudden changes of mood. Smoky industrial areas surrendered instantly to lush meadows with a mere bend in its course as it murmured and whispered on its journey from source to sea and back again in the continuous cycle. It changed with the weather and the tide. At the moment it shimmered in the sunlight, but she had seen it bubble in a storm. Now, at high tide, it lapped confidently against the green, slimy wall, but at low tide it pawed helplessly at the mud. *And it was always there.* Buildings were demolished on its banks, boats were destroyed on its waters, but the river remained. To Bella, distressed by the thought of her imminent departure, it seemed the only constant thing in an insecure world.

As she watched a cloud passed over the sun, darkening the muddy waters. Scavenger seagulls swooped and rose, and gregarious pigeons stalked around her feet. She shivered and hugged herself, feeling the material of her short-sleeved cotton dress pull across her bosom. Auntie said she was to have a brassiere soon, but not until it was absolutely necessary because of the extra drain on the clothing coupons. She turned back to Ivy House and gazed at it absently for a few moments before glancing back at the river and saying a small prayer that Uncle and Auntie might be spared for the children's return.

The damp chill of late afternoon began to fill the air and Bella knew she must make her way home. She felt better and was glad she had come. She turned away from the river and began to walk back along the promenade, unaware that she was under observation from the ivy-covered house behind her.

Chapter Two

'You seem very quiet this weekend, Dezi. Are you feeling quite well?' asked Eve Bennett from her capacious red leather armchair in the drawing room of Ivy House.

'I'm all right, Mother,' replied the young airman, turning away from the window and absently raking his fingers through his short curly chestnut hair. He was seated near the lace-curtained window just far back enough not to be visible from the towpath, since the house was raised slightly to avoid occasional flood waters. In the same way that passers-by stared curiously at the homes of the affluent, so the residents were not above a spot of casual observation themselves. There were such a variety of people out there on the promenade – dreamers, drunks, strollers, starers, punters, paddlers, potential suicides . . .

'It's ages since you've been home and you've hardly said a word,' Eve murmured reproachfully, drawing heavily on a cigarette. 'Tomorrow you'll be gone and God only knows when we'll see you again.'

'I know. I'm sorry, Mother.'

'Have you any idea when you'll next get leave?'

The steady drumming of his fingers on the arm of the

chair accelerated. 'Not until things quieten down, I suppose.'
Dezi was a fighter pilot flying Spitfires. Stationed in Kent, he
had been able to get home quite often until the long run up
to D Day, when his job had been to protect the ports and
airfields of Southern England from enemy air intrusion. After
that, with the onset of the intensive VI attacks, he had been
kept busy intercepting the weapons in the air before they
reached London. He wouldn't have made it home this
weekend but that his commanding officer had ordered him
to take a forty-eight hour pass: 'Just to keep you going, 'til
we can give you proper leave.'

Now Eve was being tiresome. 'You could try to be a bit
more sociable,' she whined.

He drew in his breath sharply. Why couldn't she see that
he needed to be left alone? 'I'm sorry,' he snapped, but noticing
her eyes moisten at his abruptness, he was ashamed. Oh God,
what was happening to him that he couldn't even be cour-
teous to his own mother? After all, he was fortunate. If there
had to be killing, he supposed doing so in the skies was pref-
erable to working with a bayonet or shooting at close range,
as was the lot of the ground troops.

When you were flying day after day the enemy airmen
ceased to be individual human beings and became mere obstacles to be exterminated, and the adrenaline flowed at such a
rate that you didn't notice the emotional side effects of a
kill – not until afterwards. At twenty, safely on ground and
on leave, Dezi felt like an old man.

He had been christened Desmond by his mother, basking
in the newly acquired refinements of a middle-class existence.
His father, Frank Bennett, for all he was a high flyer, had still
been influenced by the hard men he had grown up with in

the East End – the Berts and Syds and 'Arrys – and thought the name frankly effeminate. But rather than make ripples in the tranquil domestic millpond he had smilingly agreed with Eve's choice, immediately shortening the name to Dezi with a 'z' sound, to give it a tougher edge. The story, which was part of Bennett family history, was typical of Frank who always managed to have his cake and eat it, too. Dezi smiled wryly at the memory of his misguidedness, since one of the bravest men Dezi had known had been a Desmond.

Recently, Dezi had not felt comfortable in the claustrophobic confines of home. Flirting daily with death and living amid the boisterous camaraderie of camp life made ordinary domestic conversation an effort. But he didn't want to hurt his mother's feelings; she deserved some consideration from him. Glancing across at her he thought how much older than her forty-two years she looked, being pale and painfully thin. She smoked too much and ate too little though, since Dezi's father was as well endowed with black market contacts as he was with the cash to use them, the Bennetts' rations were substantially augmented – something which embarrassed Dezi greatly.

Mother smoked because she was afraid of the bombing. She would be less so, in Dezi's opinion, if she were to involve herself in a job outside the house like most other women who were free of young children. She darned and knitted for the troops, but she did it alone at home when what she needed was company. She had never mixed, or had much life outside the family. Dezi's father had discouraged that for as long as he could remember. Dezi and his younger brother Peter had been raised with the idea that their mother was delicate, though as far as they knew all her problems were stress-related. Dezi's entire childhood had been shadowed with hushed pleas for quiet as Mother was resting with 'one of her heads'. He had been trained to cherish her as one might treasure a Dresden ornament, to be worshipped but not cuddled or hugged. He had never had fun with her, gone for walks or played a game. She had never pushed him on a swing.

It was only in these last few years that Dezi had begun to wonder if perhaps Mother might have been happier if she had not been quite so pampered by her husband. And of course these days women who didn't pull their weight for the war effort were unpopular anyway, no matter how many doctor's certificates they produced. So unless she got out and 'did something', there was no chance of her making friends.

He realised that his mother was speaking to him. 'Please don't be sharp with me,' she said, close to tears. 'Haven't I enough to put up with with these terrible flying bombs dropping on us day and night?'

With a mixture of shame at his impatience and anger at her inability to view the war from any other perspective but her own, he made a show of remorse by going over to her chair, placing a comforting hand on her arm and saying kindly, 'Forgive me. I'm tired, I guess. Now why don't you bring me up to date with all the family news?'

Eve looked up at him through moist grey eyes set in a pale, thin-lipped face around which her greying fair hair curled wispily. Despite his irritation a rush of filial affection washed over Dezi. My father has given her everything and nothing, he thought. He has protected her from the world, but he can't protect her from the war since he has made her too dependent on him to want to go to safer pastures without him.

'All right, Dezi,' she said, taking his hand momentarily, 'you're forgiven.' And, placated, she went on happily to relate trivia regarding her younger son whilst remaining totally insensitive to the turmoil of the elder.

Dezi sighed and returned to his window seat, his glance ranging idly around the spacious and tastefully appointed room. In an attempt not to seem *nouveau riche*, his parents had furnished in traditional style. Soft chintz-covered armchairs and sofas sat on best quality Axminster in muted colours on a cream background. Finely carved occasional tables were conveniently placed, porcelain ornaments bedecked various surfaces, and original oil paintings embellished the walls. There was nothing of mere utility in the room.

'Peter will be home from school for the holidays next week,' his mother was saying.

'Will he fill the time by helping Dad at the garage?' asked Dezi dutifully.

'Oh, yes, we can't keep him away from the place. And he's a great help, apparently. Your father will be glad when he leaves school and can work there permanently, until the army grabs him.'

Fifteen-year-old Peter, like his brother before him, was away at one of the less prestigious public schools. It infuriated Frank, having striven to afford the best, to find that money alone could not breach the uppermost bastions of privilege.

'Is Dad at the garage now?' asked Dezi.

'Yes, he'll be back any minute though.' Eve sighed heavily. 'I'll start to prepare dinner soon.' She tutted. 'I'll be glad when the war is over and we can get help again. Doing everything myself wears me out.'

Dezi clenched his fists to avert an angry outburst. How could she be so blind to the hardship and suffering around her? When she lapsed into silence, he closed his eyes and found himself back in his cockpit, streaking towards a high-flying Messerschmitt. Sounds of combat split the sky as opposing aircraft locked into deadly conflict all around him. The heavens were littered with stricken planes; black smoke trails rose from victims on both sides as they fell to the ground. The sound of the guns was deafening as Dezi roared towards them ... Cold sweat broke out on his forehead and upper lip. He raised a hand to wipe it away, and was surprised to see that the hand was steady and that he was sitting safely in an armchair at Ivy House rather than in the pilot's seat of his fighter plane.

A release from the tension was what he needed. Something to blot out reality, if only for a short time. Drink or a woman, he decided. Maybe he would go to one of the Fulworth dance halls or Hammersmith Palais; there was never any shortage of available women there. And if he had no luck in that direction, he would take the other escape route and get himself blotto.

Turning back to the window he noticed a dust-smeared narrow boat heading upstream with a cargo of coal while, in marked contrast, some nearby swans gleamed whitely in the sun. He loved every aspect of the river – industrial or idyllic, commercial or residential, he was drawn to it. But today he felt nothing; even the sun glistening on the water left him unmoved.

This ruddy war is destroying my very soul, he thought, turning back to face his mother. Something outside caught his eye and he found himself swinging back sharply. There was a girl on the towpath, gazing up at the house. Nothing unusual about that. Ivy House was an impressive property, it was bound to attract attention. At first glance there was nothing particularly special about the girl either. She was an ordinary child wearing a cotton frock, white ankle socks and sandals. She was dark and slender, probably about twelve or thirteen. Her eyes, however, were certainly not commonplace. They were large and luminous and they stirred him unaccountably. Maybe it was his emotional frame of mind, or perhaps he recognised something of his own mood in her, but Dezi felt an immediate affinity with her. He knew that she was suffering some sort of trauma right now.

His mother's voice registered from far away, like a low tuned wireless. She was talking about their forthcoming meal. 'Very nice,' he muttered, having barely heard a word, and turning eagerly back to the window found himself surveying the girl's back. She was standing perfectly still with her head bowed towards the water. For a moment his heart lurched as he thought she might be going to jump in, for it wouldn't be impossible to drown along here at high tide. But, he realised, he was letting his imagination run away with him since she would almost certainly be on a bridge if she had serious suicidal tendencies.

A cloud passed over the sun. After a few minutes the girl turned back to the the house with her arms folded across her chest, shivering slightly. She looked directly at him though she didn't realise it, and despite the glass and lace curtain that separated them he felt the power of those dark eyes. She turned back towards the river, bowed her head again for a few moments, then began to walk away downstream.

Eve cocked her head, listening. 'Ah, that sounds like your father at the front door.' Her face flushed and softened as though her husband's arrival home, after just a few hours' absence, was more blessed relief than simple pleasure. No able-bodied person should be that reliant on another, thought Dezi.

As she trotted from the room to meet her lord and master, Dezi was overwhelmed with a longing for escape. He had forcibly to restrain himself from running out of the house.

His father was the last person he wanted to see just now. He needed to be at his most forbearing to cope with his father's inane insinuations to the effect that Dezi, as a young adult male, was automatically a sexual reprobate. 'I was young myself once, my boy,' he'd say with a knowing wink. Dezi intended to find a place of his own after the war, and right now he needed a respite from the family ties that seemed to be strangling him.

'I'm going out for a walk before dinner,' he called in the general direction of his parents' voices. 'I won't be long.'

Hurrying out through the back hall, he dashed down the stone steps and marched briskly in the direction the girl had taken, panic rising in him at the thought that she might be out of sight. But he could see her on the river bend near the Seagull Inn. Oblivious of passers-by he hurried after her, too caught up in his inexplicable compulsion to talk to her to realise that his actions might be misinterpreted. As if telepathically aware of his presence, she stopped suddenly and looked behind her. Seeing him flapping his arms at her, she hurriedly turned and walked on. Looking back again a few moments later and seeing him still in hot pursuit, she broke into a run. At which point the siren's woeful cry rent the city air.

With a head crammed full of warnings about sick men who tried to accost young girls in lonely places, it did not occur to Bella that her pursuer had any innocent motive. He was probably one of those dirty old men who exposed themselves in public, she thought shakily. She surmised, too, that he must be a desperate pervert to chase a girl in broad daylight when there were other people about – or at least had been until the siren went. Now, she couldn't find a living soul to enable her to adhere to Auntie's strict instructions to 'run away and tell the first person you see'.

Far more worried about the 'filthy pervert' behind her than the air-raid warning, she tore down the narrow lane and was in a road near Fulworth Green when she heard the ominous hum of the doodlebug overhead. Being faced with an imminent explosion was one thing when you were with a crowd of cheery schoolpals; quite another when you were alone. As the gravity of the situation impinged on her, Bella found herself paralysed with fear. She tried to run to the door of the nearest house but her legs refused to move. When the overhead droning stopped, indicating a few seconds 'til the explosion, her whole body turned to stone and she thought her heart would burst.

A hand on her shoulder galvanised her into action. Swinging round, she found herself staring into the light-brown eyes of her pursuer. Even now, with death a distinct possibility, indignation got the better of fear.

'Yer oughta be locked up, you do, frightening young gels! I'll 'ave me uncle on to yer, see if I don't,' she croaked, shaking so much her teeth chattered.

Undeterred, he forced her to the ground and flung himself on top of her. 'Keep still,' he urged. 'If you want to stay alive.'

Her face was squashed against the ground so that she ate the dust. Pushing her head to one side for air, she saw a flash and a half circle of fire spreading towards them. There was smoke and debris, but no sound. What was happening? Was the bomb not going to explode after all? Then there was a blast so fierce both Bella and her protector were lifted from the ground and the next thing she knew she was slumped, dazed, against a garden wall.

Chaos ensued. There was shouting and screaming and the thud of running footsteps. Thick, choking smoke burned her eyes, but she could just make out a heap of smouldering rubble on the street corner. Within minutes the area was crawling with fire engines, ambulances and police. Bella felt disorientated and peculiar, but she didn't seem to be in any pain.

'Can you sit up?' It was her pursuer, whom she now realised was dressed in Air Force uniform.

'Yeah, I'm okay,' she said, taking his hand and scrambling up. But as she put the weight on her legs they wobbled dangerously.

'Don't worry,' said the airman kindly. 'The shock will make you feel a bit strange for a while. I live near here. You'd better come home with me until you're feeling better.'

'I can't, I've gotta get 'ome. Me auntie will be worried about me.' The previous misunderstanding was bothering her. 'Look, mister, thanks for seein' me orlright. Sorry I was rude before. I thought you was one o' those dodgy sort o' blokes.' She tried to walk away through the smoking debris, but lightheadedness forced her to lean against the wall.

The airman took her weight by placing a strong arm around her. 'Where do you live?' he asked.

'About fifteen minutes' walk from 'ere. Napley Road,' she said weakly.

'You're in no condition to go there now, you're coming home with me. My mother will give you some hot sweet tea. Don't worry about your auntie, I'll let her know where you are in due course.'

'But what about you?' asked Bella. 'Ain't the explosion made you feel queer, too?'

'No, I'm fine,' he said. 'Now let's get you to my place.'

And Bella was in no condition to argue.

Even the smell of Ivy House was different from number nine. Here the air was lightly scented, like face powder with just a hint of cooking, rather than steam redolent of mealtimes past and present. Having introduced himself and his parents, Dezi settled Bella on the sofa in the drawing room with a cup of tea and some aspirin which he said would make her feel better. Then, leaving her to be tended by his parents, he borrowed his father's car and drove to Napley Road to put her aunt's mind at rest.

Whilst it was interesting for Bella to have an inside glimpse of the gracious house, she was disappointed to find that there was nothing at all gracious about Mrs Bennett. At Dezi's behest she supplied the girl with hot sweet tea, but not willingly. Fortunately he was back very soon and Bella detected a slight improvement in his mother's attitude towards her. It helped to ease the worst of her discomfiture, even if she was still terrified of breaking her paper thin cup and saucer.

Dezi told Bella that her aunt was quite happy for her to stay and have dinner at Ivy House provided he brought her home at a reasonable hour, since she had to be up early in the morning.

'Dinner!' exclaimed Bella. 'I 'ad me dinner hours ago, at dinner time.'

'Supper then, if you prefer,' said Dezi without a hint of condescension.

The dining room was at the front of the house overlooking extensive grounds beyond which lay a quiet tree-lined avenue.

The gardens were patriotically laid to vegetables and there was an elderly man, presumably the gardener, working on them in the evening sun. The furnishings in here, as in the other room, took Bella's breath away. There was a long glossy table and high-backed chairs with tapestry seats, complemented by a matching sideboard.

Elegant wooden place mats and white linen embroidered napkins replaced the traditional tablecloth that Bella was accustomed to, and instead of the food being served directly on to the plate, rose-patterned tureens were placed on the table for people to help themselves. There was none of the chipped bone-handled cutlery Bella was used to either, but heavy silver knives and forks.

It was all very grand and Bella was impressed, but having already had tea earlier her conscience was uneasy. At number nine, over-indulgence was a major crime.

'I've 'ad me dinner and me tea,' she informed them gravely, 'So I won't take much.'

And then to her amazement, since she had grown up with shortages, Mr Bennett said, 'You have as much as you like, my dear, there is plenty for everyone.'

No sooner had she recovered from the surprise than she was shocked to discover that the oxtail soup and roll and butter only constituted part of the meal. The large tureens were brimming with piping hot liver and bacon in thick gravy, potatoes, cabbage and peas. And Mrs Bennett was actually apologetic over the fare on offer. It was incredible. Why, this feast would surely feed the six Browns for three days.

'It isn't very inspiring, I'm afraid,' Mrs Bennett said, her tight little face knotted into a frown. 'We all have to make sacrifices in these hard times.' She gave a sardonic laugh.

'Liver and bacon is hardly weekend fare, but that's wartime for you.'

'It's very nice,' said Bella politely. But her cheeks were burning crossly. That woman wouldn't know sacrifice if she shared a bed with it! And how come the Bennetts had all this? Were the rich exempt from rationing or something? Anger, coupled with reaction from the explosion, culminated in a total loss of appetite and after one mouthful of the main course Bella was forced to concede defeat. 'I'm afraid I can't manage any more,' she said, far more worried about wasting the food than the malicious look being aimed in her direction by Dezi's mother.

'Oh,' said Eve in surprise, having clearly expected rapacity rather than restraint from someone of the lower orders. 'Finicky, are you?'

'No,' said Bella, refusing to allow herself to be intimidated. 'I'm just not 'ungry.'

She thought it odd that such a nice young man as Dezi should have such awful parents, and pitied him for it. Mr Bennett, a plump man with deep-set grey eyes, a pointed nose and a wet mouth topped by a bushy brown moustache, infuriated her with his air of patronising generosity. He owned a big garage in Fulworth High Street, apparently, and boasted about it for the duration of her visit. And as for his sourpuss of a wife! She had complained about everything from the drabness of blackout curtains, to that *disgusting* dark and indigestible National Loaf and the *interminably* lumpy and rubbery dried egg powder.

Neither Bella nor Dezi was saying much, since chance would be a fine thing, but when Bella was offered some sponge cake and creamy custard from a china jug, she blotted her copy book with Mrs Bennett. 'I can't manage any meself, but me sister and cousins would love me bit o' cake. So can I take it 'ome with me? It's a sin to waste food.' While Eve was still struggling to gain her power of speech, Bella damned herself forever by adding:''ow come yer 'ave so much, anyway? Are yer on different rations or summink?'

At least that brought some colour to Eve's cheeks. She turned scarlet from neck to brow. 'Good management, my dear,' she replied cuttingly.

Bella realised, of course, that she had enraged Mrs Bennett. But these were hard times; etiquette must yield to enterprise. Feeling the cold resentful waters of social disapproval rise around her, she thought she might as well drown completely. 'Can I take it then?' she asked, meeting her hostess's frowning gaze.

'Yes, all right,' was Eve's tight-lipped reply. 'I'll see if I can find something to wrap it in.'

Watching her leave the room, even her back view exuding disapproval, Bella knew that this would be her first and last visit to the beautiful Ivy House. But she certainly didn't intend to lose sleep over it.

Cursing the war which had stolen her maid, Eve sprinkled some soda into the water in an enamel bowl in the kitchen sink and began to wash the dishes, thoroughly glad to see the back of that dreadful child. Why the lower classes didn't teach their offspring manners was beyond her. After all, it cost nothing. She didn't choose to remember that twenty-five years ago she and Frank had been part of the lower echelons of society, living in rooms in a poor part of the East End. Nor did she care to recall that it was her father's earnings as a rag and bone man that had fed and clothed her as a child. Whenever these things did come, uninvited, to mind Eve used them as a yardstick against which to measure her own and Frank's inexorable progress.

Enterprising men like her husband were the backbone of the country, she thought. He had been one of the unsung heroes of World War I who had come home to find themselves jobless. Apathy had been rife, men had lost the will to work after months on the dole. But there was nothing apathetic about Frank, and although he had not had an actual job, his quick wits had never failed to put food on their table. He'd traded in the streets and pubs mostly, in those days, in watches, cheap jewellery, clothes ...

She and Frank went back a long way. They had been raised in the same street, had been childhood sweethearts and married in the early 1920s. Seeing no future in the East End Frank had worked increasingly in West London, exploiting the second-hand car market. His success had been phenomenal and within a short time he had been able to rent a yard with a small house attached in Hammersmith. From there he had bought the Fulworth site which he had skilfully built up into one of the most respected and lucrative businesses on this side of the river. With Frank's business success, the Bennetts' personal security was guaranteed and Ivy House had been their home this past fifteen years. Eve didn't consider her husband's choice of business methods to be any concern of hers. He provided well for her and that was where her interest in his work ended.

Eve did not want independence thrust on her and simply couldn't understand women who actually seemed to enjoy

doing jobs outside the home. And such appalling work, too –
cooped up in a factory all day, or working on the buses or
railways. Even the milkman was female these days. And as for
the women's services . . . well, if rumour were to be believed,
they were hotbeds of immorality. An excuse of frail health
suited Eve admirably, since the domestic chores were quite
enough for her to cope with. Besides, Frank liked things the
way they were. Eve knew he was a good man. Those who
said otherwise, and she knew there were plenty, didn't understand him as she did.

While his wife was silently extolling his virtues, Frank was
smugly congratulating himself. He was smoking a cigar in the
drawing room, happily anticipating the prospective post-war
boom in every aspect of the vehicle services industry, especially
car and petrol sales, when restrictions were lifted altogether and
motor manufacturing for the home market resumed in earnest.

Business was a consuming passion of his and he was proud
of his achievements, especially his role of provider for the
family whose material status he sought constantly to improve.
Nothing pleased him more than recalling how he had secured
a future for them in this more affluent part of London. Despite
all the reports of gloom and doom in the interwar years, there
had been money about if you searched for it. And the car-buying
middle classes had certainly not been short.

Now he was a rich man. He had a fine legitimate operation
and several lucrative sidelines that were not, perhaps, quite so
respectable. His dear Eve would never go short of anything,
he would make sure of that. The war, rather than harming
his business, had been a positive boon. Whilst it was true that

the abolition of the basic petrol ration had virtually ended private motoring, essential vehicles still had to be maintained and supplied with fuel. And as Frank had the facilities to provide both petrol and services, a government contract had not been hard to secure, especially as he had managed to retain a skilled workforce by employing older men.

His thoughts turned to one of his lesser known but highly remunerative concerns, a row of terraced houses in a poor area of Fulworth. He wondered if it was time he raised the rents of certain tenancies. People earned good money in wartime, and according to his spies in that area some of the residents could easily afford an increase. His full mouth curled into an unctuous smile as he considered the income he had enjoyed for several years from this source, which was especially profitable given the Inland Revenue's ignorance of it.

Stubbing out his cigar butt, he sauntered into the kitchen. His wife was at the sink and Frank approached her from behind, placing his plump hands on her lean shoulders, feeling her bones through her cotton dress. He loved her thinness and frailty. It appealed to the dominant streak in his nature which he saw as protectiveness.

He put his lips to her soft downy hair and said, 'Would you like to go out for a drink this evening, dear?'

Seeming almost oblivious of his embraces, she shook her head. 'I don't think so, dear,' she said in the cultured tones they had both gone to pains to acquire since discarding their humble origins. 'With all these bombs about, I'd feel safer at home.'

'Fair enough, pet,' he said, patting her shoulder. 'We've got some bottles in so we can have a drink while we're listening to the wireless.'

Eve turned to him and smiled. 'I managed to get some of

your favourite chocolate when I was out shopping too,' she said, 'thanks to the extra sweet coupons you keep us supplied with.' She dried her hands on a linen cloth. 'I was quite relieved when Dezi took that awful girl home. I didn't relish the idea of sharing our evening with her.'

'Or our chocolate,' grinned Frank, and added more thoughtfully: 'She wasn't our sort of person at all.'

'No,' agreed Eve. And they smiled contentedly at each other and went into the drawing room to enjoy their ill-gotten gains.

Bella and Dezi were still on the riverbank. Bella had wanted a last look before he drove her home.

'I've 'ad me last look, this is me very last look before I go away,' she explained. 'I won't be long if yer in an 'urry.'

'No hurry,' he assured her. 'You take your time.'

The evening was advancing and mist sat patchily on the water. 'It used to be lovely along 'ere at night before the war when the lamp posts were lit. They shone beautiful on the water,' Bella said. 'Now it's creepy.'

'Dangerous, too,' he said. 'People have drowned along here after one too many at the pub.'

She looked into the water, black now in the dusk. Ships' hooters echoed distantly and the trees on the opposite bank were shadowy and sinister. 'I never did get around to asking you why you were chasing me,' she said.

'I saw you from the window and noticed how sad you looked. I thought perhaps I might have been able to help.'

She turned and looked up at him, her eyes ineffably beautiful. 'That was good of yer,' she said, and with a total lack of self-consciousness told him all her fears.

He listened with interest and said, 'Well, you know what they say.'

'No, what?'

'Lightning never strikes in the same place twice. I don't know if it's true, but it's something to hang on to while you're away.'

'Yeah, thanks, I'll do that.' She was grateful to him for hearing her out like a fellow adult and not trying to fob her off with unrealistic assurances. Studying him, she noticed his clear-cut features, aquiline nose, firm well-shaped mouth, solid clean-shaven jawline and neck. His light-brown eyes were flecked with orange and thick lashes matched his chestnut hair, some of which was visible to one side of his air force blue forage cap he wore tilted to the left. He had told her he was a pilot and she guessed he must be very brave.

Looking at her, Dezi realised just how much he hoped things would work out for her. She was so young, so fresh, so brashly confident, yet vulnerable, too. In that moment, on the misty river bank, he wanted her to have the moon. Somehow this gauche child, so sincere in her directness, had rejuvenated him and made his job seem worthwhile again. It was for children like her he was fighting, that they might have the freedom to enjoy lamplight on the water again.

'There goes A. P. Herbert in *The Water Gypsy*,' said Dezi referring to the famous writer as he chugged by in his well-known boat.

'Yeah,' said Bella, smiling, for Alan Herbert, who lived on the river at Hammersmith, was a familiar figure on this stretch of the Thames and had served throughout the war in the Naval Auxiliary Patrol.

A pigeon waddled up to Bella and eyed her beadily. ''Ello,'

she said, looking down at the bird. She turned to Dezi. 'P'raps 'e can smell what's in 'ere.' She waved the crumpled paper bag she was clutching and, opening it, threw a few cake crumbs to the ground whereupon pigeons converged on them like crowds on an accident. 'All 'is mates are 'ere now, look. We'd better go before they 'ave the lot orf me.'

The rapport between them was palpable. Feeling inexplicably moved, Dezi said, 'Come on then, let's go to the car and home.'

When they drew up outside number nine in Mr Bennett's black Singer Saloon, Bella turned to Dezi and said chirpily: 'Thanks for bringin' me 'ome. I don't feel arf as worried about goin' away now.'

'You take care down in the country, and behave yourself,' he warned jovially.

'And you take care in that plane o' yours,' she said, reaching up and kissing his cheek.

'I will,' he said, feeling ridiculously happy.

He got out of the car and opened the passenger door for her. 'Bye, Bella.'

'Ta-ta, Dezi.'

The siren shrieked. 'Come on in now, Bella,' called Auntie, appearing at the front door. 'Thanks for bringin' 'er 'ome, mister.'

'My pleasure,' he said. And hearing his well-modulated tones contrast sharply with Auntie's unrefined ones, Bella became conscious, for the first time, of her own rough speech and decided to improve it one day.

When Bella gave her aunt the cake to distribute, Violet felt no compunction about taking it. From what she had heard those Bennetts didn't go short. Frank would be dealing in the black market if she knew anything about him. And in fact she knew plenty because she had grown up in the next street to his in the East End.

A few mornings later while Bella slept peacefully in her Dorset bed, having decided that the country wasn't half bad and their foster parents really quite nice, Dezi was in the cockpit of his plane flying over Kent on yet another operation to intercept the killer missiles on their journey from their launch sites in the Pas de Calais to London.

Firing range was crucial to the success of the mission. To shoot from too far away was to risk disabling the flying control system of the robot, which would plummet to the ground with its active warhead still intact. Too close, and the warhead would seriously disable or even destroy the attacking fighter. So the ideal distance was between two hundred and two hundred and fifty yards, which meant the lethal device could be exploded in mid air without undue danger to the fighter or to people on the ground.

Dezi curved towards his target and, reducing speed, he fired, hitting the missile but watching heart in mouth as it hurtled to the ground. Relief overwhelmed him as he glanced down to see it explode in open countryside. That must not happen again, he vowed.

Roaring onwards for a while, he noticed a colleague in combat. He hit his target, causing it to dive, then as Dezi watched in horror the English pilot rammed the warhead. The resultant explosion took the Spitfire and the brave young pilot with it. Looking down and seeing a village directly below, Dezi knew that it had been no accident. If the warhead had dropped, civilian lives would almost certainly have been lost. Bile rose in his throat and his hair and face felt sticky with sweat beneath his helmet and goggles. But he dare not lose concentration for a second or he could become another statistic.

With a presentiment of danger accelerating his flow of adrenaline, he thundered towards another target. Nerves stretched to breaking point, he drew close then reduced range and fired. A deadly flash demolished the evil intruder. Flushed with success, Dezi spun off after his next objective which he demolished, and another three besides. But after bringing his total to five he felt the control lever leap in his hand and, peering at the port wing, saw a legacy from his last encounter: a hole in the metal aileron was upsetting the balance of the plane and tilting it to the right.

The Kent countryside hurtled towards him and his stomach dropped faster than the plane. Heart pumping, but fighting to control his panic, he managed to raise the right wing by dropping the gear and using plenty of left rudder. Struggling to maintain height, he limped back to the airfield and a safe landing.

But now the horror of his colleague's death had registered properly. Dezi didn't leave the cockpit but removed his goggles and sat there in the morning mist, glad that no one was around to witness his tears. The rest of the squadron were still up there battling with the V1s.

Oh well, sighed Dezi, drying his face with a blue Air Force handkerchief, there's five of the buggers less anyway. And he found himself smiling as the memory of a young girl brightened his thoughts on this grey dawn. A skinny girl – all eyes and ankle socks. I'll bet she's livening things up in the country, he thought.

Unstrapping himself he climbed out of the aircraft and walked across to the camp office to report his friend's bravery.

Chapter Three

Bob Brown stared in dismay at the derelict shell of a building that had once been his place of work. Ned Tucker's once thriving car repair workshop, now windowless, doorless and rusted, its yard forested with stinging nettles and weeds, had deteriorated into a haven for tramps and yobs. Situated at the far end of Fulworth High Street, beyond the shopping area, it was a pathetic sight.

It was October 1945. Just a few days before Bob had emerged from the demobilisation centre wearing a brand-new suit, shirt and tie, a trilby hat, shiny shoes and a twinkle in his eyes. The war was over, he had come through it more or less unscathed, he had two beautiful daughters and he was still young enough, at thirty-six, to reshape their lives together in the free new world.

But he had quickly realised that readjustment to hearth and home was not going to be without its problems. Three years was a long time to be away from growing children. Bella had already left school and was working in the offices of the soap factory, and Pearl would soon be discarding her gymslip forever. Bob had left a couple of street happy sprouts who could be sent into paroxysms of delight by two ounces of sherbet lemons. He had returned to two budding women, more interested in cosmetics than confectionery. Father's opinions were no longer to be accepted without question, they had ideas of their own now. Not to mention burgeoning bosoms and sharp, all-seeing eyes . . .

Whilst realising that, by the very nature of things, life could never again be as it had been, he was still determined to make a home for the three of them together for as long as the girls needed it. As much as they all felt at home at number nine, it was time to move on. Being officially homeless, Bob was reasonably placed on the council housing list and wouldn't be averse to renting one of those prefabricated houses that were springing up everywhere.

His square, somewhat nondescript face creased into a frown at the scene before him. A job was essential to his plans and it wasn't going to be easy to find one immediately with countless thousands of other servicemen flooding the employment market. However, he refused to entertain the idea of another bout of unemployment. Once the country settled down properly after the war there should be no shortage of work in his trade. Already, pre-war cars were flooding back on to the roads now the basic petrol ration had been restored. They all had to be looked after. But the fact remained that his job had gone, along with Ned Tucker who had been killed in an air raid. A trip to the Labour Exchange was next on the agenda he decided, but first there was something else he must do.

'I called to see 'ow you are, Rita luv,' Bob said, resting his kindly, grey-blue eyes on Ned Tucker's widow. 'And to say 'ow sorry I was to 'ear about Ned.'

'It is nice to see yer, Bob,' she said sharing a pot of tea with him in her parlour. 'I still miss 'im somethin' shockin', and 'e's been gorn over a year now.'

'I was right choked when I 'eard, an' all,' said Bob.

Rita shook her head sadly as she poured some tea from a round brown pot and handed him a cup. 'Still, 'e went in a way he would 'ave wanted. A bleedin' doodle 'it the pub while 'e was in it.'

They both laughed and the atmosphere lightened. Ned had not been in business in a big enough way to have provided his wife with an exalted lifestyle, and Rita lived in a small terraced house not far from Napley Road. She was a plump, scruffy, middle-aged woman wearing a flowered crossover apron and a turban from which curlers sprouted at the front. Her feet were encased in dirty brown carpet slippers and her thick legs were a mass of varicose veins.

Having dealt with the condolences they chatted about more general things until Bob rose to leave, saying he was going to the Labour Exchange to see about a job. At this Rita grew thoughtful.

''Ere, 'ang on a minute, Bob,' she said, 'maybe you and me can 'elp each other in that direction.'

Bob sat down again, eyeing her quizzically. She offered him a cigarette and lit one for herself. 'Ned's workshop,' she said, tilting back her head as she drew on the cigarette. 'I wannit orf me 'ands.'

'Yer shouldn't 'ave any trouble sellin' it, but yer'll 'ave to get it done up if yer wanna get a decent price for it,' he said, absently scratching the side of his pug nose and wondering if she wanted him to do the job.

She pushed her horn-rimmed spectacles on to the bridge of her nose and peered at him meditatively. 'I won't beat about the bush, mate. My Ned left me provided for. I ain't rich but I got enough for what I need, so I ain't looking for a fortune for the place.' She cradled her handleless tea cup, sucking her slightly protruding teeth before drinking thirstily. 'So 'ow about you? Are yer interested in takin' it on?'

Being of working-class stock, Bob had never anticipated finding himself in charge of a business, however small or rundown. He was taken aback. 'Me?' he exclaimed. 'Cor, that's a laugh! Yer can't be serious.'

'Why not?' she asked.

'I ain't no businessman, luv, I wouldn't 'ave a clue about running me own show,' he said, flattered nonetheless.

Rita finished her tea then reached across and took his cup and saucer from the wide arm of his chair, and poured them both another. 'Yer wouldn't 'ave called Ned an entrepreneur, would yer? 'E was a just a tradesman 'oo 'ad 'is own place. Yer good at the job. Why not work for yerself instead of lining someone else's pockets? The car trade is pickin' up, I think you'd do well.'

Despite the absurdity of her suggestion, Bob was forced to stifle a yearning to accept. 'It's good of yer to offer me first refusal, but even if I was interested, I ain't got the dough. Me army gratuity won't be enough. Apart from the cost of makin' the building usable, I'd 'ave to 'ave enough to live on while I got started. And what about tools and equipment?'

She leaned towards him, resting her hands on her plump knees. 'Ned's gear is in store in 'is mate's shed, so that's no problem.' She tilted her head conspiratorially. 'I'll be really straight wiv yer now, Bob. I'm bein' pestered by that bugger Frank Bennett, 'im 'oo owns that great big garage the uvver side of town. 'E's after the place.'

'Well, if 'e's got the cash, why not?' said Bob.

But her eyes rolled in disapproval. 'I ain't lettin' 'im get 'is 'ands on it.'

Knowing nothing of Bennett apart from his name over a garage in a part of town he rarely visited, Bob said, 'Surely 'is money is as good as the next man's.'

'No it ain't! Not the way 'e comes by it. My Ned thought 'e was a right crook, and Ned wouldn't want me to sell the workshop to 'im.' She lowered her voice confidentially, her eyes fixed on Bob. ''E scares me, to tell the truth.'

'Is 'e threatenin' you?' asked Bob, his firm mouth thinning with anger.

'Not exactly, more like persuading, but 'e's very persistent. I think 'e plans to wear me down so that I'll let 'im 'ave the place for buttons just to get rid of 'im. I don't trust 'im at all.' She was thoughtful for a few moments. 'But I don't mind lettin' you 'ave the place cheap, 'cos I know that's what Ned would want. And at least then I could sleep easy in me bed, because once Bennett knows the place is sold 'e'll leave me alone.' She leaned back and nibbled her thumb nail. 'Yer could pay me in instalments when yer get established, if yer like, then you'd 'ave yer gratuity to get yer started. No 'urry for it, as long as I get paid eventually.'

'Well,' said Bob, brushing his straight brown hair from his brow thoughtfully and rising to leave, 'I'll certainly think it over. I'll 'ave a chat wiv me bruvver about it and let yer know.'

Whilst Violet was mildly apprehensive about her brother-in-law's proposed new venture, Wilf, an ardent socialist, was dead set against it.

'Yer'll be a fool to take it on,' he warned gravely that evening, 'You ain't the right class to be a guvnor. Yer'll lose all yer money, I'm warnin' yer.'

'I don't see why I should,' argued Bob who had grown increasingly keen on the idea since leaving Rita this afternoon. 'I know me job inside out, and thicker men than me have succeeded on their own. It's only a little workshop, not the bloomin' Woolworths' chain!'

'You've gotta think of yer responsibilities. A steady wage is what you need, mate. You stick wiv yer own class and yer won't go far wrong, 'specially now we've got a Labour Government,' Wilf lectured in his gravel voice.

Violet was more succinct. 'Get a steady job, mate,' she said.

'Me and two million uvvers,' Bob reminded her.

'There will be plenty of jobs,' insisted Wilf. 'Clem Attlee will see to that.'

The discussion was taking place in the parlour of number nine. Bella was sitting at the table doing her shorthand homework opposite Donald who was counting his cigarette cards; Pearl was outside in the street flirting with some boys; and Trevor was cleaning his bicycle in the kitchen.

'I think you should buy the workshop, Dad,' Bella chipped in, looking up and chewing the end of her pencil. 'It's a smashin' idea. I'll come and work in your office.'

All eyes turned to her. 'Thanks for yer confidence, luv,' said Bob, beaming at her.

'Take no notice of 'er,' said Wilf. 'She's just a kid.'

But his daughter's faith in him was the deciding factor for Bob. 'You and me ull make a good team, I reckon, Bella. Give me a couple of months to get started and yer can give yer notice in at the factory.'

She flushed with excitement. It was good to have Dad back home again, even though it felt a little strange. 'Really, Dad?' She smiled but eyed him cautiously. 'Do yer mean it?'

'Yep,' he said confidently. 'I mean it.'

Leaping up, Bella hugged him, recent inhibitions swept away by their sudden empathy. Then, flushed with enthusiasm, she went into the kitchen to make them all a cup of tea, followed closely by Tiddles whose calculated feline charm never failed to set Bella reaching for the milk.

She and the others had returned from Dorset at the end of March after the last flying bomb had fallen. During moments of anxiety while she was away, Bella had clung tenaciously to Dezi's 'lightning' theory. She had thought of him often on her return and hoped she might see him on her riverside walks. So far, there had been no sign and she dreaded the thought that he might have been killed in his Spitfire.

But she was too absorbed in her own life to brood, what with working all day, evening classes for shorthand and typing twice a week, visits to the cinema with Joan and long speculative talks about love and sex with her sister and classmates. Life was good. The war was over, Dad was home forever, and soon they would be moving into their own home. And as if all that wasn't enough, now she had a new job to look forward to.

'We can make ice cubes and lollies,' said Bella excitedly to Joan Willis. 'And 'ave ice cold drinks like they do in American films.'

'Ooh,' whispered Joan reverently as the girls surveyed the cream enamel refrigerator which stood glamorously in Bella's new prefabricated home. 'Innit lovely? I wish we 'ad one.'

'All the prefabs 'ave got one,' Bella informed her. 'The council supply 'em.'

She chipped some ice cubes from the metal tray and dropped a couple into a glass of lemonade which had been especially purchased for the occasion. ''Ere yer are,' she said to Joan. 'When yer come round at the weekend, we'll make some lollies.'

'Lovely,' said Joan, sipping her drink in delight.

The move to the prefab had not materialised until March 1946 and had taken place a few days ago, since when a constant stream of friends and relatives had poured through the single storey, flat-topped box to give their approval. Made of asbestos sheeting, it was situated about ten minutes' walk from Napley Road on an estate of identical dwellings known as Hawthorn Grove. The hawthorns in question separated them from a brick-built council estate. Bella thought it was wonderful, so sunny and modern with two bedrooms, a living room, and a bright kitchen and bathroom.

Joan rattled her ice cubes in the bottom of the glass. ''Oo's going to keep 'ouse?' she asked. 'There's no Auntie Vi to do it for yer here.'

'Pearl and me will do it between us,' said Bella, chewing her ice cube.

'You'll be lucky to get Pearl to take 'er turn, I'll bet,' said plump, brown-eyed Joan. 'I can't see 'er washin' the floor, or queuein' at the butcher's.'

Bella flushed. No matter how warranted, she couldn't allow criticism of her sister, not even from her best friend. 'Pearl is orlright, she'll do her share,' she said.

But Joan was right, as Bella had known in her heart all along. After several non-existent dinners, shopping that didn't appear, and dishes that congealed on the wooden draining board when it was 'Pearl's turn', Bella faced the fact that she was in sole charge. But not without constant battles with her unreliable sister who always defended herself by attacking. 'Yer should 'ave reminded me,' she'd say crossly, as if Bella was the guilty one. 'I can't 'elp it if I forgot. I'll do me share tomorrow.'

At the beginning of the year Bella had gone to work for her father and was growing increasingly close to him. She had added basic bookkeeping to her evening studies, and since her father's clerical work was growing at about the same rate as her experience, she didn't have any problem running his office single-handed. She was still in close contact with the other Browns and saw Trevor every day at work where he was employed as a trainee mechanic.

When Pearl and Donald left school in the summer of 1946, Pearl began a hairdressing apprenticeship and Donald followed his father into a factory. Whilst Trevor grew into a quiet unassuming young man, Donald became increasingly outgoing and brash. Motor cycles were a mania with him and he embarked on any number of schemes to raise enough cash to buy one when he was old enough to ride it. Anything from odd jobs to entrepreneurial ventures like selling 'lightning sketches' for one penny each which were simply jagged lines depicting lightning across a page. Since they were only ever on sale to family and friends, he was usually allowed to keep the money 'for his cheek'.

And, whilst Bella matured in her new found responsibility, Pearl became more scatterbrained and selfish. Her enthusiasm was of a different nature to Donald's, though. She attracted hordes of yobs to the gate, which would send her father rushing furiously outside threatening them with the police.

And if the boys made him angry, Pearl's inability to conform to the curfew he had set made him positively apoplectic. Bella found herself acting as permanent peace maker.

'She's probably forgotten the time, Dad,' she would say, instinctively loyal to her own generation. 'She won't be long.'

But her father would shake his head angrily. 'She's gettin' 'erself a bad name, 'angin' around street corners with yobs,' he'd say angrily. 'I won't 'av 'er disobeying me.'

Pearl's lack of remorse did not help matters either. 'I ain't a kid,' she'd say, arrogantly chewing gum while her father was reading the riot act. 'I'll come in what time I like.'

'Not while yer livin' under my roof, yer won't,' her father would shout.

'I'll leave then,' she'd fume. 'I ain't gonna stay in this bloomin' prison camp.'

But knowing on which side her bread was buttered, Pearl never did more than threaten. For all her faults, she was not without charm. Having driven Bella to screaming point, Pearl would suddenly change her ways for a couple of days. She would sweep through the house, demolishing every chore in sight, make valiant, if indigestible, culinary attempts and blow all her sweet coupons on chocolates for the family.

And Bella was enjoying life too much to be cross with her for long. As 1946 rolled into 1947 Britain was still shabby and short of everything, the cruel winter caused chaos and misery, but Bella thought peacetime was wonderful.

In the autumn of 1947 Bob Brown was feeling pleased with life, too. He had been in business for two years, had paid off his debt to Rita and had enough regular business to consider expanding his staff. Bella had proved to be a gem and ran his office with an efficiency belying her years. As well as typing all the estimates and invoices, ordering materials and looking after the monthly bills, she made up the wages, kept the accounts ready to be handed over to the accountant and dealt confidently with the customers, both in person and on the telephone. She was developing into a proper little lady with her posh telephone voice.

'I'm off now, Dad,' she said, coming to him in the workshop one evening in September. 'I've got class tonight. I'll leave your dinner ready for you to heat up if you're not in before I go.'

'Okay, luv,' he said, smiling warmly, appreciative of the fact that she managed his home with the same competence as she ran his office. He was a lucky man.

'See you later,' she said, hurrying away.

'Ta-ta, luv.'

One of Bob's daily pleasures was a pint of beer at the Lamb on his way home from work. It cleared his throat and helped him to unwind. He never stayed more than half an hour and never had more than one drink. A spot of camaraderie with the regulars was a good way to end the working day.

This evening, however, there wasn't anyone in the pub that he knew, so he stood alone at the bar, reflecting on his plans. He had gone into business with the idea of doing nothing more than making a decent living. But as things were going so well, expansion was a logical next step. Maybe he should be thinking in terms of a bank loan to modernise the workshop and later, when petrol came off ration, to apply for a retail licence.

'I understand that you're Bob Brown.' A stranger had

appeared at his side, a stout balding man with a moustache, and was thrusting a fat hand towards Bob. 'Frank Bennett.' The man paused and in the absence of a reaction, added, 'Proprietor of Bennett's Garage on the other side of town.'

Uncertainly, Bob shook his hand. Bennett had obviously done his homework to have known where to find him. But why?

'What are you having, old boy?' asked Frank, turning towards the counter.

'Nothin' for me, mate, I'm just orf 'ome,' said Bob.

Up went Frank's brows. 'Oh, come on, you can manage another, surely.'

But Bob shook his head. 'If me daughter takes the trouble to get a meal ready for me, I reckon it's me duty to eat it before it spoils.'

Frank's eyes darkened. 'Look, old boy, I would like a few words with you. And I think you'll be more than interested in what I have to say.'

A feeling of unease crawled up Bob's spine. This well-spoken man was out of place in this working-man's oasis. Here, in the public bar at this time of day, overalls were the accepted dress, not a Savile Row suit. Rita's words echoed in his head, but curiosity prevailed. 'Righto,' he said, pushing his empty pint glass forward. 'I'll 'ave arf in there.'

Frank frowned. 'Feel free to have something else – a Scotch perhaps,' he said with patent condescension.

'Just arf o' bitter,' said Bob emphatically.

Anger flared momentarily in Frank's eyes, followed immediately by an oily smile. This man is not to be trusted, thought Bob.

'I'll come straight to the point,' said Bennett as the two

men sat down at a table in the corner of the roughly furnished bar. 'I am in a position to make you a good offer for your little workshop.'

Bob might not have been a sophisticate, but he was not prepared to tolerate this sort of insolence. 'I'm pleased to 'ear that your finances are in good shape, mate,' he said, sipping his beer and enjoying the other man's annoyance, 'but I've no plans to sell me workshop, thanks very much.'

Bennett swirled the Scotch in his glass, stared into it and said, 'Oh, come on, man, you're just playing at business. I conduct the real thing. I'll give you a good price.'

'Why do yer want my place?' Bob demanded. 'Don't yer own workshops give you a good enough livin'?'

'Good God, yes!' said Bennett sharply. 'I want your little place to take my overflow.'

And the Thames flows best bitter, Bob thought. He's after my High Street position with the predicted traffic increase in mind. 'I'm not interested.' He pushed his unfinished drink away and rose to go.

Bennett leapt up and slapped a restraining hand on his arm. 'Let's stop playing games, shall we? I don't like people who don't co-operate. And I'm a powerful man in these parts.'

Though he'd never been a quarrelsome man, this sort of aggression made Bob's stomach churn. After several years in the army he wasn't about to submit to this slug of a man. Removing the clammy hand from his arm, he said: 'I don't know where you've been this last few years, mate, but this is a free country. We won the war, yer know.'

Bennett's mouth twisted sardonically. 'Don't you get funny with me!'

Bob laughed dryly. 'Just 'oo do yer think yer are?'

Drawing back from Bob, Bennett brushed his lapels with the back of his fingers as though to emphasise the superiority of his clothing. 'Is that your last word on the subject?' he asked.

'Yep,' said Bob boldly.

'You'll regret it.'

'Don't threaten me or I'll 'ave the law on yer,' said Bob confidently. But as he marched from the pub his nerves were jangling. It wasn't that he was afraid of Bennett, but he liked to live in peace with his neighbours. He had had quite enough hostility during the war.

The air outside was cool and moist, a mixture of scents permeating the atmosphere: soot, earth, wood smoke, a hint of the distant sea wafting from the river; the smell of his own particular patch of London, familiar and reassuring in his suddenly vulnerable mood. Men like Bennett were cowards, but they were dangerous, too . . .

Nonsense, Bob admonished himself, you've seen too many American gangster films. This is Fulworth-on-Thames in 1947, not Chicago in the 1920s. And as he bumped home in his dilapidated van, he banished the incident from his mind.

Frank stayed on at the Lamb and ordered himself another Scotch, idly watching a game of darts and mulling over his meeting with Bob Brown. A small crowd of men were gathered around the darts players whom Frank guessed were builders from the dusting of dry cement on their rough clothes. The tense silences while the players threw were punctuated with rousing cheers and raucous busts of laughter. This pub, with its common clientele, basic wooden furniture and sawdust on the floor reminded him of the hostelries of his youth in the East End. Though he knew himself beyond this sort of place now, Frank could feel a twinge of nostalgia at finding himself in these surroundings. It wasn't that he missed his roots; more that he felt he no longer belonged anywhere. He did not feel comfortable in company like this, but neither was he totally at home in the more elevated circles in which he now moved. Sentiment was banished with his awareness of it. The good old days were the bad old days as far as he was concerned. Good riddance to them! He wouldn't be seen dead in a place like this other than in the line of business. Thank God he could afford a more salubrious social life.

He glanced at his watch, finished his drink and left. Eve would have a meal ready for him and he hated to keep her waiting. Just thinking about her sweetened his mood. Feeling a nip in the air as he walked towards his car, he pondered happily on the fur coat he would buy her to keep her warm this winter. He had a good contact for furs, a man who didn't bother about coupons as long as you were willing to pay his price.

As he switched on the ignition, his mood blackened as his thoughts returned to Bob Brown. That man had a lot to learn if he thought he could upset Frank Bennett's plans! Frank had a rapidly expanding business and two sons working with him in it. He had big plans for the new motoring age, and a small-timer like Brown certainly was not going to stand in his way. That site was going to be invaluable as a petrol retail outlet and he was determined to have it. Bob Brown would soon learn that there was more than one way to skin a cat.

Chapter Four

'Shall we get some chips on the way 'ome, Bella?' asked Joan Willis one evening about two weeks later as the two girls collected their coats from the cloakroom after typing class.

'As long as we can walk along by the river first,' said Bella, slipping a beige velour coat over the white blouse and grey skirt which she wore with her new wedge-heeled shoes.

Joan tutted. 'But the river is out of our way. I dunno why yer always wantin' to go there, it's only a strip of dirty water after all.'

Pointless to try to explain that it was so much more – that it was the very heart of London, that it soothed yet enthralled Bella, especially now that the waterfront was lit once more. For Joan, pleasure came through food, clothes and organised entertainment. She would never understand how the sight of the lamplight shining through the willow trees and beaming gold on to the black nocturnal waters made Bella happy.

'You don't *have* to come,' she said, buttoning her coat. 'I don't mind going on my own.'

Joan sighed heavily. She was a cuddly dumpling of a girl with placid brown eyes and mousy brown hair currently resembling scorched string after an unsuccessful perm. She thought Bella's obsession with the dull old river stupid, but a visit to the chip shop was no fun alone. 'Oh, orlright, I'll come, but only if yer promise not to 'ang about for too long. I'm dying for some chips and I've gotta be in by ten.'

'I promise,' said Bella.

The tide was on its way in and, by lamplight, Bella could just make out the little rowing boats being lifted from the mud as the water pushed towards the banks. The lingering smell of paint drifted from the boatyard and the sound of singing, laughter and a honky-tonk piano resounded from the cosily lit windows of The Seagull. Strolling on to the quieter promenade and noticing the glowing windows of Ivy House, Bella found herself remembering the beautiful room behind the closed curtains.

'This is the grandest 'ouse I've ever seen in me life,' said Joan, echoing her thoughts. 'I wonder 'oo lives there.'

Bella's brief encounter with the occupants had never reached Joan's ears. Even Pearl and the boys had received only a few details. Quite why, or how, the incident had affected Bella so deeply she didn't know. Possibly because it had happened at a sensitive time it had seemed to signal a new phase in her life, but it was not something she wanted to share. 'It's the people that own the big garage at the far end of the High Street,' she said.

'Oh,' said Joan in surprise. ''Ow do *you* know?'

'Because they want to buy me Dad's business,' she said.

'Oh, I see.' Having satisfied herself as to the source of her friend's superior knowledge, Joan lost interest. The Willises, in company with the rest of the neighbourhood, thought Bob Brown had ideas above his station and was riding for a fall. 'Is 'e gonna sell it to them then?' she asked with token curiosity.

'No, he isn't!' said Bella vehemently. Until last week when

her father had casually mentioned his refusal of an offer from Frank Bennett, Bella had heard nothing of that family since her meeting with them three years ago. Upper and Lower Fulworth were two separate communities after all. Whilst remembering Dezi with warmth, his father's arrogance still registered vividly in her mind and he was the last person she wanted to take over Brown's. In fact, she didn't want it to belong to anyone but Dad because she enjoyed being involved in their own family business, and revelled in the responsibility she knew no other firm would bestow on a sixteen-year-old.

Walking back through the tree-lined avenues of Upper Fulworth to their own patch, Bella was entertained by a titillating tale of a girl in Joan's office who had 'gone all the way' with a boy recently.

The deliciously sinful story caused much feverish hilarity and by the time they reached the chip shop they were cackling helplessly, unaware that they had been followed since leaving the school.

They ate the chips under the lamp post outside the shop, savouring every salt and vinegared morsel and chattering effusively. Then they made their way home, parting company at an appropriate point along the route. Bella was still chuckling as she walked towards Hawthorn Grove through the empty streets. The lamplight shone on dewy pavements and spiders hanging plumply in webs on the privet hedges.

Startled by a sudden movement behind her, she turned to see three dark figures. Even as she opened her mouth to scream, a hard, salty hand was clamped over it. She was marched to a nearby bomb site, out of the lamplight, and as her eyes grew accustomed to the dark she could see that her assailants were men with balaclava hats pulled over their faces so that only their eyes were showing. Whilst two of them gripped her roughly by the arms, the other glared at her menacingly.

'What's going on?' she gasped as soon as her mouth was free. 'What do you want of me?'

'Ooh, listen to 'er,' said the spokesman, betraying the fact that he was not much older than herself. 'A posh voice won't impress us, darlin'.'

Her speech had improved so gradually she was barely aware of it and she now reverted instinctively to her Lower Fulworth tones. 'Lemme go,' she demanded, struggling fiercely.

'All in good time, darlin',' said the leader again. 'We've gotta give yer a message first.'

'Yeah,' came a chorus from the other two.

'You tell yer dad that Mr Bennett don't like bein' messed about by small fry like 'im. Mr Bennett wants yer dad's workshop and 'e intends to 'ave it, just you tell 'im that.'

Trembling with a mixture of fear and fury, Bella wrenched and writhed violently, but her bruises deepened as their grip tightened. 'You go back and tell your boss that we ain't selling, not to him nor anyone,' she panted.

Coarse laughter erupted around her. 'I think the little lady is a bit deaf, don't you, lads?'

'Deaf, yeah,' was the inane reply.

'You thugs just let me go. My dad will 'ave the law on yer,' she shouted.

Another roar of laughter. 'Gonna give 'em our descriptions are yer?' the leader asked sarcastically.

'They'll get yer, don't worry,' she sobbed, tears of frustration dimming her sight. 'Now just let me go.'

'All in good time, darlin', but first we want yer word that you'll explain the situation to yer dad,' said the leader.

'No,' she shrieked, almost beside herself with rage. 'Me dad ain't sellin' and that's ...'

She was silenced as the leader roughly dragged her against him. The balaclava was pulled up to release his mouth which was pressed on hers in a vulgar and repulsive action, while his other hand slipped downwards. Terrified at the implications, she pushed and kicked but since his assistants were still imprisoning her arms she was powerless. The possibility of rape seemed very real but, having apparently insulted her sufficiently, the chief thug drew back.

'P'raps that ull make you see things in a clearer light,' he said breathlessly. 'Make sure yer dad gets in touch wiv Mr Bennett to discuss 'is terms or we'll be back to finish the job. You'll get the full treatment next time, and we'll come back again an' again 'til yer dad does what we want. Get it?' His voice was as harsh as a spade on gravel.

Despite the excruciating pain from the pressure on her arms, Bella remained rebelliously silent.

'Well?' said the leader.

'No,' she rasped.

'Oh, well, it's up to you. But if yer ole man ain't come up trumps in a couple o' days, even tin drawers won't 'elp yer.' And releasing her so suddenly that she almost lost her balance, they ran off into the night.

Bella stood rooted to the spot, nauseous and shaking. The half moon, which had seemed to offer little light before, now seemed dazzling. The hateful incident had left her feeling dirty and ashamed. She vomited into some bushes before walking miserably away.

When she got home, her father was snoozing in his armchair with the wireless playing softly and Pearl was washing her stockings at the kitchen sink. All Bella wanted to do was to crawl away and hide, but she dutifully made cocoa for her father before escaping to her bedroom, wishing she didn't have to share with Pearl.

By the time her sister came to bed, Bella was buried under the covers feigning sleep, in reality wide awake and reliving the lout's evil groping, her head pounding with his threats. But she *still* wasn't prepared to tell her father. Why should he be blackmailed into something he didn't want just because of Frank Bennett's greed?

'In what way do you feel poorly? Do yer feel sick? Is it the flu? Are yer in pain?' asked Auntie Vi two weeks later, having been enlisted by Bob to investigate his daughter's mystery illness.

'I don't know,' lied Bella weakly. 'I just don't feel well enough to go out.'

On waking the morning after the incident to find herself frantic with fear at the prospect of going out on to the street, a pretend illness had seemed the only course open to her. Now she faced humiliation unless she could persuade her aunt that she was not ill enough for money to be spent on a visit from the doctor.

Every night she vowed she would go back to work the next day, but when the time came she was overcome with trembling and postponed it yet again. Added to her original burden of fear, shame at her own dissimulation weighed her down, for she knew her father needed her at the office. Alone in the house all day she peered fearfully through the net curtains, imagining the louts to be lurking just around the corner in wait for her. When the insurance man knocked at the door, she almost died of fright.

Now, Auntie Vi sighed and shook her head thoughtfully before uttering the dreaded words: 'I think we'll 'ave to get the doctor to 'ave a look at yer.'

'No, no!' objected Bella vehemently, imagining the terrible possibility of the doctor getting to the root of the trouble. 'I'll be fine tomorrow. Don't let Dad waste his money.'

Her aunt eyed her shrewdly, certain that this was a psychological problem. 'If there is anythin' you'd like to talk about, luv, it won't go any further. I won't even tell yer dad,' she said kindly. 'Us gels must stick together.'

Bella turned scarlet; did Auntie think she was pregnant? 'No, no, there's nothing, honest. I'll be fine. I promise I'll go to work tomorrow.'

Violet looked worried. 'It isn't a question of just getting yer back to work but of getting yer right. You're such a lively gel as a rule. None of us likes to see yer under the wevver.' She scratched her head.

'We'll see 'ow yer are tomorrow, but if yer still poorly we'll get the doctor and 'ave done wiv it.'

That night when Bella was thrashing around in the sheets, dreading the morning, Pearl, who was sitting on the edge of her bed painting her toe nails, asked casually: 'Whassamatta, Bel? Are yer pregnant?'

Bella sat up, white with fury. Why was everyone so convinced she was pregnant? She sniffed disdainfully. 'Of course I ain't! 'Ow can I be when I ain't even got a boyfriend?' she said, reverting involuntarily to raw Cockney, in her chagrin.

Unperturbed, Pearl continued painting, her mouth pursed in concentration. 'Orlright, orlright, keep yer 'air on,' she said without looking up. 'I was only jokin'.'

'You'd better be,' said Bella, slipping gratefully back down between the sheets. After a while she was forced to ask, 'Are you ever going to turn that light off, Pearl? I wanna go to sleep.'

'Shan't be long,' chirped her sister brightly. 'I've just gotta put me curlers in.'

Bella groaned. Pearl's bedtime routine seemed to expand nightly. There was cold cream and curlers, nail care and knicker washing. And all the while the ceiling light glared overhead.

'My boss, Louise, says I can 'ave a free perm soon,' Pearl chatted on thoughtlessly. 'One of the gels is gonna do it for me when we ain't too busy.' She swept her golden hair up and stared at herself in the mirror above the chest of drawers. 'I'm not sure wevver to keep it long, or 'ave it shorter.' She tilted her head at various angles, pouting her lips. 'What do you think would suit me best. Bel? Long or . . .'

But the relentless prattle, added to the strain of the last fortnight proved too much for Bella. 'Shut up, can't you?' she screamed, shooting up in bed scarlet with rage. 'You vain little cow! Why can't you let me go to sleep?'

The uncharacteristic violence of Bella's reply sent the colour rushing to Pearl's cheeks, but she soon recovered sufficiently to retaliate. 'You shut up yerself, yer miserable cow. It ain't my fault we 'ave to share a bedroom.'

And then, to Bella's surprise and mortification, she found herself reduced to tears and sobbing uncontrollably.

Shocked into compassion, Pearl moved to her sister's side. 'Aah, don't cry, mate,' she said putting a comforting arm across Bella's shuddering shoulders. 'I'll do me curlers in the bathroom if the light's botherin' yer that much.'

But having released some of her repressed tension in tears, Bella relented, too. 'No, it's all right, you carry on. But don't be too long.' She sank down and buried her face in the pillow.

'Why don't yer let Dad get the doctor? 'E'll give yer a tonic and yer'll soon be as right as rain again,' said Pearl, returning to the mirror.

Oh, if only it were that simple, Bella thought, but said: 'We'll see. I'm going to sleep now. G'night.'

'G'night, Bel,' said Pearl, and by the time the first metal curler was wound into place, her sister's tears were forgotten in the face of the pressing dilemma of which permanent wave to choose.

After a night of fitful sleep and frightening dreams, Bella awoke the next morning more terrified than ever but firm in the knowledge that she must meet this challenge. She must conquer her fear today or sink forever into despair.

Her father opened his workshop sharp at eight o'clock every morning, whilst Bella usually set the office into motion at nine, giving her time to clear a few domestic chores before she left. This morning, however, Bob thought a change of routine was warranted. 'Yer still look pale, Bella luv. If yer insist on comin' back to work today, why not come in the van wiv me? Save yer walkin' on yer first day back.'

It was tempting, but would be fudging the issue since she had to be alone and unprotected to free herself from fear. 'I'll be okay, Dad,' she said, smiling bravely. 'I'll take the bus for a few stops if I start to feel queer.'

And so it was that at a quarter to nine on a misty October morning in 1947 Bella left the prefab and walked towards the High Street on legs of cotton wool. Tension made her giddy and the pavements seemed to rush towards her. A cold sweat saturated her clothes and she thought her head would burst. But to the casual observer nothing about her would seem amiss.

'Mornin', Bella. A bit parky innit?'

'Morning, Mrs Smith. It is a bit nippy.'

''Ow's fings?'

'Fine. How about you?'

'Mustn't grumble, luv, ta.'

Ignorant as to the ruffians' appearances, Bella imagined every passing young male to be one of them and felt as timid as a baby sparrow. Reaching the office at last, she closed the door behind her and flopped down at her desk as gratefully as an athlete at the finishing line.

It was a medium-sized room with a window overlooking the yard outside and glass partitioning offering a view of the workshop inside. The furnishings were basic: a second-hand oak desk with a typewriter on top of it, dark green metal filing cabinets and shelving on which stationery, car repair manuals and trade magazines were piled. In the corner there was a small sink with a wooden draining board housing a kettle, teapot, cups and saucers, a bottle of milk and a packet of Brooke Bond tea.

The telephone rang and she started so violently that pain shot through her, but it was only a customer making an enquiry.

She replaced the receiver and watched her father and Trevor through the glass, happily engrossed under the bonnet of an Austin 10. Seeing them so satisfied at their work, her own problem came sharply into focus. She had braved the streets at last, but she still had not found a solution. The threats were obviously not idle ones, so did she allow those hooligans to abuse her or did she yield to Bennett's pressure? It seemed she had no choice. She would have to pass the matter over to her father.

The morning passed. Tea break came and went and still she said nothing. Desperation almost had her confiding in Trevor when he came into the office for some aspirin. But he seemed to be going down with flu so the moment passed. And then, quite suddenly, as she was sitting at her desk at lunchtime trying to tempt a nonexistent appetite with fish paste sandwiches, it happened. Boiling fury flashed through her body like electricity. How dare Bennett strike terror into her so that she was afraid to walk the streets? *How dare he?* She had been viewing the problem from the wrong angle. It was not *her* father she needed to talk to about the problem. Not now, not ever.

Telling Dad she was going to do some shopping, Bella left the office and made her way along the High Street which was teeming with people. Queues trailed from the butcher's, the baker's, the fish shop, the greengrocer's. Dusty, dilapidated shopfronts stared emptily into the promenade, for peace had not brought prosperity to the streets of London. Shabbily dressed optimists queued for new shoes and cigarettes, for fruit and fish. Had Bella been less preoccupied she might have joined the crowds on the bomb site between Lyons Teashop and Dolcis Shoes which had turned into a trading ground for spivs who mysteriously obtained luxury goods intended for export. A suitcase of nylons, or Nestles Milk Chocolate sold out in seconds here at more than twice the normal price.

Intent on her mission, however, she hurriedly threaded her way through the masses, past Woolworths, the Co-op and the wide ornate foyer of the Fulworth Empire, until eventually she reached the imposing garage and service station with 'Bennett and Sons' boldly written above the extensive buildings. Queues of cars snaked from both entrances as motorists waited to get to the globe-topped petrol pumps where a male attendant was serving. The sight of this smart, flourishing establishment further fuelled her anger. Didn't Bennett's have enough without coveting the livelihood of others?

Marching across the busy forecourt, she entered the glass-fronted reception office, a smart, carpeted room with lots of plants where a well-dressed young woman was sitting at a desk.

'I'd like to see Mr Bennett, please,' said Bella determinedly.

'Do you have an appointment?' was the haughty reply.

'No.' Bella's stare was unwavering.

'Well, I doubt he'll see you.' The girl was clearly enjoying her moment of power.

'Is he here?'

'Yes, but. . .'

'I am equally as determined to see him as you are to stop me,' said Bella, rising to the challenge. 'So unless you want me sitting out here for the rest of the day, you may as well tell me where to find him.'

Glaring coldy at the interloper, the girl picked up the internal phone. 'Who shall I say wants him?'

'My name is Bella Brown.'

Routine procedure was set in motion and the receptionist sulkily led Bella through a door at the back of the office and up some stairs to a landing housing several offices. Down below were impressive showrooms with several brand-new cars all displaying 'Sold' notices. Beyond these, through some glass partitioning, Bella could see smart workshops in which there appeared to be a large workforce. Brown's seemed insignificant in comparison.

The girl knocked on the door marked 'Manager', listened until a voice said 'Come in', then ushered Bella inside. Bella marched up to the desk with all the aggression of a boxer in mid-bout, but meeting the light brown eyes of the man behind the desk, she was thrown into confusion. This wasn't the Mr Bennett she had come to see.

Chapter Five

Bella's anger towards Bennett's had not, she now realised, included Dezi. Perhaps because she had met him while he was a pilot, she had always imagined him remaining in that role. Maybe she hadn't wanted to connect him with his father's devious tactics. Whatever the reason, it was a shock to her now to find herself confronting him as an integral part of Bennett's establishment.

But he was up and bounding towards her, his face lit with smiles. 'My word, but you've grown,' he said, taking her by the arms and observing her closely. 'You're quite a young lady now, I hardly recognised you.' His beaming smile was enhanced by shiny white teeth. 'How old are you now?'

'Sixteen,' she said, surprised and flattered that he had remembered her.

'Sweet sixteen, eh?' he laughed, moving back.

'I don't know about that.'

'Modest, too, are you?' He returned to his seat. 'Take a pew, I'll get some coffee sent in.' He paused thoughtfully, his eyes never leaving her face. 'Or would you prefer tea? A girl with a mind of her own, if my memory serves me correctly.'

'Nothing for me, thank you,' she said, but she did sit down. This unexpected development had taken the wind out of her sails. Her rage had been greatly diminished by relief that Dezi was alive and well, though why she should be so strongly affected was beyond her comprehension.

'Dare I ask if you returned from the country to find your aunt and uncle safe and sound?' he asked, frowning a little apprehensively.

She smiled stiffly. 'Yes, they were spared. Such a fuss I made that day!'

'Nonsense, it was a traumatic time for us all.' His eyes were momentarily bleak, but softened as he said, 'Pretty down by the river now that the lamp posts are lit again, isn't it?'

Hardly able to believe that he had remembered such an insignificant detail of their meeting, she smiled more easily. 'Oh, yes, it's lovely.' Then she frowned. 'Actually, I had wondered if you'd been killed in action or something. I've never seen you along there and I often pass your house.'

'Only the good die young,' he said lightly, but she sensed something else beneath the nonchalance. 'Thank you for your concern though.' He sat back and folded his arms. 'I don't live at Ivy House now. After the war, I thought it was time I moved from under the parental roof. I live on the other side of the river. Taken a little flat in Putney.'

'Very nice,' she said politely. The conversation was superficial, like talking to a stranger on a bus. It seemed to be the result of some underlying force in the atmosphere which Bella could not identify. She was uneasy, but happy, too. It was strange.

If it were possible, he was even more good-looking out of uniform. His face was fuller, his complexion healthier, with a slight tan suffusing his skin. Without his Air Force cap she could see the full luxuriance of his rich chestnut brown hair which he wore brushed back without a parting. A grey business suit, which he wore with a white shirt and blue tie, sat well on his broad shoulders, and those orange-flecked, cinnamon eyes of his were just as compelling as she remembered them.

Bringing her down to earth with a bump, he asked, 'So, to what do I owe the pleasure of this visit?'

'I came to see your father, actually,' she explained, forcing herself to concentrate on the most urgent priority.

His eyes narrowed quizzically. 'He isn't here today. Can I help?'

Bella's spirits dived. She must get this matter settled today. She simply could not bear another sleepless night. 'Well, not really.' She chewed her lip anxiously, the urgency of the affair overwhelming her. 'Could you tell me where to contact him? It is important that I speak to him today.'

'Oh?' He was obviously curious. 'Well, I more or less run the business these days. Nothing much goes on here that I don't know about. So unless, of course, it's a personal matter, why not try me?'

He was much too nice to know about it surely? But if he ran the business . . . if he knew everything that went on . . . Her cheeks burned angrily at the implication. 'Okay,' she said briskly, 'as you are in charge, will you please have your father call off his thugs? I am not going to give in to them whatever they do to me. If I don't have your assurance that I won't be bothered again, I am going straight to the police to ask for protection.' Her eyes rested on his unwaveringly for a few silent seconds. 'So which is it to be?'

He did look genuinely baffled, she had to admit. 'I have

no idea what you're talking about.' He spread his hands. 'So will you please tell me what's been going on?'

She was glad that she believed him. He had never struck her as a chip off the old block.

'Well?' he demanded.

'It's difficult ...'

'I have to know, if I'm to help.'

And so, through parched lips, out poured the whole story. She felt relieved of her burden and in control of the situation, all fear gone. 'They'd have to murder me before I'd tell my father about it,' she concluded. 'He's worked hard to get his little business going and I'll not have him put at the mercy of these blackmailers on account of me.'

It was an incredible story from a girl he hardly knew and Dezi didn't want to believe such allegations of his own father. But his uncertainty was quickly overruled by his instincts which told him that Bella Brown was not a liar.

A sudden pallor overlaid Dezi's tan and his eyes gleamed darkly. Bitterly, he shook his head. 'I am so sorry.' He clamped both hands tightly together until his knuckles gleamed white. 'And so deeply ashamed.'

Bella wanted to reach out and comfort him, feeling almost as if she were intruding in this moment of personal trauma. 'So, can I have your assurance?' she asked.

'You most certainly can. I *promise* you that nothing like that will ever happen again,' he said.

'Thank you.' And with the same instinct that she distrusted Frank Bennett, so she trusted his eldest son. She knew she was safe now. And she felt almost light-hearted as Dezi showed her off the premises.

★ ★ ★

Dezi confronted his father coldly as the older man tried to bluster his way out of trouble.

'I'm still the guvnor around here,' Frank shouted. 'How dare you order me to come to the garage and then present me with a pack of lies?'

Immediately Bella had left, Dezi had begun the business of locating his father, telephoning several of his club haunts. When he found him he asked him, on the telephone, to return to the office. There, he presented him with the allegations and was treated to a slanging match which had only served to convince Dezi of his father's culpability.

'And you'd believe some slut of a girl before your own father!' Frank continued. 'I mean, what is she? Just the daughter of some small-time git playing at business instead of leaving it to us professionals. She's probably after money.'

'She is *not* a slut and she is *not* after money,' Dezi informed him dryly. 'And I notice you don't deny knowing her father.'

'Met him once in a pub, that's all,' said Frank, his face suffused with purplish-red blotches.

'How could you bear to put a sixteen-year-old girl at risk, Dad?' Dezi demanded. He gripped the edge of his desk to curb the violence that boiled inside him. '*How could you?*'

'I didn't. How many more times do you want telling?' denied Frank, his lies hanging emptily in the air. The one thing he craved more than money was the respect and admiration of his elder son. He lit a cigarette and puffed nervously. 'Who do you think you're speaking to anyway? I'll thank you to remember that I am your father.'

'That is something,' rasped Dezi, 'that does not exactly fill me with pride right now.' His eyes were stony. 'Do I have your word that you'll call your animals off, or shall I tell Mother what you've been up to?'

Frank turned ashen. 'All this fuss over some liar of a girl,' he mumbled crossly.

Hardly able to restrain himself from striking his father, Dezi clasped his hands together. 'If that girl has any more trouble of this sort, and I shall get to know about it if she does, then I shall not only tell Mother about it but the police, too. So make sure you see to it.'

The two men faced each other in silent conflict. Dezi knew that his father would never admit his guilt. He was equally certain that he would yield to Dezi's demands. For he would do anything rather than have Eve know what he was really like. Unable to bear the man's company a moment longer Dezi rose, marched across to the coatstand and unhooked his grey overcoat.

'Where are you going?' demanded Frank.

'To the pub for a late liquid lunch – you've killed my appetite for anything else,' he said, and stamped furiously from the room.

Dezi sat at a corner table of the White Lion with a glass of light ale, mulling over the whole disgraceful business. He had never been close to his father, but now he felt totally alienated from him. He had always seen the old man as self-satisfied and far too interested in material gain, but this latest revelation had come as a shock. The man was his father after all.

Thinking about it, Dezi realised he had always felt different from the rest of the family. Mother doted on Peter who in turn would do anything to gain his father's favour: laughing at his tasteless jokes, agreeing with his ideas, and generally allowing himself to be a lap dog. Peter had always been more Eve's and Frank's son than Dezi had, yet he had often sensed that it was he whom their father actually favoured. Dezi hoped that his brother's current two-year National Service stint would broaden his horizons and make him less susceptible to their father's domineering personality.

After Dezi's demob, he had not wanted to go back into the family business and had favoured the idea of starting up on his own. But after weeks of parental lectures about family loyalty, he had felt guilty enough to concede to pressure. Since then he had practically taken the reins from his father although his directorship wasn't to be made official until he was twenty-five.

He pushed his beer aside. Even that tasted foul in his present mood. This whole Bella Brown affair had upset him more than he would have thought possible. Right now he was ashamed to bear the name Bennett.

Until today, the existence of Brown's car repair business had been unknown to Dezi. Numerous small motor workshops thrived inconspicuously in London's back streets and railway arches, one didn't get to hear of them all. The ingredient that made Brown's different and of interest to his father, Dezi assumed, was that its main road position offered tremendous business potential when petrol rationing finally ended. But Brown did not want to sell and that must be the end of the matter for Bennett's.

A vivid image of Bella floated into his mind. What a beauty she was growing up to be! Her childish features had softened wonderfully into womanhood, her skin shone like silk, her mouth now bowed sensuously, and those amazing dark eyes held ineffable depths. A world away from that skinny-legged kid in ankle socks! Bella now had a pair of the shapeliest legs he'd ever seen. And she had spirit, too. Most youngsters would have run shivering to an adult after such an ordeal, but that wasn't Bella's style at all. A smile lit his eyes. It was the sponge cake episode all over again. She'd stuck her neck out for her family then, too.

As thoughts of her lingered, he realised that he had been almost childishly pleased to see her again. But why? It wasn't as though they had any interests in common. They were not even in the same age group. Any attempt at friendship on his part would almost certainly be misunderstood, since she was only sixteen and he was a grown man of twenty-three. He did hope that chance sent them another meeting, though. The sight of her had cheered him up no end, despite the unhappy circumstances of this morning's encounter.

Back at the garage all personal thoughts were cast aside as the afternoon became fraught with problems: a customer complaint about a job, an urgent brake repair with complications, a mechanic taken sick, and a forecourt attendant not appearing for his shift. All in a day's work, he thought, changing into a pair of overalls. Any employer worth his salt must be willing and able to stand in for his staff if necessary. And Dezi went out to the forecourt and began serving the waiting motorists with petrol.

On her return to the office, Bella found herself with little time to dwell on her meeting with Dezi. Trevor had been sent home with worsening flu, leaving an urgent job half done and Dad in a flap. The telephone seemed to ring non-stop with customer enquiries, there was a panic about spare parts which meant Bella chasing up the suppliers, and numerous other routine jobs.

So it wasn't until she was walking home in the gathering

mist and recalling how very different she had felt walking these very same streets this morning, that her thoughts turned, inevitably, to Dezi. He was nice, she liked him a lot. And something more stirred deep inside her; that same peculiar ache she had experienced this morning that made her happy but simultaneously restless and desirous of something beyond her reach. Memories of his physical presence enflamed her, quickening her body. But her down to earth upbringing meant that a sense of reality was never far away. The man was out of her age group and class, so any fancy she had in that direction was doomed to disappointment. She did hope that she saw him again sometime, though.

She made a detour to Napley Road to deliver Trevor's wage packet since he had left before she had had it ready this afternoon. And the moment she set foot inside number nine, all other thoughts were swept aside by a family crisis.

Eve noticed her husband's air of gloomy preoccupation when he arrived home that evening. 'Anything wrong, dear?' she asked, reclining on the sofa with a pre-prandial sherry.

'No, just a business matter that needs some thought, nothing for you to worry your pretty head about,' he said, surveying her through a cloud of cigar smoke.

'Oh, good, just as long as you're not coming down with anything,' said Eve, not wishing to shadow her own comfortable existence by probing further.

Frank nodded dutifully, but her words barely registered. His head was crammed with angry thoughts of Bob Brown. Men like him just weren't built for the responsiblity of business. Why would he not see the logic in selling up and having all the worries taken off his shoulders? After all, nobody was asking the man to give the site away. His mood was darkened further by the fact that he would have to remove the pressure from the girl now that Dezi was suspicious.

Quite why Frank doted on Dezi, he didn't know, since the boy gave him precious little encouragement. But try as he might, he could not love Peter with the same intensity. Maybe it was because Peter's affection came effortlessly, whereas Dezi had never seemed unduly impressed by his father's achievements. Yet hadn't Frank given him plenty of cause to be proud . . . hadn't he given the family prestige through his financial success? No man could have done more to win the respect of his son. Yet Dezi always seemed more concerned about pleasing customers and staff than he did his father.

He shivered with fear at the thought of Dezi's reaction to his other sidelines should he ever discover them. House tenants with no rent books, black market coupons for every possible commodity, and the more than occasional acquisition of short supply items for resale at a high profit. Frank knew that his puritanical first born would be scandalised if he got to hear about any of it. But there was no way that he would. After all, apart from the houses, Frank employed people to act on his behalf; he himself only ever acted as a middleman.

Returning to the question of Brown's, he supposed he would have to put the matter on ice for the moment. Give Dezi a chance to calm down, regain his confidence and make him so secure in the firm he would never want to leave it. In the meantime Frank would devise another scheme, something more subtle than the last. He would wait years if necessary, but he'd get Brown's site.

★　　★　　★

Bella knew what was on her aunt's mind, since the older woman was not the sort of person to panic over a bout of 'flu, no matter how severe.

'Just because Trevor has a stiff neck doesn't mean he's got infantile paralysis, Auntie,' Bella said, facing her aunt gravely. 'It's more common in hot weather anyway.'

But Auntie shook her head. 'There's bin a case reported recently, a young fella about Trevor's age. They reckon 'e picked it up at the swimmin' baths. Trev was there last week – they've closed the place now.'

'Oh!' That was something Bella hadn't known. 'I still think you're worrying unnecessarily, but perhaps I'd better go and ring the doctor. At least you'll sleep easy in your bed tonight then.' She hugged her aunt gently. 'It's probably just good old-fashioned flu.'

But it wasn't, and by eight o'clock that evening Trevor was in the isolation hospital with suspected poliomyelitis. The next day the disease was confirmed and the family was told Trevor was not expected to live. A dark shadow seemed to fall across the whole neighbourhood, and the Browns instinctively clung together. Violet and Wilf moved into the prefab to be near the telephone which Bob had had installed when he had gone into business. The role of comforter fell to Bella, though she herself was in a state of trauma since she and Trevor had always been close.

Only Violet and Wilf were allowed to visit because of the infectious nature of the illness. After a day at the hospital they were exhausted, but unable to sleep. Since the war there had been many deaths from this terrifying disease and although the Browns were not an outwardly religious family, they all turned to prayer now. As Trevor sank deeper into coma, the end seemed inevitable . . .

It was Bella who took the call when the phone rang one evening exactly one week after the diagnosis. She had to since everyone else was paralysed with fear.

'It's the hospital,' she said shakily, coming back into the living room from the hall. 'They want Auntie and Uncle to get there as soon as possible. They didn't give any details.'

'Bloomin' 'orspitals,' grumbled Wilf, aggressive in his anguish. 'They never tell yer what yer've a right to know.'

Bob took them in the van while Bella tried to console Pearl and Donald, who were both pale with fright and crying intermittently. She made them cocoa and had just persuaded them to play a game of cards to occupy their minds when the telephone shrilled alarmingly. This time she really didn't think her legs would carry her to the telephone, since this had to be the final act in this nightmare. The three sat frozen to their seats, letting it ring, until at last Bella stumbled out into the hall. It was her father . . . Oh God, she was going to faint . . .

'We ain't gonna lose 'im,' her father said hoarsely. ' 'E's come through the crisis. They would 'ave told yer on the phone, but yer 'ung up too quick. We don't know 'ow badly 'e's gonna be paralysed, but at least 'e ain't gonna die.'

Hot, salty tears gushed down Bella's cheeks as the three youngsters hugged each other for joy. Then she threw on her coat and rushed off to tell the neighbours who had been so kind and concerned. She tore around to Napley Road to spread the good news there, calling at Joan's house afterwards. Her tearful reaction surprised Bella, who had not realised her friend was that fond of Trevor. By the time Bella got back to the prefab the whole of Lower Fulworth was buzzing with the good news. They had been spared a tragedy, this time.

Chapter Six

The 1951 Festival of Britain, planned to take place from a derelict bomb site on the South Bank of the Thames in token of the government's belief in a better future, was a very controversial event. The brothers, Wilfred and Bob Brown, disagreed heatedly over it.

'Eleven million bloomin' pounds of tax payer's money just to boost the nation's morale – it's downright criminal! I don't know what 'Erbert Morrison is thinking abaht,' grumbled Wilf in the spring of that year when he and his brother were enjoying a pint at the local together. Wilf enjoyed nothing more than a good political moan and could become as critical of his own party as any other if it meant a good argument. ''Ouses are what people need, not a bloomin' funfair.'

'Come on now, Wilf,' argued Bob. 'It's more than just a funfair. Its purpose is to demonstrate British achievment in the arts, sciences and design. If this country is going to move forward, it needs confidence – and what better way to promote that than an exhibition? Anyway, it's all down to your lot, you voted 'em in.'

'That doesn't mean I agree wiv everything they do. I'm

damned sure the Tories would 'ave made a worse mess of things.' Wilf was flushed and warming to his theme. 'Not that you'd admit to it, now that you're a capitalist.'

Bob smiled. He'd known it wouldn't be long before his business was dragged into it. Calling him a capitalist was a gross exaggeration, of course, but Bob had to admit to being at the helm of a thriving concern. He had rebuilt his workshops and increased his workforce, putting Trevor in a position of authority. After his illness the boy retained a limp but although he tired more easily than before, he was able to work normally. Brown's was able to offer a complete service now that Bob had extended his workshops to include a body work department which was headed by a skilful and trustworthy young man called John Sharpe.

Bob's most adventurous move yet was imminent. He had been granted a petroleum retail licence and was about to open his revamped forecourt, complete with petrol pumps. With this very much on his mind, he changed the subject under discussion.

'Talkin' o' business,' he said, 'what do yer think about this latest venture of mine?'

'I think yer want yer brains tested, mate,' said Wilf, eyeing his brother over the rim of his pint glass. He was wearing a trilby hat and a dark blue suit. His face was adorned with spoils from the relatively new National Health Service: owl-like spectacles and ill-fitting teeth which frequently became almost irretrievably dislodged. The two men had a high degree of mutual understanding which withstood any amount of altercation. 'I don't know why you wanna keep takin' on more responsibility.' He clicked his teeth. 'All that extra worry. Credit where it's due, you've made a go of it so far, why not be content wiv that?'

'Expansion makes good business sense,' said Bob.

Wilf swigged his beer and leaned his elbows on the table, indicating that one of his brotherly lectures was forthcoming. 'Maybe it does, but you ain't built for worry, Bob. I've seen the strain in yer eyes lately. Yer could 'ave an easier life.' He paused and his eyes became glazed. 'Now you take me. I goes to work, I does a good job and I comes 'ome leavin' the work be'ind me. I get a good wage, I've got enough for a few pints, and the missis never goes short. I'm 'appy as a king. Some of us 'ave got the stamina to be guvnors and some of us ain't. You ain't. That's all I'm sayin'.'

'Fanks!' said Bob. There was nothing new in this. He had heard it all a million times before.

But Wilf was a fair man, with his brother's happiness at heart, and he continued less aggressively, 'But since this business lark is what yer want, you go ahead and good luck to yer. Like I said, you've not gone wrong so far. Just don't bite orf more than you can chew, that's all.'

Bob's spirits lifted at this recognition of his achievements. But in his heart he knew that Wilf was right. There was something lacking in his character, in that he needed his brother's approval before he could confidently proceed with an idea. It worried Bob that he didn't have the courage of his own convictions. And although he would never admit it to anyone, he knew he was not a natural entrepreneur. But he did enjoy the satisfaction of providing first-class working conditions for his staff, which in turn guaranteed a service to the customer which in the area was generally accepted as second to none. He had created a happy firm in Brown's and it was his duty to keep it flourishing and progressing, true businessman or not.

★   ★   ★

Bella stood on Chelsea bridge one Saturday afternoon in May and surveyed the scene before her with wonder. A few hundred yards upstream, an explosion of life and colour brightened the landscape like a sudden burst of Technicolor in a dreary black and white film. A dozen Festival flags flew among a thousand pennants which were strung from the masts of tall yachts and interwoven between poles on a floating pier which jutted far into the river. Through the masts she could see the tented roofs of the restaurants and snack bars, in red, green and yellow, edging the Embankment and disappearing beneath the trees. Flourishing flower boxes bordered the cafeteria terraces and coloured umbrellas topped the tables. Distantly, above the tree tops, the Festival's symbol, the Skylon, shimmered into the cloudless heavens like a gigantic double-ended spear, towering over the thrilling silhouette of the funfair. Bella had never seen anything like this before.

'Come on, Bella, don't stand there gawpin' all day,' urged Pearl excitedly. 'We wanna get down there.'

'Yeah,' exuberantly agreed Private Donald Brown of the Middlesex Regiment. 'I can't wait to get to the funfair.'

'They say there's a grotto and a boatin' pool,' said Joan Willis enthusiastically, clutching Trevor's arm. 'Are yer all right, Trev? Yer leg ain't playin' yer up too much, is it? Yer can 'ave a sit down when we get there. They've even got beer gardens, so I've 'eard.'

The party of five moved with the crowds towards the festival gardens where they gaped at the futuristic sculptures and resplendent fountains. There was a tree walk beside a Chinese dragon, and the Guinness Festival Clock whose strike orchestrated a series of tableaux. There were grottoes and flower gardens; a piazza and a Punch and Judy Show; an aviary and an amphitheatre. Vitality and exuberance charged the air.

Whilst Bella's companions agreed to join her in her inspection of the exhibits on display in the Dome of Discovery, the message of a Brighter Britain of the Future conveyed in murals and sculpture was lost on them, since they were far more interested in the abundant pleasures on offer in the here and now. After trekking through the bowels of the earth to view the Schweppes Grotto, with its luminous walls, phosphorescent fountains and huge crystals glowing in changing colours, there was a general drift towards the funfair. Bella, however, had not yet had her fill of sightseeing so, arranging to meet the others at the Guinness Clock in two hours, she set forth alone.

Strolling along the Grand Vista, with its Chinese Gothic arcades and fountained lakes, she was happy to be on her own for a while to absorb the unique atmosphere. Later she rested a while at a riverside tea garden, watching the throngs of people, and wondering how Pearl and the others were getting on. She smiled at the thought of Joan mothering Trevor so ardently, obviously protecting her investment since she clearly intended to marry him.

His recovery had been slow but miraculous, with the paralysis finally affecting only his left foot. It was during his convalescence that the rather one-sided romance had begun. And whilst it was noticeable that Joan took all the initiative, it was also fair to say that Trevor offered no resistance and showed no interest in other girls. It was hardly the love story of the century, but Bella thought they were right together.

As for Pearl, she drew men like a magnet. Her brash prettiness, coupled with a tendency to flaunt it, rarely attracted those with serious intentions. But Pearl didn't seem to care, she liked to play around.

Then there was Donald, a soldier for nearly a year. His passions still seemed centred on his motor bike which received his undivided attention during his leaves. There wouldn't be any more of those for a while though since he was currently on embarkation leave before going overseas. They would miss his forty-eight hour weekend passes; he was like a breath of fresh air about the place. But it wouldn't be for too long, Bella reminded herself, as almost half his service was already done.

Bella herself had not been without the occasional fluttering heartbeat these last few years. There had been a van-driver who had appealed strongly for a while and a brief torrid affair with a pal of one of Pearl's boyfriends, a strong, virile bricklayer who had wanted to go 'the whole hog' with Bella in the hawthorn bushes. She had been sorely tempted, since his earthy charms had inflamed her curiosity as well as her youthful libido, but prudence, heavily influenced by the fear of pregnancy, had finally prevailed.

Now she finished her tea and continued on through the gardens. Passing the Riverside Theatre, with its Victorian-style Wedgwood-blue and white stucco, she thought how sad it was that most of these magnificent structures were only temporary. Pale sun gleamed on the river where some intrepid ducks were heading hopefully towards the clusters of bread throwers on the banks.

A light breeze lifted her long dark hair which she wore loose with a side parting. She was fashionably dressed in a red and white floral print dress which hugged her slender waist and billowed out into a full skirt. Glancing at her watch to see that it was time she met the others, she quickened her step and headed towards the Guinness Clock.

'Let's go for a look round the funfair, Dezi,' suggested Peter Bennett to his brother as they took tea on one of the terraces in the Festival Gardens. 'We might pick up a couple of girls for tonight.'

Dezi frowned. At twenty-seven, he considered himself to be well past that sort of juvenile practice. 'You are supposed to be engaged to Lucy,' he reminded Peter.

He grinned wickedly. 'What's that got to do with anything? If Lucy decides to go off to a girlfriend's place for the weekend, leaving me high and dry, she can hardly expect me to waste all my . . .' he paused as though choosing his words carefully, ' . . . considerable charms, can she?'

'I thought she'd gone because her friend is ill,' said Dezi.

There was no reply to that and he threw his brother a disapproving look. At twenty-two Peter was well endowed with looks, sex appeal, intelligence, and the money to exploit all three. 'You shouldn't abuse women,' Dezi pointed out crossly. 'It isn't right.'

'Abuse doesn't come into it,' laughed Peter, raking his long fingers absently through his curly blond hair. 'I've never had to force a girl yet. They come out with me quite willingly and I see to it that they have a good time. That isn't abuse, it's just good fun.'

Not only did the brothers differ in personality and their attitude to life, but in appearance, too. In contrast to Dezi's muscular physique and richly coloured hair, Peter was fair with greyish-blue eyes and a lean build. Dezi was fond of him in a brotherly sort of way, but irritated by him. Like their father, Peter was a taker and viewed the world as one huge playground for his use. But, of course, given their father's influence over him, despite his two years' absence, this was only to be expected.

'One of these days you'll get your comeuppance for all this double dealing,' said Dezi, sipping his tea and idly watching the passing crowds. The sound of their clamour roared cheerfully around them and rival strains of music fought tunefully on the breeze.

'Men have cheated on women throughout history,' Peter said lightly. 'We are all polygamists by instinct, it's a fact of life.'

Dezi laughed dryly. 'A philosopher now, are you? Well, don't include me in your rash generalisations.'

Peter took a gold cigarette case from his blazer pocket, offered it to his brother, who declined a cigarette, then lit one for himself. 'To hear you talk, anyone would think you were celibate,' he said, inhaling deeply and leaning back in a relaxed manner. 'But you don't exactly go short of girlfriends, do you?'

'Maybe not.' Dezi made a face. 'But I only ever have one relationship at a time.'

'You admit that there have been quite a few, though.'

'Certainly, I'll admit it. That's because I haven't met the right one yet,' said Dezi, partly to annoy his brother and partly because it was true.

'Oh, God save us!' groaned Peter. 'You sound like some puritanical agony aunt in a women's magazine.'

'Maybe I do, but it's the truth.' A breeze rustled through the trees and sent the bunting into a frenzied dance. Dezi reflected on his love life. It was true that there had been several affairs, but they had all been dogged by a feeling of simply going through a preordained sequence of events. Perhaps 'love' really was just a myth invented for the civilised continuation of the species. He knew people who thought so. But Dezi wasn't ready to accept such a cynical view. There had to be something more out there somewhere . . .

He turned his attention back to Peter who was wittering on about taking a mistress after he and Lucy were married. Dezi was bored. He and his brother had nothing in common except their shared blood and the garage, where Peter was the Sales Manager and Dezi now Managing Director. They almost never socialised together, each having their own separate circle of friends. But today Peter, at a loose end without Lucy, had persuaded Dezi to go for a drink with him at lunchtime after work and had subsequently talked him into a trip to the Festival.

Although Dezi did not find the company stimulating, the events around him certainly were. The standard of professionalism with which the whole thing had been staged was very impressive. It was good to see people enjoying themselves, though it wasn't all smiles. Nearby a small boy, having pestered his mother for one toffee apple too many, was being treated to a hiding instead. The Thames shimmered in the sunlight and the scent of sweet peas floated fragrantly on the breeze.

But then he saw *her*, and all else left his mind. His heart hammered against his ribs so violently he thought it would stop. She was the most beautiful woman he had even seen, with long dark hair flying in the breeze and tumbling on to her red and white dress. She was walking purposefully in his direction, looking towards the river. Even from a distance he knew it was Bella Brown, now grown and quite exquisite. Transfixed, he feasted his eyes on her, his mouth dry, stomach churning. She was lovely, just lovely, and she was passing by without even looking his way.

'Hey, where are you going?' asked Peter as his brother almost knocked the table over in his hurry to leave it. But Dezi had already disappeared into the crowds.

Bella thought it was Pearl tapping her on the shoulder. So, swinging round to find herself facing Dezi Bennett, she was thrown into confusion.

'I hope I didn't startle you.' He felt as nervous as a schoolboy.

'No, of course not.' She thought her legs would give way.

'Do you remember me?' He was probably shaking notice-ably and couldn't stop himself.

'Of course I do, Dezi.' What had happened to her mouth that it wouldn't stop trembling?

'I almost didn't recognise you,' he said, unable to take his eyes off her stunning beauty, those luminous eyes, the glorious figure. 'It must be about four years.'

'Yes, it must be, I'm twenty now.'

'And how beautiful you've grown.' Oh dear, he probably sounded like some awful old lecher!

'Oh!' Her eyes widened in surprise and she turned scarlet.

'I'm sorry, I've embarrassed you.'

'In the nicest possible way,' she laughed. The three miles that separated their places of work might have been an ocean, since there was never any reason for their paths to cross by chance. She had looked for him though, oh yes, there had been a time when she had seen his face around every street corner. 'Are you still living in Putney?'

He nodded. 'Here alone?' he asked.

Her hair bounced as she shook her head. 'No, I'm with my sister and cousins. They went to the funfair. I'm on my way to meet them.'

Damn! Well he wasn't going to let her go this time. 'Must you? I'd hoped you might join me for tea.' Never mind that he'd just had some, he'd drown himself in the stuff to be with her.

'I'd love to,' she said graciously, 'but they will be waiting for me at the Guinness Clock. They'll worry if I don't turn up.'

Dezi was terrified of losing her. If she went back to the clock her relatives might lure her away. He *must* have some time with her. 'If I were to get a message to them, would you consider it?'

Her eyes narrowed quizzically, a half smile gracing her lips. 'Well, yes, I don't see why not.'

He took her arm and hurried her back to the tea gardens where a puzzled Peter was about to leave.

'Ah, I thought there must be a woman about somewhere to send you tearing off like that,' he said, his eyes roving appreciatively over Bella 'I must say this one's enough to make any man run.'

'Don't mind my brother, Bella,' Dezi said witheringly. 'Manners aren't his strong point.'

Bella shrugged. 'It's all right, I took it as a compliment.'

Having obtained Peter's reluctant agreement to deliver the message, Dezi decided to chance his arm. 'Tell them that I'll take Bella home by car later on tonight. No need for them to wait.'

Watching Peter hurry away, armed with a description of Pearl, Dezi turned sheepishly to Bella. 'I've been presumptuous, I know. Maybe you already have something planned for this evening.'

But Bella smiled warmly. 'No, I would only have mooched around the funfair with the others. I can do that another time.'

They went to the high-class Riverside Rooms and laughed heartily after both admitting to having already had tea. This was a restaurant of West End standards, with a terrace edging the Thames and a wine garden with umbrella-shaded tables surrounding a circular dance floor roofed with fairy lights.

Noticing Bella's undisguised approval, Dezi said, 'Would you like to come back here later for dinner? It'll be pretty when the lights are turned on.'

'I'd love that.' Bella saw no point in holding back, since her enjoyment of his company was obviously reciprocated. Now that she was older she was able to recognise the strong physical chemistry that existed between them. There was no sense in being coy about it. She wanted him with the intensity of a longing that had begun when she was thirteen years old, albeit she had not realised it then. She nibbled a scone and dabbed her mouth daintily with a white linen napkin. Her olive skin seemed translucent, her eyes shone. 'I've never danced in the open air before.'

Her appearance was not the only thing that had changed, he thought. She was more graceful now. Her speech was softer, and whilst it retained the Cockney intonations, ain'ts and dropped h's seemed to be a thing of the past.

'Are you still working for your father?' he asked as he buttered his scone.

'Yes,' she said, passing him the strawberry jam. 'Are you still with the family firm?'

'Yes.'

'I didn't have any more trouble.'

'I know.'

An uneasy silence fell. She had felt it important to refer to the reason for their last meeting, to clear the air between them. Then she met his eyes and the moment passed. She enjoyed his overt admiration of her; she was glad to please his eye as he pleased hers.

Dezi felt euphoric. Now he could openly admire Bella, as a man attracted to a woman, not a full-grown male lusting after a young girl. He wanted her desperately and knew, somehow, that she was the only woman for him. He had thought of her often and now realised why he had never tried to stage an ostensibly accidental meeting. The feelings he had for her now were nothing new and he had been terrified of such impulses towards a girl of sixteen. Now that she was an adult, the seven-year age gap hardly seemed to matter.

He could even accept that his fascination for her went back even further, to that day on the towpath when she had been just thirteen. He knew, with absolute conviction, that she was the reason he had never had an enduring relationship with a woman. She was the magic he had waited for. But it would not be wise to rush her, even though he sensed that she felt something for him. Getting to know her was going to be an exquisite pleasure. He wanted to know all about her. What she liked to do and eat, what she thought and felt about the world. Everything from the day she was born. He wanted to get to the heart of her, to spend every moment of the day with her and wake each morning by her side. The possibility that she might already be committed to someone else was too terrible to consider, so he clung to the fact that she wore no rings.

'We are on the verge of a new venture, as a matter of fact,' said Bella, licking some butter from her upper lip. 'Dad's got an agency with the Mella Oil Company and we're about to become petrol retailers.'

Up went Dezi's eyebrows. His father wasn't going to like that at all. But Dezi didn't want to think about business. 'Good for him. You'll do very well, I should think. The increase in traffic on the roads since petrol rationing ended last year is quite dramatic.'

'Yes,' said Bella, but business was no contender for her thoughts against the more absorbing interest of the moment. She was certain that this meeting was somehow pre-ordained. If it hadn't happened today, it would have been some time soon, because something very special existed between them. Sexual attraction maybe, but there was more to it than that. And without being presumptuous, she knew he felt it, too.

She smiled across at him, thinking how attractive he looked today. He was wearing a light grey sports jacket with a snow white shirt, maroon tie and charcoal grey flannels. Very smart and middle-class. His tanned face shone like varnish against the lightness of his shirt. Their eyes met and she flushed. But it didn't matter at all.

'Isn't the Festival wonderful?' she said, sipping her tea. 'It's quite the most amazing thing I've ever seen. Like something out of an American film.'

'Why American?'

'The colour and glamour of it all.'

'Mmm, perhaps Fred Astaire and Ginger Rogers will come dancing through the crowds in a minute.'

'Now you're making fun of me.'

'No, just teasing you a little.' He glanced through the window. 'I know what you mean though. America does have a glamorous image, though I doubt if it's all like we see in Hollywood movies.'

'Of course not, but we all like to have our dreams of faraway places.' She poured them both some more tea. 'My uncle doesn't agree with the Festival, he thinks it's a waste of money.'

'There are plenty more of that opinion.' He reached across and caught her slender hand in his. 'I'm very glad they went ahead with it, though, because it helped me to find you again.'

His hand felt strong around hers. 'You would have done that anyway, somehow,' she said solemnly.

'Yes, I know,' he said as her other hand closed over his.

When Peter saw Pearl standing under the clock, he couldn't believe his luck. She wasn't in the same league as her sister, Bella's striking beauty was in a class of its own, but she was certainly a looker in a chocolate-box sort of a way. She had a pretty face, despite the thick make-up, a good figure and super blond hair. And tarty-looking girls, which she certainly was with her skintight dress and high-heeled platform shoes, always excited him.

Having introduced himself and delivered the message, he said with feigned mournfulness, 'We've both been deserted, I'm afraid.'

Pearl, liking what she saw, decided to seize the opportunity. 'Well,' she huffed, turning to her companions, 'that's nice, innit? Bella going orf like that and leavin' us 'igh and dry.'

'If she's met someone nice, I don't blame 'er,' said Joan. 'You wouldn't bother about 'er if you 'ad the chance, Pearl.'

'We'll enjoy ourselves without 'er!' said Trevor.

But Donald played right into Pearl's hands. 'I'm orf 'ome now to meet me mates. I'll come back wiv 'em later.'

'Oh, well,' grumbled Pearl, though she was beside herself with glee, 'I'll just 'ave to tag along wiv you two. But it ain't no fun bein' a gooseberry.' She turned her expressive blue eyes on Peter, who was still gawping at her with unveiled admiration. 'Thanks for bringin' the message,' she said sorrowfully.

Peter thought that brash, working-class girls like her were far sexier than the girls at the tennis club with their perfect accents and tasteful attire. And this one was sending out signals, so it was worth a try. 'Look here.' He was unable to hide his enthusiasm. 'Since we've both been dumped, why don't we team up?'

He was a cut above the usual types Pearl hung around with. Obviously well-heeled. Might even have his own transport. And a car-owning boyfriend really would be something. She could see that he was responsive to her particular brand of charm. He was practically drooling! It shouldn't take too much effort to have him eating out of her hand. It was about time she found a bloke with a nice fat wallet ...

'Yeah, okay then, I don't mind.' Her tone was deliberately casual. 'I'll see you lot later,' she said to the others, and slipping her arm through that of her new companion she guided him into the crowds. She didn't want relatives cramping her style while she went to work on Peter.

Bella was mesmerised. The Festival had been noteworthy by day, but by night it was stunning. Illuminations of every shape and colour blazed into the dark sky and set the black waters of the Thames afire. She and Dezi were standing by the Fountain

Tower, a glowing spire topped with a luminous pineapple. A continuous procession of golden spheres cascaded down its sides and vanished into a bowl of light at the base. All around them lights and lanterns winked and glittered endlessly.

'I've never seen anything so pretty,' said Bella.

'Neither have I,' said Dezi, but he wasn't looking at the lights.

They had spent the time since tea exploring, and had sampled the boating lake and all the fun of the fair. Now, having been for a wash and brush up, renewed her lipstick and dabbed Yardley's Freesia behind her ears, Bella was on her way to dine.

A chill had come into the air, so Dezi suggested a table inside by the window overlooking the fairy-lit dance floor. Lanterns hung among the trees, tinting the foliage with assorted hues and shining on the water. Whereas this afternoon they had been in the tea rooms, now they dined in the prestigious restaurant with champagne in ice buckets, waiters in full evening dress and fresh flowers in crystal bowls. They had hors d'oeuvres and steaks cooked at the table, chocolate mousses, cheese and coffee. A feast indeed after years of postwar austerity but more exciting for Bella was the dancing between courses. Dezi felt solid and vibrant against her. If she could have somehow passed through his skin into his body she would have done so, right there and then.

She felt so right with him that even words were not necessary. Later they walked hand in hand beside the river. 'I've thought about you a lot,' he said.

'And me you.'

'You were too young.'

'Yes.'

He drove her home in his Ford Consul. Outside the prefab, she responded eagerly to his first kiss. 'I have had a wonderful time,' she whispered. 'Thank you.'

'I should be thanking you.' He stroked her hair back from her brow. 'Can I see you tomorrow?'

'Oh yes!'

'I'll pick you up about two and we'll drive out to the country.'

'I'll look forward to it.'

Sunday afternoon with Dezi by the lake at Virginia Water was the closest thing to heaven yet for Bella. The lake was bathed in sunlight which filtered through the trees into the secluded corner where they sat among the buttercups and beeches. Bella's experience of picnics had, hitherto, been well-used paper bags containing doorstep-thick fishpaste sandwiches and bottles of lemonade, all stickily devoured on a rainy Southend beach.

But that wasn't Dezi's style at all. He produced a wicker picnic basket containing an impressive spread: thick lean ham, succulent tomatoes, moist cheese and crusty bread, all washed down with champagne.

'This is delicious,' she said, munching happily. 'You must have blown your entire cheese ration for the month.'

'It's worth it,' he assured her.

Having not been raised in a car-owning family, journeys into the open spaces of the Home Counties were almost unknown to Bella. 'Isn't it beautiful here? And so quiet,' she said. The few afternoon ramblers they had seen had kept to the main footpath around the lake. The only sounds were the rustle and twitter of birds and insects. 'It must be very nice to be able to drive out to these places whenever you like.'

Dezi nodded. 'Yes, a driving licence does open up all sorts of possibilities. I don't expect it will be long before you get yours, will it?'

Bella was taken aback since women drivers were still something of a novelty in the circles in which she moved. 'Well, I haven't thought of it.' As she spoke, the idea gained credibility. 'But it would certainly help Dad if I could drive, for delivering cars and running errands in the van.' She sipped her champagne. 'Maybe I'll give it some serious thought.'

'I think you should,' said Dezi.

His casual assumption that all things were within her reach boosted her confidence greatly. He made her feel cared for and capable of anything. Replete with food and sleepy from champagne, she lay back on the grass and closed her eyes. The breeze whispered through the trees and brushed her face with the scent of May blossom. Dezi's fingers running through her hair made her shiver with pleasure. Her skin burned beneath his touch and she longed for him to extend the range of his caresses. But he just gently put his lips to hers. She responded passionately and, restlessly, slipped her hands over the strong muscles of his back.

Dezi was as susceptible to the temptations of the flesh as any other normal man. Just being near to Bella was driving him wild, but he was determined not to put their relationship at risk by gracelessly hurrying her. She was far too special.

He had lost his virginity one night in France during the war, to a farmer's daughter who had sheltered him when a hit by the Luftwaffe had forced him into a parachute jump. It had been an act of generosity on her part and gratitude on his. Love had not come into it. They had drunk lots of wine and fallen asleep together in the hayloft. When he'd been smuggled away the next day they had said goodbye, not *au revoir*, since they had not wished to meet again.

Now he was in love, hopelessly and irrevocably. He wanted Bella forever and in every way. Time must be expended on building confidence and respect. They kissed lightly, delighting in each other, until the shadows lengthened. 'I think I'm in love with you,' he said simply.

'And I with you.'

They went to an old pub with oak beams on the river near Windsor, and sat in gardens rich with marigolds and pansies and overhanging lilac. They talked and laughed 'til darkness fell, then drove home, tired and happy. When he kissed her goodnight she didn't know how she would survive until tomorrow when she would see him again.

Chapter Seven

'Dezi Bennett ain't right for yer,' Bella's father stated categorically. ''E's out of yer class and 'e'll break yer 'eart.'

Bella shook her head. 'No, he won't, Dad,' she said.

'Of course 'e will! Can't yer see that men like 'im only want gels like you as their bit o' rough? Once you've given 'im what 'e's after, yer won't see 'im for dust.' His evening paper, which he was reading in an armchair by the wireless, fell to his lap and his eyes narrowed anxiously. 'I 'ope to Gawd you ain't bin lettin' 'im take liberties.'

'Really, Dad,' she admonished crossly.

'Don't yer get on yer 'igh 'orse with me, gel. What I'm sayin' is God's truth. When the party is over, Dezi Bennett won't wait around for the clearin' up.'

'And I'm saying that you're wrong. Dezi just isn't like that,' she told him hotly.

'I bet 'e is, yer know. So be told, will yer? The sooner yer stop seein' 'im, the better.' Bob lit a cigarette shakily. Bella watched him, knowing that he spoke in her best interests. But he was so wrong.

'I can't do that.'

'Can't or won't?'

'Both!'

It was three months since Bella's meeting with Dezi at the Festival, and she and her father were alone in the house. She had cleared up after the evening meal and was waiting for Dezi to call for her. Pearl had gone out straight from work.

Since that glorious day at Battersea, Bella had been absorbed in Dezi to the exclusion of all else. She had lain awake at night feverishly reliving every word, every look, every touch, longing for the hours to pass until she would see him again. She had, in fact, seen him every evening, and at each midday they grabbed a bite to eat together: sometimes just a sandwich in the park, other times a restaurant meal. The food didn't matter, just the precious moments together. For the first time, Bella's home life had been a burden to her and she resented the domestic chores which restricted her freedom. In desperation she demanded, adamantly, that Pearl should pull her weight. At home and at work Bella became moody as each minute away from Dezi seemed dull and wasted. And although she was hurt that her father was so deadset against him, it did nothing to cool her ardour.

'There's none so blind as those 'oo don't wanna see,' her father continued. He waved his hand at the room with its basic furnishings and thin temporary walls. 'But ask yerself, what would a bloke like Dezi Bennett, 'oose parents are drippin' in dough and 'oo was brought up in a bloomin' great 'ouse by the river, want with a gel from a prefab, if it ain't a spot of monkey business?'

Tears stung her eyes. He made her seem worthless. But she knew it was simply that he was of a generation more steeped in class consciousness and spoke with the voice of his own inferiority complex.

'Our different backgrounds don't matter to us,' she said. 'Times have changed since the war, Dad. People don't worry so much about that sort of thing.'

'Don't kid yourself, luv.'

'It's time you stopped undervaluing us Browns,' she told him firmly. 'You're a businessman now, you should feel equal to anyone.' Her tone was firm, but a certain breathlessness betrayed her.

He gave a brittle laugh. 'It ain't a question of bein' equal, it's a matter of bein' different. People like the Bennetts don't live to the same set of values as us, they've got rules of their own. Your boyfriend went away to public school where they teach 'em to think they are God's gift to the world. But in actual fact you're too good for 'im. Don't let 'im make a fool of yer.'

As further communication on this subject seemed impossible, Bella thought it best to call a halt now while they were still friends. 'We'll have to agree to differ on this one, Dad,' she said sadly. 'I won't lie to you, I am not going to stop seeing Dezi, but as it seems to upset you so much, I'll not encourage him to come to the house so often. I'll go to his place at Putney.'

'Yer'll get yerself talked about,' he warned, surveying her over the top of his horn-rimmed spectacles which had slipped to the end of his nose. 'It ain't nice for a well-brought-up gel like you to spend time with him in his flat alone.'

Now he was not only being unreasonable, but old-fashioned, too. 'Well, it's off this manor so you won't get to hear the gossip,' she snapped, bitterly disappointed. She had always imagined that the man she fell in love with would become a friend of her father's. In her mind's eye she had seen them enjoying an occasional pint at the local together, and teasing her, and talking about sport. She loved her father, but she loved

Dezi too. 'And it will save you having to suffer his company for any length of time. When he calls for me we'll go straight out, and when he brings me home I'll not ask him in.'

'I've never said 'e ain't welcome 'ere,' said Bob.

Now it was Bella's turn to laugh dryly since her father's chilly attitude to Dezi would have made a rhinoceros wince. 'You didn't need to put it into words,' she said.

In her opinion, Dezi had shown great patience in his efforts to win her father over, stoically ignoring the nip in the air and constantly assuring Bella that Bob was simply experiencing normal paternal protectiveness. 'He'll come round,' he'd said. 'Don't you worry.' Thank goodness for their haven from the world at Putney!

But the world, it seemed, was not prepared to be discarded that easily. One day in August, Bella and Dezi were snuggled up together on the sofa in Dezi's sitting room with Chopin on the radiogram, some crisps and cream crackers on the occasional table along with a Scotch and soda for Dezi and a gin and lime for Bella, when Dezi said, 'I've told my parents all about you and they are keen to meet you. They've invited us to tea on Sunday.'

Bella's spirits plummeted, the memory of their last meeting still haunting her. Oh well, that will be the end of 'us', she thought, bracing herself to face an afternoon of snobbery and disapproval. But she smiled and said graciously, 'How nice. I'll look forward to it.'

Outside, a warm breeze ruffled the plane trees and wafted through the open window, setting the undrawn curtains gently flapping. Dezi's flat was on the fifth floor of an exclusive block set in well-kept gardens with lawns and flower beds. The double aspect windows offered a splendid view of the

Thames beyond the intervening rooftops. In the light of the summer evening Bella could see the river traffic gliding by, the dark commercial crafts now interpersed with freshly painted cabin cruisers which were gradually reappearing and brightening Attlee's austere Britain. She could just make out Putney Embankment with its boathouses and small boat and oarmaking factories. Usually here, in the flat, she felt happy and secure in Dezi's love for her. Now she felt vulnerable and afraid.

Sometimes the strength of her feelings for him alarmed her, in that they were all-consuming. And often they caused her pain rather than pleasure since she was living under a very high degree of emotional and physical tension. As well as the conflict at home, there was the inner turmoil Bella suffered now that their embraces were becoming increasingly difficult to curtail. In this state of heightened awareness, the world seemed to shimmer around her with added brilliance.

Right now, she wanted to shut out everything but Dezi. His arm encircled her shoulders and she took his hand and squeezed it. He must have sensed her feeling of insecurity, for he held her more tightly and tilted her face up to his. 'What's the matter? Does the prospect of tea at Ivy House depress you so terribly?'

She knew she couldn't lie to him. 'Sorry, does it show that much?'

'Only to me.' He frowned. 'But we won't go if you'd really rather not.' He kissed her brow. 'Though I am rather looking forward to showing you off.'

'The last occasion was hardly the social success of the century, was it?' she reminded him.

He chuckled. 'It quite cheered up my war, actually.'

'It made your mother's worse, I think.'

He put her hand to his lips and covered it in kisses. 'She was a little taken aback by your directness, that's all.' He smiled. 'I shall never forget that gleam in your eye when you queried their access to all that food.'

She laughed, despite herself. 'It wasn't funny, though.'

'Maybe not at the time, but I thought you were wonderful.'

'Didn't you mind that I was rude to your parents?' she asked, snuggling into the crook of his arm.

'I am fond of my parents, naturally,' he said, 'but we disagree on many issues. I happen to think you were right.'

She wondered if he would take her side on more important issues, and the way things were between them at present she thought he probably would. But although there was a certain satisfaction in this, it was tinged with sadness because the last thing she wanted was to come between him and his family. With this in mind she decided to make a special effort to make the visit to Ivy House a pleasant occasion. 'Of course we'll go on Sunday,' she said. 'It will be fun.'

Pearl stared at the telephone on the shelf in the hall. Ring damn you, ring! she implored it silently. I'll do the dishes every day for a week, if only you'll bring me his call.

She had not made the same mistake as her sister, and invited trouble by bringing Peter Bennett to the house. In fact, the family didn't know who her mysterious new boyfriend was because, sure as hell, Dad would disapprove if she told them. And her plans concerning Peter were far too crucial to allow parental opposition to rock the boat. He was proving to be a little more difficult to manipulate than she had originally anticipated. When they were together she knew he was hers. Mesmerised by her physical attributes and her expertise in using them, he was putty in her hands. But they were not together often enough. Just three or four nights a week, and he was secretive about what he did the rest of the time.

The glamorous lifestyle that he took for granted, Pearl wanted for herself. Candlelit dinners at the best West End hotels, presents, punting on the river, being taken everywhere by car... Oh yes, he was her man all right. Had she not fancied him, she would not have tolerated him for all the jewels in Regent Street since the chemistry had to be right between her and a man. But the fact that she did made her absolutely determined to have him, wedding ring and all.

It might have been easier had she not fallen for him quite so strongly, though, since this impaired her judgement and made her show her hand rather too openly at times. The truth was that just the thought of him reduced her to a throbbing mass of desire. And she felt ill with despair when he didn't telephone at the time he'd promised. There was no doubt that he had the upper hand at this point, and Pearl knew that subtlety as well as sex appeal was needed to balance the situation. He had said he would call her on Sunday. It was almost four o'clock now, so where the hell was he? Her mouth was dry, her palms damp, she wanted to beat her fists against the wall in sheer frustration.

The unco-operative artifact suddenly sent shock waves through her by ringing loudly. It was Peter. She felt weak with relief, yet restored to life. He'd pick her up at their usual place near Fulworth Green at five o'clock. Perhaps they could go to see a film and have a bite to eat out?

Now Pearl could smile. In fact, she grinned stupidly from

ear to ear and wanted to tell the world. But that must wait until later, when Peter was more securely hooked.

'You're looking pleased with yourself,' said Bella, appearing from the bedroom where she had been getting ready to go out. 'Has that secret boyfriend of yours proposed, or something? I heard you talking to someone on the phone.'

In the joy of the moment, Pearl almost revealed the identity of her boyfriend. Bella was a good sort, she'd not tell Dad, and it would be fun exchanging notes about the brothers. But no tale was complete without a happy ending, so she'd wait till she had a *fait accompli*. 'That was just a girl from work. She wants me to go to the pictures with her,' she lied without compunction.

'I see,' said Bella who was far too preoccupied with her own arrangements to query her sister's story.

Pearl imagined the hullabaloo when Dad discovered that his antiquated class prejudice was doubly called into question, and she knew that she was right to bide her time. Bella's relationship might well be strong enough to withstand Dad's opposition, but hers with Peter . . . no, not yet. A shadow clouded her mood as she remembered the reason for Bella's flushed cheeks and furrowed brow. Sunday tea with Dezi's parents. The mark of his serious intentions towards her.

No such invitation had been forthcoming from Peter to Pearl, yet the duration of her romance matched her sister's exactly. And Peter still lived at home, too. He might even be present, briefly, at Bella's initiation tea party. His unreliability came to her mind, and Pearl's suspicion that some other female filled his time when he wasn't with her. Then she remembered that she was meeting him in an hour and her mood was tinged with magic again. Maybe he was seeing someone else, but not for much longer. She intended to eliminate his need for any other woman but herself.

'You look lovely, Bel,' Pearl said since her present mood of optimism allowed her to be generous. In actual fact she wouldn't be seen dead in the plain white blouse and floral dirndl skirt her sister was wearing. It was far too prissy for Pearl. But much to her annoyance, Bella seemed to be able to attract male attention without the aid of provocative clothes and layers of make up. And she seemed to have this Dezi character eating out of her hand without any effort at all. It was infuriating. 'The Bennetts ull love yer.'

'I do hope it all goes off okay, for Dezi's sake,' said Bella, glancing briefly in the hall mirror and patting her hair anxiously.

'Do you want me to get Dad's tea before I go out?' asked Pearl in one of her rare altruistic moments.

But Bella knew better than to rely on Pearl's meagre filial conscience. 'It's all ready in the fridge, he only has to cut some bread.'

'I'll do that for him before I go,' promised Pearl.

Bella thanked her, said cheerio to her father, who was dozing in the armchair behind the Sunday paper, and left the house to meet Dezi on the corner, which was standard procedure since Dad had voiced his opinion about the romance so forcibly. She made no secret of the fact that their relationship was still flourishing, but rather than damage her closeness with her father irrevocably, she thought this the wisest course for the moment, despite Dezi's willingness to persevere.

'Would you like another cup of tea, dear?' asked Mrs Bennett, smiling coldly at Bella.

'Yes, please,' said Bella with resolute brightness, annoyed at the way her hand trembled, rattling the cup in the saucer as she passed it to her hostess. Bella's throat had closed against food the instant she had felt the impact of Eve Bennett's thinly veiled hostility. Surely no one in the world could make 'dear' sound quite so patronising. Eve delivered it to Bella with the same degree of superciliousness as an irate shopper to an ill-mannered assistant, or an impatient teacher to a mentally retarded child. The false smile twitched on her tight lips, and those critical eyes ... Oh dear, groaned Bella inwardly, how am I to survive the next few hours?

'That's a pretty skirt, dear,' Mrs Bennett said as she handed the tea to Bella. 'Is it by Dior?'

'C & A,' said Bella boldly, managing to curb the childish impulse to retaliate by mentioning the fact that she had seen some dresses similar to the haute couture but frumpish one Eve was wearing in that very same store.

'Really?' Eve's tone held just enough surprise to maintain a sense of superiority. 'I haven't been in there for years.'

'I like their prices, and of course they do some nice *young* styles,' said Bella. It was only on noticing a flush suffuse Eve's cheeks that she realised she could perhaps have been more tactful. 'Like most girls of my age, I haven't the cash to go for the French clothes that smarter women can afford,' she added in an attempt to rectify the situation.

Eve's slightly warmer smile indicated the acceptability of Bella's words, but the afternoon was rapidly developing into a fiasco. The idea of feigning a sudden headache and beating a hasty retreat flashed through her mind, but she thought better of it. Arrogant and cold these people were, but their right to respect, as the parents of the man she loved, was unquestionable. She eased her parched throat with tea and forced herself to nibble a salmon and cucumber sandwich.

'Well, well,' said Eve, sipping her tea daintily and surveying Bella over the gold-rimmed, rose-patterned cup, 'you have certainly changed since we last met. All these years and our paths have never crossed, yet we live just a few miles apart.' She rested her cup on the saucer and dabbed her mouth with a starched linen napkin. 'But, of course, moving in such different circles as we do, I suppose it isn't really all that surprising.'

Which, translated, meant that Bella was from the wrong side of town to qualify for acceptance into *this* family. 'Yes, that's very true,' said Bella politely. Just let me endure this visit without strangling the old bat, just let the time pass . . .

'Dezi has been telling us that you live in one of those prefabricated houses,' said Eve, offering Bella a wafer-thin sandwich from a fine china plate. 'I have heard that they can actually be quite comfortable, even cosy, so they say. I was reading an article about them in a magazine.'

Perish the thought that she might have gained her information through personal experience, thought Bella, recognising the implication. She courteously refused another sandwich and let her glance linger on Dezi's mother, whose dress was navy blue linen with a white trim and buttons. Its plain round neck was adorned with a double row of pearls and her bosom, clearly not enjoying the benefits of an uplift bra, took a matronly dive towards her thickening waist. She was much less thin and jumpy than at their last meeting, Bella noticed. Her hair was now white but blue rinsed and set rigidly in waves pressed flat against her head.

'I find ours quite snug,' said Bella, maintaining the simulated cordiality. 'In fact, I shall be sorry to leave it.'

'Oh!' Up shot Eve's brows in surprise. 'Are there possibilities in that direction then?'

'Well, yes, I imagine so, eventually, since it is only temporary housing,' said Bella to ease the other woman's mind since she obviously feared that Bella might be including Dezi in any plans she had for a change of address.

'I see.' Her relief was visible. 'Where would you move to?'

'I expect they'll move us to a council estate,' explained Bella, beginning to relax slightly with the duration of the visit.

'A council estate?' exclaimed Eve as though she had just learned that the Browns were to be rehoused in the public lavatories.

'Well, yes, of course.' Bella's tone was not one which invited criticism.

Tension was building steadily between them. Eve filled the awkward silence by pouring more tea for them all. Then she looked up and said, 'I understand that your father is in the same line of business as us, in a small way.'

'Yes, that's right.'

'Maybe one day he'll become one of our competitors.' She laughed as though this was the most ludicrous suggestion since the flat earth theory. 'And then he'll be able to buy a house.'

'Mother . . .' reproached Dezi.

Bella's cheeks smarted angrily, but she clung tenaciously to her patience. 'Maybe he will, but certainly not for a while. My father needs his capital for business. We've just expanded, you see.' She smiled sweetly. 'And I have no compunction about living in subsidised accommodation since my father provides jobs and a service to the community through his business. When he can afford it, as you say, he'll buy a house.'

'I wasn't suggesting . . .'

'No, of course not, but these things are best clarified,' said Bella firmly, though inwardly quaking with anger.

Frank Bennett, who had been silent until now, chimed in: 'Yes, I heard that your father had gone over to petrol retail.' He smiled unctuously. 'Just tell him that if he wants any help or advice at any time, to give me a call. What I don't know about the garage game would fit on the head of a pin.'

The incident four years ago had not been forgotten by Bella, and her shrewd gaze was meant to indicate to Frank that she knew the depth of his insincerity. The flicker of unease in his eyes told her the message had registered. 'Thank you very much,' she said in a pleasant enough tone to deceive the rest of the company. 'I'll tell him. Though he is coping quite nicely at the moment.'

Feeling the tension crackle in the air, Dezi attempted to steer the conversation on to a more general topic. 'I was telling Mum and Dad how much we enjoyed the Festival, Bella,' he said, smiling warmly at her.

She returned his smile, but with a look which indicated that she was managing and didn't need help. Her earlier nervousness had now given way to rage. How dare these people condescend to her in this appalling manner? But for Dezi's sake she smiled at Eve and said, 'Yes, it really is good. Have you been along to see it?'

Eve nodded. 'I wasn't all that struck, fairgrounds are too noisy for me.'

Too common, was what she really meant, thought Bella. 'But it is so much more than just a fair. There is the cultural side of it,' she said.

This remark earned Bella a withering look from Eve. 'We

don't care for mass culture, do we, Frank?' she said turning to her husband.

He seemed lost in thought and the question was repeated. 'No, certainly not,' he said at last. Though he had, in fact, made several visits to Battersea alone, and had thoroughly enjoyed the spectacle since he was partial to an occasional spot of razzle dazzle. In the interests of domestic harmony, though, he had said nothing to Eve who would disapprove of his witnessing such vulgar displays.

But the Festival was the furthest thing from his mind this afternoon. He was far too busy milking his mind for any possible business advantage in this romance between Dezi and Bella Brown. Sadly, he could find none. Brown was not likely to reconsider his decision just because his daughter had struck lucky in her love life. And, anyway, the asking price for Brown's would be too high now to consider trying to acquire it through the normal channels. But Dezi did seem smitten with the girl and it wouldn't be wise to antagonise him by being too blatantly unpleasant to her. Noticing that she had an empty plate, he invited her to have one of the fancies from the silver tiered cake stand. 'Do have one, my dear, Eve had our housekeeper, Mary, make them specially.'

Wondering wryly if they might be laced with arsenic, but soldiering on in the interests of good relations, Bella chose a pink-iced fairy cake. Turning to Eve, a second or two later, she said, 'They are delicious.'

'One does what one can,' she said smugly.

In actual fact the cake had a very gluey consistency, but with her robust wartime constitution Bella managed to chomp her way through it. And she was feeling less nervously dehydrated now, despite the heavy silence that had once more descended like a blanket. She stared out of the window to see that the weather had deteriorated. Fine rain was falling and a grey mist floated on the river, eliminating the opposite bank. A paddle steamer chugged by and a lone fisherman on the bank looked ghostly in the uncertain light.

The shrill sound of the telephone broke the silence. Eve scuttled out to the hall to answer it and returned with the news that it had been Peter's fiancée Lucy, looking for him. 'That boy treats this place like an hotel,' she said, frowning heavily. She turned to Bella, who had received an apology for Peter's absence on her arrival, and as though realising she might have sounded too critical of one of her own in front of a stranger, added, 'He's too attractive to the girls for his own good, that's the trouble. He went to spend the day with Lucy and her parents, but left in the middle of the afternoon saying, mysteriously, that he had to come home. As we haven't seen hide nor hair of him, I suppose he's got some other girl in tow.'

Bella couldn't help wondering if her tone would have been quite so understanding if she had been the mother of the abandoned girl. 'I see,' she said.

'As long as he doesn't push Lucy too far and lose her,' Eve said anxiously.

'It would probably be the best thing for both of them if he did,' said Dezi. 'He's far too immature to be thinking of getting married.'

'Twenty-two isn't too young,' said Eve.

'No, but he's young for his years, and his behaviour indicates that he isn't ready to settle down,' Dezi pointed out.

'It would be an excellent match,' interjected Frank. 'Her father is one of my golfing pals.'

'Not to mention your bank manager,' said Dezi, and Bella could see from his thunderous look that this was a sore point with him. She felt very much an outsider.

'So,' challenged Frank, 'what's wrong with that?'

'Nothing per se, but everything when you use it as grounds for encouraging Peter's marriage as a means of safeguarding your access to capital,' Dezi said, pale with temper. 'Peter should be encouraged to get a flat and stand on his own two feet for a while before he takes on the responsibilities of marriage.' He turned to Bella and smiled tightly. 'Anyway, we'll discuss it another time. Bella doesn't want to listen to us squabbling.'

'It's all right, really,' she assured him.

Eve, who had recently refilled the pot, set about pouring more tea. 'Let's hear what Bella has to say on the subject.' Her grey eyes rested stonily on the young woman. 'Don't you agree, dear, that similarity in backgrounds is essential to any couple contemplating marriage?'

Poor Mrs Bennett, thought Bella, all these insinuations about class, and she doesn't even have the breeding to incorporate a little diplomacy into her setdowns. Bella met her gaze. The afternoon had not been a success. Should she make one last attempt at placating Mrs Bennett and pay lip service to her snobbish opinions? Was that what Dezi wanted of her? She knew the answer to that even before receiving his reassuring wink. And had his wishes been otherwise, she doubted if she could have conceded.

'No, I don't agree at all. I think love is the only essential ingredient. If that is there, everything else can be resolved.' She moved her eyes slowly around the table until they came to rest on Eve. 'The man hasn't been born who is good enough for me, in my father's eyes, Mrs Bennett, so whoever I marry will be a disappointment to him. But I think it would be wrong for me to let that influence my decision, if I really love someone.'

Silence fell like cold penetrating rain. Bella felt emotionally drained. This had been the worst few hours of her life. But she felt better now, much better. 'May I have another of those delicious cakes, please, Mrs Bennett?' she asked sweetly. 'They really are rather good.'

Dezi thought Bella had risen to the occasion magnificently. All his protective instincts towards her had been poised ready for action against his mother's acerbic tongue, but Bella's terrific spirit had made them redundant. His parents should be proud to have her at their table.

He watched her daintily nibbling a cake and making polite conversation with his father, while his mother went to the kitchen for a sherry trifle and, no doubt, to recover from the girl's speech. Bella looked fresh and girlish in her summer attire, her firm breasts etched against the plain white blouse upon which her dark hair loosely tumbled. Her flushed cheeks, the throbbing vein in her slender neck and her dark eyes smouldering with rebellion, betrayed the fact that she was not so calm as her exterior pretended, which made her even more admirable. He loved her prickliness, her refusal to acquiesce. Soon, when he thought she was ready to consider it seriously, he would ask her to marry him.

His filial affection still existed, but was clouded by his sense of fair play and hatred of his parents' snobbery. It would be pleasant if they approved of Bella, but the fact that they obviously didn't made no difference to his feelings for her. He was far beyond their influence. 'I'll join you in one those cakes, Bella,' he said, smiling at her warmly.

★   ★   ★

'It won't last,' Frank Bennett assured his wife later when the visitors had gone and they were enjoying a drink together in their elegant drawing room. 'He'll soon get tired of her.'

'I'm not so sure,' said Eve miserably. Dezi was obviously infatuated by the wretched girl. Making a spectacle of himself by gazing at her like a lovesick schoolboy all afternoon – it was ridiculous! 'He seems totally besotted by her.'

'Animal lust,' opined Frank. 'She is, after all, a very pretty girl. He's just sowing his wild oats, that's all.' He laughed dryly. 'He's too sensible to tie himself to someone like that permanently.'

'He is twenty-seven though, Frank. High time all the oats were sown.' Eve drew on a cigarette and sipped her sherry. Peacetime had wrought a great improvement in her nerves, but she still smoked from habit. 'It's time he found someone suitable to settle down with.'

Frank fanned clouds of cigar smoke with his hand and shrugged. 'This thing with Bella Brown will peter out, just you wait and see.'

But Eve sought further reassurance. 'You don't think he's contemplating marriage, do you?' She shifted slightly in the capacious armchair in search of further comfort.

'Good God, no,' said Frank emphatically. He knocked the ash from his cigar into the ashtray. 'He's just having a fling.' He paused thoughtfully. 'Once this thing has run its course I'll get him introduced to someone more appropriate. Archie Dent's daughter, for instance.' His eyes lit up at the prospect. 'Now that would be useful for all of us since Archie owns one of the largest garages in London. I've been mulling over the idea of a merger with Dent's for some time. It would give us, and them, a great deal more wholesale buying power.' His brows rose meditatively 'Not that we need mention any of this to Dezi, my dear.' He smiled at his wife. 'Given how he disapproves of using personal relationships to further business interests, he wouldn't give the girl a second glance on principle. I will bide my time on that one. But obviously Archie would be more open to my ideas if we were all one big happy family.'

'At the moment, even a date with a princess won't lure him away from Bella Brown,' said Eve mournfully. After all Frank had done to raise the family to society's higher echelons, Dezi had repaid him by getting involved with a guttersnipe. Couldn't he see that someone like her, who didn't even know how to behave in company, would wreck his life? Why, she was downright ill-mannered, daring to imply that Dezi might not be considered good enough for her by her father! The man should be damned grateful that Dezi was bothering with his daughter at all.

Although Eve could hardly bear to admit it to herself, her rage was tinged with fear. She felt threatened by Bella. Not only did the girl have youth and beauty on her side, but she refused to treat Eve with the deference she expected from any girlfriend of her son's. Others that Eve had met had recognised her as an ally. They had flattered her and coveted her lifestyle. She had all the things a potential wife of Dezi's should desire – a beautiful home, expensive clothes and jewellery, and the power that money bestowed. They had made her feel envied, and, therefore, superior. In making it clear that these things didn't matter to her, Bella had made Eve feel uninteresting and vulnerable.

This led her to wonder if Bella actually did reciprocate Dezi's feelings. Surely if she wanted him as a husband she would have made more of an effort to get along with his parents. After all, Dezi was far more of a catch for her than she for him. He was rich, handsome and charming. So where was the deference that Eve craved so badly? She set her sherry glass down on the carved antique table and plumped the cushions behind her. 'My back is aching,' she said, grimacing. 'All that effort I made entertaining someone who would have been more at home with just a loaf of bread slapped down on the table.'

'Don't let her upset you, my dear,' said Frank in concern. He rose and gathered a cushion from another chair. 'Come on, old girl, let's make you more comfortable.' He shook the cushion and eased it gently behind her back. 'Better?' he asked.

'A little, thank you, dear.' Her spirits rose. This sort of pampering was what she expected and deserved. That Bella Brown was a nobody and Eve wasn't going to waste any more energy thinking about her.

'They hate me,' said Bella, back at Dezi's flat.

'Of course they don't,' he assured her. 'No one could do that. Mother isn't used to having anyone stand up to her, that's all.'

Still reeling from the magnitude of the disaster, Bella held her head. 'I'm so sorry, Dezi. I didn't intend to let you down. But I found it impossible just to sit back and let her walk all over me. Were you horribly embarrassed?'

'Only by Mother,' he said, but a frown creased his brow as he felt the burden of conflicting loyalties. 'I thought you were splendid. I don't know what makes Mother behave the way she does. She's always been very sensitive . . .'

But only to her own feelings, thought Bella, who was also of the opinion that the woman might have a happier life if she did something with it instead of sitting around all day luxuriating in imagined aches and pains. But she was Dezi's mother, so Bella just said, 'I hope I didn't upset her too much, but all that nonsense about class rankled.'

They were ensconced on the sofa by the window, with Dezi's arm around her shoulders. 'The day had to come when someone refused to suck up to her,' he said. 'I was proud of you. Now stop worrying about it.'

But Bella felt no sense of victory. She wanted to love and respect Dezi's parents, not score points over them. The young couple had been back at the flat for quite some time and darkness had fallen. Through the rainsoaked window Bella could see dark rooftops etched broodingly against the night sky, tinted orange from the serried ranks of suburban street-lights. Distantly the strings of coloured bulbs outside the river-side pubs were reflected on to the velvet black waters. 'I just wanted to get along with them,' she said.

He tilted her face up to his. 'There will be other times,' he told her.' 'But remember that I love you, just as you are. Not how my mother wants you to be.'

She snuggled against his chest, feeling his strength encompass her. It was cosy in here with the rain pattering on the window. The room was long and tapered into a dining alcove at the end with a serving hatch to the kitchen. Cream embossed paper adorned the walls which fell to a rich red carpet covering most of the polished parquet flooring. The furnishings were of contemporary style – long low coffee tables with winged ends, and a sleek beige moquette three-piece suite with spindly legs.

Dezi kissed her gently at first, then harder as his passion rose and he caressed her ripe body.

Just the thought of him made Bella throb with excitement. She had been ready for him for weeks. But now, in the aftermath of an emotional onslaught, wasn't quite the moment. She moved his hand and pulled her skirt down.

'Sorry,' he said hoarsely, cursing his bad timing.

'It's all right.' She was trembling and her eyes were feverishly bright. Tension had arisen between them. She felt weighed down by outside influences. 'It's just, after this afternoon ...'

'I know,' said Dezi. He had a sudden impulse to ask her to marry him now, but was it the wrong moment for that, too? His parents had obviously hurt her deeply. Dare he take the risk when that might influence her decision? Deciding against it, he hugged her with more affection than passion. 'I know Mum and Dad are not the easiest people to like. But whether or not you do eventually win them over is irrelevant to the way I feel about you.'

She smiled and kissed him, but the shadow that had fallen over the day persisted.

Pearl's goodnight to Peter, in the back of his Morris Oxford parked out of the light on some waste ground near Fulworth Green, was somewhat less restrained than her sister's to Dezi.

'I 'ope yer mean it when yer say yer love me,' she whispered breathlessly.

'I do, I do,' Peter ardently assured her. And at that very moment it was quite true. He simply couldn't get enough of her.

'Only I don't let other boys do this, yer know. You do believe me, don't yer?'

'I believe you.'

'It's only 'cos I love yer.'

'Yes ... yes ...'

'Oh, Peter!'

Chapter Eight

Bob Brown liked to pre-empt that 'Monday morning feeling' by going to bed early on a Sunday night. So Bella was surprised to see the lights still blazing in the prefab when Dezi drove her home that night.

'I expect Auntie and Uncle popped round to see him and they got talking politics,' she explained to him. 'That's about the only thing that would keep Dad up after ten-thirty on a Sunday.'

'Shall I come in with you to make sure everything is all right?' he offered willingly.

'No, there's no need,' she assured him.

But immediately she stepped into the hall she knew something was terribly wrong. The sounds of anguish echoed alarmingly from the living room: throaty, weeping, sorrowful voices. With legs like jelly she entered the room to see her aunt and uncle perched stiffly on the sofa. Wilf had his arm about Vi, who was sobbing violently. Bella's father was administering brandy, left over from Christmas, and an ashen-faced Trevor hovered awkwardly nearby. Bella stood fearfully in the door as her grim-faced father informed her, 'Yer'll 'ave to be brave, luv. Donald's been killed in action in Korea.'

Trevor caught Bella as the room swayed horribly around her and she was vaguely aware of choking on some evil-tasting liquid. 'Killed, Donald? No!' Her voice rustled in her ears like paper and her mouth felt as if it had turned to stone. It was as though she had crashed into a wall at high speed; she was numb, yet hurting, too. Maybe she should have been prepared for this, but somehow, after the impact of World War Two, the significance of this more limited war had never really registered. She was devastated!

Yet seeing her dear Auntie Vi crushed and broken like a wounded bird, Bella realised that her own grief must be just a fraction of what the other woman was feeling. She went to her with open arms. 'Auntie, I'm so sorry. Our dear, lovely Donald.' She clasped the other woman's trembling hands. 'He will never truly leave us, because he has left us so much laughter.'

'He went as an 'ero, that would have tickled 'im pink,' said Uncle Wilf with tears streaming down his face.

Pearl arrived home and went into immediate hysterics on hearing the news. Her father slapped her face and Bella held her close, both sisters shedding copious tears. None of the family wanted to take their grief to bed, so it was a long night of purgatory and well-meant platitudes as they searched to justify the tragedy. 'At least 'e's safe now,' they told each other sagely, and 'Maybe he would 'ave only lived to suffer.'

It was also a time of unselfish family unity as the despairing group found solace in each other. Aware of a strength she had not known she possessed, Bella assuaged her grief in concern for the rest of the family. It was Bella who comforted and coaxed them into eating. It was Bella who took time off from work to stay with Auntie. And Bella who arranged a memorial service to replace the funeral that had been made impossible by the fact that Donald was buried on some Korean battle-field.

Absorbed in family duties, her personal life ceased to exist. 'I'm sorry, Dezi,' she explained during one of his frequent telephone calls, 'I can't see you this evening, I have to go and see my aunt and uncle. They've been knocked sideways by Donald's death.'

'I want to be with you through all this, Bella, don't shut me out,' he implored her.

Tears smarted in her eyes. God knew she needed Dezi by her side right then but in their sadness the family would close ranks against him and make him feel even more of an outsider. 'You know how it is with families at times like these,' she told him. In illuminating the Browns' unity, her cousin's death had really brought home to her the problems of a relationship unblessed by parental approval. Would he always be excluded from her family life in this way? She hated herself for hurting Dezi, but this was no time for bridge building. 'As soon as things settle down a little, I'll be in touch.'

It was early September before that happened and Bella hadn't seen Dezi for over two weeks. Things were far from normal for the Browns, indeed Bella wondered if they ever would feel ordinary again after the tragedy, but at least everyday life had resumed again, albeit only with a kind of desperate resignation. And so it was that Bella caught a bus to Putney one late summer evening, intent upon surprising Dezi.

In the glorious anticipation of seeing him, her troubles seemed to slide away as she walked along the avenue beneath the plane trees and quivering poplars already beginning to change colour. Sunshine bathed the mature gardens and glinted on the large windows of the white- fronted Edwardian houses, some of which had been converted into flats. She was trembling with excitement as she turned into Acacia Court and, heeding the notices to 'Keep Off the Grass', made her way to the entrance. Ascending in the lift, she realised just how deprived she had felt without Dezi. She needed his strength through the ordinary and awful things of life as well as the rosy and romantic. Her nerves were fluttering as she pressed his door-bell. No reply. Oh well, it was her own fault, she should have telephoned first. She was about to turn away when the door opened and he stood there wearing a black brocade robe, a towel in his hand, his hair sticking damply to his head.

She fell, rather than walked, in and they were in each other's arms even before the door closed behind her. In the sitting room Ravel's 'Bolero' played on the radiogram, and the scent of soap from his bath sweetened the air. 'Something to drink, or eat?' he asked, turning the volume of the music down, almost child-like in his joy at seeing her.

'No, nothing thanks. You are all I want. Oh, Dezi, I've missed you so much.' And to her shame, the relief of seeing him and the tension of the last two weeks culminated in a tidal wave of tears.

He held her close and eased her down on the sofa where he cuddled her and gently mopped her cheeks. 'Donald was so full of life, I still can't believe he's gone,' she sobbed.

Words would have been inadequate, so he just sat quietly beside her, holding her hand and letting her cry until she was calmer. 'It probably isn't the right time to ask, but if I wait for that I may well wait forever,' said Dezi, stroking her hair.

'Please marry me, Bella. I want to be a part of your life, the bad bits as well as the good. I want to look after you.'

'I would love to marry you, Dezi.' Now they were both crying for joy as they stumbled to the bedroom. Sounds and smells wafted through the open window – the smoky scent of early autumn, the click of heels, the slam of a car door, the distant sound of jazz music from a passing riverboat and laughter echoing on the tide. Here, as the mystery of sex was revealed to Bella for the first time, everything registered with dazzling clarity as though to be forever synonymous with this night.

It was an experience of ineffable beauty and voluptuous pleasure. 'I am so happy,' she whispered before falling asleep in his arms.

She came to with a start. Seeing it was after midnight, she leapt out of bed and scrambled into her clothes.

'Oh God,' groaned Dezi. 'Can't you stay the night?'

Bella giggled. 'Can you imagine the uproar at home if I did?'

'We must get married at once,' he said, swinging out of bed and gathering clothes from various drawers and cupboards. 'This sort of thing is positively uncivilised.'

'I must say I do feel rather degenerate,' laughed Bella, hurriedly fastening hooks and buttons.

But Dezi was not amused by the situation. He did not like losing the woman he loved to her own bed and the demands of her family. 'How soon can we be married?' he asked.

'Well, it will take a bit of time to arrange,' said Bella.

'We could get a special licence.'

Bella tensed as all the problems that must first be resolved poured into her mind. 'Let's talk about it on the way home,' she said. And as Dezi's eagerness for a quick wedding increased during the drive, Bella knew she must introduce a note of common sense. 'If I married you tomorrow it wouldn't be soon enough for me, Dezi, but I don't want our life together overshadowed by family resentment, which it will be if we don't use a little diplomacy.'

'Sounds as though you are putting me off.'

'You know that isn't true,' she said softly, resting her hand on his knee. 'I just think we should give the families a little time to get used to the idea of us as a couple. You wouldn't want me to have to choose between you and my dad, I'm sure.'

'Of course not, but what are you suggesting?' he asked, his voice heavy with disappointment.

'I think we should get officially engaged at Christmas and have a spring wedding. We'll tell no one of our plans until then and in the meantime we carry on as we are, but more outwardly, with you coming to the prefab again. By Christmas everyone will be more or less expecting an announcement,' she explained, looking at his firm profile as he concentrated on the road ahead.

'Why can't we get engaged right away?' he asked.

'Because a formal engagement will mean some sort of a celebration, a meeting of the two families, perhaps. And I don't think mine are up to anything like that right now – it's too soon after Donald's death. But you and I will know that we are engaged and that is all that really matters, isn't it? Christmas is less than four months away, so why don't we just enjoy the fun of anticipation?' She paused. 'Please don't misunderstand me, Dezi, I will marry you without my father's blessing if it comes to that, but I would be so happy if the two of you became friends.'

'A Christmas engagement and a spring wedding, is that a promise?' he asked with raised spirits.

'It's a promise,' said Bella.

Realising that Dezi should not be the only one to make an effort, Bella took a firm line with her father, explaining that she wished to have her boyfriend come to the house without being made to feel uncomfortable.

'He means a lot to me,' she said, 'so please don't let me down.'

'I s'pose yer'll be gettin' ideas about marryin' 'im,' her father mumbled.

Resisting the temptation to reveal all, she said, 'Maybe, all in good time. But right now I'm asking that you be civil to him and stop blaming him for being who he is. He didn't ask to be born a Bennett, and he isn't anything like his parents.'

'It's in the blood,' Bob grumbled.

'Nonsense!' Having made her position so clear to Dezi, she knew she must do the same thing to her father. 'I love you, Dad, and I want us to stay friends. But I'm not a little girl any more. I'll be twenty-one next year. I need a life and friends of my own, and I want to be able to bring them home without fear of embarrassment. If you make life too difficult for me, I shall just have to move out.'

Her father gasped as though he had just heard that she was expecting triplets. 'Go an' live with 'im, yer mean?' he exclaimed.

'Not necessarily, no,' she said since she was making a point rather than referring to her impending marriage plans. 'I would probably take a bedsitter on my own.'

Another sharp intake of breath. 'Decent gels don't live away from 'ome till they get married,' he said solemnly.

'If that is how you feel about it then make sure you don't make it impossible for me to stay at home,' she said firmly.

'It's 'im 'oo's changed yer! Yer'd never 'ave thought of anything like that before yer met 'im.'

'I've grown up, that's what's happened. I can't *only* like the people you approve of.' She went to him and hugged him to assure him that he wasn't excluded from her affections by her new love. 'You and me are pals, Dad, and I want it to stay that way. Give Dezi a chance.' She stood back and searched his worried face. 'Please.'

'Well, maybe I 'ave bin a bit orf.' He scratched his balding head. 'Oh, orlright, I can't promise to like 'im, but I'll see 'e's made to feel at 'ome 'ere.'

'I love you, Dad,' she said wrapping him exuberantly in another bear hug and smacking a kiss on his cheek.

And as the summer sharpened into an autumn of nippy mornings and evenings, strung together by glorious sunny days, Bella and Dezi's romance blossomed and strengthened. They enjoyed themselves in any number of ways. There were walks by the river; dinners at the Savoy and Claridges; West End shows; the back row of the Fulworth cinema eating popcorn; and sometimes just a quiet evening at Bella's place with her father. Dezi took to joining them for Sunday lunch at the prefab and her father gamely invited Dezi to join him for a preprandial pint at the local. A token gesture maybe, but it was a start.

Anxious to match the effort Dezi was making with her parent, Bella was the soul of tact when asked to dine at the Bennetts', even though she guessed it was an invitation born of pressure from Dezi rather than enthusiasm on his parents' part. For his sake she feigned interest in Eve's latest new dress, most recently acquired malady and gossip about the members of the Bennetts' social circle. She bit her tongue and pretended not to be hurt by the older women's superior attitude, reminding herself that delusions of grandeur were simply an inferiority complex in disguise. She couldn't like the woman but she learned to pity her which meant she could cope, provided she functioned only at a superficial level. The moment she allowed herself to operate from the heart she would be lost. Bella saw both of Dezi's parents as silly, greedy children and often wondered how they had managed to produce such a kind and caring son.

One weekend in late September the opportunity arose for Bella and Dezi to take a break from the strain of all this dutiful socialising. While Bella's father went for a long weekend with Vi and Wilf to Vi's cousin Mabel in Brighton, with the aim of 'perking Vi up', Bella left Pearl at the prefab and joined Dezi on a blue and white cabin cruiser called *The Pretty Lady*. Happy in the knowledge that her father could not disapprove of something he knew nothing about, she stood on deck beside her fiancé in the morning mist as they chugged away from the smoke and grime of the capital, past the elegant tranquillity of Kew Gardens, through Teddington lock and out to the gentle non-tidal reaches of the Thames heading for Windsor.

It was early afternoon when they moored on a secluded wooded bank outside the town with the impressive Round Tower of the castle looking down over the tree tops. The sun was gentle like warm milk, the air sweetened by a misty chill. Plump, furry bees droned lazily over the wild flowers on the bank, and river flies skimmed the water beneath the over-hanging willows. Lunch was the product of a hilarious double act at the tiny Calor gas cooker in the cabin. The chops burned, the potatoes went to mash and the gravy had the consistency of blancmange. But never had a meal, eaten on deck in the sunshine, been more delicious.

'I didn't realise that solid gravy could taste so good,' Dezi teased, since she had been in charge of the Bisto department.

'And you must let me have your recipe for charred chops,' she riposted, aiming a nearby teatowel in his face.

They made a handsome couple, she in a white fluffy jumper and blue slacks and he in an Aran sweater and beige casual trousers, both wearing navy blue deck shoes.

Bella finished her champagne, fed some hovering ducks with the rest of her bread roll and settled back in her deck chair, surveying the scenery. 'Oh, isn't it beautiful here?' There were hawthorns and hazels, silver birches and copper beeches, aflame with glorious autumn colours.

'Uhmmm.' He sighed contentedly and relaxed back in his chair with his hands behind his head.

'I'm surprised you don't have a cruiser of your own,' she said, since he had told her he had just hired the boat for the weekend.

'I've never got around to it,' he explained. 'Dad had one for a while before the war, but he never took to it. He isn't really the outdoor type.' He stretched lazily. 'Maybe we'll get one after we're married. I'm assuming that neither of us will want to buy a house far from the river.'

They had not yet discussed the practicalities of their life together, and the realisation that Dezi could afford to buy both a house and a boat with more ease than she could invest in a new winter coat, put the gulf between their backgrounds sharply into focus. 'See how we feel about it nearer the time,' she said evasively, embarrassed by her own meagre resources. The future must be planned sometime soon, but this weekend was for fun and romance.

The dishes were left in the sink while they rambled through the meadows, damp underfoot with the advancing afternoon. Ripe crimson-brown berries hung like clusters of beads from the hawthorn bushes and a carpet of russet leaves cushioned their steps.

'Would you like to visit the town and the castle?' he asked, when they arrived back at the boat glowing from the exertion.

'Well . . .' She grinned wickedly. 'Maybe tomorrow, but now I'll go down to the cabin . . .' her eyes caught his knowingly '. . . to do the dishes.'

She didn't, of course, not until much later. With the last of the daylight dimmed by the drawn chintz curtains, the unwashed dishes in the sink, the gentle water lapping against the side of the boat, they luxuriated in the most exquisite intimacy.

'Love among the dirty dishes,' Bella giggled later as she languished on the pull-out bed which doubled as a table by day. 'How dreadfully decadent we are.'

'Yes. Wonderful, isn't it?' he chuckled, and caught up in the joyous mood of the moment they collapsed into a heap of helpless laughter, rolling and roaring until their sides ached. Bella had never been so happy.

Eventually they washed the dishes and had a candlelit supper of sausages and mash, since they were too hungry to fiddle with anything more elaborate, and too lazy to go out to a restaurant. The next day they trekked around the pretty little town, with its quaint shops and cobbled streets, and indulged in a guided tour of the castle which included a trip to the Curfew Tower with its tri-hourly chiming bell. After a magnificent lunch of traditional roast beef and Yorkshire pudding at one of the town's restaurants, they set off for home, happy and refreshed.

Bella stood beside Dezi at the wheel as they glided through the gentle wooded countryside of the Thames Valley, rich and colourful in autumn dress. The breeze was cool in her face, lifting her hair and exhilarating her. 'I love the autumn, don't you?' she said, though she felt it was not without a certain poignancy.

'Yes,' agreed Dezi. His tanned hands were firm on the wheel, his hair blown flat to his head. 'But I find it sad somehow, too, with everything dying away.'

'I had the same thought myself, but think of all the good things of winter: cosy firesides, stew and dumplings, Christmas.'

He laughed. 'Trust you not to mention burst pipes and coughs and colds.'

'Nothing is perfect,' she reminded him.

As the sylvan landscape began to yield to the wharves and warehouses of London, Bella noticed a sudden tension in Dezi, as though some problem he had shelved for the weekend was now dominating his thoughts.

'What's the matter?' she asked. 'I seem to have lost you.'

'Nothing,' he said, rather too hastily to convince her.

'I'd like to help,' she said, observing his tense profile, the grim line of his mouth.

'Yes, you're right, there is something. I haven't wanted to worry you with it but I suppose you should know.'

Her heart lurched. 'Oh God, that sounds ominous! Don't tell me you've a wife and children stashed away somewhere.'

He gave a tight little laugh. 'No, of course not, it isn't about us actually. It concerns my brother. I've discovered that he's playing around with Pearl. I saw them together in his car, and confronted him with it. It's been going on since that day at the Festival, apparently.'

'Oh! I knew she was seeing someone, but Peter was the last person . . . you know, being engaged to Lucy.'

'Which is exactly why I'm worried.'

'You don't think he's going to break it off with Lucy then?'

'No, he's too keen to keep on the right side of the old man,' Dezi explained, his anger manifest in the tightening of his grip on the wheel.

'So I suppose he's just using Pearl?'

'He's just using them both, I think, but sure as hell some-one's going to get hurt and I've a terrible suspicion it will be your sister. I've read the riot act to him but I'm not sure if there is anything else we can do – they are both adults after all. But I thought you ought to know. Maybe you can warn Pearl so that she is one step ahead of him.' He paused and glanced at her momentarily before turning his attention back to the steering. 'I'm not sure if I've done the right thing in telling you. You're obviously upset.'

Too right! She was insulted on Pearl's behalf and furious with the order of priorities which discarded her sister in favour of some rich bitch with a useful father! She and Pearl might not always be the best of pals, but Bella's blood instinct-ively stirred in her sister's defence.

'And because us Browns are not useful to you Bennetts, Pearl doesn't stand a chance, is that what you mean?' she rasped, eyes dark with rage.

132

She saw her jibe hit home and hated herself for it.

'Yes, I'm afraid that is what I mean,' he informed her coldly. 'Because that is the way Peter is, the way my father is. I don't share their values or opinions but I can't change the way they are. My only concern in all this is you.' His voice trembled slightly. 'If your sister gets hurt then it will hurt you. And your happiness is the most important thing in the world to me, you must believe that.'

'I do believe you, and I'm sorry,' she said resting her hand gently on his arm. 'Thank you for telling me.'

'It is a delicate situation, but maybe forewarned is forearmed in Pearl's case. You must be the judge of what is best for her,' he said, his tone warm again. Evening was approaching as they moored at the boatyard. The waterside buildings, with London gulls lining the rooftops, seemed oddly threatening after the open spaces. 'But we must make sure that whatever happens between them doesn't come between us.'

Wise words indeed, given her recent eruption, she thought.

Bella lay in bed that night waiting for Pearl to come home. She knew it must be late because it had been past midnight when Dezi had finally left, after becoming embroiled in a discussion with her father about the forthcoming general election.

Having carefully considered what Dezi had told her about Peter, Bella's duty was miserably obvious. At last she heard a key in the door and as soon as the bedroom light was switched on (it would never occur to Pearl to fumble about in the dark out of consideration for Bella), she sat up, noticing her sister's smudged make-up and dishevelled hair.

'Oh, 'ello,' whispered Pearl, mindful of the fact that their father slept in the room next door. 'Can't yer sleep?'

Her happiness was obvious; so was the huge love bite on her neck. 'Can we have a chat?' asked Bella.

Pearl yawned contentedly as she started to undress. 'It's a bit late, we've gotta get up for work in the mornin'.' She slipped her cotton nightdress over her head and gazed dreamily into space. 'Still, yer can talk to me while I do me curlers if yer've got somethin' on yer mind. 'Ang on while I pop to the bathroom and wash me face.'

The temptation to leave her sister in blissful ignorance was strong during the interim period. But when Pearl settled at the utility dressing table mirror with her nocturnal ironware and said, 'Okay, mate, I'm all ears. Whatsamatta? You got problems with Dezi?' Bella knew she must speak up.

'No, but you have with Peter.'

'Peter?' There was conspicuous hiatus, like the gasp before a sneeze. ''Oo's Peter?'

'I know you're seeing Peter Bennett,' Bella explained. 'Dezi saw you with him in his car and Peter has admitted it.'

'Well, so what if I am? It ain't a crime, is it? I didn't want you and Dad to know about it yet 'cos Dad is so bloomin' paranoid about the Bennetts.' A lock of hair was firmly rolled into place and she turned to face Bella, scarlet blotches staining her cheeks and her blue eyes flashing defiantly. 'But there ain't no problem, we get along fine.'

'Haven't you ever wondered why he is so keen for your relationship to remain a secret?' asked Bella, casting about for the gentlest way to break the news.

'To please me, I suppose,' she said, doubt beginning to hover in her eyes. 'Why?'

Bella shook her head. 'He doesn't want anyone to know about you because he is engaged to someone else.' Her heart thumped horribly. Compassionately, she just couldn't bring herself to rob Pearl of all hope. 'I thought you ought to know, so that you can ask Peter to choose which one of you he really wants.'

Pearl's face was ashen as she stared at Bella in horror. Then, with a heartbreaking display of nonchalance, she swallowed hard, turned back to the mirror and said, 'You ain't told me nothin' I didn't already know. Peter told me all about that other gel, but 'e's gonna finish with 'er, 'cos it's me 'e loves.'

And respecting her sister's way of coping with her trauma, Bella said, 'Oh, that's all right then, just as long as everything is okay.' She had done what she could, the rest was up to Pearl. But, to Bella, her sister seemed like a delicate china ornament balanced precariously on a high shelf. It couldn't help but fall, it was just a matter of when. All Bella could do was to be around to glue together the pieces.

Guessing that her sister was desperately in need of privacy right now, Bella said, 'I'm going to make some cocoa, would you like some?'

'No, thanks. I wanna go to sleep when I've finished doin' me 'air.'

Regretfully Bella knew that cocoa was no panacea for this sort of ill. And drinking hers at the kitchen table, leaving Pearl to shed her tears alone, she thought about her sister's selfishness over the years. She had used boys as toys since she had been old enough to know how. So, maybe Peter Bennett would be the one in need of glue, after all!

★　　★　　★

'What do you want to talk to me about, Mother?' asked Dezi, a few days later as he sat down to lunch with Eve in the dining room at Ivy House.

Eve served him with a grilled pork chop and left him to help himself to vegetables from the tureens. 'Can't a mother invite her son to lunch without having an ulterior motive?' she asked, spooning some baked potatoes on to her plate.

He smiled at this game she liked to play. 'Maybe another mother can, but when mine extends an invitation to me it usually means that she has something on her mind.' He poured some gravy on to his meat. 'But let me guess. Would a certain Miss Bella Brown have anything to do with it?'

She made a performance of daintily slicing her meat before looking up. 'Well, since you mention her, I would like a word, yes.'

'Fire away,' said Dezi, eyeing her warily. He was not expecting praise for Bella.

'Don't you think the time has come to stop playing silly games?' she said, laying down her knife and fork. 'This play-acting has gone quite far enough. The longer you continue to see her, the more deeply she will be hurt when you do finally end the affair.' She poured some water from a crystal jug. 'I can't pretend to like her, but I don't like to see anyone get hurt.'

Stifling his chagrin, Dezi said as gently as he was able, 'I *am* a grown man, you know. It's high time you stopped worrying about the way I conduct my life. I'm sure you would learn to like Bella if only you would allow yourself to get to know her.'

Eve threw him a black look. 'The girl will get too fond of you if you lead her on,' she warned.

Damn it, his mother would try the patience of a saint! 'Far from hurting Bella, my only aim is to make her happy.' Because he was still susceptible to the promptings of filial affection and duty, he could not remain as calm as he intended and his heart pumped anxiously. 'I'm sorry if this doesn't please you, but it's the way it is.'

Eve gulped her water, her hand trembling slightly, with rage rather than nervousness, Dezi suspected. 'You do not intend to give her up then?' she said.

'On the contrary, I intend to marry her.' He was angry with himself for being goaded into breaking his word to Bella. 'It isn't generally known yet because she wants her father to be given time to get used to the idea.'

The prim and proper Eve could become very vulgar when sufficiently roused. Her fist thumped the table, knocking the water jug over. 'You damned fool,' she said, mopping at the spilled liquid with her napkin. 'Can't you see that she's using you?'

'I thought you were concerned about her getting hurt,' he challenged.

'I was just being kind,' she snarled. 'She's after your money. Her father is probably hoping for a business merger once he's got his foot in the door. As if your father would bother with a tin pot little firm like his.'

If he had not been so angry Dezi might have laughed at the ludicrousness of the suggestion. He gripped his hands together under the table. 'You may find this hard to believe, but Bob Brown is dead set against our relationship. I am having to treat him with kid gloves to try to get him to accept me.'

'That is outrageous,' she fumed. 'You shouldn't go crawling to the likes of him.'

'I'm doing it to make Bella happy,' he said. 'And on the subject of effort, Bella made plenty of that on her last visit here, I would appreciate it if you could do the same. Try being a little less patronising.'

'I'll do no such thing,' declared Eve.

'In that case, Mother, you must expect to see much less of me,' he said firmly.

Beside herself with frustration, Eve rose and marched around the room with her hand clasped to her brow. 'So this is how you repay your parents for giving you a privileged upbringing,' she sobbed. 'Your father and I didn't grow up with all the things you took for granted as a child. Frank worked every hour God sent so that you boys could have the best of everything.' She mopped the angry tears from her eyes. 'And you insult us by expecting us to accept a guttersnipe as a daughter-in-law.'

She had gone too far and she knew it. Dezi leapt up from the table and marched from the room.

'Dezi,' she was running after him, 'where are you going?'

'As far away from here as possible,' he shouted without turning around.

'What about your lunch? I had Mary make it 'specially, and I asked Frank to eat at the club so that we could be alone . . . Dezi, please!' It was the plea of a frightened woman, but still he marched on towards the front door. 'Dezi, I'm sorry. I didn't mean those things.'

Torn, he turned slowly around. His mother looked small and ageing in her good grey twinset and pearls, standing forlornly in the imposing hall. A plethora of confused feelings for her besieged him. Pity and protectiveness, fury and hate, followed immediately by guilt. She *was* responsible for his

138

existence, whatever her shortcomings. 'Don't ever speak of Bella in that way again,' he said in a half whisper, 'or you'll not see me again.'

He saw her lips tremble and his heart lurched instinctively. But he knew that it was because she couldn't bear to be beaten. She wasn't used to it. She had never had any competition, until now.

'Goodness, it won't come to that,' she said, terrified by the fear of losing him altogether. 'Maybe I haven't tried hard enough to get to know the girl. Come on, let's finish our lunch.'

Dezi nodded and followed her back into the dining room, but his appetite had fled.

'All right, so I'm engaged to someone else,' said Peter, 'but what is all the fuss about? I have never told you that I *wasn't* engaged, have I?' But even he knew he was treading on thin ice.

It was a few days after Bella's revelation, and Pearl and Peter were in his car parked in a Fulworth side street near the river, having spent the evening in the back row of the cinema. Strategically placed out of range of the streetlights, they were still at the mercy of the bright moon which shone through the swaying poplars, sending a pale undulating light into the car's interior. Pearl had stifled the urge to rush hysterically at Peter with her accusations the next time she had clapped eyes on him, deciding that the situation would best be served by using cleverer tactics, because she had no intention of conceding defeat to his other woman.

'You led me to believe that I was the only one,' she said coldly, brushing his hand away as it landed on her thigh.

'Well . . . er, perhaps I did, but Lucy means nothing to me and I didn't want to upset you, Pearl, honestly.' He slipped an arm around her soft, rounded shoulders. It was instantly removed. 'Let's go somewhere more private, we can't talk here.'

He didn't want to talk any more than she wanted him for his mind. 'No, not yet,' she told him firmly. 'We're not going anywhere until this thing is settled.'

Oh God, he groaned inwardly. Why couldn't women just enjoy love without complicating things by demanding a commitment? He didn't insist on fidelity from Pearl, did he? She was free to do as she pleased when she wasn't with him. But wincing from a stab of pain at the thought of her with another man, he was forced to admit that Pearl had caused such havoc in his life, he didn't know his own mind any more. And, if Pearl did but know it, Lucy was the more deceived since he spent an increasing amount of time telling lies to her so that he could be with Pearl.

He had drifted into the engagement with Lucy to please his folks. And she was a nice girl. She didn't turn his guts to water, or make him laugh like Pearl did, but he had been quite happy to think he would marry her until he'd met Pearl. But whereas Dezi didn't care how much he upset the apple-cart with Father by dangling Bella under his nose, Peter wasn't prepared to take the risk of losing what little credibility he seemed to have with the old man, over a mere woman.

Peter admired his father enormously and craved his respect. Dezi was the favourite, of course, which was odd since he kept his distance and made it obvious that he had nothing in common with Dad. Peter took heart in the fact that he was now in his father's confidence far more than Dezi who knew nothing of the sidelines – the rented houses and the dealing in dubious

140

watches, wireless sets and jewellery. Dezi was only excluded because Dad knew he would disapprove, but at least it gave Peter a chance to build his role of trusted pal. He thought his father was the epitome of a real man: strong, worldly, a rough diamond with all the style and panache of a gentleman.

But Pearl was saying: 'I ain't playin' second fiddle to some other gel, so if yer wanna carry on seein' me, you'll 'ave to finish with 'er.' But now she reminded him of just what he had to lose by putting her hand on his knee and nuzzling her head against his shoulder, drowning him in clouds of Evening in Paris. 'Depends which one of us yer love, 'cos yer can't 'ave us both.'

'I'll get rid of her,' he assured her breathlessly, weak from the onslaught. She really was the cuddliest, sexiest girl he had ever met. He couldn't possibly give her up.

'When?'

'Right away,' he whispered.

'There's no point in you lyin' to me,' she said, ''Cos I can find out the truth from Bella.'

Now things really were getting complicated! Two women ... one a practical asset, the other a compulsion. Not only did he have Pearl on his back, but Dezi, too. Oh, why had he had the bad luck to be seen with her? Now he would have to play for time while he thought things through and worked out a long-term solution.

'I don't think it is a good idea to let Bella know that you are still seeing me because word might get back to my parents,' he said slowly. 'They're not going to like my broken engagement one bit because Lucy's father is a friend of the family. They'll blame you, which will make things difficult for you when we get married. You don't want to start married life at loggerheads with your in-laws do you?'

'Married! Do you mean it?' Unlike her sister, Pearl was not in the least sensitive to the suggestion that she might not quite match up to his parents' expectations for him. If it meant getting her man, complete with all the trimmings, she'd crawl like a good 'un.

'Of course I mean it,' he said, pleased with this stroke of genius. 'As soon as there's been a cooling off period after my finishing with Lucy, we'll be down that aisle like a shot.'

'You'd better not be muckin' me abaht,' she warned him.

'Would I do that to the woman I love?'

'Well . . . I 'ope not. Don't forget I could blow the whistle on yer good and proper, then you'd be right in the cart.'

Which was something he had to insure against. 'I promise I won't let you down. So will you promise to tell Bella that we're finished.'

'I promise.'

'And you'd better not start trying to check up on me or Bella might get suspicious. The best thing is to act like the Bennetts don't exist as far as you are concerned. It won't be for long, just 'til Mum and Dad are over the shock. Then we'll get engaged properly.'

Pearl kissed him in her own inimitable way, making him tingle all over. 'Okay, I'll trust yer,' she said. 'Now shall we move to somewhere a bit more private? The sooner you get a place of yer own, the better!'

Chapter Nine

Frank Bennett stood in the shabby parlour of a house in Factory Street, Fulworth, one late afternoon in November 1951. The furniture was ugly and worn, the lino had more craters in it than the moon, and the stained wallpaper was peeling. The smell and feel of damp hung sourly in the air and steam rose from the washing that was drying on a fireguard in the hearth.

A pale, thin woman of about thirty, with a sty in her eye, sat at the table with two small boys, an infant girl in a high chair and a baby on her lap. The boys were eating thinly sliced bread, the toddler sucking a crust, and the baby was feeding from a bottle. The woman wore an apron over a jumper with holes in the elbows and her lank brown hair was scragged back from her face with hair grips.

Looking up at Frank, she asked, in a monotone, 'And how are we expected to find the money for this rent increase, Mr Bennett? You just tell me that.'

'Come, come now, Mrs Smith, your husband is in work, I'm sure you'll manage.' He spread his hands in a gesture of helplessness. 'Anyway, what else can I do? I have my overheads to pay like everyone else. I can't afford to rent out these houses at a loss.'

Reliable sources informed him that Syd Smith could afford a bit more each month. Oh yes, Frank had done his homework, there was no point in trying to get blood out of a stone.

'You, runnin' at a loss!' she snorted. 'That ull be the day.' She winded the baby on her shoulder. 'It's criminal, that's what it is. Syd's only just 'ad a rise and you're gonna take it orf us. We need that bit extra.'

Frank's visit coming so close to Mr Smith's increase in pay was no coincidence. Up-to-date information wasn't difficult to come by for the price of a few pints. And Frank's conscience was clear. After all, he was going to leave them with *some* of the increase. 'We all have to pay our way, my dear,' he said, brushing some imaginary dust from the sleeve of his overcoat. He could feel the smell of poverty permeating his clothes, and was anxious to conclude his business and leave.

The baby stopped feeding and began to cry. Mrs Smith patted its back against her shoulder, her hands red and chapped. 'You knew Syd 'ad 'ad that rise, didn't yer?'

'Now how could I know a thing like that?' he asked innocently.

'I dunno, but I know yer did. Yer're a slippery one, Frank Bennett, and no mistake. Yer'd take our last bleedin' penny. And I notice yer don't call to break the news when Syd's 'ere, do yer?'

'I didn't deliberately avoid him,' lied Frank. Only a fool would leave himself open to physical attack by coming on this sort of an errand when the man of the house was at home.

'Oh no, not much.' She cast a critical eye around the room. 'Yer put the rent up easy enough, but yer don't maintain the property, do yer?'

'I think I fulfil my obligations adequately,' argued Frank smoothly. 'You are never left with burst pipes or blocked drains.'

She lifted the baby on to her shoulder and went to the window, raising the drawn curtains to reveal huge areas of black mould growing up the walls. 'You could grow bleedin' mushrooms in 'ere, it's so damp. And it's worse upstairs in the bedrooms. It ain't 'ealthy, the kids 'ave got bad chests 'cos of it'.

'You can't expect a palace on the rent you pay me,' he informed her, turning away from the diseased wall for fear a troubled conscience might weaken his position. 'But no one is forcing you to stay on here. If you are so dissatisfied, why not try your luck elsewhere?' The council housing list in this area was a joke, it was so long. He lit a cigar to suffocate the offensive stench. 'You won't offend me, my dear, I've a waiting list as long as your arm for these places.'

Mrs Smith turned scarlet. 'You know we've nowhere else to go,' she said with a frightened sob in her voice.

Frank drew on his cigar and surveyed her coolly, since he held every single ace in the pack. 'Yes, but that isn't my fault, is it? I don't run the country. I am a busy man and I don't have the time to stand around arguing. If you're not prepared to pay the extra rent, I'm afraid I shall have to ask you to look for somewhere else.'

Her hold on the baby tightened protectively and she stared at Frank with resignation and hatred. 'We'll pay,' she said, close to tears.

'I thought you'd probably see my point of view in the end.' He smiled indulgently and spoke as though with genuine concern. 'Perhaps the change of government will improve the housing situation and make things easier for you people.' He looked at her silent, resentful face. 'My man will be along at the end of the week to collect the rent as usual. You'll have the correct amount ready for him, won't you?'

She nodded wearily and scuffed to the front door in her trodden-down carpet slippers to see him out. She hated him and herself for yielding to his demands. But with the housing shortage in London as it was, what alternative was there? She couldn't have the kids put into the street for the sake of telling the landlord what she thought of him. Her moment of mild rebellion was the furthest she dare go.

'Goodbye, Mrs Smith.'

'Goodbye, Mr Bennett.'

She closed the door against the cold, damp November air, deposited the baby in a pram in the narrow hall and wiped the tears from her cheeks with the back of her hand.

Frank got into his car, smiling broadly. This little enterprise of his was a real goldmine.

'Wasn't it a super show, Dezi?' said Bella as they drove through the bright lights and bustle of the West End. They had been to see *South Pacific* followed by supper at the Savoy Grill. 'I just loved the music and the colour.' She stretched pleasurably against the seat. 'Oh, it must be wonderful to go to a real sun-drenched beach.'

The traffic moved slowly because of the homebound theatre and cinema clientele. But the restaurants were still busy and people poured into the clubs hugging themselves against the cold night air, laughing and chattering vivaciously in party mood. Dezi covered her hand with his for a moment. 'We'll go abroad for our honeymoon, if you like.'

She turned to him, smiling. 'I'd love that, though I doubt if we'll even notice the location!'

'*Bella!*' he reproached laughingly.

'Just you and total privacy is all I want for my honeymoon,' she giggled. 'I shall need at least two weeks before I shall want to bother with the outside world.'

'It's men who are supposed to say things like that,' he laughed.

'So, I've broken with tradition!' And they both roared with laughter.

As the dazzle of the neon signs gave way to the gentler glow of suburbia, they fell quiet, both engrossed in their own thoughts. It was a month before Christmas and in three weeks' time they were going to make their announcement, to give the families time to mull it over during the holiday period. Last week they had gone to Regent Street and Dezi had purchased a diamond cluster ring which he was keeping safe until it was time to slip it on Bella's finger.

Now, they drew up outside the prefab and Dezi sighed deeply. 'How I wish the time would pass,' he said. He found conventional courting a strain. Apart from the hole and corner love making, there were the restrictions of Bob Brown's domestic curfew, and the lack of privacy. He supposed he was bound to be more irritated by it than Bella because he was older and resented having to conform to another man's rules. He wanted Bella to have all the trimmings of a trad-itional wedding because that would make her happy. But, oh, this awful period of limbo!

'The time will soon go,' she said, taking his hand and putting it to her lips. Her thoughts mirrored his. The strain of conducting a love affair in the face of so many potentially damaging outside influences was weighing heavily on her.

Right now she wanted to slip away and get married, with or without her father's approval. But she said, 'This time next month we'll be an old engaged couple.'

The news was greeted with a kind of plucky resignation by Bella's father. 'I've bin expectin' it,' he said. 'I can't say that I think yer're suited, but since you've made yer minds up, I wish yer both all the luck in the world.' And to show the extent of his magnaminity, he raided the sideboard for the fruits of his Christmas Club and poured them all a drink before dragging them off to the local to celebrate. Bella was thrilled and knew they had done right to wait a while.

The Bennetts reacted with a stiff upper lip. 'Well, this is good news,' said Eve having been falsely but faultlessly pleasant to Bella ever since her altercation with Dezi. 'Pour some drinks, Frank.'

And there was some consolation for Frank, Bella thought wryly, in that it gave him the chance to dive behind his new American-style cocktail bar (with real optics and strip lighting) to serve them all with drinks. Though in all due credit to the couple, they both put up a good front, kissing Bella and welcoming her to the family, for which she was grateful. A stranger might even have thought that they liked her.

The real fun began, however, when Eve said, 'We must meet your folks, Bella dear. Are they free tomorrow evening?'

It was all-out war. A verbal battle without any actual harsh words or tempers being visibly lost. Armed with irony and insinuation, the older generation Browns and Bennetts went at it hammer and tongs, with the former's determination not to be impressed in direct proportion to the latter's obstinate intention to the contrary. Had Bella not been so closely associated with the participants of this burlesque show, she might have thought the whole thing hilarious. As it was, it seemed to be the longest evening of her life.

The Browns, comprising Bob, Bella, Pearl, Wilf, Violet, Trevor and Joan Willis (who was practically engaged to Trevor), were greeted effusively at the door by their hosts and offered champagne from a silver tray by the stalwart Mary, dressed for the occasion in a black dress and starched white pinafore. The contest then got off to a flying start when Eve, in her anxiety to demonstrate her acquired *savoir vivre*, only succeeded in showing the most appalling lack of it.

'I don't know if champagne is quite your sort of thing,' she said with blatant condescension, 'but this being a special occasion ...'

Wilf, obviously feeling compelled to dispense with manners in favour of retaliation, replied rudely, 'I've more respect for me guts than to fill it wiv glorified lemonade. I'd rather 'ave a brown ale.'

'He's very particular, is my old man,' chimed in Auntie Vi. She was wearing her smartest emerald green woollen dress, the round face above it flushed and shiny and her freshly washed hair wildly escaping from the customary hair grips.

'Oh,' riposted Eve, immaculate in blue *crêpe de Chine* with a Peter Pan collar, a fresh blue rinse enhancing her stiff, symmetrically waved hair, her heavily powdered face mask-like with rouged cheeks and cherry red lipstick. 'I'm afraid we never keep anything of that sort in. No call for it among our usual guests.' She smiled indulgently. 'I'd quite forgotten that people still drink it, actually. It's no problem, though. Frank will pop out and get some, won't you, dear?'

'Certainly,' said Frank. He smiled at Vi. 'How about you, my dear. Would you prefer milk stout or something? I know you people often prefer that sort of thing.'

'Champagne will do fine for me, ta very much,' replied Vi, courteously disregarding his snipe.

The score was even in round one, Bella thought, as coats were taken and small-talk made until the guests were shown into the dining room and invited by Eve to, 'Help yourselves when you're ready. It isn't anything very much, but I thought a little buffet would be less formal than a sit-down meal. Give us all a chance to get to know one another.'

The 'little buffet' would not have been out of place on the pages of *Good Housekeeping*, and was a clever presentation of style without the superfluity which might have enraged guests in these times of lingering rationing. Pencil slim cheese straws were on offer among sausages on sticks, vol-au-vents, savoury topped toast fingers, skewered cheese and pineapple, open rolls, pork pie wedges and a range of pickles, all displayed on a starched white cloth. Bella awarded Eve full marks. It really was an excellent spread. 'It looks beautiful, Mrs Bennett,' she said, since she was a great believer in giving credit where it was due. 'And so much more fun than sandwiches.'

'Oh, it's really nothing,' Eve replied, throwing the compliment back in Bella's face. 'Things on sticks are quite old hat nowadays.'

Maybe so to the members of the *nouveaux riches*, but they were still a novelty to Bob and Wilf, to whom cheese was only acceptable in a sandwich and pineapple in a sea of evaporated milk, and never the twain should meet, leastways not in their stomachs. But, to Bella's relief, they didn't let the side down by saying so, though they studiously chose the cheese straws and rolls.

Back in the drawing room, the food was eaten amid stilted conversation laced with awkward silences. Pearl wasn't helping matters by flirting outrageously with Peter Bennett under the very nose of Lucy, a plain girl with a good figure and long brown hair tied back in a ponytail. Eve's murderous looks were lost on Pearl who seemed to be full of devilment and thoroughly enjoying herself. Her sister's antics surprised Bella, as she had been told Pearl wanted nothing more to do with Peter.

'Nice place yer've got 'ere,' said Bob to their hosts, deliberately coarsening his tone, Bella suspected, in a kind of inverted snobbery. In actual fact Bob was feeling a sensation of power because he knew he had the one thing that Frank Bennett coveted: his garage site. And four years after Bennett's offer to buy, Bob was doing very nicely, thank you.

'We like it,' said Frank, popping a sausage into his mouth.

'I'm thinkin' of buyin' a place in a year or so. A little semi ull do me, though. I won't need too much space now the gels are of an age to leave 'ome.' Bob looked from Frank to Eve, sitting beside him on the sofa. 'Don't yer get fed up with rattling around in this place, just the two of yer?'

'Peter still lives at home,' Eve quickly pointed out.

'Only just,' muttered Bob, looking at Peter who was sitting uncomfortably between Pearl and Lucy on another sofa.

'No, we like plenty of room, and of course we do have help in looking after it. Mary is an absolute treasure and we have a local man come in to do the garden.' Eve smiled victoriously. In trying to belittle her grandeur, Bob had provided her with the perfect opportunity to enhance it.

Auntie Vi, who had been quietly nibbling some cheese straws, said to Eve and Frank, 'I should think yer *would* appreciate all this after what yer came from.' The couple stared at her quizzically while an echoing silence filled the room. 'A bit different to the old days down the East End, ain't it?' She paused and looked from one to the other. 'Yer don't remember me, do yer? Well, I can't say as I'm surprised, I only ever knew yer by sight and it was a long time ago. And o' course yer were both that bit more well known on the manor than me.'

Eve nervously cleared her throat. 'As you say, it was a very long time ago.' She turned in panic to Frank. 'Why not put some music on, dear?'

But Vi wasn't deterred that easily. 'I grew up in Berry Street, just round the corner from yer. Terrible living conditions, wasn't they? No bathroom, or 'ot water, even in the kitchen.'

'I've a terrible memory for faces,' Eve said. She had turned pale, but wore a trouper's smile. Damn the woman! Why couldn't she leave the past where it belonged, dead and buried?

Vi was determined to make the very most of her opportunity. People who put on such airs and graces about a fortune acquired off the backs of others, deserved to be toppled off their perch. 'Have you really? Well, that's where I've got you beat 'cos I never forget a face.' Her blue eyes twinkled at Frank who had abandoned his food and was trying to hide behind a cloud of cigar smoke. 'Many a dance I had wiv you up the Town Hall, Frank. Bit of a rascal wiv the gels in those days.' she sipped her sherry daintily. 'Small world, ain't it?'

Frank choked. 'It's all so long ago . . .'

'I always knew you'd do well, though. Yer were a sly bugger, even as a kid,' Vi said by way of a finale. She had made her point, she didn't want things getting out of hand and upsetting Bella.

'Time we had a toast to the happy couple, I think,' said Frank, rising, determined to silence the dratted woman.

And so the evening moved on. But whilst the Bennetts remained staunchly sober, the Browns became increasingly exuberant. And spotting the baby grand piano in the corner, Bob said: ''Oo plays the joanna?'

'Well, the boys had lessons as children, but no one plays now,' Eve warily explained.

'What a shockin' waste!' exclaimed Bob loudly. 'Wilf ull give us a toon. 'E plays by ear, don't yer, mate? Just sing any toon to 'im and 'e'll play it.' He turned to Eve. 'Go on, luv, sing any song yer like to 'im.'

'I rather like Chopin's Mazurkas,' said Eve, clinging tenaciously to the last shreds of her painfully acquired cultural pretensions.

'You tell me 'ow it goes and I'll play it,' said Wilf, installed now at the piano.

'There are several,' said Eve scornfully.

'Choose yer favourite then, gel, as long as it's got a good toon, so we can all sing,' said Wilf.

'It isn't the sort of music for a sing-song,' she hissed in exasperation.

'Oh, that's no good then. We'll 'ave to 'ave something else,' said Wilf cheerfully.

'"The Bells Are Ringing For Me and My Gel",' suggested Vi, breaking into song.

At this point Eve made her point by sinking into an armchair and eyeing the proceedings with disdain, her lips pursed together in contempt.

Bella's heart sank even deeper. It was definitely time for the Browns to leave. She went over to Dezi, who had been acting as barman all evening and was pouring some drinks at the bar. 'I think it's time we were on our way.'

'Just when the party is livening up,' he said. 'I don't think you'll be very popular if you drag them away now.'

'It's a farce.'

'Give it a little longer,' he urged her. 'I'm sure you'll find the evening will end in a draw.'

An hour or so later the room rocked to the sound of music and laughter, with a flushed Eve leading the company raucously in a splendid version of 'Daisy Daisy', while Frank waxed lyrical, to anyone who would listen, about the previously taboo 'old days'. After that, the proceedings either improved or deteriorated, depending on personal taste, and ended with Eve lifting her skirt as well as her knees in 'Knees up, Mother Brown'.

'Okay, Dezi, so what did you put in their drinks?' Bella asked as they managed a few moments alone in the kitchen.

'Just enough vodka to loosen them up a little,' he grinned.

'You're a wicked man,' she giggled, kissing him, 'but I love you.' She drew back and smiled up at him. 'Thank goodness this is just a one-off, I don't think I could stand a repeat performance.'

He laughed loudly and hugged her tightly. 'You must brace yourself then, my darling, because your father has invited us all for a return bout at your place on Boxing Day.'

'Oh no!' she exclaimed, making a face. 'He must be drunk.'

'You can't win 'em all,' he reminded her.

Bella was not the only one who found the evening a strain. For Peter, having failed to dissuade his mother from inviting

Lucy, the party had been hell. It was unforgivable of Pearl to flirt with him under Lucy's nose like that, threatening to tell her everything if he didn't respond. And she'd only done it for revenge because he had not broken his engagement. He had managed to square things with Lucy when he had taken her home by telling her that he had only played up to Pearl out of courtesy, since her sister was about to become one of the family. But events had forced a watershed because Pearl was not going to be so easily placated. There was nothing else for it, he would have to make a choice.

Pearl was the first to admit that she was not academically gifted. She never read a book, could barely add up her clients' bills, and avoided films that demanded concentration. But she had a practical mind and recognised the value of her two main assets – her talent for hairdressing, which earned her living, and her powerful sex appeal. Hopefully, the latter would eliminate the need for the former by enabling her to hook Peter Bennett. If horsy Lucy thought she was going to win, she was sadly mistaken. Peter had broken his promise to Pearl and for that he must pay. By the time she had finished with him he would be down on his knees *begging* her to marry him.

'I want nothing more to do with you,' she said when she found him waiting outside the salon for her after work the following evening.

'Pearl, please.' He stood in her path. 'Look, I can explain about Lucy. I just hadn't got around to breaking it to her.'

She marched around him. 'I 'ave to get 'ome. It's late. I've been rushed off me feet all day with everyone wanting their 'air done for Christmas.' She had already begun some self-improvement on her speech, since she wanted to feel equal to her new role when she took it on. It wasn't perfect yet, but given time ...

He followed her and grabbed her arm. 'Pearl, just let me give you a lift home. Lucy isn't pretty like you. I couldn't bring myself to hurt her feelings.'

'And *my* feelings don't matter, I suppose?' she said with calculated calm. 'But it really isn't important. You are free to do whatever you damned well like with Lucy.'

'I haven't touched her in weeks,' he said.

'Hardly the behaviour of an engaged man,' she said. 'But that's your business not mine. I have to go 'ome and get ready to go out.'

'Where are you going, and who with?' he asked frantically.

'Mind your own business!' She pushed past him and swung off down the street, her high heels clicking against the pavement, her golden hair shining in the lamplight.

He wanted to let her go. Lucy was by far the wisest choice. But desperate with jealousy at the thought of Pearl with another man, he tore after her. 'Please give me another chance. I'll do anything you want, anything.'

Ah, that was better. He was beginning to get the idea. 'All right. You can drive me 'ome,' she said.

Immediately they were inside the car, he tried to take her in his arms. 'No,' she said, pulling away.

'Just a kiss,' he begged.

She shook her head. 'I think it's about time I made something clear to you. I do not intend to continue to be your, or anyone's, fancy piece. Unless you are prepared to make a definite commitment to me, I shall not see you again.'

'You want us to get engaged, we'll get engaged,' he said.

She laughed dryly. 'Words are easy. You think you can tell me another pack of lies and I'm yours again. Well, it isn't going to be like that any more, mate.' She paused, looking at him. Even by the dim High Street lighting she could see on his face his fear of losing her. Up until that moment he had held the stronger position in their relationship. Now she knew that *she* was in control. It was an exhilarating feeling. 'When you 'ave finished with Lucy, and bear in mind that I shall check with Bella, contact me again.' She reached for the door handle. 'Until then, I want nothing more to do with you. And I'll walk home, thank you, since you can't be trusted to behave like a gentleman.'

He reached for her, only to be pushed away. 'How can you do this to me, Pearl? I love you.'

'Then prove it by doing as I ask.' She slipped her arms around him and kissed him in such a way as to leave him in no doubt of the effect she still had on him. 'But I don't intend to wait around too long, so unless you want this to be a goodbye kiss you'd better get cracking.' And, intoxicated with power, she left the car and clattered down the street.

Gloomily, he watched her disappear, cursing the force that enslaved him to her and dreading the deed that must be done.

But by some perverse working of fate to reward the undeserving, he was pre-empted by Lucy who, tired of his neglect, broke the engagement later that very evening. Lightheaded with relief, he reported the incident to Pearl, adjusting the story to make it seem as though it had been he who had given Lucy her marching orders.

'So how is the petrol side of the business shaping up, Bob?' asked Frank Bennett conversationally.

'Pretty good,' replied Bob.

'I suppose you employ forecourt staff on a shift system to cover the weekends, do you?' Frank said chattily.

'No, I've got one permanent man an' I use casual labour at weekends. A young fella who needs the extra cash,' explained Bob.

'Casual labour can often be a bit too casual. They move on once their finances have improved,' said Frank.

Bob nodded. It was the evening of Boxing Day and the proceedings at the prefab were well underway. Bob still didn't like Frank Bennett, but felt it was his duty to be civil for Bella's sake. And it was useful to be able to bridge the cultural gap by talking business. 'Yes, I've noticed.'

'Still, an ad in the local paper usually brings a response. There's always someone needing a few extra pounds,' suggested Frank.

'Yes, I usually find my casual staff that way,' said Bob, and he was so busy playing the congenial host he didn't notice the sly glint in Frank's eye.

Bella watched the two fathers chatting with a sense of relief. This gathering had been far less harrowing than its forerunner. There had been one or two snipes about the prefab from Eve. 'Isn't it amazing what one can do with a spot of ingenuity? You've made it into a little palace, Bella dear. I can't imagine how *I'd* manage with so little space.' But generally speaking the folks were behaving with dutiful tolerance knowing that they would not be forced together again until the wedding. And the Bennetts seemed a little subdued, something Bella attributed to Peter's broken engagement, which she guessed had not pleased them.

It didn't seem to have left *him* too broken-hearted though, she noticed, watching him jiving with Pearl at the end of the room to 'Twelfth Street Rag'. Pearl seemed in fine form and had been determined to introduce a younger note into the proceedings by dragging her new record player out of the bedroom. 'We 'ad enough of the old songs last time,' she'd announced earlier. 'It's the young ones' turn tonight.'

Not that age was any barrier to Auntie and Uncle who were jigging around in their own version of the jive, as were Trevor and Joan. Bella and Dezi had taken a break from the dancing for some refreshment, and he was now in the kitchen getting a drink for his mother, who was sitting watching the dancing. Bella gazed at the beautiful token on her left hand with a feeling of elation that her engagement to Dezi was now official. The families might not approve, but at least they accepted it. The spring couldn't come soon enough for her.

And the end of the evening couldn't come soon enough for Eve. Sitting here in this shed of a place while people cavorted about like fools in a space no larger than her broom cupboard! Thank goodness there would be no more of these occasions. She and Frank had done their duty by Dezi and suffered two large helpings of his *awful* future in-laws. Her line of vision focused on the dancing. You'd think Peter would have the grace to look a little less jubilant after what had happened, too. Her heart suddenly turned to stone at the look of joy on the faces of both Peter and Pearl as they came together in the dance and laughed at some private joke. Oh no, it couldn't happen twice, could it? One Brown in the family was bad enough!

Chapter Ten

'There are two chaps from the Weights and Measures Department in the office to see you, Dad,' Bella called to her father who was in the workshop inspecting the underneath of a car which had been raised on the hydraulic ramp.

'Oh!' said Bob in surprise, wiping his hands on some mutton cloth. 'I wonder what they want.'

'A routine check of the petrol pumps, I should think,' said Bella who had a good comprehensive knowledge of the business.

The official deputation consisted of a tall lamppost of a man with a pale face and horn-rimmed spectacles, and a short dapper man with a neatly clipped moustache and a trilby hat. Both wore dark business suits.

'Come to check the pumps already, 'ave yer?' asked Bob. 'I ain't been using 'em a year yet.'

'Just the middle-grade pump,' said Lamppost.

'Oh!' Bob's eyes narrowed quizzically. 'Why just the one?'

'We are following up a complaint, sir,' said Trilby Hat in the monotone of a radio newsreader.

'*What*!' Bob turned pale. 'What complaint?'

'Someone has alleged that you are serving short measure from your middle-grade pump,' Lamppost explained calmly.

Dumbstruck, Bob stared at them. 'Who's made the complaint?' he asked at last.

'I'm afraid we are not at liberty to say, Mr Brown,' said Trilby Hat.

'I don't believe this,' exploded Bob, his temper rising. ''Ow the hell can I be serving short measure when the pumps were checked an' sealed by your people before I started using 'em?'

'My dad would never cheat his customers,' intervened Bella hotly.

'You'd best get on and check the pump. The quicker this mistake is sorted out the better,' said Bob, marching out to the forecourt with the two men following.

He was as much hurt as angry as he waited in the office with Bella for the verdict. When he thought of the times he had actually lost money on a job rather than charge for additional labour! When he thought of how hard he tried to keep his prices down! And this was his reward for trying to please the public – one of his customers trying to make trouble for him with bureaucracy. Thank God he had nothing to fear. Those two stuffed shirts had better not be stingy with their apologies.

It was March 1952 and Brown's Garage was now a smart establishment offering an all-round service. The buildings were white rendered with blue paintwork, the service island topped with a blue and white canopy, and in the front of the forecourt there was a lawned area with flower borders and a tall 'Mella' sign. Brown's Garage was written in large blue letters along the front of the main buildings.

'They must have come to the wrong garage,' said Bella, noticing her father's pallor. 'They'll soon realise it, don't worry.'

But the men looked grave when they returned to the office. 'The pump is short measuring by about five per cent. We have checked it several times with our own measuring cans. Although the meter clock on the pump is registering a gallon, that amount is not reaching the customer's petrol tank. The complainant apparently called here with a gallon can to take to a friend who had run out of petrol on the road. That was how it came to light.'

Bob dragged a handkerchief from his overall pocket and mopped his suddenly damp brow. 'In that case the pump manufacturers are at fault, those pumps are still under guarantee.'

'Not against alteration, Mr Brown,' said Lamppost solemnly.

'*Alteration?*' he gasped incredulously.

'The pump has been tampered with,' said Trilby Hat. 'The mechanism has been reset to serve less than the reading on the outside of the pump.'

'It just ain't possible,' rasped Bob.

'Let us show you,' suggested Lamppost.

'I think you'd better!'

And sure enough the lead seal inside the pump had been broken and cleverly replaced. 'But who ... and why ...? It doesn't make sense.' Bob stared at the officials. 'Yer think I did it, don't yer?'

'Of course he didn't do it,' interrupted Bella emotionally. 'Why would a man, who has built a reputation for fairness wreck it by doing a thing like this? After all, it was sure to be discovered sooner or later, wasn't it?'

The men exchanged glances. 'It isn't for us to make

judgements, miss, we just report our findings back to our superiors, they decide what action is to be taken,' Trilby Hat informed her.

'*Action*! What do you mean, action?' she cried.

'As the proprietor of this establishment, Mr Brown,' said Lamppost, turning to Bob and addressing him formally, 'these pumps are your responsibility. You will be hearing from our department in due course. Good afternoon.' And, taking their official copper measuring cans with them, they left.

Over a cup of tea, Bella and Bob racked their brains for the culprit. 'It must have been someone who knows about garages and how the pumps work,' said Bella. 'But none of the staff would have a motive since they wouldn't stand to gain by it. So who and why?'

'Someone 'oo wants to make trouble for me,' said Bob, shaking all over. A more ruthless businessman might have been able to cope. But just the thought of an unknown enemy made him feel ill. 'Gawd knows 'oo.'

Bella shook her head. 'I still think there must be another explanation. No one would do a thing like that.' She hugged her father sympathetically, feeling him tremble against her. 'Don't worry, Dad, it will be all right.'

But a few days later Bob received an official letter saying he was suspected of contravening certain trading standards and he was to be taken to court by the Weights and Measures Department.

Despite the fact that Bella had no connection with the Universities of Oxford or Cambridge, their annual boat race from Putney to Mortlake was as much a part of her calendar as Whitsun or August Bank Holiday. Each year, excluding the war, whatever the weather, she and her sister, her cousins and friend Joan had joined the crowds on the towpath to cheer their favoured crew.

On this boat-race day of 29th March 1952, the poignancy of Donald's absence was cushioned by the presence of both Bennett brothers. And far from the event being a traditional forerunner to summer, a blizzard swept across London, deterring all but the hardiest of spectators, and driving many of those inside to view the race from the windows of the riverside pubs.

And so it was that Bella found herself among the polished mahogany and brasses of the Gull and Sparrow at Chiswick where there was no shortage of boat-race spirit, albeit that the flesh was weak. The room was awash with boat-race favours and scarves in contrasting blues, and a hubbub of conversation and laughter rose and fell around them. The pub was packed to the doors and Bella and her companions were squashed together, standing up, eating hot pies and drinking punch.

'Are we going out on to the towpath when the crews appear?' asked Bella. 'We won't see a thing from here and you can't get anywhere near the window.'

'In this weather?' said Pearl ruefully. 'I should cocoa.'

'It isn't the weather to be outside,' agreed Peter, his face glowing redly from the punch.

'Me and Trev will stay in 'ere, eh, Trev?' said Joan, pink and giggly from the drink. 'We'll find yer a seat in a minute.'

'Suits me,' said Trevor. 'It's snowin' out there.'

'Where's your sense of sportmanship?' asked Bella jovially.

'The east wind 'as frozen it to death,' laughed her cousin.

A roar from the crowd at the window indicated the appearance of the crews. Bella grinned at Dezi. 'Well, are you coming with me or staying with this bunch of sissies?'

Dezi made a face. 'Is there a choice?'

'Not if you want to retain your strong masculine image,' she laughed.

He slipped his arm around her. 'I must be mad, but come on then.'

The piercing east wind nearly blew them off their feet and flurries of snow drove into their faces as they braved it on to the towpath. Bella drew her duffel coat hood over her head, shivering. 'Spring, huh? That's a joke.' The wind whipped across the river, making it choppy. 'The crews must be freezing,' she said.

'They won't be bothered about the cold, it's the wind that will make the going tough,' said Dezi.

But as the crews came into sight amid cheers from their much diminished but loyal following, they rowed with their usual precision, faces raw and screwed up in concentration but evincing no lack of enthusiasm.

'Come on Oxford,' yelled Bella who had sworn her allegiance as child because she preferred their colour.

'Cambridge, Cambridge,' roared Dezi, with good-humoured rivalry. And recognising the unacceptability of changing allegiances for any reason whatsoever, they fell into giggles as they slipped and slid on the mud along the edge of Dukes Meadows which today was more like the frozen wastes of Iceland than green and gentle parkland. When they got to the finishing line, a little ahead of the crews who had overlapped throughout the course, they were breathless and hoarse from cheering.

It was the most exciting finish Bella had ever seen. The crews were level, moving with the speed and grace of fish. Then, in the last few moments, Cambridge's cohesion began to deteriorate and suddenly they were floundering instead of forging ahead, while Oxford gained new energy and crossed the finish about ten feet in front.

'Hurrah, hurrah!' shrieked Bella, jumping up and down and hugging Dezi. 'Never mind, darling. Both crews put up a super show, well worth braving the weather for.'

And Dezi had to agree. 'The most exciting boat race in years,' he said.

After cheers and commiserations back at the pub, Bella's group went back to Dezi's place for coffee and sat around playing records.

'Let's all go dancing at Hammersmith Palais tonight,' suggested Peter.

'Yes, let's,' urged Pearl.

Joan looked at Trevor enquiringly and he smiled. 'We'll go if yer fancy it,' he said. 'I can always retire to the bar when me leg gives out.'

Normally Bella and Dezi were too keen to spend their precious time together to want to share it with other people, but caught up in the festive mood of the moment they agreed. And swaying around the crowded dance floor with her head on Dezi's shoulder, beneath the dimmed, softly changing lights, Bella was glad they had come. For with the velvet sound of the clarinet, the silky saxophone, the male singer crooning 'Some Enchanted Evening' and Dezi's arms around her, the worry of home, since Dad had received that dreadful letter, seemed far away. It was a brief but much needed respite.

'I've enjoyed myself enormously today,' she said, looking up at him, her dark eyes glowing warmly and cheeks flushed from the fresh air. 'Have you?'

'Mmm.' He smiled down at her. 'God knows why. First you try to give me pneumonia and then you have us come here to get trampled to death among the masses in the Saturday night crumpet hunt.'

She roared with laughter. 'You'll survive.' They moved together as one, a handsome couple, she wearing a white blouse and a full skirt in pink, supported by underskirts in the new crackle nylon, he in a light-grey lounge suit. 'Are you glad your hunting days are over?' She paused and grinned up at him 'At least I hope they're over! They'd better be.'

'Well. . .' He seemed about to tease her, but changed his mind and said, 'I've found the only girl that I want.'

She sank happily against him and closed her eyes, enjoying the undemanding nature of the slow foxtrot. But the problems at home refused to be blocked from her mind completely and a stab of pain caught her unawares at the thought of how the allegations against her father had changed him. He had become moody and depressed, unreachable somehow. And the long wait until July for the court case didn't help.

Dezi had been a tower of strength to her and her father. He had gone with Dad to see the solicitor and had spent hours trying to persuade Dad that problems were an integral part of business and this wasn't the end of the world. Dezi could not accept that an act of sabotage had been committed and seemed to think a more logical explanation would be discovered in due course. He was as worried as Bella about the effect of all this on her father's health, however. 'Let's hope it will toughen him up,' he said. 'It doesn't do to be ultra sensitive in the garage business. There are too many hard men about.'

Now Bella pressed closer to him, overwhelmed with gratitude for his love and friendship. For in all her life she had never had a friend like Dezi, someone she knew she could rely on whatever her problems. The music ended.

'Shall we go to the bar for a drink?' he suggested.

'Lovely,' she said.

They went upstairs to the bar and sat at a table looking over the balcony at the swaying, bobbing sea of humanity below. The hunters and the hopefuls of both sexes stood around with feigned nonchalance, chewing gum or smoking cigarettes beneath the ornate archways, while a mass of quick-steppers tripped around the floor to the tuneful beat of 'My Truly Truly Fair', and jivers twirled close to the band. It was a cross section of young, working- and lower-middle-class society; secretaries and shop assistants; clerks and carpenters. There were the Teddy Boys in drape jackets and drainpipe trousers, and conventionally dressed men like Dezi in sports jackets or suits. Most of the girls wore skintight pencil skirts and stand-out collars, or overly stiff flared skirts like Bella's.

'I wonder how many of those people down there will end up marrying their partners,' she said, looking down thoughtfully.

'What a romantic you are,' he said fondly.

'Yes, I admit it,' she said. 'I think this place must be London's most successful marriage bureau. Auntie Vi met Uncle Wilf here, you know.' She looked up at him. 'I think I know one couple down there who will marry.'

'Who is that?'

'Trevor and Joan.'

'Yes, they seem to belong together somehow,' agreed Dezi.

'What do you make of Pearl and Peter?' she asked.

'I rather think they deserve each other,' Dezi laughed. 'After all my fears for Pearl, I think she's more than capable of handling my brother.'

When the dance ended, Peter and Pearl gave Trevor and Joan a lift home, leaving Bella and Dezi free to drive down to the river for a few moments before going back to the prefab. Here, while the lights of the traffic moved distantly over Kew Bridge and a bright moon sent splinters of silver into the black waters, they luxuriated in lingering embraces. The affinity between them was stronger than ever these days. 'Not long now,' said Dezi referring to their wedding which was set for May.

'Just two months,' she said.

The living-room light was on in the prefab as they drew up outside. 'Dad's up late,' said Bella, guessing that Pearl would not be home yet. She was singing under her breath as they tripped up the path. '*Some enchanted evening, de de de . . .* Hi, Dad,' she said as they entered the room. 'We've had a great ti –' Her words petered out at the grim expression on her father's face. 'Whatever is the matter?'

He looked past her to Dezi. 'Get out of my 'ouse, you Bennett trash,' he growled. 'Go on, get out, yer bleeding scum!' And to Bella's horror he lunged at Dezi with his fists up.

Separating them with her body, she said furiously: 'Now what's all this about, Dad? What's Dezi done to deserve it?'

''E's Frank Bennett's son, that's what, 'e's full of bad Bennett blood. I don't want 'im, or 'is brother, in this 'ouse ever again. Scum of the earth, that's what they are.'

Trembling and close to tears, Bella held one hand to her father's chest and the other to Dezi's. 'This is my fiancé you're attacking,' she said, her voice shrill and hysterical. 'So tell me what's happened, for God's sake.'

''Is father 'as set me up. It's Frank Bennett 'oo's behind this trouble I've got with the Weights and Measures people. That weekend forecourt attendant I took on a few weeks ago, 'e was workin' for Bennett. It was im 'oo altered the pump.'

'How do you know?' asked Bella.

'It's obvious. The bloke's done a runner now 'e's done what Bennett paid 'im for. Disappeared without trace.'

'Dad, you are being paranoid,' said Bella.

'No, I'm not,' he barked. 'You think about it. Bennett waits 'til he sees me advertisin' for a weekend forecourt assistant. Then he sends bloke number one to apply for the job and bloke number two to come in with a gallon can as soon as bloke number one has done the business with the pump. Then bloke number two takes the evidence to the authorities. That's why 'e was askin' me about my forecourt staff, at Christmas. I should 'ave smelled a rat.'

Bella tutted. 'Really, Dad, your imagination is running away with you.'

'It ain't, yer know.'

'Okay, so why would Mr Bennett go to all the trouble of sending a man to work for you? If the man is so clever with pump mechanisms, why didn't he break in and do it under cover of darkness?'

'Because the pump is in a prominent position and 'e'd 'ave needed to use a torch. The chances of 'im bein' noticed by a police patrol would 'ave been 'igh. Whereas no one would be suspicious of a forecourt attendant tinkerin' with a pump while the garage is open.'

Bob mopped his blotchy face with a handkerchief. 'It never occurred to me not to trust the bloke to look after the forecourt alone. As long as I go to collect the takings at the end of the day and lock up, I thought I'd be safe.' His face contorted with rage and his breathing was ragged. 'And all this to discredit me so that business will drop off an' I'll end up wantin' to *give* the place away! My God, I didn't think Bennett would go to these lengths, though 'e warned me five years ago that 'e didn't wish me well.' He put his hand under his chin. 'I'm sick up to 'ere with it. Greedy bugger! 'E's got enough – why can't 'e be content.'

'Hey, steady on,' said Dezi, instinctively defensive, stubborn family ties deterring him from accepting what he knew, in his heart, was true.

'Shut up,' retorted Bob rudely.

'*Dad!*' Bella felt nauseous and faint with tension but her father looked worse. His skin was patched with red and mauve blotches and beaded with perspiration. She slipped from between the two men and took her father's arm, hoping to coax him out of this nonsense. Her emotions were confused. She was hurt and embarrassed at Dad's appalling treatment of Dezi, but worried about her father's health. 'I know you're upset, we all are, but making wild accusations isn't going to solve anything. Of course Dezi's father didn't do it. You're letting the whole thing get out of proportion.'

She reeled under the blow of Bob's fury. 'Yer can mock me all yer like, me gel, but what I say is the truth. At first I thought it must be someone who 'ated me enough to wanna make trouble for me. Then I realised that greed, not hate, was the motive. Frank Bennett wants my garage an' 'e wants it cheap, that's what all this is about.'

Dezi, who had been wonderfully patient, said quietly, 'You ought to watch what you're saying, Bob, you've no proof.'

'Proof,' he exploded, pulling away from Bella and staring furiously at Dezi. 'I know your father for what 'e is, that's all the proof I need.'

Through all this, Bella had hoped for some miracle to bring her two men together on the same side. But, to her despair, she heard Dezi – quite naturally, she supposed, since blood was supposed to be thicker than water – establish himself firmly in his father's corner. 'You can't go around slandering people like that, it's against the law.'

'It ain't slander, it's the truth.'

Seeing Dezi's pallor and the slight twitch of his mouth, Bella knew that he was exercising supreme control for her sake. 'You'd better go, love,' she said.

'Too true 'e'd better go, an' don't yer ever come back,' shouted Bob.

With miraculous self-restraint, Dezi said, 'Good night Bob.'

But her father turned his back like a sulky child and remained silent.

At the gate Bella said, 'I'm sorry, Dezi, it was a disgraceful display. I think he must be heading for a breakdown.'

'Don't you worry about me,' he assured her, holding her gently in his arms, 'my back is broad. I don't think he realises the seriousness of what he's saying, though.' He kissed her lightly. She could feel the tension vibrating through him. 'I'll call round for you tomorrow.'

'No, it's probably best if you don't come to the house. It upsets me when he's so rude to you. I'll come to your place.'

'As I said, my back is broad, but I don't want you to be upset,' he said.

Back in the house, Bella confronted her father. 'I have never been so ashamed,' she said.

'And neither 'ave I, that a daughter of mine would side with someone against me on an important issue like that. Yer know me, luv, I'm not a vindictive man. But I know that Frank Bennett 'as set me up,' he told her.

'It's a serious accusation.'

'I'm in serious trouble.'

'But even if Frank Bennett is behind it, which I very much doubt, is that any reason to be horrid to Dezi? He isn't to blame for his father's behaviour,' she pointed out.

'Yer can't be raised by a man like Frank Bennett without 'aving 'is wickedness rub orf on yer.' He sank weakly into a chair and for a moment Bella thought he had collapsed. But he seemed stronger suddenly. 'I'm sorry if it upsets yer, but I meant what I said. I ain't 'avin' either of those Bennett boys in this 'ouse. I can't stop yer seein' 'im, but if yer marry 'im yer won't see me at the wedding, or any other time for that matter.'

'It's me you're hurting, Dad, not Frank Bennett. Please don't punish me for something that isn't my fault. Dezi has never done anything to harm you.' She was hurt by her father's disregard for her feelings, and distraught at her own power-lessness over the destructive forces which plagued her rela-tionship with her fiancé. 'It's Dezi I'm marrying, not his father.'

But Bob remained adamant. 'Same thing,' he said.

And realising that in his present frame of mind he was incapable of accepting reason, she just said, 'I didn't realise that my father could be so lacking in understanding. Goodnight.' And she marched from the room.

She stayed awake to tell her sister what had happened. Pearl didn't see it as any kind of problem. 'It doesn't worry me if Peter can't come to the 'ouse. I never feel comfortable when he is 'ere anyway, with Dad going out of his way to be more common than he really is just to prove some sort of a point to Peter. Me and Pete managed before without 'im coming to the 'ouse, we'll manage again. But if Dad thinks I'm giving 'im up, 'e's got another think coming. I'm not 'avin' my love life wrecked just because the two fathers don't get on.'

But whereas Pearl was able to dismiss the matter and go to sleep, Bella lay awake turning it over in her mind. There was a black memory that had hovered on the edge of her thoughts ever since her father had made his accusation. It was something he knew nothing about; the events of five years ago that made his allegations about Frank Bennett seem almost certain to be true.

For surely any man greedy enough to arrange to have a sixteen-year-old girl assaulted was more than capable of organising the sabotage of a petrol pump? She didn't want it to be true and tried to dismiss the notion as fantasy, but it grew more credible with every passing moment. She hated its implications: that she was marrying into a family headed by a dangerous enemy, though in all honesty she had known that even before this latest piece of tyranny. It had simply been pushed to the back of her mind by her love for Dezi.

The situation was far more delicate than five years ago when she had gone to Bennett's full of rage, without thought of the consequences. Frank Bennett had been more subtle this time. He would have insured against being found out. And there were the laws of slander to consider. After a wakeful night, Bella rose with a pounding headache, but no solution to the problem in sight.

She did feel, however, that a few conciliatory words with her father were necessary and took him his usual Sunday treat, a tray of tea and biscuits in bed. Sitting on the edge of the bed and pouring them both a cup, she said, 'I've been awake most of the night thinking about your accusation, and I agree with you about Frank Bennett being behind the trouble.'

'Oh? Why the sudden change of heart?' he asked, sitting up and plumping his pillows behind him.

Since it would have been foolish to fan the flames of revenge by telling him, she just said, 'No particular reason. I've given the matter a lot of thought, that's all.'

Dark smudges shadowed his eyes, and a peculiar pallor suffused his skin like a fine dusting of flour. 'I knew you'd see sense, that man's a—'

'*Dad!*' she cut him short. 'The best thing you can do is to keep your thoughts to yourself. I know it's hard, but you'll just play into Frank Bennett's hands if you give him the chance to put you in court for slander.'

Her acceptance of his judgement seemed to calm him. 'Maybe you're right, I'll talk to my solicitor about it.'

'Good idea,' she said. But her heart was heavy. What could a lawyer do against a slippery customer like Frank Bennett? 'All we can hope for is that the magistrates will be able to see that you have been set up, even without proof.' She handed him a cup of tea, noticing the tremor in his hand as he took it. 'After all, there are plenty of people willing to stand up in court and give you a character reference: Your friends, the staff – you're not on your own.'

'Thanks, luv. I'm sorry I went on at yer last night, you're a good gel.'

Their reconciliation washed over her in a warm, sweet tide.

He seemed acutely vulnerable in his blue- and white-striped winceyette pyjamas, and she was reminded of the times she had nursed him through flu and bronchitis when he had been the centre of her world. Gentle times, simple times, now achingly poignant because they had gone forever. She would always care for him and look after him in sickness and old age, but he could never be her whole existence again. She must establish her right to her own life as an adult human being.

'Because I agree with you about Mr Bennett, doesn't mean I agree with you about Dezi though,' she said, sipping her tea. From the front door came the sound of the newspaper dropping on to the mat and the chirpy whistle of the delivery boy echoed into the silence of Sunday morning in the street. 'I love him and I still intend to marry him.'

His face muscles tightened. 'Just don't talk to me about it,' he said.

'Okay, I won't,' she said. And so that he would not see the degree of her hurt at his unbending attitude, she went to the front door to collect the paper and the milk, her eyes smarting with tears.

'You're not serious?' said Dezi.

'Perfectly serious,' said Bella. 'I am certain that your father is behind my father's present trouble.'

It was the afternoon of the same day and Bella was having tea at Dezi's flat. She had decided that secrets were not a good idea between a couple who were about to embark on matrimony. His reaction, however, made her question her judgement. Evidently family loyalty, even among the Bennetts, was a very powerful force.

'Good Lord, I know my father is no saint but what you're suggesting is outrageous,' he said, blinded by a lingering sense of filial duty. His face was pale and tight. 'I'm surprised you've allowed your father's paranoia to influence you.'

'My father has nothing to do with my reasoning. In fact, he knows nothing of what happened five years ago.'

Dezi flinched and his eyes hardened with memory. 'Oh, that. Well, yes, I agree that what he did then was wicked.' He pushed back his hair anxiously, torn between love for Bella and a compulsive need to defend his father. 'But that doesn't mean he should be automatically blamed for everything else.'

They were sitting in the dining alcove by the window. Outside, the trees were burgeoning with acid green new leaves, and all along the street daffodils and tulips splashed the gardens with colour. The leaden skies of yesterday had brightened and pale sunshine poked uncertainly through a gap in the clouds, glinting on the river where a pleasure boat cruised by, the distant voice of its guide audible on the breeze.

'It makes him a major suspect though,' Bella said.

'Not at all,' snapped Dezi, burdened by the suspicion of his father's guilt. 'You're just looking for a scapegoat.'

'Huh!' snorted Bella furiously. 'As you are incapable of viewing this matter objectively, I may as well go.' And with flaming cheeks she leapt up and marched towards the door.

'Bella!' He was up and after her, catching her in the hall where she was reaching for her coat off the peg. 'We mustn't let family squabbles come between us.'

'Family squabbles! Is that what you call it?' she bellowed, wrenching his hand away from her arm. 'Don't you realise that my father's health is being affected by all this?'

'Well, yes. I. . .'

'I can see now that I should have kept my thoughts to myself,' she ranted. 'But it seemed dishonest not to tell you. I thought, mistakenly it seems, that you would understand. You must know, in your heart, that my father has been set up.'

He stood between her and the front door as she furiously shoved her arms into her pink poplin raincoat. 'Yes, I suppose I do know that, but that doesn't mean I have to accept that my father is to blame for it.' He paused and stared into her fever-bright eyes. 'But supposing he is? That isn't my fault. Are you going to let it come between us?'

Her hands dropped to her sides, and her mouth fell open in the realisation of what was happening to them, almost despite themselves. She shook her head and fell into his arms, shedding tears of relief. 'No, no, of course not. Oh, Dezi, hold me. Don't let our parents part us.'

'However bad things get between them,' he said, kissing her, 'we'll never let that happen.'

Frank Bennett laughed in Dezi's face. 'Oh, really, son! That girlfriend of yours is turning you soft. Do you honestly think I would go to all the trouble of setting someone up, least of all your future father-in-law? I mean, he isn't even competition, not really. There's enough business to keep half a dozen garages going in Fulworth.' He drew on his cigar. 'Not that I don't feel sorry for Brown. A thing like that could do his business a great deal of harm.'

Dezi searched his face for a sign of guilt. But the deep-set eyes did not waver from their look of concern, the mouth did not twitch, the speech did not falter. Dezi had been awake most of the night thinking over Bella's accusation. He *had* to know the truth. So as soon as his father had arrived in his office this morning, Dezi had confronted him.

'I am very hurt that you should doubt me, son,' Frank said, turning the situation to his advantage. 'Very hurt indeed. I've never pretended to be whiter than white. Perhaps I did indulge in the odd harmless fiddle during the war, but it was always for the well-being of the family. Everything I've ever done has been for you boys and your mother.' He paused and shook his head sadly. 'But to suggest that I would deliberately try to bring about another man's downfall . . .' He sighed heavily and looked reproachful.

Into Dezi's mind came that other confrontation and how his father had lied then. But Dezi had known Bella was speaking the truth then; now neither of them could be absolutely sure. And faced with his father's wounded expression, suspicion was swept away on a wave of remorse and family feeling.

'I'm sorry, Dad,' he said.

'We shall have to postpone the wedding,' Bella announced miserably, two weeks later.

'Oh no,' groaned Dezi. 'Why?'

'Isn't it obvious?' she snapped. Did he think she was enjoying this? She wanted to rush off into the sunset, leaving all her troubles behind, every bit as much as him. But how could she with Dad making himself ill over this wretched court case and hating the entire Bennett family more with every passing second?

'No, it isn't obvious,' he said crossly. 'You won't be the first girl to marry a man her father disapproves of.'

'It's more than just that, and you know it,' she said, her

179

temper frayed by the pressures at home and her disappointment at having to delay the wedding.

'We agreed we wouldn't let our fathers come between us,' he growled, frustration making his tone abrasive.

'I am not cancelling the wedding, just putting it off until after the court case,' she pointed out, her voice shaking with emotion. 'Can't you see that I have no choice?'

'The court case isn't going to change the way your father feels about me, whichever way it goes,' he reminded her. 'So what then?'

'Maybe he'll perk up after it's over. I can't desert him now, while he's so low.' She paused and spoke more calmly. 'My uncle once said that Dad didn't have the stamina for business and I think he was right. He just can't cope. I'm very worried about him.'

But Dezi was more concerned about Bella. Her eyes were shadowed and she was losing weight. He wanted to relieve her of her burden, not add to it by pressurising her into something that would trouble her conscience. So, managing to stifle his own disappointment, he said more warmly, 'Of course you are, darling, but you mustn't neglect yourself in all this. Okay, I'll accept the postponement of the wedding, but the time is going to come when you'll have to make a choice, because your father is *not* going to give us his blessing. You may as well accept that.'

'I know,' she said, reaching for his hand across the table in the Seagull. It was a soft April evening and the wedding was to have been a month hence. Spring-scented air gusted through the open window and the towpath buzzed with the fresh vitality of a new season. People cleaned and painted pleasure crafts, and riverside strollers discarded their pinched and hurried look of winter and yielded to a slow, relaxed amble. Her velvet dark eyes rested warmly on him. 'Thank you for being so patient. I need you so much. Seeing you is the only thing that keeps me going.'

He sighed, heavy with the fear of losing her. He hated having to deliver her to her father every night like a child. Dezi thought Bob wrong to stand in the way of his daughter's happiness and knew that his behaviour reflected the depth of his trauma, since he had not struck Dezi as a selfish man. Unfortunately, he could not intervene between them without causing more trouble for Bella.

'I shall make it my responsibility to see to it that you have some fun. Otherwise your father is not going to be the only one in danger of cracking up under the strain.' He finished his gin and tonic. 'Come on, let's take a walk before it gets dark. The fresh air will do us both good.'

On Saturday 5th July 1952, Bella, looking stunning in a yellow silk dress and a matching picture hat with trailing ribbons, sat beside Dezi, wearing a striped blazer and white flannels, in his car coasting through the lush green Oxfordshire country-side en route for the finals of the Henley Regatta. Approaching this oldest of Oxfordshire towns via its handsome stone bridge, she caught her breath at the splendour and pageantry around her. The sunlit river was filled with boats, and edged by an interminable ribbon of people. Behind them a forest of brightly striped tents spread across the meadows.

Dezi's longstanding connections with the Regatta ensured them a welcome in the exclusive steward's enclosure where they were immediately surrounded by friends eager to drown them in Pimm's, which was flowing in true Regatta tradition.

Initially, Bella had been a little daunted. But not for long. Far from feeling excluded, she found herself the star of the show, with Dezi eager to show her off to all and sundry. Shaking so many hands she began to feel like royalty. And the admiring male glances told her she was equal to the feminine competition around her.

Fortunately, they managed to lunch alone at a table under the trees. They had champagne and caviare, fillet steak and salad with tender new potatoes and a variety of local grown vegetables, followed by strawberries and cream. 'Mmm, delicious,' said Bella, 'I'll be tiddly by teatime though, with all this booze.'

He laughed, pleased to see her relaxing. 'We'll concentrate on watching the rowing this afternoon, or I'll be accused by serious rowing men of coming just for the socialising.'

The sun shining from a clear blue sky gave the scene a picture postcard quality: the men in blazers, club ties, caps of many colours; the women in fashionable dresses and colourful hats.

'All this makes me even more aware of the difference in our backgrounds,' she said. 'Until today Henley Regatta was out of my league, like Royal Ascot.'

'You are the most beautiful woman here,' he said, smiling fondly at her.

'Flattery will get you everywhere,' she laughed. 'But what I really mean is that there is still so much about you that I don't know. I didn't realise that you were quite so well connected.'

'I did a little rowing before the war and I'm on the committee of my old rowing club,' he explained. 'And until recently I used to give a hand with the staging of the Regatta. The whole lot, stands and all, has to be erected and removed each season. And practically all the work is done by amateurs for no payment whatever. The standard of organisation is the envy of the world.' He sipped his champagne. 'This is one of the oldest river regattas in the world. The first was in 1839.'

'Why did you stop helping with it?' she asked.

He tilted his head thoughtfully. 'The usual reason – pressure of work.'

Glancing absently around, she asked, 'Who are the official-looking men in dark suits and straw boaters with black bands?'

'Oxford University scouts,' he told her. 'They are traditional. A week's duty here is regarded as a paid holiday by them.'

'Scouts!' She looked puzzled. 'Aren't they getting on a bit for that sort of thing?'

'College servants,' Dezi explained. 'They call them scouts.'

'Didn't your parents want you to go to Oxford?' Bella asked.

'They would have liked it, yes, but I'm no intellectual,' he explained 'And a place at Oxford is something that money alone cannot buy. Anyway, the war put paid to any chance of university for me.'

'I see.' She grinned at him. 'So, how many other interests do you have that I know nothing about?'

His eyes twinkled as he caught her playful mood. 'Oh, just womanising, a spot of crime, nothing very interesting.'

'It's a good job you're joking.'

He leaned across the table and took her hand, gazing solemnly into her eyes. 'Nothing is kept from you intentionally. My life is an open book.'

'I know,' she said. Around them was the buzz of conversation, light, exuberant, casual. He was devastatingly handsome today, she thought, his skin tanned, eyes sparkling, the sunshine bringing red lights into his hair. She had not been unaware of admiring glances being cast in his direction from the most stunning of females, and she wondered why he had chosen her, totally unaware of her own dark, luxuriant beauty so striking in the yellow outfit. 'Sometimes, when I'm at home, I feel distant from you though.'

'You know the answer to that – marry me,' he challenged.

'Soon,' she said softly, her eyes darkening as she remembered her father's case next week.

Feeling a part of her withdraw from him, he cursed his impulsiveness. These last few weeks he had stifled his impatience and tried to help her by providing affection and escape in the form of outings such as this one. 'Come on,' he said lightly. 'Let's go to the river bank and get a close look at the races.'

There were cheers and commiserations as the skiffs cut the water in the various contests, on a course lined by a multitude of colourful, bunting-strung boats. The event of the day, which some were calling the race of the century, was between an English and an Australian crew, with the home craft eventually triumphing. But the Thames Challenge Cup went to the USA when Pennsylvania beat Christ's Cambridge.

The excitement was infectious and Bella became flushed with elation. On the way home her mood deteriorated. The day had been a pleasant diversion, and she appreciated Dezi's attempts to lighten her burden. But with the court case and her father's strange mood shadowing her life, it was impossible to escape her problems for long.

Chapter Eleven

A tense silence filled the courtroom as the magistrate's decision was awaited. Bob Brown stood very still, his face drawn, his stocky build reduced to lean haggardness. Bella's muscles ached from strain and her heart had bumped unevenly throughout the hearing.

On one side of her sat her aunt and uncle, and on the other her father's trusted bodyshop foreman, John Sharpe. Trevor had been here earlier and had spoken up on behalf of his Uncle Bob, but was now holding the fort at the garage while John stayed on to give Bella moral support since, for obvious reasons, she had not wanted Dezi to attend. The embarrassment of seeing her father in the dock had proved too much for Pearl, and after a token appearance she had gone back to work.

' . . . and you are obviously a hardworking and honest man normally and have plenty of people willing to testify to this,' the magistrate was saying. 'But it is your responsibility to ensure that your petrol pumps comply with the law and serve the public fairly. This has not been done and we therefore must find you guilty as charged. You will pay a fine of £75.'

A shocked murmur rippled through the court and John's

steadying hand on Bella's arm was welcome as her legs buckled. She saw her father flinch and turn ashen.

'It could be worse,' whispered John sympathetically. 'It ain't too huge a fine.'

'The money doesn't matter,' she said. 'It's being found guilty that will floor him.'

John drove them back to the prefab in his ancient Austin 10. The atmosphere was warm with concern for Bob, but uncertain. As at a bereavement, no one quite knew what to say.

'Bleedin' magistrates,' said Wilf, who was sitting in the back with Bella. 'What do they know?'

'They took the line that the pumps are Bob's responsibility no matter 'oo tampered with 'em, didn't they?' said Vi, who was sitting next to Bella. 'You must forget about it now, Bob, and look to the future.'

'Vi's right,' agreed John. 'Those people who matter know that you were set up, let the others think what they like.' He inclined his head slightly towards Bob, who was sitting in the front. 'I've got a really tricky job in the workshop. I'd value your opinion on it if you're comin' into the garage later on today.'

Bella warmed to him, thoroughly approving of his tactics since her father had done far too much moping at home recently. Involvement was what he needed, but she suspected he'd need a great deal more persuasion. So she was pleasantly surprised when he said, 'Orlright, mate, I'll have a cuppa tea, change me clothes, then I'll get meself down there.'

Relief lightened the atmosphere like sunshine after rain, and Bella caught John's eye in the driving mirror and winked. She had work to do at the garage, too, and after they had all had a cup of tea and a sandwich at the prefab, she travelled there with John, while her father took Vi and Wilf home in the van.

'I appreciate what you did earlier,' she said.

''Is advice will be useful,' said John.

'But not essential,' she guessed.

'No one is indispensable, but I think 'e needs to feel that 'e is, right now,' John said. 'There's nothin' like work to 'elp yer forget.'

'Thank you for all the extra work you have put in while Dad has been having so much time off,' she said.

'Glad to 'elp,' he said amiably. 'By the end of the week the whole thing will be past 'istory, I reckon.'

And that may very well have been the case had the local press not splashed the story all over the paper, in such a way as to paint a picture of her father very different from the one Bella knew. PETROL FRAUD — GARAGE PROPRIETOR FOUND GUILTY, was the headline.

Forecourt sales dropped dramatically, snide remarks were made to the family in the street, the shops and pub.

'It will be a five-minute wonder, Dad,' Bella sensibly pointed out. 'This time next week someone else will be news.'

But Bob did not have his daughter's indomitable spirit or the resilience of youth. He became more morose than ever, chain smoking, barely eating enough to stay alive, and plagued with nausea and headaches. The doctor diagnosed stress and prescribed tablets to calm him, but they seemed to dull his spirit even more, Bella thought.

As his deteriorating health kept him increasingly out of action, Bella's business responsibilities expanded accordingly. Along with her own clerical duties, she now found herself responsible for hiring and firing staff, albeit with the guidance of Trevor and John, maintaining stock levels, chasing overdue accounts from the large companies whose vehicles Brown's were contracted to maintain, and any number of other everyday tasks befitting a garage proprietor. Fortunately, the repair side of the business was scarcely affected by the adverse publicity, because a large proportion of the work came from within the trade, where Bob's reputation for quality was too well respected to be unduly harmed by any article in the local paper.

Because of the drop in petrol sales, Bella was forced to dispense with weekend forecourt staff until business picked up again, as she was determined it would. She retained one part-timer for the busy weekday periods and counted herself very lucky in that the family, and John, rallied round and offered to take turns with her to cover the rest. As well as taking her turn at the pumps, Auntie Vi also assisted Bella with some routine office work for an hour or so after she had finished work at the school. Camaraderie was strong and Bella thanked God for them all, particularly Trevor and John who, as well as shouldering the responsibility of the workshops in her father's absence, were generous with their help and advice in many other ways.

Even Pearl did a stint at the pumps, though, without being cynical, Bella suspected that it was more gain than pain for her in that forecourt duty provided a perfect opportunity for her to indulge her natural inclinations as a flirt. The fact that she was heavily involved with Peter was no deterrent, it was simply a game to her.

As the heavy, humid late summer turned to a soft bronze autumn, the added strain took its toll on Bella, finally culminating in her falling asleep whilst dining out with Dezi one

Friday evening. They were in a West End restaurant having been to see Terrence Rattigan's *The Deep Blue Sea*, during which Bella had snoozed unnoticed in the plush comfort of the theatre. But her brush with slumber in the restaurant was more noticeable since her head nodded momentarily on to her chest while Dezi was in mid sentence, between dessert and coffee.

His concern for Bella was tinged with despair because he had felt pushed to the periphery of her life for weeks. She either cancelled their arrangements because of pressure of work, or was too tired to be any sort of company when they did meet. And his offers of help had been declined because she felt that would exacerbate the situation with her father. Dezi was tired of being hidden away like a guilty secret. '*This* is the last straw,' he declared, anguish hardening his tone. 'I am not going to stand by and watch you kill yourself with work. We are going to spend tomorrow afternoon together, whatever happens. We'll drive out of London somewhere to give you a break, God knows you need one.'

'I have to work the forecourt until mid-morning.'

'I shall be working until then, too,' he interrupted firmly. 'And I'll pick you up at the garage at eleven.'

'I have to go home and get Dad's lunch,' she said, chewing her lip anxiously.

'Let him get his own lunch for once, he isn't helpless,' declared Dezi.

'Well, I . . .'

'No arguments,' commanded Dezi crisply. 'Take your clothes to work and you can change at my place. If you go home first, you're sure to get caught up in some duty or other.'

His rich brown eyes held hers firmly and Bella knew that

she had pushed him to the limit of his patience. 'All right,' she said. 'I'll be ready at twelve.'

John Sharpe usually spent Saturday afternoon with his mates. Sometimes they went to watch a football match, especially if Chelsea was playing at Stamford Bridge. Or, if there wasn't a game they fancied, they would mooch around Fulworth, call in at the Billiard Hall, go to the café for a cuppa and a bun, hang around the record counter at Woolworths 'til it was time to go home for tea and the soccer results. Saturday afternoon was a time for buying clothes, too, something he always did with the approval of his pals. Because John's gear had to be acceptable to his peers.

But today, like most Saturdays recently, his routine was upset by the fact that he had agreed to look after the forecourt after his stint in the workshop. He had had a quick wash and was eating his sandwiches in the small staff room before relieving Bella from duty. He didn't really mind helping out. In fact, it made him feel surprisingly good, like one of the family. He liked the Browns and thought it was rotten luck Bob getting set up like that. Trevor was a real pal, and Vi and Wilf were both good sorts.

And then there were the girls. Both terrific lookers and strongly fancied by all the lads. Pearl was a right little cracker in a brassy sort of a way; Diana Dors, the boys called her. But Bella, now she really was special. Those dark, sultry eyes, that rich glossy hair, that stunning figure. She was the most beautiful girl he had ever seen.

Glancing at his watch and seeing that it was time he reported for duty, he made his way outside where Bella was working at the pumps, holding the nozzle to the filler tank of a Morris and chatting to the driver, apparently unaware of the man's admiring glances. A Fair Isle sweater and black calf-length pants clung curvaceously to her slender form, and her long hair glinted in the autumn sunshine as she flicked it back from her face. John's heart beat faster. She was the perfect woman: beautiful but not conceited; confident but not bossy; kind but not sloppy; and a fighter. Oh yes, this business would not fail while she held the reins.

'Hi, Bel,' he said, approaching her with a smile. 'I'll take over now if you want to get away.'

She grinned, displaying milk-white teeth. 'I'll just finish serving this customer and I'll see you in the office to give you an update.'

In the tiny forecourt office, which was kept solely for the use of the duty attendant, Bella said, 'There's plenty of small change in the safe and Auntie Vi will be here about five to relieve you. So if you're going out this evening, you'll have plenty of time to get ready.'

She had a smudge of oil on her cheek which John longed to wipe away with his finger, trembling inwardly at the thought of touching that smooth, translucent skin.

'That's good,' he said, for want of a more interesting remark.

'Are you going anywhere nice this evening?' she asked conversationally.

He knew that this was just an exercise in staff relations to her, but he still felt warmed by her attention. These recent months must have been a worrying time for her, but she never failed to show an interest in other people. 'Only out with me mates for a few pints and a creep round the dance floor at the Palais,' he explained, feeling an infuriating blush burn his cheeks. At twenty-three he should be able to converse with a girl without schoolboy embarrassment. After all, he wasn't totally inexperienced. There had been a few girlfriends and he'd almost got engaged once when he was doing his National Service, though it had petered out after his posting to Cyprus. But Bella wasn't just any girl.

'You'll be looking for female company at the Palais, I suppose,' said Bella lightly. Though John seemed more the type to prop up the bar with his mates than chase the girls, she thought. He was nice but definitely not a lady killer. Being in roughly the same age group as herself, she thought of him as a friend, rather than an employee. He was a rock of a man with broad shoulders, a solid chest and thickset neck and jawline. Of medium height, but taller than Bella, he had fair hair worn unparted with a quiff, warm brown eyes, a broad nose and a firm mouth which curled frequently into a crooked smile. He liked to dress in Teddy Boy style and hang around with a crowd. But she didn't feel threatened in his company as she might with another young man of that ilk. She remembered him telling her once that his father had been in the motor trade and had been killed in action in the war. He lived with his mother, a charlady apparently, in a council flat. He was from the same working-class background as herself and she shared her father's trust in him.

'I dunno about that,' he replied chattily. 'We go for a laugh more than anything.'

'One of these Saturday nights you'll meet some girl who'll make you wonder what you saw in going out with a crowd of blokes,' she teased.

The ping of the service bell, indicating that someone had driven over the rubber tubing which stretched the width of the forecourt, made them both turn to the window. Bella's face was illuminated with a sudden radiance as a gleaming Ford Consul streaked past the pumps and stopped in the far corner. If it had been anyone else but Bella, John might have thought it was the Bennett style and cashflow that was the attraction. But he knew that it would take something other than that to impress her.

'There's my date,' she said excitedly. 'So, I'll get my coat and be on my way.' At the door she turned and blew him a friendly kiss. 'Thanks for everything, John, you're a real pal.' And leaving him staring stupidly after her, she swung across the forecourt.

Observing Dezi Bennett from the window, and noticing that he was dressed in a casual cream sweater and beige slacks, John recognised his charisma even from a distance. He didn't dress in the manner that John thought was 'cool', but the man's style was manifest in the ease and confidence with which he carried himself. As Dezi turned to see Bella approaching, the man's whole being radiated with the same light that John had just seen in her. John was no expert on being 'in love' and supposed it was some sort of a mixture of lust and friendship, but he had never seen two people so right for each other.

As they fell into each other's arms in greeting, John turned away filled with a deep and inexplicable loneliness. Suddenly he felt clumsy and immature. He was not a man to be bothered by envy as a rule, being happy with his lot. He enjoyed his work and earned a decent wage, he had good mates and a kind Mum who never interfered in his life. And he didn't begrudge Dezi Bennett his money or magnetism. But he would do *anything* to have Bella Brown look at him in that way.

★   ★   ★

The dreaming spires of Oxford were bathed in hazy sunshine and finely traced against a misty blue sky as Bella and Dezi entered this historical town, a beautiful hotchpotch of old and new, of academic and industrial, where ancient houses of learning mingled with modern chain stores and a car factory. They parked the car near the meadows behind Christchurch, with its greyish beige stone buildings and the silver grey dome of Tom Tower presiding majestically, and after lunching at a place in the town they ambled towards the river. Term was in progress so the colleges were not open to sightseers, but through various gaps and gateways they could see the cloistered lawned quadrangles and occasional figures hurrying through the archways with black gowns flowing like vicars' vestments.

A hint of woodsmoke scented the air and the afternoon sunshine was seasoned with a faint mist that caught the back of the throat. The river was dotted with punts moored close to the banks, and a crew of oarsmen were being instructed through a megaphone by a man on a bicycle on the towpath. Pairs of earnest students walked briskly by, engrossed in conversation. Somewhere a gramophone played a popular tune and a bell chimed out the hour above the distant rumble of traffic. They sat on a wooden bench on the edge of the meadows, which were carpeted with fallen leaves. For a long time they silently absorbed the ambience, then Bella turned to Dezi and said, 'Thank you for bullying me into coming. It's wonderful here.'

'We both needed a break,' he said.

'I'm sorry I've neglected you lately,' she told him.

Instead of the expected reassurance, he just said, 'Come on, let's go and have tea.'

Back in the city, they wandered through narrow cobbled

alleyways, passing bow-windowed book shops and tea rooms, and clusters of parked bicycles. Already, cosy patches of light were beginning to appear in the solemn college buildings and the shops and cafés glowed appealingly.

They went to a homely tea shop with red-and-white checked tablecloths and trim waitresses in traditional uniform. The air was warm with the smell of toast, the comforting tinkle of tea cups and the pleasant hubbub of conversation. As they tucked into toasted tea cakes and crumpets, Bella thought she would burst with love for Dezi.

But he was in a strange, preoccupied mood which deterred her from telling him so and led her to ask instead: 'What's on your mind, Dezi?'

'I'm tired of the situation between us,' he said. 'I want us to get married right away.'

And so did she. But marriage to Dezi meant problems she didn't know how to handle. She couldn't hurt her father, no matter how unreasonable his behaviour, especially when he was so depressed. 'You know how things are for me right now,' she said.

'I know that you are allowing your father to wreck our lives, yes,' he snapped, and she could see the deep lines of strain around his eyes.

She wasn't being fair to him, she knew that. But still her instinct forced her to fly to her father's defence. 'You talk about *my* father, when if *yours* hadn't . . .' She checked herself, just in time.

'Another quarrel,' Dezi pointed out with a sigh. 'I'm tired of being dominated by the hatred between our parents. Surely we're entitled to be together, to have a life of our own. I know marriage to me will not be easy for you because of your father, and God knows, the last thing I want to do is to come between the two of you. He might want to stop you seeing me, but I can assure you that I'll never try to stop you seeing *him.*'

He sighed heavily. These last weeks had been hell as he had felt her being dragged away from him like a prisoner behind enemy lines. 'I know things are tough for you and I don't want to make them worse. But we can't go on like this any longer. You and I were meant for each other and I'm not prepared just to stand by and see our chance of happiness destroyed by other people.'

Bella sipped her tea, her throat suddenly parched. 'I haven't delayed our wedding plans lightly,' she explained. 'I know how much I have hurt you and I hate myself for it.' She set her cup down into the saucer and shook her head despairingly. 'But Dad isn't the man he once was and I do have a duty to him. He is my father, after all.'

'I'm not asking you to desert him. You can have him live with us if you'd feel happier.'

'You know he would never agree to that.'

'Call and see him three times a day then,' Dezi suggested.

'He doesn't want to see me at all if I marry you, you know that,' she reminded him.

'He'll come round once he gets used to the idea.'

A group of duffel-coated students clattered in, their exuberant presence filling the room. They were of both sexes and all about Bella's age. They were laughing and flirting vociferously, casually having fun. Bella felt a stab of envy. She was twenty-one, but she might almost have been of another generation.

Dezi was right in everything he said. Few men would have been so patient. And she was tired of being torn in two. It must be worse than having an affair with a married man. Even though she never actually concealed the fact that she was seeing Dezi from her father, she didn't refer to it either, given his current frame of mind. And Dezi deserved more than that.

'Can we go back to London now?' she asked suddenly.

He looked surprised. 'Rather have dinner in the West End?'

She shook her head. 'No, I'd rather eat at your place. We could get some fish and chips.'

'Okay,' he said.

Back at Putney they dined deliciously on the unlikely combination of fish and chips and sparkling white wine, eaten in front of Dezi's gas fire. 'I love you,' she said, 'and I'd like to get married as soon as it can be arranged.' She felt stronger immediately the words were out. 'Dad will just have to get used to the idea.'

They made love in exquisite abandon, relief at having made the decision to marry adding to their passion. 'We can live here at first rather than delay things while we look for somewhere else,' she said afterwards, eager now that the decision was made. 'The sooner we are married, the better. I'll tell Dad first thing in the morning.'

A few days later Bob Brown sat hunched up over the electric fire in his office at the garage. For weeks he had felt frozen to the core and no amount of external heat seemed able to thaw him out. Through the glass to the side of him he could see Bella in her office next door pounding away at the typewriter. She, and everyone else, shimmered in a bright, faraway world of sunshine and happiness where Bob longed to be if only he could find his way through the cold grey mists which he seemed forced to inhabit.

His head felt fuzzy, his thoughts incoherent, and his stomach was tied in knots. All around him the garage hummed industriously. He knew he ought to show his face in the workshops, but the blackness in his mind acted as a millstone, adding to his guilt at the burden he was placing on others, yet leaving him powerless to change the situation. As he observed his daughter, some forgotten fact tried to re-establish itself in the jumble of his mind. Something painful. Oh yes, Bella was getting married, that was it. She was leaving her father to marry the son of a crook and a bastard.

Time fell away from Bob. As the sound of an air-raid siren screamed in his head, he pressed his hands to his ears to try to shut it out. London was blazing – fire-duty – flames – bodies – heat. Phyllis – he must find her in the debris . . .

His wife felt very close to him suddenly. He'd talked to her a lot lately. She was the only one who understood how wretched he felt, the only one who made him feel warm.

'Are yer comin' for a quick pint at the Lamb after work tonight, with John an' me, Uncle Bob?' asked Trevor, who had come in from the workshop and was standing over him.

Bob blinked to try to erase a terrifying feeling of unreality. 'The Lamb . . .' he began with a bewildered look.

'Yer always used to come with us on a Friday, just for half an hour or so. It will do yer good,' Trevor reminded him.

A flash of sunlight appeared momentarily through the fog as Bob received a mental image of himself and his two trusted colleagues laughingly playing darts. It all seemed so long ago. 'I'll think about it an' let yer know this afternoon,' he said, eager to be left alone with his thoughts.

'We're gonna nag yer into it, mate,' warned Trevor. 'A laugh an' a joke is just what yer need.'

Bob nodded. Please go away Trevor an' leave me in peace, he begged silently.

'Do yer wanna cuppa tea, yer look cold?' said Trevor in concern.

'No thanks.'

'Sure?'

'I'm sure.' Just go away, Bob's inner voice implored.

Immediately the door closed behind Trevor, Bob closed his eyes and luxuriated in memories of Phyllis and the proximity he now felt to her. 'Mummy is safe now,' he'd told the girls that day in 1940. 'Nothing can hurt her.' Suddenly, the way forward seemed dazzlingly clear to him.

He picked up the telephone, dialled Bennett's number and asked for Frank Bennett. 'Meet me in the King's Arms at twelve-thirty,' he commanded in a tone that did not invite argument.

'I'm lunching at my club, old boy . . .'

'*Be there*,' demanded Bob.

'All right, all right,' Frank agreed.

'So what's all this about?' asked Frank Bennett, facing Bob across a table in the corner of the King's Arms.

'I just want yer to know that I know it was you 'oo set me up with the Weights an' Measures,' said Bob, enjoying the freedom to speak the truth at last.

Frank's eyes narrowed. 'You ought to be more careful what you say,' he warned.

'Do I? Why is that?' said Bob, feeling almost light-hearted.

199

'Because I could put you in court for slander,' Frank barked, his voice rising angrily. 'And don't think I wouldn't.'

'I don't doubt it,' said Bob, infuriating Frank with his show of confidence. 'But you'll never get hold of my place, *never.*'

'What makes you think I want it?' asked Frank.

'Yer wanted it enough to threaten me,' said Bob.

Frank laughed dryly. 'That was years ago. And I didn't threaten you. I was merely establishing my position in the business community. Some you win, some you lose. Yours I lost and I didn't give it another thought afterwards.'

'I suppose you're waitin' for the dust to settle after the court case before yer make yer next move,' Bob continued as though the other man had not spoken. 'Because if yer were to approach me too soon, it would look suspicious. After a decent interval, but while my business is still sufferin' the effects, you'll get someone to put in a nice low offer for the place. Oh yeah, yer wouldn't be fool enough to approach me yourself.'

Frank looked towards the table next to them where two men were playing shove ha'penny. 'Keep your voice down. I don't like having my reputation smeared in public.'

Bob laughed loudly. 'Your reputation! Phew, that's a good 'un. Yer make Al Capone seem like Snow White.' Bob had not felt so well and happy in ages.

'I don't have to sit here listening to this trash,' said Frank, rising to go.

Down came Bob's fist on the table. 'Sit down.'

A hush descended on the bar and all eyes turned in their direction. Frank looked around uneasily then sat down. 'Finish what you have to say and have done with it,' he said.

'You'll *never* get my place, *never.* Maybe I 'aven't the guts for business, but my daughter Bella 'as, an' she'll never let it go to you,' Bob said emphatically.

'What has Bella got to do with it?' asked Frank curiously.

'Never you mind. Just accept that you'll never get the place.'

Arrogance was Frank's downfall. 'Don't bet on it,' he taunted. 'I warned you years ago that I don't give up easy.'

Bob smiled. 'That's as good as an admission that you 'ad me set up,' he said.

'I admit nothing, you pathetic little man.'

And then the regulars at the King's Arms were treated to a lunchtime cabaret as a man they knew only as quiet and unassuming threw a pint of beer in his companion's face. And while the latter was reeling and spluttering from the shock, Bob clipped him on the jaw with his fist, marched to the bar and handed the landlord some money for any damage. Then he stalked from the pub, leaving a stupefied Frank Bennett sitting nursing his face.

That afternoon Bob spent a long time writing at his desk, then joined Trevor and John for half an hour in the Lamb before going home. After dinner, when both the girls had gone out, he propped a letter addressed to Bella in front of the clock on the mantelpiece and left the house. Arriving at the garage, he unlocked the workshop doors, drove his van inside and closed the doors firmly behind him. Then he went to the stores to find a piece of rubber pipe.

It was a grey, misty day in late October when the small gathering stood at the graveside to pay their last respects to Bob Brown. In life, he had been a popular man; in death he had disgraced himself to many who saw suicide as a sinful cowardly act, thus diminishing the show of public mourning. The sad, darkly clad group looked to each other for comfort, Vi and Wilf supporting each other, Pearl leaning heavily on Peter, a tearful Joan clinging to Trevor. Only Bella stood unsupported, having brushed aside Dezi's attentions. They had closed the garage as a mark of respect and John Sharpe headed the solemn staff delegation.

The choking fog swirled around them, prickling noses and throats, its penetrating damp seeping through clothes and flesh to the bone beneath. It's got all the makings of a pea souper, Bella thought with the curious sense of detachment that was carrying her through the proceedings. Inwardly she was numb, functioning in a blur of unreality. Outwardly she was practical and efficient, organising the official side of things and comforting the others, for the instant she allowed her own feelings to surface she knew she would be lost.

She had felt like this ever since that terrible night a week ago when she had returned home with Dezi to find the police waiting for her outside the prefab. Someone had reported an engine running inside the workshops, but when the police had got there her father was already dead at the wheel of his van. Carbon monoxide poisoning, the coroner had called it, inhaled directly from the exhaust pipe by means of a rubber pipe inserted through a narrow gap in the van window.

She remembered every word of his last letter. It would be forever engraved on her mind.

Dear Bella

I'm so sorry, love, to desert you, but I can't go on any longer feeling wretched and making your and everyone else's life a misery. Your mother is waiting for me and I am going to her. The business is yours, lock, stock and barrel. You deserve it, you've worked hard to help me make a go of it and I know that you have the strength that I lack to put it back on top once the court case scandal has quietened down. All I ask is that you never let Frank Bennett, who admitted his guilt to me today in the pub, get his hands on it.

You will be well advised to take Trevor and John Sharpe into the business with you. They both have a sound technical knowledge and will be a great help to you. I trust them both implicitly. Pearl has never pulled her weight at home or in the business, so she is to expect nothing from it. But if she is ever in need, you must help her.

I know I am weak but I might just have made the grade as a businessman had it not been for that trouble. Forgive me. Love to the others, and look after each other.
Dad.

Now the brief ceremony was coming to a close. The funeral procession walked slowly back to the cars. Back at the prefab Bella had laid on a modest spread of sandwiches, bridge rolls with salmon and ham, fruit cake, tea, and an assortment of alcoholic drinks. With flawless composure she hosted the occasion, consoling her aunt and sister, tactfully suggesting that Peter take Pearl off somewhere, chatting to everyone in turn, thanking them for coming and eventually ushering them out.

Finally, when only she and Dezi remained, Bella sank into an armchair by the fire, watching the orange and mauve tongues of flame rise gently from the smouldering coals. She was vaguely aware of Dezi sitting down nearby. She turned towards him, suddenly intensely aware of his well-cut dark suit, black tie and hand-sewn shoes so incongruous against the worn leatherette furniture. Until that moment she had not known what she intended to say. Now the way ahead seemed crystal clear.

'It's over,' she said.

'Yes, and I don't expect you're sorry,' he said, misunderstanding her. 'Miserable things, funerals.'

Pale and tragic in a black jersey suit, she said, 'I don't mean the funeral, I mean us. I'd like you to go now and never come back.'

He was on his feet at once. 'Bella, what are you saying?'

She twisted the ring from her finger, rose and handed it to him. 'My feelings have changed, I no longer want to marry you.' But though her voice was dull and flat, feelings were beginning to penetrate her deadened senses for the first time in a week. A dull pain began somewhere at the core of her being and flooded right through to her skin. She ached all over. 'I hate you,' she said, more emotionally. 'What I once thought was love has turned to hate.'

'You're in shock,' he said, coming to her and taking her gently by the arms. 'You're saying things you don't mean.'

'Yes, I am in shock,' she said into his face, making no attempt to shrug away his hold on her. 'But I mean every word.' Each syllable cut into her like a razor, but it was as though she needed the hurt, welcomed it almost.

'Bella darling,' he said and she could see the anguish in his face, 'we're engaged.'

'Were engaged. I've told you, it's over.'

'What has happened to make you do this to me?' he asked, his arms dropping to his sides.

'I should have thought that was obvious,' she said abrasively. 'I can't marry the son of my father's murderer.'

'*Bella*! That's a terrible thing to say.'

'Maybe, but it's true.' She looked at him unwaveringly. 'Oh, I know the technical cause of death was suicide, but your father killed him as surely as if he had knifed him in the back. He caused the trouble that made Dad sick.'

Now Dezi was distraught. 'Don't wreck our lives, Bella,' he beseeched her. 'Don't let your hatred for my father become an obsession, like it did with your dad.'

'Maybe he did become paranoid,' she said, 'but there was a basis of truth to it all.' As she stared at Dezi, it was as if she saw his father's face superimposed on his. 'You're his blood and I want no part of you.' Hurting him, she felt she was hurting his father. It gave her a perverse kind of satisfaction.

She was paper white with deep shadows under her eyes. The blackness of her clothes emphasised her pallor. Yet Dezi had never seen her look more strikingly beautiful.

'Don't you care how much you hurt me?' he ground out angrily. 'Are you too wrapped up in your own feelings to think about mine?'

'I don't know,' she said, suddenly bewildered. 'All I do know is that my feelings towards you have changed. Please go. I'm very tired.'

He came to her and put his hands on her shoulders. 'Bella, please . . .'

For a moment the magic they had once shared, the intimate pleasure of being together, overwhelmed her. Close to him she saw his bloodshot eyes and the lines of tension clearly etched on his face. His pain racked her body like a physical assault. She wanted to put her arms around him and soothe away the hurt she had inflicted. But she had made the decision to part from him, and she intended to carry it out. 'I'm sorry, I did love you once but not any more,' she said at last. 'Please go.'

He moved back, grim-faced. 'All right, I'll go,' he said, his word endings clipped with emotion. 'I'll not stay where I'm not wanted.'

Agonised, she heard the front door slam and his car roar away. Sinking into an armchair, she huddled over the fire, raking the coals for extra warmth. She felt frozen to the very soul. Too restless to sit still for long, she rose, instinctively feeling she ought to be busy with some chore or other. But there was no Dad to prepare food for and no Dezi to hurry to. There was only emptiness.

Bella forced herself to look at her father's chair, tilted towards the fire as though he was still in it. Unable to bear the sight any longer, she went to the kitchen, boiled a kettle, filled a stone hot water bottle and put it in her bed. Still shivering, she took her nightdress into the living room and undressed by the fire, the low flames rippling over her lean form.

Then, checking that the front doorkey was on the end of a string inside the letterbox for Pearl, she hurried to the bedroom and climbed into the icy sheets, burning herself on the bottle in her feverish search for comfort. With fists clenched and teeth chattering, she buried herself beneath the covers, hugging the bottle ardently.

And then the tears came, hot salty floods of them. It was the first time she had given way since her father's death. As her violent sobs filled the house, she was glad they had come when Pearl was not at home. And when her pillow was soaked and her body drained of emotion, she realised, with a sense of shame, that she had been weeping for the loss of Dezi as much as for the loss of her father.

Chapter Twelve

'I expect you will have been wondering what is to happen to Brown's now that Dad is no longer with us,' Bella said to John Sharpe, seated at the other side of her desk. 'Whether or not you still have a future with the firm.'

'It 'as crossed my mind, yeah,' John admitted frankly. 'I thought perhaps yer might decide to sell up.'

Bella shook her head firmly. Today she was perfectly groomed in a grey pencil skirt with a red sweater and matching court shoes. Her hair was swept up into a chignon and fastened with a plain red clip, a modest amount of make-up giving her appearance an added lustre. Since she had been forced into a career as a businesswoman, she felt she must look the part. She needed the boost to her confidence because, although she was prepared to face a challenge, she had not underestimated the difficulties of heading a company within such a male-dominated sphere. Maybe, at some time in the future, she might consider putting the business under management in order to be free to tackle something of her own choosing. But not until she had adhered to her father's wishes and put Brown's back on top.

It was two weeks since the funeral, a hectic fortnight during which Bella had thrown herself into making plans for the company's future and left herself with little time to brood. The days had been filled with lengthy meetings with her solicitor and accountant, and the evenings spent at the office catching up on clerical work. She realised now that her father's diminished responsibility in his last months had stood her in good stead for the massive task in which she was determined to excel.

'If I was to sell, Dad would turn in his grave,' she said in reply to John's suggestion. 'No fear!' And at his look of surprise, she added, 'Well, don't look so shocked. I am capable of taking control, you know.'

'No one is in any doubt about that, after the way you've performed this last few months,' he assured her. 'It's just that runnin' a garage ain't traditionally a female occupation, an' I thought you might rather sell up an' buy a dress shop or somethin'.'

'Not on your life,' she laughed. 'Well, not for a good few years anyway. Maybe I wouldn't have chosen a garage, but since Dad left me this place with the idea that I would return it to its former, pre-scandal glory, I intend to do that and much more. I plan to raise it to its full potential before I even consider the idea of turning my hand to something a little more feminine.'

'Good for you,' he said, admiring her spirit enormously. 'I'm sure the rest of the staff will be more than 'appy with your decision.'

'I shall need to delegate much more than my father ever did though,' she said, leaning back in her chair and clasping her hands together on her lap, 'since my role will be mainly managerial.'

208

He waited, raising his brows quizzically.

'In my father's final letter to me he showed his great respect for you and Trevor by advising me to offer you both directorships,' she informed him solemnly.

John flushed and gave a little gasp. 'Oh!' he said.

She smiled. 'And I have decided to take his advice and make you an offer. Trevor, having been with the firm longer, will have slightly more equity than you. He has already accepted the terms I offered him,' She paused, noticing his obvious delight. 'Do I need to give you time to think about it?'

'Not bloomin' likely!' he said, beaming. 'Yer can take my acceptance as read.'

'Excellent,' she said. 'I'll have my solicitor draw up a contract. In the meantime, let me give you a brief outline of how the new company structure will work.' She rested her slender hands on the arms of the chair. 'I, as Managing Director, will be responsible for the overall running of the business. You and Trevor will be joint managers and will have full responsibility for the workshops and the forecourt, including the hiring and firing of staff. And, since I do not intend to learn how to fix cars, you will get no interference from me in the workshop.'

'Fair enough,' he said.

'My job,' she continued, 'will comprise all financial matters, customer relations, the promotion of our services, maintaining existing contracts and seeking new ones as well as generally keeping things running smoothly. The three of us will have regular meetings and although I shall have the final say on company policy, your ideas and suggestions will be thoroughly discussed and used if of value to the firm. I shall no longer have time to cope single-handed with routine office work, so

I will be taking on a secretary.' She met his gaze. 'Any questions?'

'No.'

'I know that you and Trevor are good pals and I'm sure the three of us will work well as a team.' She rose to indicate that the interview was at an end. 'As soon as I get the contract drawn up, we shall have another meeting. I'm sure you'll be happy with the terms, though.'

'Right . . . fine . . . thanks very much.'

'If you have any queries, don't hesitate to come to me,' she said in a mature way which belied the fact that she was two years his junior. She laughed. 'All the trouble must have aged me. I sound just like a mother hen.'

Lost for words, he just stood there, grinning. 'Well,' he said at last, 'I'd better get back to work.' And as he left Bella's office he was beaming. Him, a director! Well, what a turn-up for the books.

Immediately the door closed behind him, Bella's smile died. Outwardly cheerful and efficient, inwardly she felt like hell. Up until three days ago she had been besieged by letters and flowers from Dezi, all of which had been returned, and the telephone receiver replaced at the sound of his voice. Now, apparently, he had decided to accept her decision because all communication had stopped. She should be pleased, but she was hurting too badly to appreciate the respite. Her eyes smarted at the thought of him. How could she still love someone she had every reason to hate? It didn't make sense. She was over-emotional in her bereavement, that must be the problem, because the Dezi Bennett era of her life was definitely over.

Mindful of one matter from the past which must be dealt

with immediately, she put a sheet of paper into the typewriter and typed a letter to Frank Bennett, addressing it to his office, marked 'Personal'.

Bella stood on Kew bridge looking upstream towards the beautiful waterfront of Strand-on-the-Green. But the trees, which she remembered as green and splendid in July, were black and skeletal on this raw November day. Overhead was a dark threatening sky, and the biting wind cut bone deep through her red velour coat. There was a considerable amount of traffic on the river, mostly commercial at this time of the year, tug boats and lighters and larger cargo crafts travelling to and from Brentford Docks. The tow path, so crowded in summer, was almost deserted except for a few dog-walkers, their faces screwed up against the bitter wind.

She looked at her watch. Almost one-thirty. He should be here soon. Staring down into the dark flowing waters had a curiously soothing effect, despite their murkiness and the assortment of flotsam and jetsam. The wind stung her cheeks and whipped icily through her hair. She dragged her coat collar up around her ears and plunged her gloved hands deeper into her pockets. Her skin was cold, yet she felt feverishly hot inside. Not nervous exactly, but eager for the meeting to be underway.

'I'm right on time, I think,' said a voice beside her and she turned to see Frank Bennett, smartly accoutred in a dark overcoat with a white silk scarf and a trilby hat. His full-lipped mouth twitched into a wary smile. He clapped his leather-gloved hands against the cold. 'Have you been here long?'

'Just a few minutes,' she said in an even tone.

'I don't know what you want to see me about,' he said, shivering violently, 'but whatever it is I'd rather not stand about here getting pneumonia. Let's go to a pub or a café.'

But Bella did not want the impact of what she had to say dulled by outward distractions. She had not expected the weather to be so cruel and had intended them to take a walk. She looked at his pinched face, already showing a blue tinge, and was reminded that he was not a young man.

'Where's your car?' she asked.

'Just around the corner.'

'We can talk in there. I'd rather not say what I have to say in public,' she explained with a firm edge to her voice.

Sitting about in a car with a young woman on a public highway had doubtful connotations that did not match the respectable image Frank liked to project. But her commanding attitude made him reluctant to argue. 'All right,' he said.

Inside the car, he lit a cigar. 'I'd appreciate your getting straight to the point. I'm a busy man,' he said, waving the clouds of smoke from his face. 'Something to do with Dezi, I suppose. Eve and me were very sorry to hear you'd split up.'

Bella laughed sardonically. 'Liar!' she said. 'You must be absolutely delighted. You hated the idea of Dezi marrying me.' She paused for a moment, fanning the smoke away. 'But no, it has nothing to do with Dezi. We're finished forever.'

'You were always far too sensitive about your background, you know,' Frank said in a condescending manner.

It didn't suit Bella to rise to the bait, so she said calmly, 'Overproud maybe, but never ashamed.'

'No, never that.'

'Not like you are of your own humble beginnings,' she challenged him.

'Well, I . . .'

'I don't know why you go to such pains to hide them,' she interrupted. 'After all, you are the proverbial working-class boy made good, and people admire that sort of success. They see it as a sign of hope for themselves, that the glittering prizes are up for grabs for everyone, not just the elite few born to money.' She watched his affront turn to complacency.

Frank had been uneasy ever since he had received Bella's letter. He didn't quite know how, but he had suspected that she meant to make trouble for him in retaliation for her father's death. He had only pretended to think she might want to see him about Dezi. But now, soothed by her reminder of what a clever fellow he was, he relaxed.

'Yes, you are indeed one of life's winners,' she continued brightly. 'It's a pity you've detracted from all the good things you've achieved by allowing your greed to drive you to murder.'

Frank stared fixedly ahead along the street. The stripped trees creaked in the wind and some lingering autumn leaves scudded along the pavement. Bella saw him stiffen, but it was some moments before he turned to her. She had expected a show of outrage from him, so was surprised to see fear shadowing his deeply sunken eyes. Well, well, perhaps he did have a conscience after all? But it was a mere momentary lapse and almost immediately he reverted to type. 'I haven't the faintest idea what you're getting at,' he said crossly. 'But that is some big accusation, lady. You seem to be as ignorant of the slander laws as your father was.'

'There's nothing I don't know about you, Mr Bennett,' she said firmly. 'You were behind the incident leading to my father's court case, which eventually drove him to suicide.' She stared directly into his wary eyes. 'Of course, you were not to know that my father did not have the same thick skin as you. I doubt if you expected things to end as they did. As a result though you won't get your hands on our site, because it belongs to me and I would *never, ever* sell to you, under any circumstances or for any price. So, you've wasted your time.'

'You're mad,' blustered Frank, his hand trembling as he knocked his cigar ash into the ashtray. 'You can't blame me because your father saw fit to take the easy way out. I was very sorry to hear about his death.'

'I expect you were. Guilt is a powerful emotion.'

'This is preposterous,' growled Frank. 'I think grief must have addled your brain.'

'On the contrary, my mind has never been sharper,' she said. 'But I think yours will begin to deteriorate when you start to have sleepless nights. Because, one of these days, you will find that you do have a conscience. Yes, even you won't be able to rest easy with what you've done.'

Frank's icy stare concealed a troubled mind. He had been more affected by Brown's passing than he cared to admit. When he had organised that scheme to discredit him, he had wanted the man's business premises, not his death. How was he to know Brown would let the whole thing get on top of him? 'Oh, shut up, you silly woman,' he said.

'Not before I've finished,' she told him briskly. 'I must warn you that it would not be wise for you to try any of your tricks on me. My father didn't have the stomach for a fight, but I do. And although you have money and contacts behind you, I have something infinitely more valuable, something that you can never have again. I have the power of youth. I am bright, energetic and fit. You try to wreck my business and you'll see just how strong I am.'

He made as if to strike her but stopped himself in time, suspecting that any such attack would be positively welcome to her as ammunition to use against him. 'I think your talents would be better used writing crime fiction,' he said, with a tremor in his voice. 'You certainly have the imagination for it.'

She smiled, intoxicated with her newfound sense of power. 'You are beaten, Mr Bennett.'

'Get out of my car, you maniac. Go on, get out.'

'Certainly,' she said, and almost as her feet touched the ground, the vehicle roared away.

Needing to calm herself before returning to the office, she went down to the river and began to stride briskly along the towpath, euphoric with victory. But the feeling soon evaporated, leaving her full of self-loathing for what Bennett had forced her to become, a woman filled with hate and bitterness. So engrossed in her own thoughts was she, she barely noticed the malty aroma from the brewery carried on the wind, or the wolf whistles from the men unloading some grain from a barge at a small quay.

Her heart was heavy with regret at having to use a family tragedy to score a point off Frank Bennett. It had been shabby and vulgar, and the fact that it had been necessary did not make it right. Her eyes stung with tears as she recalled his remark about Dad taking the easy way out, an opinion she knew was shared by many, out of her hearing. But outsiders couldn't know that Bennett, not her father, was really to blame.

Passing Ivy House, she quickened her step as the memory of that first day when Dezi had watched her, on this very spot, threatened to overwhelm her. One day she would be able to think about it without feeling pain, but not now. She made a slight detour on her way back to Fulworth and walked through the lush parkland of Duke's Meadows, bleak but beautiful in winter dress. The grassland undulated in myriad shades of green as it blew in the wind beneath bare, swaying trees.

Fulworth High Street was quite a contrast with its rumble of heavy traffic and crowds of people. As she approached the garage she saw several vehicles on the forecourt. Business was already picking up. This valuable asset was hers to command but right now it felt like a trap.

Frank Bennett stopped at the first pub he saw after leaving Bella and downed a double Scotch. It was quite ridiculous but that silly bitch of a girl had unnerved him and he felt as shaky as a leaf. The very idea of him being to blame for her father's death was ludicrous! Brown was the sinner, not Frank. If only the stupid man had listened to him years ago, when he'd offered to buy him out, he'd probably still be alive now. But no, the fool had insisted on staying around in the business for which he was totally unsuited.

He ordered another whisky, glad that he was not known in here for he was in no mood for company. The alcohol calmed him. In fact he felt quite drowsy, which was not surprising considering the fact that he had recently become an insomniac. Well, yes, perhaps Bella Brown had been right, maybe his conscience was a little troublesome in the small hours. The night was a strange thing; thoughts became magnified, shadows became ghosts, and death seemed just a heartbeat away.

'Murder,' she had said. The word made him shiver. A horrendous image of Brown's body, in his van, blue-tinged with staring eyes, filled his mind; he saw a coffin from which Brown rose, pointing an accusing finger in his direction. The phantoms of the night were now haunting him by day. He began to sweat and shake. His breath seemed to desert him. He drank the whisky and gradually anger replaced his fear. How dare that wretched girl threaten him? She was a nobody, a nothing. He doubted if Brown's would last six months under her supervision. She would soon find that the business world was no place for weaklings and amateurs.

'Let's get married without telling anyone,' suggested Pearl eagerly.

'That's a bit drastic,' said Peter nervously. 'It isn't as though you're pregnant.'

'If we wait for our people to approve, we'll wait forever,' Pearl pointed out. 'Bella won't 'ave anything to do with you because she 'ates your whole family to 'ell. Your parents don't think I'm good enough for you. So, if we do the deed and tell them afterwards, they can't spoil it for us.'

Peter fell into a worried silence. Pearl had been exerting pressure on him for some time, using her own special brand of blackmail. It was marriage or nothing, she'd told him. Either he made an honest woman of her, or he didn't make her at all. It wasn't that he didn't want to marry her, but the situation frightened him. Marriage to her would make life very awkward with his parents; they wanted Pearl as a daughter-in-law like they wanted TB.

'Well, Peteykins?' persisted Pearl in her sexiest, little-baby voice. 'It's a month until Christmas. If we get a special licence, we can be married by then. Won't that be romantic?'

They were in Peter's car, parked in the shadows near Fulworth Common, Pearl having become tactically puritanical about making love in his recently acquired flat in Barnes.

'It's a big step,' he said at last.

She nibbled his ear lobe. 'Don't you want to marry your Pearlykins?'

'Of course I do,' he whispered huskily, his heart hammering wildly at the touch of her hand on his thigh.

'Let's do it then,' she said in a more practical tone. 'We can live at your place at first. And just imagine all that privacy. We can stay in bed all day on Sundays.'

Oh God, she really was irresistible. Everything seemed possible when she was near. And he had to admit to being sick and tired of the present arrangement. They were like a couple of outcasts, with Bella not allowing him into the prefab and his parents making life so uncomfortable for Pearl that she refused to visit them at all. All of that would have been tolerable if it hadn't suited Pearl to have sudden qualms about her reputation and make life even more uncomfortable by refusing to spend any length of time with him at his flat. If that wasn't closing the stable door after the horse had bolted, he didn't know what was, but she was adamant. As a result, they spent all their time in theatres, cinemas, restaurants, pubs, or the car.

'That would be lovely,' he said feebly.

'You see, it's like this, Peteykins,' she cooed, playing her trump card, 'I'm no slut. I can't let you make love to me any more without a ring on my finger.'

'We could get engaged,' he suggested hopefully.

'Getting engaged is kid's stuff,' she stated categorically. 'I don't wanna bother with any of that nonsense.'

'Oh!' Her hand moved tormentingly on his thigh.

'Of course, if you don't wanna know, then say so outright. Though plenty of men would jump at the chance,' she reminded him.

And didn't he know it! He rather enjoyed the lustful glances she attracted from other men when they were out together. It made him feel superior and manly. But the idea of her actually going off with one of them was too awful to bear. Steeling his thoughts against the carnal delights she was implicitly offering, he looked ahead to the practicalities of such a match. Sure, his parents would hate it, but what could they actually do about it? After all, Peter was a legal director of the company, so they couldn't throw him out without breaching his contract of employment. And anyway, Dad found him far too useful to want to fall out with him permanently. Who else would collect the slum rents and assist with the disposal of certain questionable artifacts from time to time?

His infatuation with Pearl was entirely physical, he accepted that. But what else drew couples together, initially, except biological chemistry? Other things came later, he assumed, but right now he could not see beyond the magnetism of her sex appeal. And what did it matter if her horizons were limited to popular music and fashion? He wasn't exactly Brain of Britain himself.

'Okay, let's get a special licence,' he said, warming to the idea now that the decision was made. 'I think marriage to you will be a lot of fun.'

'Whoopee,' she squeaked, jubilant in victory. 'I love you, Peter.' And she did love him, almost as much as the lifestyle which she knew he would provide.

★　　★　　★

'You've done what?' asked Bella furiously, a few weeks later.

'I've married Peter,' Pearl explained. 'Aren't you going to congratulate me?'

'Where is he?'

'Outside in the car.'

'Frightened to come in and face me, I suppose,' snorted Bella.

'No, not at all. I told him not to come in, because I knew you'd try to spoil our day by making a scene.' She was wearing a red coat with matching pill box hat and black patent high-heeled shoes and accessories. 'We knew you would disapprove which is why we waited until afterwards to tell you.'

'My God, you're selfish,' said Bella, facing her sister across the hearth in the living room at the prefab. 'How could you marry into that family after what they did to Dad? And him barely cold in his grave.'

'Peter didn't do anything to Dad,' Pearl pointed out. 'What 'appened between his father and Dad is not my quarrel. You were a fool to give Dezi up because of it. He could have provided well for you.'

'Is that why you've married Peter, for his money?' Bella asked coldly. She felt betrayed and utterly alone.

'Not *only* for that,' Pearl explained boldly. 'We get along well together.'

Bella stared at her sister incredulously. 'But the money is a consideration?'

Pearl exuded insolence. She wanted to hurt Bella for having the power to make her feel guilty. 'And what's so terrible about that? It is just as easy to fall in love with a rich man as a poor one.' She turned nonchalantly to check her stocking seams.

'How you can have such a flippant attitude towards something as serious as marriage is beyond me,' Bella snapped. 'But that's not the issue. The fact is it was disloyal of you to marry into *that* family.'

'Dad is dead, Bel, he didn't think about us when he killed 'imself. I don't like Mr Bennett or that cow of a wife of 'is any more than you do, but I 'aven't married them. If you want to make a martyr of yourself by throwing away your future with Dezi, that's up to you. I'm not that stupid.'

But Bella's animosity towards all the Bennetts was implacable. 'You've betrayed your father.'

'I 'ave my own life to live and I want to live it with Peter,' Pearl said. 'Okay, so I like the idea of 'is money, but that doesn't mean that I don't love 'im, in my own way. I know how to make 'im happy and I'll be good to 'im.' As her sister turned away in disgust Pearl continued, 'Anyway, you're a fine one to lecture about love.'

'And what is that supposed to mean?' said Bella, turning back sharply.

'If you'd *really* loved Dezi you'd not 'ave made 'im suffer for something that's not 'is fault.'

Bella was suddenly assaulted by a vivid recollection of Dezi's despair the day she had broken off their engagement. 'My feelings towards him changed. Anyway, you're not marrying Peter because you feel he might suffer if you don't. You're doing it for reasons of greed.'

'Be that as it may, I certainly wouldn't give 'im up for some ridiculous matter of principle. Peter is alive and wants me; Dad is dead and doesn't. It's as simple as that,' Pearl informed her vehemently.

'In that case there is nothing more to be said,' said Bella

coldly. 'You are a Bennett now, so stay on your own side of the fence.'

'Don't be like that, Bel.'

'Go to your husband, Mrs Bennett,' rasped Bella bitterly. 'And don't come back. I never want to see you again. Collect your things when I'm not here.' And before her sister could say another word, she marched into her bedroom and locked the door behind her.

Sitting rigidly on the edge of the bed in the freezing room, she ignored Pearl's calls to her and finally heard the front door close and the click of her sister's heels hurrying down the path. Three people she loved were now lost to her. She had never felt more alone and isolated. Pearl's words pounded through her head until it hurt: 'If you'd really loved 'im, you'd not have made 'im suffer ...' Well, maybe Pearl was right, maybe she had not really loved him. But Pearl always measured everything in terms of self. She and Peter Bennett deserved each other.

Still memories of Dezi persisted and Bella knew that Pearl had been wrong. She had loved Dezi, more than anything in the world. Why had it changed, why? And as she remembered, her mind became a blur of bitterness and resentment.

Chapter Thirteen

It was midday on Christmas Eve and Brown's Garage was about to close for the holiday. Bella had just shared a Christmas drink with the mechanics in the workshops, but guessing that her presence put a damper on the men's merrymaking, she had made her appearance brief.

'Would you two like to join me in the office for a drink?' she said to Trevor and John as the gathering began to disperse.

'Much as I'd like to, Bel, I must rush orf,' said Trevor. 'Joan an' me are gonna to do some last-minute shopping. I'll see yer at 'ome later.'

Although normally keen on Christmas, this year Bella's natural inclination was to crawl into a corner out of range of the celebrations. But such a negative attitude stood little chance of survival against the positive side of her nature, and feeling dutybound to spread cheer and goodwill to those around her she forced herself to say to John, 'How about you? Do you have time to share a little festive cheer with me? Dad always invited his management team into the office for a drink on a Christmas Eve, as you know, and I don't want to break with tradition.'

'I never say no to a tipple,' beamed John. 'I'll join yer when I've seen all the blokes orf the premises.'

'Lovely,' said Bella, her face set in the smile she felt obliged to wear in deference to the season.

Back in her office, she took some bottles and glasses from the hospitality cupboard and set them down on her desk. For convenience' sake she now used her father's old office, leaving the adjoining room free for her secretary, Beatrice, a married lady who had been given today off in consideration of the mountain of mince pies and sausage rolls her family would expect to eat tomorrow.

Bella had been obliged to change her domestic arrangements, too, in the light of Pearl's defection. No longer eligible, as a single person, for the tenancy of the prefab, she had moved back into number nine with her aunt and uncle. It was purely a temporary measure though, for whilst they all got along very well, Bella was of an age where freedom beckoned, and she intended to find a place of her own after the holiday. Though with rented accommodation still so scarce in London, it was not going to be easy.

Pouring herself a small sherry to pass the time while waiting for John, she found herself feeling unexpectedly nauseous at the smell of alcohol. Shakily putting the offending liquid down, she part-filled another glass with Tizer and sipped it slowly, aware of a cold sweat breaking out all over her.

John breezed into the office, overalls discarded, face freshly washed, hair combed neatly into place.

'Have they all gone home?' she asked cheerily, though feeling like death.

''Ome via the pub, I reckon,' he laughed.

'What would you like to drink?'

'A beer, ta,' he said, and seeing her brush a hand across her moist brow, added, ''ere let me do it. Yer look a bit peaky. Are yer orlright?'

Sinking gratefully into her chair, Bella said, 'I'm okay, just a bit tense. Christmas is weighing heavy this year. It's too soon after Dad.'

He nodded sympathetically. 'It must be awful for yer. Well, if it's any 'elp, I've a good strong shoulder an' it's yours if yer need it.'

'It's good of you to offer,' she said, 'but I'll be okay once Christmas is over. It isn't the best time for the recently bereaved.'

Raising his glass to her, he said, 'Well, 'ere's to yer survivin' it, if yer can't manage to enjoy it. 'Appy Christmas, Bella.'

'Happy Christmas, John,' she said, lifting her own glass.

'What are yer doin' over the holiday?' he asked, sitting down on a chair opposite her.

'I'll have a quiet Christmas at home with Auntie and Uncle. My social life is non-existent these days,' she admitted.

He sipped his beer thoughtfully. 'I 'eard that you and Dezi Bennett 'ad split up.'

'Yes,' she said, and immediately diverted the conversation to a less dangerous topic. 'So, what festivities lie in store for you?'

'Oh, the usual things, yer know, general overindulgence an' lazin' around.' He paused and studied his knees for a few moments. 'I was wonderin',' he said, looking at her, a strawberry blush creeping up his neck, 'if yer might like to ... er ... What I mean is, if you ain't doin' anythin' special on the evenin' after Boxing Day, would yer like to come out somewhere?' Noticing her look of surprise, he added quickly:

225

'No strings, just a friendly outin'. It might cheer yer up to get out of the 'ouse.'

Bella felt she ought to refuse. The last thing she wanted was a date with John Sharpe, or anyone else for that matter. But she was very lonely and a night out might relieve her sense of isolation. And it wouldn't be a date, as such.

Bella needed young company right now. Pearl had taken her at her word and collected her belongings from the prefab while her sister was at work. Any visits to number nine were made when Bella was absent. Although she hated to admit it, she missed her little sister though she could not forgive her and had no plans for a reconciliation. Joan and Trevor would be around over the holiday, but they were closer than butter on bread these days and talking of an engagement next year, which only emphasised Bella's loneliness.

Now John was saying, 'We could go to see a film, if you'd like to.'

And persuaded by his kindness, she said, 'I'd love to.'

And, indeed, the magic of the cinema proved to be a panacea. The compelling charm of the big screen blotted out the real world. Doris Day, shimmering with health and vitality, trilled tunefully, aided by an assortment of beautiful clothes, glamorous settings and romantic misunderstandings en route for the rapturous happy ending without which no film of hers would have been complete.

Christmas Day at number nine had been predictably gloomy, despite a magnificent culinary effort by her aunt who found solace among the baking tins, unlike poor Wilf who was still devastated by his brother's untimely demise. Pearl's absence contributed to the lack of Christmas spirit, try as everyone might to exude happiness and cheer. Even the Willises' party, after tea, had brought little solace to Bella, for the guests had been predominately of an older generation. So, by virtue of his youth alone, John was welcome company. And, fortunately, he kept his distance.

On the way home in his old Austin, feeling at ease with him, Bella admitted to having enjoyed the break from home. 'I love my aunt and uncle dearly, but we need time away from each other.'

'Yeah, being indoors all the time can get yer down. Mind you, I 'ad a good night out with me mates on Christmas Eve, so I was quite 'appy to stay at 'ome Christmas Day and Boxing Day wiv me mum.'

Inevitably, Bella found herself comparing John to Dezi, who would be bored rigid by the idea of endless nights out with a crowd of men. John was very immature in comparison, though just a few years younger than Dezi.

'You get on well with your mother then,' she said conversationally.

'Oh, yeah, she's one o' the best. All me mates love 'er.'

Stifling a mild feeling of irritation at his frequent references to his 'mates', she realised that Dezi's sophisticated ways had ruined her for more ordinary men. John was two years her senior, yet she felt by far the elder. But he was kind and they got along well enough.

'I know of a nice little pub near Kew where they have a jazz band on a Saturday night,' he said later, as they drew up outside number nine.' Would yer like to come along with me on Saturday?'

Well, where was the harm? He was a good friend. 'Yes, that would be lovely,' she said.

★   ★   ★

'Would you like more coffee, Carol?' asked Dezi of his companion in the Savoy Grill the evening after Boxing Day.

'Yes please,' said the young woman sitting opposite him.

He smiled and called the waiter.

'It was a lovely meal, thank you,' said Carol Dent.

'My pleasure,' he assured her. 'Though it's a wonder our taste buds are still able to function after the Christmas onslaught.'

Watching her small round face crease into a polite laugh, Dezi was very much aware of the fact that he felt no male response to her whatsoever. An alarming discovery for a man who had never been lacking in the libido department. Bella Brown had a lot to answer for.

Carol was the daughter of a friend of Dezi's father. Archie Dent was a garage proprietor in business in Wimbledon where the family lived. Dezi had met her for the first time on Christmas Day when she had called with her parents for a seasonal social gathering at Ivy House. With Peter being absent in favour of a connubial Christmas, Dezi and Carol had been drawn together by the fact that they were the only singles, amid a collection of middle-aged couples.

Now Dezi studied her, seeing a moderately attractive woman of twenty-six, small with a trim figure smartly dressed in a simple black cocktail dress. Her mid-brown hair was cut fashionably short and feathered around a face with small, ordinary features and clear blue eyes. She was not beautiful but easy on the eye in a gentle, homely sort of a way. She was well spoken without being affected, and had a quiet natural charm.

Quite why he had invited her out he wasn't sure, since Bella's was the only female company he wanted and he certainly had not given up hope in that direction. He supposed he had been driven to it by loneliness. Bella needed time to get over her father's death. When she came out of shock, she might see things in perspective. Until then he would leave her alone, whatever it did to him.

Since that terrible day when she had ended their engagement, Dezi had alternated between anguish and anger. He had tried several remedies to assuage his grief. He had deadened his brain with alcohol on weekend benders through the pubs and clubs of London. But these inevitably left him feeling more depressed. Then he had tried to resuscitate his battered ego by calling an old flame. They had wined and dined. She came back to his flat and had been more than willing to help restore his confidence in his own attractiveness. But when it had come to the crunch, his self-loathing for the way he was using her had been so acute he had not been able to follow through. He had not called her again.

Then there had been the solitary phase. Long evenings and weekends spent lying on his bed with classical music on the record player and thoughts of Bella running through his mind so persistently that his brain ached. He refused to accept that she did not love him, yet was unable to deny the evidence to that effect. Surely, if she had *really* loved him she would not have allowed any outside influence to affect her feelings. Had the situation been reversed, he did not honestly think he could have given her up if her father had knifed his in his sight. The only possible explanation was that shock had temporarily made her see things out of focus. But this theory, whilst keeping hope alive for the future, did not lessen the anguish of the present. Some days Dezi sank into a well of despair. Christmas Day had been one such day, which was probably the reason he had turned to Carol for company.

He felt comfortable with her. It was like being with an old friend. She had a soothing effect on him and he guessed she must be very good at her job as a nurse.

Becoming aware of the need for some effort on his part (undemanding or not, she deserved some attention), he said, 'So why is an attractive woman like you alone at Christmas time?'

'I was jilted,' she explained, surprising him with her honesty. 'I was engaged to be married. Everything was arranged. Church and honeymoon booked. Invitations sent out and answered. Then, two weeks before the big day, he broke it off. He'd met someone else.'

'I'm so sorry, that must have been awful,' he said, the discovery that he was not alone in his rejection somehow raising his spirits.

'Don't be,' she urged him, 'it's all in the past. But I've never wanted to make that sort of commitment again. I've just drifted along solo, you know.' She paused as the waiter poured her some coffee. 'I understand from my parents that you were engaged too.'

Her sincerity prompted him to talk freely. 'Yes, that's right. But if your version of the affair came via my parents, you'll have heard that I'm better off without her because she was just a cheap little tart who only wanted me for my money.'

Carol seemed worried by his fiery response. 'Oh dear, you *are* on the defensive. But I didn't actually get many details, just the impression that your folks aren't too disappointed that it's over.'

His eyes darkened angrily. 'They're quite wrong about her. Bella doesn't give a toss about money. It might be simpler if she did. At least then I could try to woo her back with it.'

'You're still in love with her,' deduced Carol.

Had it been anyone else but her asking the question, he might have denied it out of pride. But her reassuring frankness led him to say, 'Yes, I'm afraid so.' He surveyed her over the rim of his coffee cup. 'Is it the same for you with your ex?'

She sipped her coffee thoughtfully. 'Not now, no. At first I thought I would never get over him, but time is a great healer and it was over a year ago.' She placed her cup on the saucer and propped her chin on her hands meditatively. 'Now that I am able to see things clearly, I sometimes wonder if it was my heart or my pride that was damaged most.' She eyed him directly. 'Mine was the opposite situation to yours in that my parents were heartbroken when it ended. They thought he was wonderful and loved the idea of having a doctor for a son-in-law.' Her gaze became distant. 'I met him in true story-book fashion. He hadn't long qualified and was working on the wards in the hospital where I was nursing. He's a GP now.' She re-focused her eyes on him. 'My confidence was practically non-existent for some time after we split up.'

'I can imagine,' he said with immediate empathy. 'I'm still suffering that way.'

'It doesn't show,' she assured him. 'You seem supremely self-possessed.'

He was relieved to know that his inner torment was not visible to the outside world. 'One puts up a front,' he said.

She nodded. 'Oh, yes. But it's easier for a man. You can go out and find company. If a woman goes to a pub or club alone she's classed as fair game.'

'Yes, I can see that it must be more difficult,' he agreed. 'But you seem to have got your confidence back now.'

'Oh, it doesn't do to let that sort of thing take hold. And my work was a great help. I love it, you see.'

'Snap,' he smiled, feeling increasingly comforted by her natural warmth. 'I'm a bit of a workaholic myself.'

'We must meet again and compare notes,' she said, the mischievous sparkle in her eyes suggesting that something more than friendship would not be unwelcome.

'Yes.' He was flattered but wary.

'Don't worry,' she laughed, 'I'm not going to seduce you. I know your affections are still with Bella. But I'm a very good listener, or so my patients tell me.'

And realising that he trusted her implicitly, he found himself baring his soul to her.

'Would it be presumptuous of me to ask if there might be any truth in Bella's suspicions about your father?' she asked, after hearing the whole story. 'I'm not terribly familiar with business, but I know that devious tactics are sometimes used.' She leant her head forward and lowered her voice. 'Obviously, this is just between us.'

Surprised at her directness, he said, 'Dad denies it. But whether or not he was involved should not be an issue between Bella and myself.'

'Maybe not in story books or films, but in real life of course it would have a devastating effect on your relationship, at least initially. Bella's was a normal human reaction, I should have thought.'

'I don't think my feelings for her would have changed if the situation had been reversed.'

'But from what you've said, you aren't as close to your father as Bella was to hers. You're measuring her filial feelings against your own when in fact there's probably a world of difference between the two cases. It must have been a traumatic experience for her, losing him like that. I think you're right to leave her alone for a while. But not for too long, because when she comes out of shock she is going to need you like never before.'

Her assumption that Bella was not lost to him forever cheered him considerably and he felt overwhelmed with gratitude. In fact, the entire evening was having a therapeutic effect on him and he felt he had made a valuable new friend. 'I'll bear that in mind,' he said, smiling at her. 'You've been a real tonic. Thank you for listening.'

'My pleasure,' she said graciously. 'Any time. Any time at all.'

Much to Bella's surprise, she rather enjoyed herself on Saturday evening. The jazz band played in a crowded, smoky cellar beneath a riverside pub with a bar in the corner and tables surrounding a small dance floor. They jived a good deal and, although Bella was not *au fait* with the technicalities of jazz, she enjoyed the music enormously.

Afterwards, they bought chips and ate them in the car outside the shop, huddled into their coats, for it was a cold frosty night. Steam from the hot, newspaper-wrapped packages, and their warm breath, misted the windows as they sat and chatted happily. Bella was just thinking how much she was enjoying John's undemanding company when he abandoned his supper in favour of giving her a salty kiss, which he planted clumsily and greasily on her lips. Cursing her naivety in not having foreseen this complication, she drew back sharply.

'No strings, you said,' she reminded him awkwardly.

'Sorry, I didn't intend . . . I got a bit carried away.' He had drawn back and was nervously screwing the piece of newspaper into a ball.

'It isn't that I don't like you,' she began, in a bid to allay his obvious sense of rejection.

'It's orlright, I get the message, no need to explain,' he interrupted quickly.

'I don't think you do, not quite,' she said.

'I broke me word.'

'Please listen to me,' she urged him, 'I have something important to tell you.'

'That sounds ominous.'

Outside, the yellow glow from the streetlamps poured over the frosty pavements like simulated sunlight. It was getting late, the chip shop had just closed. Only occasional squares of light beamed reassuringly from the dark, slumbering houses beyond the shopping parade. 'It is rather,' she said, wrapping the remainder of her now unwanted chips into a tight newspaper ball. 'I accepted your invitations because I am lonely and look upon you as a friend. But I won't be going out with you again.'

'That's a bit drastic. I 'ave said I'm sorry,' he blurted out.

'I know, and rather than have you think my decision has anything to do with any lack in you, I will tell you the reason. I am having a baby, Dezi Bennett's baby.'

After his shocked 'Oh! I see,' an uncomfortable silence closed around them like a fog. John didn't look at her but stared ahead, his hands resting on the steering wheel.

'So, since my life is about to be turned upside down, I won't be going out on dates with anyone,' she said at last.

'Are yer going back to Dezi Bennett?' he asked.

'No!'

'The bastard,' he said, drawing the wrong conclusion 'leaving you in the lurch. I'll soon sort 'im out . . .'

She placed a restraining hand on his arm. 'No, it was me who ended our affair, not Dezi. He doesn't know about the baby. I have only just accepted my pregnancy myself.'

'Are yer goin' to tell 'im?'

'No!' she said emphatically.

'But surely,' said John, his allegiance changing at this new development, ''e's got a right to know.'

'It is *my* baby,' she said, her voice rising. 'I shall carry it, and care for it. The child's paternity is a mere technicality. I have my reasons for not wishing to tell Dezi, but I do not want to discuss them.'

'Okay, okay, don't get yer knickers in a twist. It's none of my business, I know,' he said. 'I'm just concerned about yer.'

'Sorry, I shouldn't have screamed at you.'

''s orlright,' he said. 'But what will yer do?'

'I shall find myself somewhere to live, then break the news to Auntie and Uncle. Then I shall set about building my life as an unmarried mum.' It was only yesterday that she had forced herself to face the fact that her sickness and missed period were symptoms of pregnancy not tension. A daunting realisation, indeed, but becoming less so with her acceptance of it. The future was not going to be easy, but no matter how difficult it became she would keep her baby and not allow it to be raised as a Bennett. It had their blood, but it would not be tainted by the evil of its grandfather while she lived. She would keep the truth from them at all costs.

'Perhaps your aunt an' uncle will let yer stay on with 'em,' John suggested hopefully. 'That would make things easier for yer.'

'I think they will probably offer, but I won't accept. Auntie and Uncle have already had a double helping of kids about

235

the place, being lumbered with Pearl and me when our mother died. I think they are entitled to some peace now.'

'They don't seem the sort to want peace an' quiet,' he pointed out.

'Maybe not,' she admitted, 'but I need my independence. And later on, as the business expands, I'll probably be able to buy a little house with a garden.'

John sucked in his breath anxiously. 'It'll be very hard for yer. Unmarried mothers ain't exactly pampered in our society, are they? The baby will find it tough, too, later on. Yer know how cruel kids can be.'

Stifling sudden guilt pangs, she said sharply, 'We'll survive. Anyway, I've no choice since I'm not prepared to turn to Dezi.' She found this discussion very painful but strangely therapeutic. Didn't they say a problem shared . . .? 'And I'm luckier than many women in my predicament in that I'll have an income from the business. I shall work for as long as possible before the birth and return to the job afterwards. But at least I won't be tied to fixed hours and some boss complaining if I take time off. A lot of the time I shall be able to work from home. It isn't an ideal situation, but I'll manage.'

'Well, if there's anything I can do to 'elp,' offered John, 'just let me know.'

Impulsively, she leaned across and planted a sisterly kiss on his cheek. 'You've helped already, by listening to me. It's cleared my mind. And I have enjoyed our outings.' As he turned his attention to the business of driving her home, she added: 'But there is something else you can do for me.'

'Anything,' he said, turning on the engine.

'Don't tell anyone my secret until I've told my aunt and

uncle. And even then I'd appreciate your keeping the details to yourself.'

'My lips are sealed,' he said.

John drove her home automatically. He felt shaken, as though he had just had news of a death. He supposed he had in a way: the death of his hopes. Now he knew what people meant when they talked about the pain of love. He was in love with a woman who not only did not reciprocate his feelings, but was expecting another man's child into the bargain. He had not realised, until now, just how strong his feelings for Bella were. What a mess!

Chapter Fourteen

Dezi sat in his car at a surveillance point in a Fulworth street and furtively watched his father disappear into one of the houses, a shabby property with mud-coloured paintwork and curtains. How he loathed this odious activity! It was a dreadful thing to be driven to spy on your own father but the issue could be fudged no longer. He *had* to know whether or not he was the son of a criminal.

It was early in February 1953. After listening to Carol's opinion of Bella's reaction to her father's death, Dezi realised that his own behaviour had been lacking in sensitivity. He had been so absorbed in his love for Bella, he had not paid proper attention to her suspicions or considered how, quite naturally, they might affect her decision to marry him. Whereas he regarded his parents as independent human beings, the more family-minded Bella could not help associating him with his parents' actions. And no matter how dissimilar he was to Frank, Dezi *was* the fruit of his loins. It was hardly surprising, he saw now, that in her grief Bella had found it impossible to marry a man who shared a murderer's blood.

So it was that the new year found Dezi in the role of sleuth, tailing his suspect in a series of unrecognisable hired cars. By the end of the first week he had discovered one reason for his father's frequent unexplained absences from his office. A visit by Dezi to some houses in Factory Street, after his quarry had made several calls there, had proved to be most revealing ...

Now, he pulled his overcoat more closely to him as a cold wind rattled around the car, sending icy draughts right through the interior. It was a mere breeze in comparison to the cruel northerly gales that had swept across the country last weekend, causing floods on the East Coast in which many had lost their lives.

Dezi wondered if his father owned this street, too, but when he emerged from the house he did not call anywhere else but went straight to his car and drove away, waved off by a young man wearing a drape jacket and drainpipe trousers. Waiting a few minutes, Dezi strode across to the house and knocked at the door.

'Yeah,' said the thickset, pimply young man whose features strongly resembled a bulldog's. 'What d'yer want?'

'I'm Frank Bennett's son,' said Dezi.

Bulldog's sudden change of attitude spoke volumes. 'Oh, right,' he said, smiling in a servile fashion. 'Come on in. Did yer ole man leave somethin' behind?'

Dezi nodded and stepped into the narrow hall which was sourly scented with the smell of boiled cabbage.

''Oo is it, Joe?' came a rough female voice from the back of the house.

'Just someone about business, Ma.'

'If 'e wants a cuppa, just give us a shout,' she said against a background of clattering pots.

'Righto.' Joe turned to Dezi. 'So what did 'e leave?'

'His lighter,' lied Dezi, detecting a familiar whiff of lingering cigar smoke beneath the overpowering culinary stench.

'Okay, mate, let's go an' 'ave a look for it. Come on upstairs.'

And assuming he would have nothing to hide from a member of his boss's family, Joe led the way upstairs to a small backroom. Dezi stifled a gasp of horror for the room was being used as a warehouse. Cardboard cartons were piled from floor to ceiling, some opened to reveal gilt cigarette cases and lighters, electric irons, jewellery, and some of the new portable radios that were all the rage.

Immediately the door closed behind them, Dezi stopped pretending. 'I'm not here about my father's lighter,' he said. 'Information is what I'm after.'

Joe narrowed his eye suspiciously. 'What sort of information?' he asked.

'Tell me about my father's part in this operation,' said Dezi, waving his hand to indicate the treasures on display. 'That will do for starters.'

''Ere, what's your game, mate?' Joe exclaimed angrily. 'If yer really *are* Frank's son, why not ask 'im? Or Peter?'

Up shot Dezi's brows. He might have known Peter would be stupid enough to allow himself to become involved. Handing Joe one of his business cards, he said, 'I am who I say I am, and unless you answer my questions I shall have no hesitation in telling the law all about your little storeroom.'

Joe turned pale. 'If yer do, you'll drop your old man right in it.'

'I know that' said Dezi.

'You'd shop your ole man, your own flesh an' blood?' He sounded incredulous.

'If necessary, yes,' Dezi informed him. 'So, start talking.'

'You're a cool one, yer are, mate, but yer family affairs ain't no concern of mine,' Joe said with a shrug. He offered Dezi a cigarette, which was refused, and lit one for himself. 'There ain't much to tell really. Your dad is the guvnor an' me and the lads do what we're told. 'E gets the gear through a contact an' we sell it through the pubs an' clubs or on the street, for which 'e pays us a good commission.'

Not half as good as he pays himself, Dezi thought. 'And I suppose it's all as bent as the letter S,' he said.

'I dunno nothin' about that, mate,' Joe said, shaking his head and tapping the side of his nose. '"Ask no questions, 'ear no lies," is my motto. Know what I mean?'

Oh yes, Dezi knew what he meant all right. Joe and his pals did all the dirty work while Father coined in the profit. As much as this weasel of a man repulsed him, Dezi could see that he was a victim of exploitation. But this was all secondary to the *real* purpose of his detective work. 'Do you do other jobs for my father?' he asked.

'Uvver jobs?' Joe asked cautiously.

'Meddling with other people's machinery, for instance?'

'Not me, guv,' Joe chirped nonchalantly.

Dezi grabbed him by his velvet lapels. 'What do you know about an incident at Brown's Garage last year, a matter of a petrol pump being altered? Tell me, or I'll get straight on the phone to the police.'

'Orlright, orlright, I'll tell yer what I know,' he said, nauseating Dezi with breath which smelt like burnt cauliflower. 'I didn't do it meself, but I arranged it with a couple o' the lads on your ole man's instructions.'

'A man died because of you,' Dezi said vehemently.

'Not me, mate,' Joe said. 'I only play in the band. You want the orchestra leader.'

Without another word Dezi marched from the house and drove straight home, unable to face the garage until he had had time to recover from the shock of hearing his suspicions confirmed. Feeling sick and shaky, he plunged into a hot bath to try to erase the lingering odour of that dreadful house.

At last he knew the truth. He was the son of a cheap crook, a man who would stop at nothing to satisfy his own greed and didn't even have the courage to take his own risks. Dezi felt like someone in possession of a dreadful inherited disease. No wonder Bella had turned her back on him.

At about the time that Dezi was drying himself and planning his next move, Bella was having lunch with John Sharpe in a coffee bar near Brown's. Outside, a cold wind whistled through the shop doorways and lurked in wait around corners. Inside, the ambience was bright and cheerful with yellow and black laminated tables and chairs set among a forest of indoor plants. Weak sunshine shone fitfully through the windows and the coffee machine snuffled steamily on the counter.

This was the first time John had spent any time alone with Bella since their evening at the jazz club over a month ago. They had seen each other during the course of the working day, but he had been noticeably restrained towards her. She assumed it was because her condition embarrassed him and had been surprised when he had invited her to join him for lunch.

''Ow are yer feelin' now that all the excitement of Christmas is over?' he asked, picking at the hamburger and chips he had ordered.

'Oh, I'm fine,' she said, nibbling the hot buttered toast she had become partial to in pregnancy. In fact, she felt drained of energy and cold despite the café's steamy warmth. Before meeting John, she had taken a couple of aspirin.

'Are yer, honestly?' he persisted. 'You're not just putting up a front?'

'No, I'm on top form,' Bella said in the bright manner which was becoming second nature to her and which was entirely false. But she could not tell John, or anyone, that life for her without Dezi was empty and meaningless, that she felt like hell without him.

'Yer must be sure to take care of yourself and not work too hard,' he warned anxiously.

'I'm pregnant, John,' she laughed, 'not suffering from TB. And work is my salvation. Without it my problems would seem much worse.' She paused and eyed him shrewdly. 'Why have you been so offhand? Was it because you were so shocked to discover that I'd been a naughty girl?'

'No, it wasn't that,' he said solemnly.

He seemed oddly ill at ease and she noticed he was only playing with his food. In a bid to ease the tension, she wagged her finger playfully at him and said. 'You're not eating. Tut, tut.'

Ignoring her attempt at levity, he said, 'I didn't mean to be offhand. I've been quiet because I've been doing a lot of thinkin'.'

'Oh dear,' she said lightly, still hoping to brighten his mood. 'Too much of that can damage your health.'

But her attempt at humour fell on deaf ears. 'Please be serious, Bella,' John said with surprising firmness. 'I have something important to say to yer.'

Duly reprimanded, she said, 'Sorry, go ahead. I'm all ears.'

243

'Will yer marry me?' he gabbled, gulping at his coffee as if his life depended on it and surveying her reaction over the rim of the cup.

'*Marry you*!' she exclaimed, unable to hide her astonishment.

'Is the idea so revoltin' to yer?' he asked bitterly, overreacting in his disappointment. 'I know I'm not in the same league as Dezi Bennett, but I could make yer a good husband.'

And Bella had no doubt about that. Her father's judgement of John's character had proved to be correct. He had a seriousness about him which belied his flashy dress. Increasingly, she had noticed how skilful and conscientious he was about his work; how well he coped with the responsibility of management; how highly regarded he was by the other workmen.

Annoyed with herself for hurting him by the hastiness of her response, she leaned across the table and rested an affectionate hand briefly on his. 'I don't doubt that you would make someone a wonderful husband, but we've only ever been out together a couple of times, we hardly know each other. I'm very flattered, of course ...'

'I know you're not in love with me or anythin' like that but I'd be good to yer, I promise,' he said.

Whilst appreciating the kindness of the gesture, she hated to feel herself an object of pity. 'It is very sweet of you to ask but there's no need to go to such lengths, honestly. I am quite prepared to face the future alone.'

He studied his expandable metallic watchstrap closely for a few moments, then looked up and said with a kind of desperate determination, 'I'm not bein' sweet or gallant. I didn't ask yer because I'm sorry for yer.' He paused to draw breath. Not naturally gifted with eloquence, emotional speeches like this did not come easily to him 'Haven't yer guessed, Bella? I love yer and I'd do anythin' to make yer 'appy.' He looked into her eyes and reached across the table to clasp her hand. 'I'd be good to yer an' love yer baby as me own. If yer give me a chance, I promise yer won't regret it.'

Bella was lost for words. She had guessed that he liked and desired her, but the depth of feeling that this passionate effusion revealed was a complete surprise. In her vulnerable state it was reassuring, but oppressive too. She wasn't sure if she could cope with being the object of such deep, unrequited love. The need to escape overwhelmed her but she stifled the urge to snatch her hand away, knowing it would hurt his feelings. Oh dear, how could she reject him without wounding his pride irrevocably?

'Look, there's no need to give me an answer now,' he said, letting go of her hand. 'Think it over for a few days. Just promise me one thing.'

'If I can,' she said, grateful for the reprieve.

'Please don't dismiss the idea without givin' it due consideration. It will make life much easier for yer an' the baby. An' you'd make me the 'appiest man alive,' he told her ardently.

'I promise to give it serious thought,' she said, smiling warmly at him.

Aware that the febrile achiness she had woken with this morning had returned with the decreasing effect of the aspirin, she didn't go straight back to the office with John, but took a walk by the river to try to clear her head. She walked from Fulworth to Chiswick Mall with its grand historic houses facing the wooded contours of Chiswick Eyot, a nesting place for swans which was well known for its annual crop of osiers used for basket making. The cold wind and the exercise had an invigorating effect on her, and on returning to Fulworth, determined not to be intimidated by the possibility of seeing Dezi, she indulged a whim and extended her journey to Ivy House which brightened the landscape at this colourless time of the year with its fresh, white-painted woodwork shining smartly against the red brick and ivy.

Memories abounded. As she stared into the water she could almost see Dezi's face reflected there. Despite their parting, he filled her entire existence. It did not seem possible, in that desolate moment, that she could survive another second without the comfort of his physical presence. A cloud passed over the sun and she shivered, just as she had on that first day . . . Reluctantly, Bella pulled herself back to the present. As reality swept over her in a bitter tide it was no longer Dezi's face she saw, but his father's.

Her biggest fear for the future was that Frank Bennett might somehow learn the truth about her child. That they were linked by blood was bad enough. If Frank discovered the connection he was quite capable of taking a possessive interest in the baby, trying to mould it in the hated Bennett ways.

Walking back to the office Bella turned her attention to John's proposal, realising that it offered not only protection for herself and her baby from the scorn of society but also guaranteed the child's safety from the evil influence of its paternal grandfather, since it would be raised as a Sharpe. The practical value of such an arrangement was tempting. But she did not love John and knew she never could, as a wife should. So the answer must be a negative one. And it wasn't fair to allow him to hope in vain, so she would tell him at the earliest opportunity this afternoon.

But an hour after arriving back at the office, she found

herself sinking under the onset of a virulent bout of flu. By mid-afternoon she had no alternative but to leave the office in Beatrice's capable hands and go home to bed. For several days she was ravaged by illness and plagued by hallucinations in which Frank Bennett snatched her child from her. When her temperature finally returned to normal, she was left feeling drained and depressed.

During the period of recuperation, when her powers of coherent thought had returned but not her physical strength, she was plagued by fears for her baby and a strong sense of panic about the situation in general. It was already February and she still had not found anywhere suitable to live. And as she did not intend to break the news about the baby to her aunt until the accommodation problem was solved, Vi and Wilf remained in blissful ignorance, something that could not continue since she would begin noticeably to change shape soon.

And so it was that John found her in low spirits when he visited her during his lunch break one day.

'Well,' he said, handing her a bag of grapes and some magazines, 'do yer think yer'll live?'

'Just about,' she croaked painfully, having been robbed of her voice by the malady. 'I'll be back at work in a few days.'

'Don't come back until yer properly better,' urged John, 'or yer'll be susceptible to any other bugs that are around. Yer gotta take special care.'

Her aunt and uncle were both out at work so they were alone in the house. 'Don't worry, I won't do anything to harm the baby,' she said, weakness bringing tears to her eyes.

'It was *you* I was thinkin' about, not the baby,' he said kindly.

'I'm sorry, John,' she said. 'The flu has left me feeling very low.' She was lying on the couch downstairs wearing a pink candlewick dressing gown. Auntie Vi had draped a blanket over her and Tiddles lay asleep by her feet. Her hair was tousled, her face flushed and shiny, and her nose red raw. She brushed her hair wearily from her face with her hand. 'I must look awful, I haven't looked in a mirror for days.'

'Yer look wonderful,' he assured her from his seat on the nearby pouffe.

'Thank you.' His gentleness, added to her current sensitivity, brought tears to her eyes again. She blew her nose. 'Take no notice of me. I'm a real wet blanket today.'

He put a comforting hand on hers. 'It's understandable. You've a lot on yer plate. An' flu does take it out of yer.' He moved back and studied his shoes for a while before looking up. 'I know this is probably the worst possible time to ask, but 'ave yer got an answer for me?'

'I have,' she told him. 'But sadly it must be no. I'm fond of you, but not in love with you.'

'I know that an' I told yer it doesn't matter,' he persisted.

'Maybe not to you. It does to me,' she explained. 'It would cause problems eventually, whatever you think now.'

'I wouldn't demand too much of yer. I may not make your heart flutter but I'd be a true friend. At least the baby would be raised in a stable family environment. Surely that's worth somethin'?' he said, his brown eyes alight with sincerity.

Bella sighed. 'John, you are *too* nice. Men like you don't happen outside of films.'

'Aw, gee,' he joked to hide his emotion.

'Are you *really* prepared to marry me and bring up my child as your own, knowing that I will probably never love you as a wife should?'

'Yes!'

'But what would be in it for you?' she asked.

'The pleasure of 'avin' you near,' he said simply.

And she heard a voice that didn't seem to belong to her, saying, 'In that case, I would love to marry you.'

He was all smiles. 'Oh, Bella,' he said, leaning forward and kissing her cheek, 'You've made me so 'appy. I promise yer won't regret it.'

God help me, what am I doing? she asked herself, panicking at the enormity of this unexpected decision. But despite her dreamlike state of mind, she knew the answer to that question. It was for the good of her child so it couldn't be wrong. And she would make this tenderhearted man happy or die in the attempt.

'It's a nice place you've got here, son,' said Frank Bennett, casting an approving eye around Dezi's lounge. 'I've often thought that your mother and me ought to move to this side of the river. Putney has such class.'

'I didn't ask you here to discuss the social nuances of the district,' said Dezi coldly.

'Oh dear, you *do* sound stern,' laughed Frank to hide the fear in his heart. 'Is your old Dad in the doghouse?'

Dezi had been more affected by his discovery of the truth about his father than he'd expected, and had postponed their confrontation for a few days until he felt calmer. He had asked Frank to come to the flat to ensure that no one else would hear what he had to say. 'That's putting it mildly,' he said, grimly eyeing his father sharply. 'The game's up, Dad. I know all about your undeclared income from Factory Street, and the stolen goods you peddle with a man called Joe.'

The blood drained from Frank's face. 'Oh Gawd,' he said, reverting to raw Cockney in his anxiety. 'I can explain, son . . .' He stood by the window, his balding head more egg-like than ever in the flood of light. 'They're just little earners belonging to a mate of mine. I just help him out.'

'Don't insult my intelligence by telling me a pack of lies. You're a cheap crook and I'm ashamed to be related to you.'

Frank's face turned from white to an angry red. 'Well, that's a fine way for a son to talk to his father,' he blustered.

'I also know the truth about the petrol pump affair at Brown's,' said Dezi as though his father had not spoken. And as Frank began to deny it, he added: 'Save your breath, Dad. Joe told me everything.'

'Oh, well, if you'd rather believe riff-raff like him . . .'

Barely able to breathe, he was so angry, Dezi rasped: 'He's good enough to take all the risks for you, and yet you have the arrogance to call him riff-raff!' He mopped his moist brow with a handkerchief. 'And to think that I believed you instead of Bella and her father.'

'Oh, them,' Frank began disparagingly.

'Don't you dare say a word against either of them. They're worth a million of you,' Dezi ground out. 'Bob Brown died because of you.'

'I didn't intend him to,' said Frank, sinking weakly into an armchair as the now familiar symptoms of stress overwhelmed him. He was trembling and sweating, and his heart palpitated.

'You wanted his business for buttons and if he had to be eliminated to that end, then so be it,' barked Dezi.

'It wasn't like that.'

'Maybe not, but that's how it ended. You're despicable, do you know that?'

'What do you propose to do now?' asked Frank, grey with fear. 'Are you going to shop me?'

This was a dilemma that had kept Dezi awake this last few nights, since even now the idea of betraying his own flesh and blood was abhorrent to him. Finally, he had decided on a solution of more practical value than a phone call to the police. 'If you don't abide by certain conditions, yes,' he said.

'You ought to be ashamed of yourself, threatening your own father,' mumbled Frank.

'You're lucky not to be in custody, so cut the complaints and listen,' roared Dezi.

'Oh, all right.'

'Firstly, I want your word that you will *never, ever* try to harm Bella, or her business, or any member of her family again.'

'Huh! Your girlfriend has beaten you to it, she's already threatened me. Bloody cheek. She's got no proof.'

'But I have,' Dezi reminded him. 'And if Bella gets so much as a hint of trouble from you, I shall go to the police and the Inland Revenue.'

'This is your *father* you're talking to,' Frank blustered, but it was an empty protest. He knew his halcyon days were over.

'Don't remind me, I'm ashamed to be associated with you,' Dezi informed him. 'Nothing would please me more than to get out of your life forever.'

Frank flinched visibly. 'You wouldn't. It would break your mother's heart. She knows nothing of this.'

'I'm not leaving,' Dezi assured him. 'I *have* to stay to make sure that the business, which I've worked hard to build, is run in a reputable way. Without me around, God knows what sort of dodgy establishment you'd turn it into.'

'The garage has always been squeaky clean,' said Frank, lighting a cigar and puffing heavily on it.

Yes, a useful, respectable front, thought Dezi. 'I wouldn't trust you to run a church bazaar, so listen to the rest of my proposition,' he said.

'There's more?' said Frank miserably.

'Yes. As well as leaving the Browns alone,' Dezi continued, 'you also clean up your Factory Street operation. Do the houses up, get rid of the damp, put heating in, adjust the rents to a fair amount, give the tenants proper rent books and declare the income. You will probably have to sell some of the houses to pay the outstanding tax that will be owing. You will finish dealing in stolen gear altogether.

'Unless all these things are done, and I shall keep a careful eye on the situation, I will consider it my bounden duty to share what I know with certain authorities. So, do we have a deal?'

'It's all very well for you to preach at me,' said Frank dismally, from behind a screen of cigar smoke, 'but it isn't that simple. I've had those houses some considerable time. How can I declare them now without being prosecuted for tax evasion?'

But Dezi was prepared for this. A few minutes with his solicitor had proved most informative. 'As a penalty, you will be liable for a much larger payment than is actually due in tax. But if you pay that, I doubt if they will prosecute. When will you go and see them to start the ball rolling?'

'Give me a chance.'

'First thing tomorrow morning is as good a time as any.'

Frank sighed irritably. 'Okay, I'll go tomorrow.'

'Too right you will!' Dezi assured him. 'And I'll go with you.'

'Don't trust me, eh?'

'No! Never again.'

'Anything I've done, I've done for the family,' Frank said shakily.

'Don't pass the buck, Dad,' Dezi said icily. 'You didn't need extra cash. The garage was already providing a good enough living to keep us all in style. You did what you did out of greed.'

And to Dezi's amazement his father said, 'You're probably right. I'm sorry, son.'

Dezi looked down at a pathetic heap of ageing humanity, bloated from too much good living. So now that his father had apologised, presumably Dezi was expected to pat him on the head and tell him that all was forgiven. Well, he would not. One man had died and two other lives were potentially ruined because of him.

But to Dezi's astonishment, a lump gathered in his throat and he was forced to swallow hard before saying, 'I should damned well hope you are. But don't think that will get you off the hook. I am going to work now, but I suggest that you make a start on cleaning up your affairs. I'll pick you up tomorrow morning and we'll go to the Inland Revenue office together.'

Eve was reclining in an armchair by the log fire in the drawing room when Frank arrived home in the early afternoon.

'Have you had lunch?' she asked. 'Or do you want Mary to get you something?'

'I don't want anything,' he said, going to the bar and pouring himself a large Scotch. He had come straight from Dezi's flat and still felt shaken from the ordeal.

'Anything wrong, dear?' Eve asked. 'You look a bit pale.'

'Just a bit of a headache,' he said absently, sipping his drink by the bar and staring glassily into space.

'A cup of tea and an aspirin will do you more good than whisky,' she chided. 'Are you staying long enough for Mary to make a pot, or going straight back to the garage?'

'I'll be here for a while,' he said.

'I'll tell her to put the kettle on then,' she said, putting down her glossy magazine.

'That will be nice,' he said dutifully.

Watching her trot across the room in her staid navy twinset and grey skirt, he thought how shocked she would be to know the truth about her husband. Her neat, matronly form exuded snobbish respectability. Even when they had been poor, he remembered, she had had the air of someone who bought the week's groceries from Harrods' Food Halls.

Frank drained his whisky and sat down, leaning his head back and closing his eyes. He knew he would never forget the hatred and scorn he had seen on Dezi's face this morning. In the aftermath of disaster, Frank tried to fathom why, with no financial need to excuse it, he had resorted to such murky business methods.

It all came down to power, he decided. He'd wanted the feeling of superiority that came from employing a gang of no-hopers like Joe and his mates, and the intoxicating sense of importance in wielding power over the people of Factory Street. He'd become dependent on this sort of dominance. His victims' and sidekicks' reliance on him had been his strength. Even his dear, colourless wife had satisfied this need in him.

Bob Brown had been Frank's downfall. In obstructing him, Bob had provided the spur to Frank's overweening need for power. As a result he had lost the chance of ever earning his firstborn's admiration and respect. The truth seared like a whiplash. He hadn't wanted Brown's site nearly as much as he'd wanted Brown to fail. Another man's success had been anathema to him and had to be thwarted.

Feeling utterly wretched, Frank slipped quietly upstairs to the elegant bedroom that he shared with Eve and lay down on the satin-covered bed. He had never been a religious man, but lately he had been beset by fears of retribution from beyond the grave. *Murderer, murderer*...The word pounded through his brain and he clamped his hands to his head in an effort to shut it out. And then he did something he had not done since he was a child. He began to cry – deep, penetrating sobs of self-pity.

'Frank ... Frank, where are you? Mary's made you some tea,' Eve called from downstairs.

He sat up and dragged a handkerchief from the pocket of his business suit, wiping his eyes and blowing his nose guiltily. He had been raised to believe that tears from an adult male were totally unacceptable. Eve must never see him like this, for if she realised he was not infallible and lost her respect for him, too, he was finished altogether. Clearing his throat, he called, 'I'm in the bedroom, dear. I came up to get a clean hanky. Be down in a minute.'

He swung off the bed, straightened his tie in the mirror, brushed his suit with his hands and went down to take tea with his wife, his damp handkerchief safely tucked away in his pocket.

Chapter Fifteen

Such was his vicarious shame at the suffering his father had caused Bella, Dezi agonised throughout February about his next move towards a reconciliation with her. After all she had been through, he was loath to add to her pain by pressurising her before she was ready.

Finally, he decided that a letter would be the wisest form of communication, since it would allow her to give due thought to her response before replying. The possibility that she might not share his wish to be reunited was not a serious consideration since he was certain that their love was too strong to be extinguished permanently. As Carol had pointed out, when Bella's grief subsided she would need him. This was the belief to which he now clung.

It was a letter written from the heart, assuring her that Dezi now knew the truth about his father who would not bother her again. He reiterated his own feelings for her, ending, 'My love for you remains constant. Without you I am nothing. Please say we can be reunited.'

He posted it in late February addressed to the prefab, since, as far as he knew, she still lived there.

★   ★   ★

Peter was too deeply immersed in the pleasures of married life to give any thought to his brother's problems. As far as Peter was concerned the affair between Dezi and Bella was over. What little news of his sister-in-law he did have, given the girls' estrangement, he maintained a diplomatic silence over in accordance with customary procedure following the parting of a couple. By far the wisest move, he thought, until he was sure there were no lingering sensitivities.

And so it was that one day in March Dezi found himself devastated by a piece of information which emerged during a quarrel with his brother. The storm blew up after a telephone call from a customer, with whom he had been negotiating for some time over the sale of an expensive new car, to say that he wanted to call to see Peter that afternoon. The man was obviously ready to close the deal, so Dezi was not pleased when his brother blithely said he was taking the afternoon off.

'I told you last week that I wouldn't be here this afternoon,' Peter reminded him.

'Be that as it may,' said Dezi firmly, 'this is more important. The customer is about to spend a large amount of money with us. He won't like being fobbed off with one of your staff. It could turn the whole deal sour. God dammit, the man is entitled to the attention of the Sales Manager when he's spending that sort of money. Take tomorrow off instead. It can't matter that much, surely.'

'No, I can't alter my arrangements,' said Peter firmly. 'I'll call the guy and change the appointment to tomorrow.'

'You can't do that,' barked Dezi. 'We're running a business here, not a game of Ludo.'

'I'm sorry,' said Peter. 'I wish I could change my plans, but I can't. What about you, Dezi? Can't you see the customer? Surely to have the Managing Director at his disposal would please him.'

The two men were facing each other across Dezi's desk. The latter frowned darkly. His mood had been deteriorating daily. Each morning he feverishly awaited the postman, and when he failed to bring the anticipated reply from Bella, Dezi spent the rest of the day breaking into a sweat at the sound of the telephone. Now, he sighed irritably. 'No, I can't stand in for you, I have an appointment with one of the top brass at the new engineering factory about the service contract for their fleet of company cars, which will be a real coup for us. Obviously, it would be foolish to postpone that interview. God knows when I'd get another one.' He looked accusingly at Peter. 'I suppose Pearl is dragging you off to look at property,' he said, knowing that the couple were about to invest in a house. 'Well, that will have to wait until tomorrow.'

'No, it isn't that,' said Peter, finding himself on the horns of a dilemma. In actual fact, he would much rather stay here and complete the business than go to Bella's wedding, which was to be a very low-key affair, apparently. A registry office do, with the reception at Napley Road. Yuk! They'd be lucky to get a glass of Tizer, let alone champagne. The whole thing would be ghastly, with the Browns barely managing to be civil to him. Because the invitation had not come until last week, he assumed that Bella had only invited him and Pearl as a last-minute sop to her conscience. Anyway, it was a damned nuisance because if he did not go with Pearl, she would be furious, and he would rather be in the doghouse with his brother than his wife. 'It's all a bit awkward . . . Can't Dad stand in for me?'

'No, he's busy at the accountant's office.'

'I'm sorry, I really am.'

Down came Dezi's fist on the desk. 'Oh, go on and enjoy yourself in your usual lighthearted fashion and leave me to sort out the problems.'

But the fact was that Peter was not being deliberately unco-operative. Dezi's taunt proved too much for him and he snapped, 'All right, I'll tell you why I can't change my arrangements. I have to go to Pearl's sister's wedding and I don't think she'd take too kindly to my asking her to postpone it 'til another day. It's a bloody nuisance, but Pearl will be upset if I don't go with her. She and Bella aren't what you'd call bosom pals at present, so she needs my moral support.'

Dezi's knuckles turned white as he grasped the edge of the desk for support. 'Bella . . . getting married?' He sank shakily into his chair, his voice a whisper.

'Yes, at two o'clock.' Peter saw the blood drain from his brother's face and regretted this words. 'Some chap who works at Brown's apparently. I wasn't going to say anything . . . wasn't sure how you felt now . . . you know.'

'Don't worry,' Dezi said, white-faced.

'So you see, as it's a wedding . . .'

'You go,' interrupted Dezi, wanting only to be left alone with the ruins of his life. 'I'll sort things out here.'

'Are you sure?'

'Quite sure. Go as soon as you like. Have a good time.'

'Not much chance of that, but thanks.'

Alone at last, Dezi sat at his desk, numb with pain and shock. At two o'clock today Bella was marrying another man . . . another man . . . another man . . . The words reverberated in his head again and again until he thought he would lose his mind. Anger, born of anguish, consumed him. The woman who had been everything to him had turned out to be as trivial and frivolous as ribbons on a party frock. She hadn't wasted any time. He pictured her showing his letter to her husband-to-be, the two of them laughing over it before throwing it on the fire. But still, somewhere in the deepest corner of his heart, there was an obstinate whisper which refused to allow him to accept that Bella did not love him.

His thoughts raced chaotically. Somehow the work of the day was done, with Dezi functioning mechanically. Telephone calls were taken, appointments changed, customers placated, until at last, somehow, the afternoon ended. He picked up the telephone and dialled a number.

'Carol, it's Dezi. I need a friend. Are you free this evening?'

'Well, it went off quite well, I thought,' said John to his bride. 'I enjoyed it. Did you?'

'Yes,' said Bella, perching on the edge of the bed in the furnished bed sitter they were renting until legal completion of their house purchase. It had been a hectic month since she had accepted John's proposal. Speed being of the essence, they had arranged the wedding for the earliest possible date, both sets of relatives being led to believe that the reason for the haste was John's eagerness, a story he gladly confirmed.

John's mother, a forthright, cheerful woman from whom he had obviously inherited his kind heart, was more worried about Bella's superior position within the firm than the reason for their early wedding. 'I think yer'll 'ave more than your fair share of problems, with Bella bein' the boss. But since you've been an' gorn an' done it, I wish yer all the luck,' she had said.

Auntie Vi, however, was more astute. 'You've got a good 'un in John. Not many men would be willin' to take on another man's child. He thinks the world of yer, that boy.'

'How did you guess?' asked Bella.

'I know you like you were me own daughter. An' I've watched you an' Dezi together,' Vi told her. 'You'd not get yourself pregnant by someone else so soon after.'

And since she hated to lie to her aunt, she did not deny it, only extracted a promise of confidentiality. In a strange way she was glad her aunt knew the truth. It made her feel less alone, somehow.

'You don't think that Uncle Wilf has guessed the truth, do you?' Bella asked.

'Lord, no. He doesn't have such a suspicious mind as me,' Vi had assured Bella. 'He just accepts things at face value.'

And so Bella had conditioned herself to play her part in a real life drama. It was a role she intended to carry off convincingly and she slipped into it every day as a matter of course, behaving affectionately towards John and feigning enthusiasm for their life together, whilst actually dying of loneliness inside. Fortunately, they shared a practical streak and had agreed that their circumstances called for a quiet wedding. Only close relatives had been invited. Bella felt better for asking Pearl. It wouldn't have felt right without her, even though she still had not forgiven her.

The couple had decided to spare themselves the expense of a honeymoon in favour of buying furniture for their house. Now, just back from the wedding reception, Bella could feel the dark waters of depression rising around her. She tried to banish the feeling by reminding herself how lucky she was to be married to such a kind and responsible man as John.

She glanced idly around their temporary accommodation, a spacious, high-ceilinged room which provided open plan sleeping, living and dining areas and a tiny kitchen behind a partition. Clean and freshly decorated with a pink floral wallpaper, it was really quite cosy.

John flopped down on the bed beside her, smartly dressed in a grey suit with a white carnation in the button-hole, a snow-white shirt, blue tie and squeaky new shoes with a mirror shine. His wife's modest bridal attire was a cream suit and feathery hat with coffee-coloured accessories.

'Well,' he said, taking Bella's hand, 'you're lookin' very thoughtful. No regrets, I hope.'

'No regrets,' she said, forcing back the tears. Don't even think about Dezi, she warned herself.

Tenderly, John tilted her face towards his. This marriage meant so much to him, she mustn't spoil it for him. 'Would yer like some supper?' he asked. 'I'll make us somethin', if yer like.'

'Maybe later. It's early yet.'

Sensitive to her mood, John turned away. 'Look, with the baby an' everythin'...I don't mind...I mean, I'll understand if you'd rather not...yer know.'

'Thank you, John,' she said, appreciative of his thoughtfulness. 'Let's just let things take their course, shall we?'

Later, when she had climbed into bed, prettily attired in a pink frilly nightdress, John appeared from the kitchen in his new red-and-white striped pyjamas, carrying supplies of the two things Bella craved most in her pregnancy: cream soda and a large packet of marshmallows. 'Champagne would have been more romantic,' he said with a grin, 'but as alcohol upsets you at the moment, I thought yer might like these instead.'

Humbled by his kindness and burdened by the fact that he was worthy of more than it was possible for her to give, her eyes moistened. 'I don't deserve you,' she said, kissing him lightly and noticing the fresh scent of toothpaste and new cotton.

'Let me be the judge of that,' he said.

They toasted their future in cream soda and sat up in bed munching marshmallows and listening to Geraldo on the radio. Then, knowing that she owed it to her husband to steer things on to the natural course, Bella took a deep resolute breath and slipped her arms around him.

Since Christmas, Carol Dent had become Dezi's valued confidante. Heartened by her depth of understanding and eagerness to listen, he had seen her regularly and held back nothing of his feelings for Bella. It wasn't that Carol soothed the pain so much as that she diminished his sense of isolation. For the first time in his life he knew what it was to share a burden.

And so it was that a despairing Dezi dined with Carol in a small riverside restaurant in Richmond on the evening of Bella's wedding day.

'I just can't believe it,' he lamented as he picked at his food. 'I would have staked my life on the fact she loved me. Huh, it doesn't say much for my judgement.'

Carol was wise beyond her years, with the ability to see hope in the most desperate situation. But Dezi needed plain speaking right now, however unpalatable, or he'd run the risk of wasting his life hankering after the unattainable.

'Your judgement isn't necessarily at fault,' she said. 'Human nature is a very unpredictable thing. Bella must have her reasons for marrying this man. On the rebound from you while still in shock, is my guess. But the sooner you accept that, for whatever reason, she *has* married someone else, the sooner you will begin to feel better. You must admit to yourself that it is over between you and build your life, without her.'

She saw his face muscles tighten as her comments hit home, and hated herself for causing him pain. Dezi was a dazzling man: charming, kind, handsome, a respecter of women as equals – unlike many of his contemporaries. Since Christmas they had built up a good platonic friendship: long conversations and the merest brush of her cheek in occasional kisses. The sooner he stopped wasting his energy in pining for Bella Brown, the better it would suit Carol...

'I know it's hard, but it will get easier with time,' she said comfortingly.

He sighed. 'I suppose you're right.'

'I am, take it from someone who knows,' she assured him.

'Yes, of course,' he said warmly, the reminder of their mutual heartache re-establishing the empathy between them. 'I must have become an awful bore. All I ever talk about is Bella.'

'As I've said before, I'm happy to listen.' She paused and met his eyes purposefully. 'But now, in the light of today's event, you have to start taking my advice.'

'Yes, ma'am,' he said with a mock salute, managing a faint smile.

Although Carol was a kind and concerned person, she was also a passionate woman who had fallen deeply in love with Dezi. And now that Bella Brown was out of the picture, Carol intended to develop her relationship with him along more satisfactory lines. She would always be second best to Bella, of course, but she loved him enough to cope with that. She hoped, with love and attention, gradually to heal his wounds. Persuading him that he wished to share his life with her would be a task which called for the utmost dedication and subtlety. But she was confident of victory. She might not inspire passion in him, as Bella had, but she could make him happy. And that was worth fighting for.

She wagged her finger at him playfully, deliberately introducing a lighter note. 'You need taking in hand and I am just the one to do it.'

He was still very pale, but smiled dutifully. Realising that he had burdened her with his problems for long enough, he asked, 'How was your day?'

'It was okay,' she said, giving the shy smile which brought dimples to her cheeks. 'Injections, bedpans ... an average sort of day on the ward with the usual percentage of emergencies.' She paused thoughtfully. 'No one died though.'

He felt a glow of admiration for her. 'Such worthwhile work,' he said. 'It makes the business world seem rather shallow by comparison.'

'Nonsense,' she said, reaching across the table and taking his hand, accepting that the initiative must be hers. 'We all have our part to play.'

'Does your work ever depress you?' he asked, absently patting her hand before releasing it.

Her eyes darkened. 'When I had my first death on the ward, I was devastated for weeks. It was a child, a road accident victim. I had allowed myself to become too involved. I didn't think I had the strength to cope with something like that ever again. I was about to leave the profession when a senior colleague took me aside and told me that I had the makings of a good nurse and I should not waste my vocation. She reminded me of something I had overlooked – the vast majority of patients who are cured.

'Anyway, I stayed and I've never regretted it. There are moments of sadness, yes, but great joy too. Lives begin as well as end in hospitals, remember. And even in terminal cases, skilled nursing and the relief of pain count for a great deal. So, no, my work doesn't depress me.'

Dezi was impressed. 'You're quite a woman,' he said sincerely.

'Thank you.'

When they left the restaurant, she said, 'Shall we go back to your place for a while? Play a few records, drink some coffee. I don't feel like going home to bed yet.' She did have her own car, but Dezi, considering transport to be his responsibility, had collected her from her home in Wimbledon, where she lived with her parents. 'Unless it would be too much of a bother to drive me home later.'

'I'd be delighted,' said Dezi, who dreaded being left to his own thoughts.

They drank coffee and listened to Chopin in comfortable silence for a long time. Then Carol perched on the arm of Dezi's chair and slipped her arms around him, leaving him in no doubt as to what was on her mind.

For a moment he was tempted to take her up on her silent invitation, but instead, he took her hand and kissed the back of it. 'I value you too highly to want to use you, Carol.' He rose and slipped his arms around her, brushing her brow with a kiss. 'You've been a lifeline to me these last few months and you're a very dear friend. Now, finish your coffee and I'll drive you home.'

Later, as she lay in bed considering his rejection, she couldn't help but love him more for it. And she was not downhearted. It was, after all, very early days...

'It's a real little palace,' said Auntie Vi one Saturday afternoon in April soon after Bella and John had moved into their small house in the Napley Road area. 'You must both be thrilled to bits.'

'We are pleased with it,' said Bella, setting down a tray of tea and scones on the table. And she had reason to be proud for she and John had worked hard on it, staying on in the bedsitter for a few weeks after the house was legally theirs and spending every spare moment painting and papering it. John had even modernised the kitchen. Now, the property exuded comfort and cosiness. Downstairs was carpeted red with a pretty cretonne three-piece suite in autumn colours and slimline dining furniture. Upstairs, their bedroom was done in pink, with deep pile carpet and a satin bedspread. 'But there's still plenty of work to do on it. We have the baby's room to decorate yet.'

John was out at a late season football match, so the two women were alone. 'Is it to be pink or blue?' asked Vi, to whom house-owning was still an alien concept since she and Wilf had only ever been tenants.

'Neither,' said Bella, pouring the tea from a white, gold-edged china pot. 'We thought pale lemon.'

'Good idea,' agreed Vi. She buttered a scone, and gave her niece a thoughtful look. 'No regrets, eh, luv?'

Bella shook her head. 'I'd be a fool if I had. John's a perfect dear.'

'I'm so pleased. Gawd knows, yer deserve some 'appiness.' Vi sipped her tea. 'Looks like we'll be 'aving another weddin' in the family next year. Trevor an' Joan are talkin' about tyin' the knot.'

Bella nodded. 'Yes, so Joan was saying.'

The two women chatted happily. Suddenly, Auntie glanced at the gilt-edged clock on the wall. 'I must go. It ull soon be time get Wilf's tea,' she said. 'I've a nice piece of smoked 'addock for us.'

The younger woman smiled, able to feel the special essence of number nine emanating from her aunt; its warmth, its sense of family. That was the atmosphere Bella aimed to create in her own home: laughter, love, security. 'Uncle Wilf will enjoy that,' she said.

'Oh yeah, 'e's partial to 'addock with a knob of butter for Saturday tea is Wilf.' Vi smiled thoughtfully. 'At least we can get it now, not like those dark days in the war, eh, Bel?'

'You're right,' she agreed, smiling affectionately at the memory of the rough and tumble of those days. She was suddenly filled with optimism for the future. If Auntie had managed to maintain a happy home despite all the deprivations, then surely she could make a good life for John and the baby.

At the door Auntie began to rummage in her handbag. 'I nearly forgot. A letter came for yer.' She tutted. 'It's been to the bloomin' moon an' back before catchin' up with us. It's postmarked the end of February. Addressed to the prefab, it was. The new people there must have left it layin' around for weeks before sending it on to the forwardin' address yer left with them.' She burrowed deeper into the capacious black bag. 'Ah, 'ere it is,' she said, handing Bella a crumpled envelope. 'Ta-ta duck, see yer tomorrow.'

'Ta-ta, Auntie.'

How her legs carried her inside, she didn't know for they had weakened at the sight of that familiar handwriting. Trembling, she stared at the red coals in the hearth, knowing that she should feed the letter to them, unopened. But the anger and hatred that had spurred her to ignore Dezi's earlier communications had been replaced by a profound and lasting sadness beneath the cheerful exterior. She simply could not do it. She looked guiltily towards the door, as though John might appear and catch her in her moment of disloyalty. Then, very much against her better judgement, she scurried upstairs to the bedroom and tore open the envelope.

His words were so vivid they brought Dezi clearly to mind. She could almost see him as she read: 'Without you I am nothing. Please say we can be reunited.'

It was the final straw. After months of doubt and uncertainty, Bella faced the agonising truth. 'My darling Dezi, what have I done to you? What have I done to us?' she sobbed into her pillow.

It was like waking from an illness to find herself cured. And she realised that she had indeed been sick in her mind until reading the letter. Now, she could picture Dezi and his father as two separate people and it was a wonderful feeling. Her instincts cried out for her to go to Dezi, to beg his forgiveness and drown in his love.

'Bella, where are you. I'm home.' John was back from the match.

Scrambling off the bed, she mopped her face with a handkerchief and hurried out to the landing, stuffing the letter into the pocket of her slacks. 'I'll be down in a minute. Just doing my hair.'

'Okay, love. I'll put the kettle on for a cuppa.'

And with the realisation of her true feelings for Dezi, came horror at the trap she had allowed to close around her. It did not seem possible for her to stay with John for another moment, but to leave him would be to destroy him. She could never do that. Besides, the main reason for her marriage would endure for as long as Frank Bennett still lived.

After washing her face Bella took the letter out of her pocket and sadly re-read it, realising that she had no choice but to destroy it and ignore its contents. Explanations would serve no purpose. Better for Dezi if he hated her, for then he might find happiness with someone new. Her duty lay with John and the baby now.

Regret piercing her, sharp as a razor, she tore the letter into tiny pieces and put them in the bottom of her handbag, ready to burn at the earliest opportunity. Then, she wiped her eyes again, combed her hair and went downstairs.

'How was the match?' she asked, finding John making tea in the smart blue and white kitchen he had made for them.

'Smashin',' he beamed, his cheeks glowing from the fresh air. 'An' all the better for havin' you to come 'ome to.'

'It was a beautiful ceremony,' said Carol to Dezi on the 2nd June 1953. 'And a lovely procession. A pity about the weather, but it didn't seem to dampen anyone's spirits.'

'We had the best and the dryest view, I reckon,' he said, referring to the fact that they had viewed the Coronation of Queen Elizabeth II on his new television set.

'You're probably right,' she agreed. They had indeed had good close-up pictures of the scene in Westminster Abbey, and the camera had brilliantly captured the festive mood of the crowds along the route. Carol glanced towards the bulky, walnut cabinet in the corner, its doors now closed across the screen. 'It's a wonderful invention. I'm glad you decided to get one.'

Dezi had joined the thousands of others who had invested in a set for the Coronation. The low social status of 'the television' didn't worry Dezi. The snobs who refused to have a set on the grounds that viewing was a pastime, suitable only for those of lower intellect, didn't know what they were missing. As well as entertainment and a wider news coverage, the television also brought culture to the masses. He thought it was great and would eventually become a part of everyday life.

As the day was an official public holiday, Dezi had been able to make a real occasion of it by inviting some non set-owning neighbours in. He had provided a buffet and they had all toasted the Queen in champagne. It had been very pleasant. But now, in the early evening, Carol wanted to sample some of the real fun.

'Let's go up West and capture some of the atmosphere,' she suggested excitedly. 'The celebrations will continue well into the night up there. It will round the day off nicely.'

'Good idea,' said Dezi.

As she went to get ready, he found himself reviewing the last three months since Bella's wedding. Rather than decreasing with time, his hatred of her for so easily rejecting him had festered inside him. He was also still plagued by desire for her.

Through all of this, Carol had provided pleasant, undemanding company, whatever his mood. Her presence soothed him, and he respected her more than any other girl he knew. When

271

she had admitted her feelings for him, he had told her that he didn't feel able to enter into an affair, feeling as he did about Bella. He had urged her to seek romance elsewhere, but she had seemed content to let things continue between them on a platonic basis. But, for all her forbearance, Carol was no paper doll, ready to agree with his every opinion. On the contrary, their debates on a broad range of subjects were often conducted at fever pitch. She was, in fact, a perfect companion.

Tonight more than ever she looked the part, wearing a beige raincoat over her summer dress, her short hair freshly brushed, her cheeks flushed from soap and water. 'Let's get going then,' she urged him, her eyes alight with anticipation.

Guessing that they wouldn't stand a cat's chance of getting the car anywhere near the West End, they took a taxi to the outskirts and joined the masses milling towards the centre of festivities. There were no buses and the crowds strolled unhampered by traffic, ignoring the occasional intrepid taxi and private motorist foolishly trying to beat the congestion. Somehow, by dodging and weaving, Dezi and Carol managed to reach the dense crowds outside Buckingham Palace in time to cheer themselves hoarse as the Queen and the Duke of Edinburgh appeared on the balcony.

Then, having heard on the loudspeaker that the Queen would not appear again until later, they waited with the masses for the broadcast of Her Majesty's speech. Only the decorations rustling in the wind could be heard during these few spellbinding minutes. Afterwards there was an emotional rendering of the National Anthem by the huge gathering. After some more exuberant community singing of patriotic songs, the Queen and her husband appeared again on the now floodlit Palace balcony. After waving happily to the crowds for a few minutes, the Queen pressed a switch which gave the signal for the illuminations to be turned on.

London was ablaze with light and colour as Dezi and Carol made their way to Trafalgar Square among the exuberant cosmopolitan crowds, their spirits unaffected by the intermittent showers. People from all over the Commonwealth sat on the steps of Eros: eating, drinking, joining in the fun. The wet pavements resounded with the sound of singing and dancing. Revellers in comic hats and rosettes bobbed and boogied, shuffled and swayed. They crooned and conga-ed and called for more. The less hardy poured into the theatres and cinemas out of the cold wind.

'Oh, isn't it wonderful?' cried Carol.

'Yes,' agreed Dezi, smiling down at her and keeping a tight hold on her arm for fear of losing her in the crowd.

In actual fact, the intense communal joyfulness of the moment had, in some strange way, lowered Dezi's spirits, like the effect of a sunny day on someone with a depressive illness. He could see Bella everywhere, in every face, around every corner. She filled his mind and body like a drug. What was she doing now? Was she well? Was she here somewhere?

Determined that Carol's day should not be spoiled by his melancholy, he strived to seem as though she, and the patriotic fervour of the day, filled his thoughts. But after watching the finale to the festivities, a firework display along the Victoria Embankment, it was a blessed relief to climb into a home-bound taxi and no longer force out exclamations of interest and enjoyment. He was angry. Damn Bella, damn her! Was he to spend the rest of his life in this pit of despair?

'What is the matter, Dezi?' asked Carol, resting her hand on his arm.

'Nothing,' he said innocently.

'Oh, come on. Don't shut me out.'

And he reeled from a sudden painful flashback to another day, another woman querying his strange mood. He was back in Oxford with Bella, the day she finally agreed to postpone the wedding no longer. He could feel the autumn sunshine in Christchurch Meadows, smell the bonfire scent of the air. He smiled at the memory of that unsophisticated supper back at the flat.

'Mr Churchill calls his dark moods "black dogs", you know,' Carol was saying. 'I read about it.'

And as the present swept over him in a cold, painful tide, he knew that he had finally reached the moment of acceptance. Bella Brown was no longer a part of his life. It was over.

'I love you, Dezi,' Carol said in her slightly husky voice, 'and I'd do anything for you. Why not let me really help you?' She slid her arms around his neck and raised her lips to his, kissing him firmly.

Her patience and generosity brought tears to his eyes. He was ashamed of the suffering he must have caused her with his wretched self-pity. Simultaneously, he was acutely aware of the depth of his regard for her. In a strange way she was the tender mother he had never had.

'Will you marry me, Carol?' he asked.

'Yes, Dezi, I will,' she said, without query or hesitation.

As the taxi rattled away from the feverish festivities of the West End, still crowded with merrymakers partying beneath the shimmering decorations, Dezi experienced a moment of doubt. He could not help questioning his motives for taking such a step. After all, he wasn't 'in love' with Carol and knew he never would be. But, the answer came at once, he *needed* her. In return, he vowed there and then, he would make her happiness his prime concern.

'How romantic,' she crooned, snuggling into the crook of his arm. 'When our children and grandchildren ask if I can remember the day that you proposed, it will be easy: the day of Queen Elizabeth's Coronation. I shall call our first daughter Elizabeth.'

He chuckled, relaxed now that the decision was made. 'How many daughters are you planning on having?' he asked.

'I'd like a large family,' she said.

'Looks like I'll be kept busy then.'

'Oh yes,' she said, and she was far too happy to worry about the fact that he had not actually mentioned love. That would come, in time.

Chapter Sixteen

The Bennett–Dent wedding, a glittering occasion extravagantly covered in the local press, took place in August 1953, quickly followed by the Bennett–Dent business merger, which also attracted its fair share of publicity.

Whilst Frank Bennett was officially a reformed and somewhat mellowed character thanks to Dezi's ultimatum, he had not been able to resist promoting the idea of the two companies joining forces. It was what he had hoped for all along, his reason for introducing his son to Dent's daughter. As soon as the engagement was announced, Frank had swung into action.

'As we are about to be almost related, Archie, old boy, I wonder if you and I might join forces in the business field, too. A combined operation would be of enormous benefit to us both; give us more bargaining power without increasing our overheads.'

'How, exactly?' asked Archie, a plump cheerful man with a ruddy complexion and a shock of white hair.

'If we were to function as one company, whilst retaining

our own independent units,' Frank explained, 'we would be able to negotiate sizeable discounts from suppliers. And, of course, there are many other advantages to a combined operation. Being able to help each other out with staff, for instance, and raising capital for further expansion if necessary. More power to the elbow generally, in fact.'

Archie, a keen but clean businessman, had been quick to see the merit of such a scheme, which left only the other directors of both companies to be persuaded. Since the proposed merger made such excellent business sense and had absolutely nothing to do with his own reasons for marrying Carol, Dezi agreed to it.

When Bella read about both events in the newspaper and saw the link, she guessed who was behind it, knowing as she did that Dezi would never exploit his personal feelings to further his business ends. She hugged her small son closer to her. Stevie was a fine July-born child with shandy-brown, orange-flecked eyes. She thanked God that Frank Bennett would never know her son's origins.

Motherhood had matured Bella. Personal regrets dimmed in the glorious light of this new responsibility. Stevie was an embodiment of the past, of course, but she trained herself to think of him as John's son, something which was helped considerably by her husband's devotion to him and modern attitude towards parental responsibilities in which he took a practical role. Since Bella was required to honour business commitments as well as maternal ones, John's assistance in the nursery from time to time was more than welcome. His willingness to take his turn with nappy changing and night duty not only gave her a break, but forged a bond between him and Stevie. No child could have a more dedicated father, nor wife a more considerate husband.

Bella knew she was very lucky.

March 1954 was an eventful month. Trevor Brown married Joan Willis, Pearl gave birth to a daughter, and Dezi Bennett arrived at the garage early one morning to find his secretary weeping outside the office doors...

The Brown–Willis wedding was a church one, with Joan radiant in white, bridesmaids shimmering in pink, and Bella, as Matron of Honour, elegant in blue. It was a jolly occasion with a reception at a local hotel and a party for the groom's relatives and friends at number nine afterwards. The little house bulged at the seams and throbbed with bonhomie. The families tittered and roared, jitterbugged and jived, and argued boozily about ancient family disputes, while Winifred Atwell's party hits thumped melodiously from the record player.

Pearl, heavily pregnant and glued to her husband's side, remained on the fringes of the party, viewing the boisterous atmosphere with disdain. She, who had once danced on the table and led a conga around the block! Why, she carries more airs and graces than Eve Bennett, Bella thought. Protective of her aunt's and uncle's feelings, she took her sister to one side.

'Pregnancy is no excuse for bad manners, Pearl,' Bella informed her firmly. 'This sort of thing might not be to your taste any more, but there's no need to behave as though we are a crowd of lepers. You're spoiling the day for Auntie and Uncle.'

'Huh!' Pearl retorted. 'They're too busy letting their hair down to notice what I'm doing. It's so damned vulgar! The risqué wedding jokes, the terrible music. Peter must think he's in the public bar of some backstreet pub.'

Bella wanted to slap her. 'You've married into the Bennett family, Pearl, not royalty.'

'You're just jealous because you lost your chance to escape from all this,' her sister snorted, turning scarlet.

'I don't want to escape, as you call it,' said Bella, 'I enjoy the company.' She paused, sipped her sherry and noticed John across the room, laughing with Uncle Wilf and some distant cousins. He fitted in with the Brown clan as though born to it. She turned back to her sister. 'Better yourself, by all means, but don't bite the hand that fed you. Everything we are now, we owe to these people. I don't give a tinker's cuss how much you look down on me, but don't hurt Auntie and Uncle.' And she left her sister for the more congenial company of the other guests.

She saw no point in pursuing a relationship with her sister even though she no longer blamed her for her marriage to Peter. Their tastes had always differed, she realised sadly. Now the gulf was too wide for them to be friends.

But when Pearl gave birth to her daughter, a few days later, family feeling prevailed. Bella sent a greetings telegram followed later by a telephone call in which she arranged to visit mother and baby one afternoon. Liberated from the trials of public transport by her driving licence and newly acquired small Austin Saloon, Bella drove to Pearl's prestigious new address in Barnes. She took Stevie in the babyseat and a gift for her new niece, Sandra, who had already been nicknamed Sandie.

'Wow!' she gasped as they swept into the drive of a beautiful white house in a high-class riverside location. It was a double-fronted property with wide windows and well-kept gardens. 'Come on then, Stevie,' she said, as she lifted her sweet-smelling son from the car. 'Let's go and introduce you to your new cousin.'

Bella had always to juggle with her busy schedule in order to fit in a little socialising. She was dressed casually and practically in a white Sloppy Joe sweater and black trews, her long hair loose about her shoulders. By contrast, Pearl opened the door wearing a red jersey dress which tightly hugged her waspie-girdled form. With it she wore matching mules with a bow on the front and seamless stockings. Her freshly coiffured hair was laquered stiffly to her head in a short curly style. All this for a cup of tea and a natter with her sister! Eve Bennett, you've a lot to answer for, Bella thought.

The sitting room was luxuriously appointed in green and gold. Deep-pile carpet, soft mint green gilt-edged furniture, and pale gold walls and velvet curtains. Slumbering amid this film-set sophistication, in a carry cot on the sofa, was Sandie. The baby seemed oddly incongruous in the setting, like an oven glove worn to a ball.

'I kept her downstairs in your honour,' explained Pearl, appearing from her luxurious American-style kitchen with a silver tray of tea. 'If she's asleep I usually leave her in her cot upstairs.'

Bella duly admired her little pink relative, sat a squirming, pre-crawling Stevie on the floor with some building bricks, speedily acquired from the visiting-with-baby-survival kit in her bag, and set about the business of enduring this tea party.

'Thanks for Sandie's little outfit,' said Pearl, having unwrapped the gift. 'It's lovely.'

'It's my pleasure,' said Bella, feeling as awkward as if she was with a stranger. She was lost for words with her own sister. How awful! Resorting to trivia, she said, 'You've got your figure back, I see.'

'Yes, thank goodness,' said Pearl girlishly, her red lips curling into a dazzling smile. 'Did it take you long to get yours back after Stevie?'

'Not long, as I remember, but more from the hectic lifestyle than anything else,' said Bella casually. 'Having a baby *and* a business can be pretty exhausting.'

'Peter wouldn't like *me* to have a job,' said Pearl, implicitly critical of John, her frosted pink nails flashing against the fine china pot as she poured the tea. 'He likes to spoil me. He even insists on me having someone in to do the housework.'

And remembering Pearl's dire domestic attempts at the prefab, Bella thought it was probably just as well. She felt as though she was inside an advertisement for some high-class brand of furnishings in a glossy magazine. A beautiful room, a sleeping baby, a perfectly turned out hostess. Only Bella and Stevie, who had chosen today to be tetchy and was already grizzling to be picked up, spoiled the illusion. This was not her sister beside her but a member of the Eve Bennett club for class climbers. Pearl had found her happy ending.

'It must be simply awful to have to go out to work,' said Pearl, determined to belittle her poor, overworked sister.

Equally resolute that she would not succeed, Bella picked up her doleful, dribbling son, guessing from the sudden oppression in the air that he had been busy in the basement. 'I don't go out to work as such,' she pointed out blithely, 'I merely keep my beady eyes on those who work for me. I thoroughly enjoy the involvement, actually,' She wiped her son's wet face with a tissue, completing the operation by smacking a kiss on his plump cheek. 'And he doesn't suffer, do you, buster?' She threw her sister a cheerful look. 'Being my own boss means that I can be flexible. I fit my day around him. It all seems to be working out very well. And if business and baby do overlap, then Stevie stays with his adoring Great Aunt Vi, who spoils him rotten.'

Stevie's answer to all this attention was to erupt into a series of chuckles which sent Bella into similar paroxysms of delight, but left Pearl resolutely unamused.

'But surely that husband of yours can look after things for you at the garage,' she said.

'He can and he does whenever the occasion arises. He would take over completely for me if I wanted it. But I don't want it. No one, least of all Stevie, suffers because I am the Managing Director of Brown's.' And just in case this opinionated apology for Deborah Kerr still felt inclined to pity her, Bella added. 'I'm perfectly happy, I can assure you. And I'd rather you didn't refer to John as "that husband of yours". He does have a name.'

But Pearl was undeterred and continued as though Bella's last request had not been made. 'It wouldn't suit me,' she persisted, moving over to her own little angel, thus distancing herself from Stevie's murderous miasma. She stared absently into the carry cot and back at Bella. 'I like to have all my needs taken care of. Peter might have been a bit of a lad with the women before we got married, but he's a wonderful provider.'

Implying that John was not, of course. But Bella didn't rise to the bait since she had no need to defend him further. 'So you've got what you wanted. The power and prestige of Peter Bennett's cheque book,' she said coldly.

'And what if I have? Peter got what he wanted, too – me.

He and Sandie are number one in my life. I would never put anything else before them.'

Not unless it suited her, Bella thought, but seeing no point in continuing the visit, said, 'Is there somewhere that I can change Stevie's nappy? Then I'll be on my way.'

'Sure,' said Pearl, and while Bella was reaching for her capacious bag, she added, 'Dezi and Carol have bought the most fantastic house in Putney. They've got superb furniture and the kitchen is like something out of an American film, with all the latest gadgets.'

Knocked off balance by the mention of Dezi's name, Bella only just managed to force out a reply. 'That's nice for them.'

'I bet you're sorry you let him go, aren't you?'

'No, of course not,' retorted Bella, blushing furiously at her sister's appalling lack of sensitivity. 'Why should I be? John and I are very happy.'

'Really?' Pearl continued impertinently. 'I always thought you married him on the rebound. After all, he must seem awfully dull after someone like Dezi.' She lowered her voice confidentially. 'Mind you, I reckon Dezi only married Carol to get even with you. She's nice enough, but very plain and dowdy in her dress.'

Bella laughed dryly, astonished by her sister's shallowness. 'I'm sure the shape of her face and cut of her clothes will not bother Dezi unduly,' she rasped. 'He always looked for inner quality rather than glossy packaging.'

Anyone else would have winced at Bella's acid tone, but Pearl was far too dense to notice. 'You could have had it all, Bel,' she said.

'I've got it all, thanks, sis,' replied Bella. 'And I'm happy with my lot.'

Incredibly, Pearl continued, 'But your little business is just toy-town compared to Bennett's. I bet you still have to watch the pennies, Managing Director or not. Whereas, I, as a Bennett wife, can have the best of everything. I know things now, Bel, about style and good taste. Eve's taught me all about china and furnishings, and how to dress well.'

Which was why Pearl looked forty instead of twenty-two! By now emotionally drained and seeking only an early departure, Bella forced a laugh and said, 'If that sort of thing enriches your life, good luck to you! Personally, I couldn't give a tuppenny toss for anything Eve Bennett says.'

'She isn't so bad, when you get to know her,' said Pearl.

Which obviously meant that Pearl spent a lot of time sucking up to her mother-in-law. 'Perhaps,' Bella said, still poised with baby and bag, 'but on the subject of Brown's, it will be a far cry from a toy-town business when I've finished with it. It will really be worth something then. And when I can afford Dior clothes and Chanel perfume, I shall have the satisfaction of knowing that I, with the help of John and Trevor, made it possible. There's no glory to me in living off someone else's achievement.'

'Men bring home the bread, women bring up the children,' retorted Pearl. 'That's the law of the jungle.'

'But not the law of the land. If I choose to do both, that's my decision.'

'I don't like to think that John is not looking after you properly, that's all,' said Pearl smugly.

'Don't waste your pity on me,' Bella warned. 'You'll need plenty of that for yourself when you're bored with all this. I know you, Pearl. Caring for a home and family is fulfilling enough for many women, but you're just *playing* the rich housewife. It's all a game to you. Sooner or later, you'll realise that money alone doesn't guarantee happiness. Anyway, I must change my son and be on my way.'

Driving through the elegant ambience of Barnes to noisy, grimy Lower Fulworth, Bella felt an overpowering sense of loss. It was as though the last remaining connection with Pearl had gone. Her sister had always been infuriatingly selfish, but there had been a vitality about her before, a certain comical charm that had made her endearing despite the faults. Now she was an empty, humourless woman with whom Bella had nothing in common. Their paths were firmly set in opposite directions and Bella doubted if she would see her sister again. The realisation made her sad.

No one could ever accuse Dezi Bennett of not pulling his weight at Bennett and Dent's. He was usually the last to leave in the evening and always the first to arrive in the morning.

One particular March morning he left home particularly early. He had been up at the crack of dawn administering hot tea and aspirin to his wife. She suffered dreadfully every month and the physical pain was compounded by sadness at her failure to conceive.

From day one of their marriage she had been eager to have a baby and since Dezi was almost thirty, he had agreed not to wait. But whereas he could remain optimistic when it didn't happen and see that it was still very early days, Carol became frantic.

After seven months, his marriage was making him happier than he'd thought possible. Carol was a wonderful companion, a warm and passionate lover, and a dear friend for whom his affection increased with every passing day. It was she who filled his thoughts as he drove into the forecourt to find that he had been pipped to the post this morning by his secretary, Janice Johnson, who was sitting on a suitcase outside the main office building.

'Well, well,' he said brightly, oblivious to the drama that was about to unfold. 'You're an early bird this morning, and with your suitcase too. Have you left home or something?'

Whereupon Janice collapsed into floods of tears and sobbed, 'My Dad has chucked me out.'

Upstairs in his office, Dezi sat her down and made more hot sweet tea, giving her his full attention. She was a blue-eyed redhead of twenty-one. When it wasn't red and swollen with tears, her face was moderately pretty.

'Why has your father told you to leave?' Dezi asked when she was a shade calmer. 'Was there a family quarrel?'

'I'll say there was,' she informed him miserably. And ten minutes later he had the whole story. Sadly, an all too familiar one. She had been having an affair with one of the mechanics, George, a married man with three children whose interest in her had ended on hearing that she was pregnant. '''E's claimin' that the baby ain't 'is,' she wept. 'Because he doesn't want to leave 'is own wife an' kids.'

'Oh dear,' said Dezi kindly. 'You are in a mess, aren't you? But no problem is insuperable. I'm sure we'll work something out between us. The first thing we must do is to get your father to reconsider his decision. I'm sure he will, once he has calmed down.'

She shook her head. 'No 'e won't. I've brought shame on him, you see.'

Dezi frowned, irritated by the harshness of the man's

attitude. 'Would you like me to have a word with him?' He was at a loss to know how best to deal with this delicate matter. Meddling in other people's lives was never advisable. But someone had to help the poor girl.

'I'd sooner you spoke to George, Mr Bennett,' she sobbed. 'Make 'im see that 'e can't just leave me in the lurch.'

'I'll see what I can do,' he assured her. 'But in the meantime, you're obviously in no fit state for work.' He hesitated, reluctant to disturb Carol while she was sleeping. 'Take yourself off to the staff room for a while and I'll arrange for you to go to my place later.'

Having packed Janice into a taxi to spend the day with Carol, who was much recovered by mid-morning and off duty today, Dezi had an unsatisfactory interview with the guilty party which ended in George's tendering his resignation. The man refused to accept responsibility, claiming that any number of men could be the father of Janice's child. He also made it clear that he had no intention of having his marriage put at risk.

'It will do Janice no good to try to make trouble for me with my wife,' he said bluntly, 'because I'll deny everythin'. I only went out with 'er a few times anyway. But it won't be comfortable for me around 'ere with 'er about, so I'll have my cards an' be on my way.'

And despite his personal disgust at the man's irresponsible and selfish attitude, Dezi knew that the problem would not be solved by further discussion. He was glad to see him off the premises for good.

A later visit to Janice's parents proved equally unavailing. Her father was an odious loudmouth with as much compassion as a meat cleaver. He assured Dezi that he no longer had a daughter, while Janice's downtrodden mother stood by his side in terrified silence.

But if Dezi felt burdened by the situation, his wife certainly did not. He arrived home that evening to find her happily mothering the tearful Janice. In the absence of any alternative, they agreed to extend their hospitality to her until other accommodation could be found, and put the poor girl's mind at rest by promising not to desert her in her trouble.

Carol's maternal instincts came to the fore over the next few weeks. She fed Janice with iron pills and orange juice and pampered her with breakfast in bed. And one night, in the privacy of the marital bed, Carol snuggled up to her husband and whispered, 'Janice wants to give her baby up for adoption straight after the birth. I want us to take it.'

'But, darling,' said Dezi, fearing heartache ahead for her, 'we'll probably be expecting a baby of our own soon.'

She stared at the undulating silver patterns on the ceiling, created by moonlight shining through the dancing branches of the trees outside. 'Yes, but that doesn't matter. I'll still love Janice's child as my own.'

Dezi still saw the plan as an emotional minefield. 'Is Janice absolutely sure she wants to give the baby up?'

'Yes. All she wants is to take up her life as before, unencumbered. I've made some enquiries, and apparently she cannot officially agree to a placement until the baby is six weeks old. Adoption could not be made legal until the baby had been with us for at least three months, so she would have time to change her mind.'

Her eagerness to enter into the whole difficult business alarmed Dezi. 'We've been married less than a year,' he reminded her.

She switched on her bedside light and leaned over him, smoothing back his ruffled hair. 'I've thought carefully about this. I am not some do-gooder or a broody woman who has given up hope. This child is unwanted by its mother. With us it would have love and security. And it isn't in me to discriminate, when, and if, we have children of our own. I think you know that.'

The pale glow from the lamp shone across her face, the warm caring eyes, the soft curve of her gentle mouth. He knew he had been wrong to doubt her. 'If that is what you want, then I want it, too.'

And so a relieved Janice was told of their carefully thought out plan. She was to live with them until the birth and for a while afterwards. She would continue to work for Dezi for as long as she wished until her confinement. If she still favoured the adoption after the statutory period, Carol and Dezi would legally adopt and Janice would leave the area. She accepted their proposition without hesitation.

The arrangement worked according to plan. Janice gave birth to a daughter in November 1954, and continued to live with Carol and Dezi. Since she had no interest in the child whatsoever, Carol and Dezi found themselves taking immediate responsibility, naming the baby Elizabeth. Three months after Janice had left the area, when the baby was nearly five months old, Elizabeth Johnson legally became Elizabeth Bennett.

'We're a real family now,' said Carol as she and Dezi gazed into the cot at their beautiful red-headed daughter.

'No child could wish for a better mother,' said Dezi emotionally.

'Or father,' Carol said. And they hugged each other, at the side of the cot, laughing and crying for joy.

Chapter Seventeen

'Can we go to Heathrow Airport to look at the planes when Dad's finished his business in Staines, Mum?' asked ten-year-old Stevie one Friday afternoon in November 1963, as he sat with his mother in her red Mini on the forecourt of Brown's. 'We'll be so near to it.'

'Yes, I don't see why not, love,' agreed Bella cheerfully. Elegantly casual in an emerald green sweater and matching trews topped by a sporty, three-quarter length coat in cream, she was waiting for her husband who was to drive a new car to Staines to deliver to a customer there, a service Brown's included as a matter of course. As Bella was to go along in her own car to bring him back, and Stevie had been given the afternoon off from school because of a special teachers' meeting, it made sense to mix business with pleasure. A spot of country air would do them all good, despite the cold showery weather. 'We'll have tea out, if you like.'

'Fab,' said Stevie excitedly.

The improvement in roads into the capital had not only made the countryside more accessible to Londoners, but had widened the commuter belt too. A plane-spotting trip at London airport, or an afternoon at Runnymede or Windsor, was no longer a novelty. Neither were customers from leafier parts, for they poured into Fulworth's thriving commercial concerns every day, often finding it more convenient to have their motoring needs catered to during the working day. And Brown's, now being a main agent for Craven cars, attracted business from far and wide.

'Dad's a long time,' said Stevie, fidgeting with childish impatience, 'Shall I go and ask him to hurry up?'

'Off you go then,' said Bella. 'But keep out of the workshops. It's dangerous for you when the men are working.'

'Okay, Mum,' he conceded brightly.

A warm feeling of pride engulfed her as she watched him walk across the forecourt, his eager, purposeful stride a poignant reminder of his origins. He was a handsome boy with finely formed features, a complexion resembling her own, rich brown eyes and curly hair a few shades lighter than hers. More Brown than Bennett, perhaps, but his eyes were pure Dezi. Though, if John noticed it, he hadn't said so, and Auntie Vi kept diplomatically silent. He was a bright, affectionate child and Bella thanked God for him.

Seeing him disappear into the main office building, she found herself viewing the premises as a stranger might, and she was not displeased with what she saw. The firm had certainly come a long way since her father had first taken over that derelict workshop. Retaining the blue and white colours which were their trademark in the area, Brown's had moved with the times. The reception area was glassier and more angular, in keeping with modern tastes; the workshops well maintained and equipped. And to the side of the premises was Bella's baby, a streamlined, hyaline car showroom in which gleamed a brand new range of Craven cars.

Taking on the Craven agency had been Bella's idea. The building of a suitable showroom, and the large amount of money tied up in stock, had made it a vast financial commitment and one which had frightened her co-directors. But she had finally allayed their fears, and three years on they had no regrets. The business was now one of the finest in the area and with the two car family on the increase, as more and more women took to the wheel, trade seemed set fair for the future. All due credit to John and Trevor, of course, but whilst they were good and stable colleagues with whom she had an excellent business rapport, they both tended to be limited in outlook and would be the first to admit that Bella was the driving force behind Brown's.

Combining motherhood with a career had not been without its problems, but things had worked out well, by and large. She stuck to one simple rule: Stevie came first. Business was important – Brown's kept them, after all – but during school holidays and while Stevie was ill, it had to manage without her. Good back-up staff and a trusted mother's help were the answer.

Nowadays, Bella saw herself as co-ordinator, public relations person and occasional dogsbody. Although she was often to be found negotiating at director level with large companies with regard to fleet vehicle servicing contracts, and taking major policy decisions on behalf of Brown's, she wasn't above pounding the typewriter or even working at the petrol pumps if the need arose. Team spirit was the essence of a successful family business. Far from harming Stevie, she felt her working pattern, hectic though it was, set him a very valuable example.

And, of course, the success of Brown's had meant a raised

standard of living for its directors. Bella and John now lived in a spacious character house overlooking Fulworth Park, a mature, traditional property standing in large gardens, while Trevor and Joan preferred the camaraderie of a new housing development nearby for their young family, Kevin, Christopher and Beverley.

Pearl, Peter and their children, Sandie and Brett, had moved out to Surrey years ago. A Christmas card each year had been the only communication with Bella since that last meeting. The specially printed cards, inset with a picture of their stylish house, spoke of the considerable luxury in which Pearl continued to live. Bella often thought about her sister and wished that they had had more in common.

But now her son was marching towards her in his dark, tight-fitting Beatles-style trousers and blue fur-lined jacket. John ambled after him, casually dressed in a smart navy quilted car coat over grey trousers. Nowadays he only donned overalls in times of emergency.

'Sorry to keep you waiting, love,' he said to Bella, his fair hair blowing in the wind. 'I just couldn't get away. One of the blokes had a problem with a job, you know how it is.'

'Don't I just, after eleven years!'

John clapped his hands boisterously against the cold. 'Before anyone else catches me, let's be on our way.' He turned to Stevie and did some mock shadow boxing. 'Are you coming in the car with me, or with Mummy?'

'With you,' said the boy, having already inspected the shiny new vehicle nearby.

'Traitor!' teased Bella. 'I'm not so sure I'll let you come back in my Mini after that.'

'Oh.' Stevie looked uncertain. 'If you want me . . .'

'Go on with you, you horror,' she laughed. 'I'll be glad of the peace and quiet.'

After the completion of the business, they all piled into the Mini and headed for the airport where they parked on a grass verge at a popular vantage point for plane spotters.

Stevie and John clambered out with binoculars to cries of 'Not too long now, in this cold wind' from Bella, and stood by the chain link fencing with the airport buildings and aeroplanes clearly visible. Watching her little family from the shelter of the car, side by side at the fence, talking, laughing, taking turns with the binoculars, John's hand resting companionably on Stevie's shoulder, Bella experienced a moment of supreme happiness. The bond that John and Stevie shared, and from which even she was sometimes excluded, was very special and she admired John for nurturing it. Many a biological father would have given much for such a friendship with his son.

'Cor, did you see that Boeing 707 take off. Mum?' gasped Stevie, breathless with excitement as he climbed back into the car, his cheeks glowing from the wind. 'Wasn't it fab?'

'Fab,' she agreed.

'And what about that Trident coming in to land? Cor, wait 'til I tell my friends.'

Bella and John exchanged glances, united in happiness at their son's pleasure. 'Where shall we go for tea?' she asked.

'Can we go to Windsor?' asked Stevie. 'It's nice there with the castle and the river and everything.'

'Windsor it is,' said Bella.

'Fab,' said Stevie.

'Would you like me to drive?' asked John in his usual considerate manner.

'You can take over after tea,' she told him.

And that was the essence of their relationship: easygoing and unencumbered by excessive passion. They had their quarrels, of course, like anyone else, but mutual respect and effort had resulted in a good, stable marriage. Even the fact that Bella had not conceived with John didn't seem to matter. They were both content for their lives to revolve around Stevie.

Windsor huddled in the shadow of the castle, its narrow streets crowded with shoppers. Early Christmas decorations already brightened some of the shop windows on this wintry day. They went to a tea shop in a cobbled sidestreet. The room with its antique furniture and oak-beamed ceiling was packed with people laden with bags and packages, but they managed to find a table in the bowed window.

'Mmm, hot cheese scones and butter and home-made fruit cake,' said Bella, glancing at the menu. 'Just what I fancy.'

'That ull do me, too,' said John.

Stevie, a true child of the sixties, studied the menu rather more carefully. 'Have they got any hamburgers or baked beans?' he asked.

'No they haven't, and don't show us up by asking for them or I'll crown you,' Bella said firmly.

'Why not?'

'Because this is a tea shop not a burger bar! Now choose something from the menu.' My God, when she was his age she'd have gone down on her knees for a fraction of what was on offer here. It was a different world.

'I'll have hot buttered toast then, please,' he said politely.

Bella tutted and glanced at the waitress, who had been hovering nearby. 'Honestly, he'd eat a table mat if it had baked beans on it,' she explained in a woman-to-woman manner.

The waitress nodded sympathetically. 'You don't have to tell me, dear,' she sighed. 'I've got two of my own and they'd live on hamburgers and beans if I let 'em. Another craze from America.' She smiled down at Stevie. 'Well, sonny Jim, I can't oblige with the hamburger, but I might be able to find a few beans to go on your toast.'

'Thank you,' he beamed. 'That would be fab.'

'No, no,' Bella urged her. 'Don't let him con you, he'll have what's on the menu and be thankful.'

But the woman was a lost cause. 'Doesn't hurt to spoil 'em now and then, does it?'

And, conceding defeat, Bella and John exchanged fond glances. 'I suppose not,' they chorused, glowing from the congenial atmosphere. In that moment Bella felt very close to her husband. Thanks to his managerial position, John had changed over the years. He would never be a sophisticate, but he certainly wasn't the rough diamond she had first known. Though he still had an unmistakable Cockney lilt in his speech, John was a gentleman through and through, and she was proud of him.

After their early tea, it was still light when they emerged from the café so they took a brisk walk by the river, hugging their coats around them against the penetrating cold. The tow path was almost deserted. The cruisers creaked emptily in their moorings, and the gusty wind whistled through skeletal trees. The area was at its best in summer, but Bella found a certain beauty in its quiet winter ambience.

Glancing up at the castle, oddly threatening against the grey skies, she remembered an autumn day long ago when she had walked on this very spot with another man. The dark moments still came when she was caught off guard by some sudden memory. But she could cope, most of the time.

John insisted on taking the wheel on the homeward trip, though the small town was congested with traffic as he tried to leave.

'Oh Gawd,' he sighed, poking his head out of the window to inspect the long tailback. 'There's miles of it. We'll be stuck here all night.'

Bella sighed, too. For although John was normally an easygoing man, his intolerance of traffic jams was well known to his family. He always tried to beat the unbeatable by making a random exit with the idea of taking another route, and invariably got them lost.

'It doesn't matter,' she pointed out. 'We're not in any particular hurry.'

'Well, no, but it's a waste of time sitting here twiddling our thumbs.' The words had an alarmingly familiar ring. 'We'll be better off doubling back. I'll turn off as soon as I get a chance.'

'Oh no,' she groaned.

'We should have brought a compass,' teased Stevie, entering into the joke.

'Oh, well, at least we've eaten. God knows when we'll get our next meal,' laughed Bella.

'Oh ye of little faith,' said John, taking a turning out of the traffic. 'I'll have you home in no time, you just wait and see.'

Three-quarters of an hour later, with dusk hovering, they were lost in a maze of country lanes.

'We can't be far off the beaten track because we can still see the castle,' said John, scratching his head and looking towards the turretted outline on the horizon.

'It will be dark soon,' said Bella.

'I can see a house,' Stevie said, excitedly pointing to the side of him. 'Look, you can just see it through the trees. We can ask directions there.'

'Thank goodness for that,' said Bella, and they rolled gratefully towards habitation, drawing up outside the locked metal gates of a neglected mansion bearing the name Lakewood Manor.

'Looks deserted to me,' said John gloomily.

'Someone must be living there,' said Bella, experiencing an unaccountable frisson of excitement. 'There's a thin spiral of smoke coming from the chimney, see.'

'So there is,' said John with relief. 'I'll climb over the gates. You two wait here.'

'Okay,' they chorused.

Their predicament paled into insignificance for Bella in the instant fascination she felt for the house. It was stone-faced and bordered by a verandah, the first floor having parapeted balconies, while attic windows poked inquisitively from the red slate roof. Wide steps from the extensive, untended grounds led to double front doors. Curiously intrigued, Bella left Stevie in the car and wandered further along the perimeter, hoping to catch a glimpse of the rear aspect in the fading light.

To her joy she could just make out the eponymous lake, dark and compelling, through the bare trees. It was the most interesting property she had ever seen and she was thoughtful as she hurried back to the car.

'We are only a few minutes from the main road, would you believe?' said John. 'Let's get going before it gets dark.'

But Bella was still staring dreamily ahead of her. 'Isn't it the most amazing house you ever saw?' she said.

'It would be all right if it was looked after,' said John casually, 'but the place is falling down.'

In her mind's eye Bella could see beyond the peeling paintwork and dusty windows, to wood-panelled rooms and log fires burning in the hearth. 'I think it's beautiful,' she said. 'So dignified despite everything, like a grandparent in need.'

'In need of a good few thousand pounds spending on it,' said John in his down to earth way. He eyed his wife shrewdly. 'You don't fancy it for us, I hope, because the idea of rattling around in a draughty mausoleum like that doesn't appeal to me.'

'Nor me,' piped in Stevie who, sensing something afoot, had got out of the car. 'It's too lonely around here.' He glanced around him at the gathering dusk. 'And creepy.'

'A house like that needs lots of people to breathe life into it,' she said to herself more than to them. 'It would be wasted on us, but would make an excellent hotel.'

John laughed. "Ever the businesswoman, eh, love?'

'Perhaps!' She was unsure of the reason for her interest in the property. 'Who lives there?'

'An elderly couple. Why?'

'Just idle curiosity,' she said.

'Come on, Mum,' urged Stevie, clambering back into the car. 'It'll be dark in a minute.'

'I'm coming,' she said. But she was reluctant to leave. Despite her acceptance of the fact that it would never be a part of her life, the house still exerted a powerful influence over her. Later that evening, however, something happened which shocked the world and removed all other thoughts from the mind.

She was making coffee in the kitchen when an ashen-faced John appeared by her side. 'President Kennedy has been shot,' he told her gravely. 'It's on the telly.'

The china jug that she was holding fell and smashed on the tiled floor. '*What*! Is he ... ?'

He nodded, barely able to say the words. 'He died in hospital.'

'But ... who ... why?'

John shook his head despairingly, too affected to speak. And going with him into the other room to watch the television reports, Bella's eyes, too, filled with tears. She felt as though she had lost a friend.

She was still in a morbid mood when she went to bed that night, the television pictures of the horrific scenes in Dallas haunting her thoughts. But when she woke suddenly from a confused, dream-filled sleep to find herself sitting up in bed, drenched with sweat and reaching out with her arms, her cries were for someone closer to home. In her dream Dezi had been weeping and calling to her. Something was terribly wrong, she was sure. *Dezi needed her!*

'What's the matter, love?' grunted John sleepily.

'Just a bad dream,' she told him shakily. 'I'm okay. You go back to sleep.'

As he began to snore gently, she slipped out of bed and went downstairs to her streamlined kitchen to make some cocoa. Sitting at the formica-topped breakfast bar, cradling the mug in her hands, she could feel Dezi's proximity like a living presence in the room. And he was in deep despair. So what are you going to do, my girl? she asked herself. Conjure up his address from thin air and tear across London in the middle of the night to your ex-lover? Leave your husband to sleep on? Oh, do grow up, woman.

The hot cocoa calmed her and her sense of panic eased. It's the Kennedy shooting that's unsettled you, she told herself. But still she felt uneasy when she went back to bed. Glancing at the luminous hands of the bedside clock, she saw that it was almost 2.30 a.m. I need to get some sleep or I'll be like death warmed up tomorrow, she thought.

★　　★　　★

On the afternoon of 22nd November 1963, Dezi Bennett stood in a blustery wind at the gates of his daughter's school, waiting for her to emerge. It was an ordinary, everyday event, a man collecting his nine-year-old child from school, but because it was a duty that didn't come his way very often in their normal family routine, Dezi was alive with excitement and pride. He was deputising as mother and thoroughly enjoyed the experience of taking Lizzie to and from school, doing the shopping and cooking their meals. They hadn't seen much of him at the garage, but that couldn't be helped.

Today being Friday, there was a feeling of holiday in the air. He and Lizzie would have tea by the fire in the drawing room, toasted buns and buttered crumpets probably. Then, later, they would visit Carol in hospital, and perhaps get a Chinese take-away for supper on the way home. Lizzie would enjoy that. This time next week Carol would be back home with them, thank goodness. He missed her dreadfully. Still, he mustn't complain. It wasn't as though she had some awful illness.

Dezi had been doubtful about Carol having surgery on her fallopian tubes because, although the removal of narrowed sections was expected to increase the chances of conception, it could not actually be guaranteed and he had not wanted her to suffer in vain. But Carol was eager to try anything, since medical tests on them both had shown no physical reason why there had been no pregnancy.

'I never think of Lizzie as other than my own child,' Carol had assured him. 'But I want a larger family. I always have.'

He had booked her into a London clinic where, the previous day, she had had the operation.

But now Lizzie was swinging towards him, her long red hair bright against her navy blue school raincoat, her face shining pink from the cold. 'Hi, Dad,' she said, kissing his cheek and climbing into the passenger seat of his Lagonda Rapide.

'Hello, darling,' he said, beaming at her. 'Had a good day?'

'All right thanks,' she said, her blue eyes shining brightly in her small face. 'Did you?'

'Not bad.'

'Any news of Mummy?' she asked.

'Yes, she's fine. Coming home some time next week.'

'Fab,' she chirped, rummaging in her satchel and producing an apple. 'I didn't eat this at break. Do you want a bite, Dad?'

'No thanks, love,' he said, enchanted by her youthful exuberance.

'We had art today and I made Mum a welcome home card,' she informed him chattily.

'That's a kind thought,' he said, weaving carefully through the post-school crush of children and traffic.

Lizzie knew that she was adopted. He and Carol had thought it best to break it to her at an early age to avoid problems later. She had received the news almost nonchalantly, as though far too busy living life to worry how she came by it.

'And guess what?' she continued excitedly. 'I got an "A" for last week's art work.'

'Again!' he exclaimed. 'Well done.'

His daughter had a natural talent for drawing and, even at this tender age, could do lightning sketches with amazing accuracy.

The London rush hour was already underway as offices closed early for the weekend. Along Putney High Street the traffic was bumper to bumper, the shops glowing brightly in the gathering dusk.

'My friend Mandy's invited me to tea tomorrow, Dad,' she said, taking a hearty bite from her apple. 'Can I go?'

'Yes, of course.'

'I'll stay and keep you company if you'll be too lonely. I mean, with Mummy being away . . .'

Warmed by her kindness, he said, 'Don't you worry about me, I'll be fine.'

'Mandy has got her own record player,' Lizzie announced excitedly. 'How simply fab! And she's got the new Beatles record.'

'Has she now?' He smiled. Such sophistication, so young! How times had changed since the strict climate of his childhood. And thank goodness for it! Not for Dezi the figurehead father role of yesteryear. He preferred a friendlier relationship with his daughter.

'Yeah,' she gasped, duly reverent at the mention of the British pop group that had conquered the world. 'I can't wait to hear it. Her own player. Wow!'

'You'll have to be careful not to upset Mummy and me, won't you?' he teased gently. 'With Christmas coming up.'

'A player . . . might I . . . would you . . . ? Oh, Dad!' she whispered wistfully.

'Mummy and I will have to think about it,' he told her. Thank heavens he and Carol had never spoilt her unaffected joy in a gift by over-indulging her, which was all too easy for rich parents in a consumer boom.

Lizzie chewed her apple thoughtfully for a while, then said, 'Mandy has a little brother. He's a real terror, but ever so sweet.' She tilted her face towards her father. 'Do you think that we'll be having a baby now that Mummy has had the operation?'

'I sincerely hope so,' he said. 'After all the trouble she's gone to.'

'It would be fun.' Lizzie lapsed into silence for a while then said: 'Are you sure you won't be lonely without me tomorrow? I'll stay at home if you like.'

His eyes moistened. She might not share Carol's blood, but she had certainly learned from her unselfish example.

They had tea in the drawing room by the log fire, a spacious high-ceilinged room tastefully decorated in reds and browns with soft cretonne-covered sofas and chairs. Lizzie chatted effusively throughout the meal and her father teased her a little. 'I shall have a nice sedate tea tomorrow while you're out. It will be wonderfully quiet,' he said.

'You!' she reproached, rolling her eyes but smiling.

Going to the window to draw the curtains, he experienced an unexpected moment of nostalgia at the sight of the riverside lights gleaming on the Thames. He was a happily married man and loved his wife and daughter dearly. But still sometimes it happened: a sharp moment of regret for what might have been. He turned away quickly and returned to his armchair.

Lizzie had changed from her school clothes into a white fluffy sweater over red trousers. She was sitting on the sofa with her feet tucked underneath her, drawing. He opened his copy of *The Times*. The atmosphere was warm and comfortable. The fire crackled, tea cups chinked and his newspaper rustled softly. Dezi felt like a very lucky man.

Carol seemed upset when they arrived at the hospital. She was pale and had obviously been crying. His heart lurched. Was it bad news? Had they discovered some dreadful disease?

'Darling,' he said, taking her hand, 'whatever is the matter?'

She waved a hand towards the television set in the corner of her private room.

'I had to turn it off, it was so upsetting.'

'Why, what's happened?'

'You haven't heard?'

'Heard what?'

'Someone has shot President Kennedy.'

'Oh, my God!'

The news from America could easily have dominated the visit. Neither Dezi or Carol could think of anything else. But Carol's maternal instincts were never far away.

'And how is my Lizzie?' she asked, hugging her daughter fondly and curbing her own tears. 'I want to hear all your news.'

Lizzie needed no second asking. Out it all poured, ending with, 'But we do miss you, Mum, and we're looking forward to you coming home. Aren't we, Dad?'

'Me, too,' Carol laughed, her colour now restored. 'Roll on next week.'

After her visitors had left, Carol leaned back sleepily against her pillows. The doctor had warned her that she might feel drowsy for a couple of days after the anaesthetic.

'What a lucky woman you are, Mrs Bennett,' said the nurse, squeaking in on her rubber-soled shoes to bring her patient some cocoa and biscuits. 'Such a considerate husband and beautiful daughter.'

'Yes,' beamed Carol proudly. 'They are rather gorgeous, aren't they? My daughter has a talent for drawing, you know.'

'Really? How splendid.'

'Yes, isn't it?' Carol said, yawning.

'You look tired, dear,' the nurse said, straightening the bed covers.

'Mmm, I do feel sleepy. Visitors are tiring. And the dreadful news from America shook me up.'

'Me, too. Terrible, just terrible.'

'I think I'll pop along to the loo, then settle down for the night,' said Carol. She swung out of the bed and slipped her feet into her pink, fluffy slippers. Oh dear, she did feel a little strange. . .

'What is it, Mrs Bennett?' said the nurse urgently, and hurried to catch her as she slumped to the floor.

Dezi decided to have an early night. This was the time of the evening, after Lizzie had gone to bed, that he missed Carol most. The house felt empty without her. He had a long hot bath and sank into bed with a book. To his surprise, the telephone on his bedside table rang. It was the hospital, asking him to come at once. A complication had arisen with Carol. Sick with alarm, he telephoned a neighbour and asked her to stay with Lizzie, who was sleeping.

'It's probably just some minor setback,' he explained to quell his own fears. 'It will all be sorted out by the time Lizzie wakes. No point in alarming her unnecessarily.'

At the hospital he was inconsolable. 'But she can't have died,' he said disbelievingly. 'I was with her just a few hours ago. She hasn't even been ill. She was coming home next week.'

'I'm so sorry,' said the doctor.

'But *how* could it happen? How?' Dezi badgered grimly. 'Just tell me that.'

'Thrombosis can happen at any time,' explained the doctor gravely. 'We do try to get patients moving as soon as possible after an operation to lessen the risk. I really am very sorry, Mr Bennett.'

Afterwards, Dezi never knew how long he stayed at the hospital drinking tea, or how he got home. When the neighbour had gone, he sat hunched in a chair by the dying embers of the fire, thinking of Carol who, like President Kennedy, had still had so much to give.

How was he to tell Lizzie? She would be heartbroken. He reached for an envelope on the mantelpiece. 'Mummy' it read, in Lizzie's handwriting. Untucking the flap he took out the product of her art class. It was a picture of a house with a man, a woman and a girl by the front door. They were unmistakably his own little family. Underneath, in bold lettering, were the words WELCOME HOME MUMMY. It was unashamedly sentimental and the most moving thing he had ever seen. As his tears began to fall, he replaced it in the envelope and put it back on the shelf.

That unassuming, big-hearted woman had become an essential part of his life. What was he to do without her? And yet, oddly, it was Bella to whom his anguished thoughts now turned. Help me Bella, help me, he cried in his despair.

The fire was dead, the room cold. He must pull himself together and prepare for life as a single parent. Lizzie was going to need him like never before. He dragged himself out of the chair and went to the kitchen to make some coffee. The clock on the wall said almost 2.30 a.m. He couldn't face bed. He'd light the fire and sit in the chair until morning. And then he would break the news to Lizzie.

Chapter Eighteen

It was the spring of 1968 and the horrors of adolescence were making themselves felt in the Sharpe household. Five foot six of rioting hormones sulked and slammed through the home in an explosive tide, leaving Bella and John miserable and exhausted. At fifteen, Stevie was long-haired, short-tempered and downright impossible!

Now that he was 'one of the lads', the balance of power in his life had shifted from his parents to his wise and wonderful pubertal pals. They visited in droves, like another species, close-banded and cliqueish; lusty together, listless apart. Parents were regarded with indifference, and the family home treated as an hotel. It was exasperating!

But having spoken to other parents of teenagers and read enough about the condition to know that it was neither permanent nor peculiar to the Sharpes, Bella gritted her teeth, clung tenaciously to her confidence, and longed for her adored son's eventual return to the human race.

'Times have changed since your day, Mum,' he informed her patiently one day, having been told to get his hair cut. 'No one has short hair these days.'

'Your father does,' she said, and realised at once she should have known better.

'Oh, well,' he said predictably, 'that's different. He's old.'

'Why, he isn't even forty yet!'

'Oh God, he's positively ancient,' Stevie sighed, peering at her solemnly through curtains of hair like some junior guru.

'Cut out the blasphemy and get yourself down to the barber's,' she warned him. 'Or I'll be getting a letter from your teacher.'

'Teachers,' he said. A shuddering sigh shook him from his toes to the top of his head. 'What do they know?'

'They know that you can't do your work if you can't see what you're doing for hair,' she told him chirpily. 'So go and get it done, or I'll take you there myself.'

She knew that would do the trick since it wasn't done to be seen out with a parent. 'Oh, all right,' he agreed. 'But I'm not having it too short. I don't wanna be a laughing stock.'

That amused her, since he couldn't look more comical than he did at this moment, bless him. Rather like a sheepdog with a shaving rash, she thought, but remained diplomatically silent on her side of the generation gap as, puffed up with pique, he swaggered from the room, his denim jeans rustling stiffly as he walked.

For all his fashionable show of indifference towards the school room, however, Stevie was a bright and industrious pupil. Homework and swotting for exams was done, albeit reluctantly and often at the eleventh hour. Definitely a candidate for college or university later on, Bella and John were informed by his teachers. And loving him as they did, against the current odds, his parents were very proud.

But life lived against a background of pop music and rows

put a strain on Bella's relationship with John. For whilst *she* could accept, with difficulty, that it was just a phase, John feared that his bond with his beloved Stevie had gone forever. And because he was hurt by this sudden exclusion from his son's life, he retaliated by constantly lecturing the boy about family loyalty and respect for the older generation, which only exacerbated the situation in that it sent Stevie thundering upstairs to his bedroom, the door slamming behind him.

'Try not to overreact to these moods of his, John,' she urged. 'He doesn't mean to hurt us. He feels alien to us at the moment, but it will pass. Constant lectures about how we behaved when we were his age only make matters worse. It's his hormones.'

'Hormones be buggered!' exploded John. 'It's sheer thought-lessness. And if you think I'm gonna sit back and let him treat us like dirt for the next four years, or however long this nonsense is supposed to last, you've got another think coming.'

'That isn't what I meant,' she informed him. 'I just think that you should try not to react to his every mood. He hasn't stopped loving us, you know. He'll come back to us, eventually.'

'And in the meantime, we're supposed to just sit back and let him look down his nose at us.'

'We all went through it at that age,' she reminded him.

'Nonsense! We'd never heard of hormones when I was a lad. If I had a fit of the sulks, I got a kick up the arse to help me out of it.'

'Yes, but society has moved on since then,' she reminded him. 'We're all more informed now.'

'And you, I suppose, are the expert on the parent–teenager relationship,' he said with uncharacteristic sarcasm.

'Of course not,' she snapped wearily. 'All I'm asking for is a little more tolerance from you, that's all. You lecture him so often it's like water off a duck's back.'

And so it went on. Battles with Stevie, fights with John. It began to tell on Bella, who longed for a break. Although, throughout her marriage, she had maintained a business life outside the home, she had never socialised much without John, or wanted to go away to business conferences or holidays without her family. Now, she felt she would lose her sanity if she did not get away on her own for a while. Just a few days' breathing space, that was all.

Fortunately the perfect opportunity presented itself. In June the Craven Car Company were to hold a four-day sales conference and awards dinner at an hotel in Paris. Bella, in her capacity as Managing Director of one of Craven's top sales outlets, had been invited. Many other such invitations had come her way over the years, all either declined or attended with John. This time it had to be different!

'I'd like to go, if you don't mind holding the fort at home, John,' she said.

He eyed her shrewdly, noticing that she had not suggested that he accompany her, though that could easily be arranged with Craven. A knot of anxiety tightened his stomach. Was he losing her? The fact that she had been a good and loyal wife had never erased that fear. Now, with sophistication added to her beauty, she was even more stunning than she'd been as a girl. Any man would want her. John had always been painfully aware that he was second best. Did her wish to go away without him indicate the beginning of the end? Would she enjoy the freedom and demand more of it? Her reason for marrying him would soon be old enough to leave the nest. Would she follow Stevie?

Panic-stricken, he longed to go with her and watch over her but sensed, somehow, that in order to keep her he must let her go alone. 'I don't mind, love,' he said with feigned cheerfulness. 'A few days away will do you good.'

She returned his affectionate smile, a lump gathering in her throat at his generosity which allowed him to respect her need to spread her wings a little. 'I hope you and Stevie don't murder each other while I'm away,' she laughed.

'You go and enjoy yourself and forget about us,' he told her. 'It won't do us any harm to fend for ourselves for a change.'

'I'll get my acceptance in the post right away, then,' she said, hugging him fondly.

Having felt a little nervous at the prospect of flying alone, when John had seen her off at Heathrow, Bella now felt exhilarated as she sat in a taxi in the Paris traffic en route for the hotel. The amazing city bustled magnificently around her – elegant, tree-lined boulevards, smart shops, stylish people taking refreshment in the sunshine at the tables of pavement cafés. She could feel its vitality pulsing through her and gasped at her first glimpse of the Eiffel Tower gleaming in the sun, eminently more impressive in reality than its picture postcard image.

The hotel was situated in a tree-lined square not far from the Champs Elysées. It was an imposing white-fronted building with ornate stonework and a marble-floored reception area. Everywhere there was a profusion of indoor plants and trees, and walls bedecked with original paintings. Bella's room was on the third floor and was a miracle of comfort in cream and gold, with a balcony overlooking the square and the spires and domes of Paris beyond.

She unpacked her clothes and put them away in the white, gilt-edged fitted wardrobes and cupboards, then sank on to the white lace-covered bed and browsed through her programme. Cocktails were at seven. It was five-thirty now. Plenty of time to get ready. After a brief refreshing nap, she bathed in the opulent bathroom and washed her hair under the shower.

What to wear? Since formal dress was not required, her safest bet was something smart but not businesslike; glamorous but not gaudy. She finally decided on an emerald green satin dress, with a strappy top and a bolero. It was plain, straight and short. A little slinky perhaps. Well, why not? This was Paris, after all. She wore large white earrings and white shoes, and her bobbed hair shone. She was a little nervous, she realised. After all, she didn't know a soul here.

'Ah well, Bella, into the breach,' she commanded herself, and with a Craven identity badge pinned to her bolero, she made her way to the lift.

'Hello,' said a man standing just inside the cocktail lounge as Bella entered. He looked at her badge. 'Mrs Bella Sharpe, I see. Pleased to meet you.'

She thrust forward her hand, having noted his name: Mr Edward Brooks. 'Nice to meet you, too, Edward,' she said.

'Ted, please,' he said, holding her hand for longer than was necessary and suffocating her with a superfluity of Old Spice. 'Edward is much too formal.'

'Fair enough,' she agreed, her glance moving around the room which showed a predominantly male company. The sprinkling of women present were probably wives or secretaries. Bella doubted if there would be many other females here in the same capacity as herself.

'Quite a place, isn't it?' said Ted, looking around the room.

'It is indeed,' she agreed, her glance moving over the gold-coloured walls with gilt-edged mirrors, wicker chairs and sofas with Provençal print upholstery, bowls of fresh flowers on tables and luxuriant indoor plants, all set on a sea of cream-coloured carpet.

'I'll say this much for Craven,' said her companion, 'they certainly do things in style.'

'Yes,' she agreed. Only the top grossing agents were invited to Craven's conferences which were always held in overseas locations, the theory being that people were more motivated to qualify if they thought they had a chance of a foreign trip at Craven's expense.

'Is your hubby still getting ready?' asked Ted Brooks. 'Sent you on ahead, did he?'

'I'm here alone,' she said.

'Snap,' he said, an unctuous smile lighting his face which was long and thin and surrounded by brown hair carefully styled to disguise a receding hairline. He was about forty-five, she thought, and ostentatiously dressed in a beige, lightweight lounge suit, cream shirt and shocking pink tie. He eyed her quizzically. 'Let me guess . . . hubby is too busy to get away, so you've come in his place. Right?'

'Wrong,' she informed him triumphantly. 'It was my name on the invitation.'

'Oh?' He raised his neatly clipped eyebrows and thought about this for a moment, then clicked his fingers victoriously. 'I've got it. He's put his business in your name for tax purposes.'

'Wrong again,' said Bella, putting him neatly in his place. 'I was invited because I negotiated the Craven contract and am officially the agent. I am the Managing Director of our company, you see.'

'Good God,' he exclaimed as though she had just admitted to heading some international crime syndicate, 'Do you *have* a husband?'

'Oh, yes.'

'How does he feel about all this?'

'Perfectly happy,' said Bella, thanking God for John. He might not be the most dynamic man alive, but at least he wasn't a blatant chauvinist. 'We have worked together for years.'

'But is he lower in status then you?' Ted Brooks asked incredulously.

'Well, technically yes, but we have separate responsibilities so that isn't a problem.'

'Huh!' he snorted, his grey eyes sparking with disapproval. 'It wouldn't suit me to have a women telling me what to do.'

'Are you married?' she asked.

'Divorced,' he said, swigging his wine speedily. 'I got in from work one evening to find my wife had packed her things and gone. Just like that, after all I'd done for her. I'm damned if I know why.'

Your sort never does, Bella thought, but remained politely silent. Having decided that her unencumbered presence in Paris gave him licence for unveiled lasciviousness, Brooks began to try to persuade her to accompany him on a tour of the city's nightlife. Fortunately she was rescued by the chairman of Craven and his wife, an immaculate couple in late middle age.

'Mrs Sharpe,' said the chairman, having researched the guest list thoroughly beforehand, 'I'm delighted to meet you.' He introduced her to his wife as one of their valued agents and chatted at a superficial level for a few minutes before passing on to Ted Brooks.

Seizing the opportunity to escape from the repulsive rake, Bella moved away and introduced herself to a female of about her own age who was alone and looking hopefully around her. But Bella soon realised that what she had mistaken for shyness was tactical observation.

'There's more than enough talent for the both of us,' said the vivacious Molly, after learning that Bella was here alone. 'I've only come for the men. I knew there would be plenty of spare ones. Always are more men than women at these do's.'

'The car trade does tend to be male-dominated,' agreed Bella. 'But you'll get no competition from me, I'm not interested.'

Molly threw Bella an odd look. 'Don't tell me you've come because you want to learn how to increase Craven's sales figures?'

'Only partly,' explained Bella. 'The conference seemed like a good excuse for a break.'

'Too true,' Molly giggled, her startling blue eyes flashing wickedly as she guzzled her wine. 'A change is as good as a rest, I always say. Why let the under twenty-fives hog the swinging 60s?'

'Quite right,' said Bella, though she suddenly felt like a nun in a nightclub.

They exchanged a few personal facts. It seemed that Molly worked part-time in her husband's garage in Hampshire. 'He's a staid old stick, never wants to go off anywhere. But I'm first in the queue when anything like this comes up. A fling with a Frenchman will set me up a treat.'

They drank some more wine, then moved separately around the room, mingling with the other guests. Bella enjoyed meeting new people from all over the UK. She was talking to a pleasant, middle-aged man, who had several garages in Devon, when she glanced idly over his shoulder and found herself reeling with shock.

'Are you all right, my dear?' asked her companion as she gripped the back of a chair to steady herself. 'You're as white as a sheet.'

'I'm fine,' she said, her voice no more than a whisper. 'Carry on with what you were saying.'

But she didn't hear a word. For switching her glance back to the Marketing Director of Craven Cars, she saw that she had not been imagining things. The man he was talking to was Dezi Bennett. As she stared, unable to drag her eyes away, he glanced up and caught her eye.

'Car manufacturers must blend practicality and comfort with style in today's market. The public wants something it can afford to run without losing status,' the Marketing Director was saying. 'Don't you agree Dezi, old boy?'

Dezi nodded. 'Yes, you're quite right.'

'Do you get much demand for metallic?' the Marketing Director asked.

'It is popular, yes. People seem prepared to pay the extra,' Dezi replied absently.

'I like it myself,' said the Marketing Director. 'Gives a car a touch of class.'

Dezi's eyes feigned interest while his mind drifted off. His company now owned six garages in the London area, but being a main agent for another car company he was a guest only in his role as president of an association of car retail agents. In this capacity he was to present the awards at the dinner on the last night. Had it not been a business occasion, wild horses wouldn't have dragged him here. Since Carol's death he had used work as an excuse to avoid any social encounters. Lizzie nagged him about it constantly.

'You ought to get out and about more, Dad,' she lectured. 'Find some female company. Mummy wouldn't want you to spend the rest of your life alone. What about when I leave home? You'll be really lonely then, if you haven't found anyone else.'

'I'm perfectly happy as I am,' he told her repeatedly, becoming increasingly set in his ways.

When Lizzie had heard about the conference, she had been delighted. 'Mix business with pleasure,' she had urged him. 'Let your hair down a little. Use your charm. Find a partner and have some fun.'

Of course, Lizzie was at the age of assumed wisdom. Quite the young lady, in fact, at fourteen, with her head full of pop music and fashion. Her talent for art had continued to progress and her teachers were hopeful of a place at art school for her eventually. A charming girl, though at that moody stage.

Dezi's companion was saying again: 'Isn't that so, old boy?'

Having lost track of the conversation completely, he nodded hopefully, and seeing a potential diversion in the fact that both their glasses were empty, looked around the room for the waiter. And then the walls closed in on him and the air left his lungs. Bella was here! Mature, sophisticated, stunning. On the heels of shock came a surge of excitement of the sort

318

that he had thought never to feel again. Gradually, over the years, his animosity towards her had lessened under the soothing influence of his love for Carol. He had begun to believe that it was really over. Now sixteen years disappeared like frost in a flame, and he knew that there had only ever been one woman in his life. There was no room in his heart for recriminations, only joy.

'Ah, there's the waiter. Over by the door – look,' said the Marketing Director.

Dezi caught the waiter's eye, supplied the other man with a full glass, then said, 'If you'll excuse me, I've just seen an old friend.'

And he wove his way through the crowds towards her as eagerly as he had that Saturday afternoon in 1951, on the South Bank of the Thames.

'Bella!' His voice shook.

'Dezi!' It was a tremulous whisper.

'I didn't expect to see you here. I'd no idea you'd signed up with Craven.' Struggling against emotion, his words sounded oddly impersonal, as though he had just met a casual business acquaintance. His skin was damp, his throat dry. 'It must be about sixteen years,' he said.

'Yes, it must be something like that.' Sixteen years come October, to be exact, she thought, but cleared her throat nervously and said: 'I didn't expect to see you here either.' She eyed him quizzically, since Brown's were sole Craven agents for the Fulworth area.

Explaining his connection with the conference, he studied her face which was no less beautiful for the fine lines around

319

the eyes and mouth. She had changed, though. Success in business had made her supremely confident.

'Oh, I see,' she said, and attempting to ease the tension in the air, smiled and added: 'Just as long as Craven haven't contravened my exclusive territory rights.'

At that moment she couldn't have cared less if Fulworth was awash with Craven agents. All she could think of was Dezi's proximity. At forty-four he was handsome and charismatic. His chestnut hair, now dusted with grey and thinning very slightly at the temples, was worn fashionably, a shade longer and styled back from his face. There were lines, of course, especially around his eyes, and a slight thickening of the neck and waistline. But he was still very muscular and his eyes were even more compelling. Stylishly dressed in a light-weight, continental style lounge suit in light grey, with a white shirt and pale grey silk tie, he looked better even than she remembered.

There were so many things Bella wanted to say to him: how sorry she was for making him suffer for his father's sins; how much she still missed him, even now. All she could manage was, 'How have you been?'

'Mustn't grumble.'

'I was sorry to hear about your wife,' she said. 'I read about her death in the paper. So young. It must have been dreadful for you.'

He wanted to say a million things to her – about them, Bella and himself, not Carol – but he felt as though a closed window stood between them. 'Yes, it was,' he said through parched lips. 'She was a wonderful woman. My daughter and I still miss her. But life has to go on. It was a long time ago.'

Bella saw the pain in his eyes and guessed that he had loved

320

his wife deeply. It didn't hurt, merely filled her with compassion. An error of judgement had robbed him of one woman; death had taken another. Conversation between them died. A hubbub of laughter and chatter rose and fell around them. She heard herself saying, 'Yes, a long time.'

'How are things with you?' he asked formally.

'Not so dusty.'

'Husband and family okay? I remember hearing, years ago, that you had a child. I expect you've expanded on that by now.' Oh God, why was he behaving like a stranger to the person he loved most in the world?

'No, just the one,' she said, frozen by guilt. 'A son.' Your son, screamed her conscience. 'Yes, he's a fine boy, but currently driving us nuts with his teenage moods. Thinks he knows it all, you know how they are. How we all were.'

He smiled and the atmosphere seemed to thaw a fraction. 'Don't I just! My fourteen-year-old daughter is the same. They're so much more informed about everything than we were at their age, aren't they? And not afraid to air their views.'

'It's stopping them that's the problem,' Bella laughed. Oh dear, they sounded like a couple of regulars at a PTA evening. But at least this undemanding chit-chat offered her the opportunity to gather her wits and face the trauma of seeing him again so unexpectedly.

It was time to eat and they were ushered into a sumptuous dining room, exclusive to the Craven party. Tables for four surrounded a small dance floor. A small band played background music on a circular stage. Dezi was whisked away to dine with the Craven uppercrust, while Bella sat at a table with Molly, Ted Brooks and the man from Devon.

The meal was superb. *Soupe à L'oignon, moules marinière*, and *boeuf en croûte*, followed by *meringues à L'orange*. But it could have been grilled gumboot for all that Bella tasted of it. Her heart and mind was at the Craven management table to which her glance constantly strayed. It was no use reminding herself she was married, either. She ached for Dezi to seek her out again. Perhaps after the meal . . . ?

'Did you know that Bella here is the Managing Director of her company?' said Slobberchops Brooks to Decent from Devon.

'I didn't, no,' said Devon, smiling politely at her.

'Women in the boardroom, whatever next?' complained Brooks. 'They'll get above themselves and start to think they can run the country if us men aren't careful.'

'They'll do more than just think about it one of these days,' said Bella lightly, pouring cream on to her dessert. 'You just wait and see.'

'Hear, hear,' said Molly.

'Rubbish!' said Brooks.

During coffee, the chairman of Craven gave a speech. 'We would like to welcome you, our top agents, to Paris. I'm sure you will all find time to enjoy some of the delights of this great city. Although we shall keep you busy during the day, we hope to finish by about four each afternoon, and the evenings are your own. Except for our last night when there will a gala awards dinner dance. Enjoy the rest of the evening, ladies and gentlemen.'

People began to take to the floor. Bella saw Brooks' eyes glisten ominously, but mercifully Dezi pre-empted him and led her on to the floor where couples were dancing energetically.

He pulled a face at the spectacle.

'Do you fancy a walk?' he asked.

'Yes please,' she said, and they left the hall separately, she having feigned a headache to Brooks and Co.

The night was warm with a light breeze rustling through the trees in the brightly lit square. People sat on benches under the trees among flocks of hopeful pigeons as the couple made their way towards the heart of the city. It glowed against the sky, every monument, church and square beautifully illuminated.

'No wonder they call it the City of Light,' said Bella breathlessly as they strolled along the broad, tree-lined Champs Elysées and gazed at the Arc de Triomphe which was bathed in gold. Everywhere there were lights; everywhere people. Humanity washed around them in an exuberant tide, gazing at the sights and thronging the tables of the pavement cafés. Bella felt the strain between herself and Dezi melt away in this warm, vibrant atmosphere.

'You've come a long way from that Fulworth back street,' he said. 'I take my hat off to you, Bella.'

'Thank you,' she said politely.

But as they drank coffee on a pavement terrace lined with wicker flower stands and red umbrellas, she decided that it was time to dispense with the small talk. They couldn't pretend the past had never happened. 'It's so good to see you, Dezi,' she said in ludicrous understatement.

'And you,' he said softly, his face gleaming in the fluorescent lights. Then his voice hardened. 'I hated you for a very long time, though, after I heard you'd got married.'

She pressed her lips together. 'I don't blame you. I hated myself, too.' The sound of spoken French hummed musically around them. 'And what about now? Have you stopped hating me?'

He nodded. 'Oh, yes. My wife helped me a great deal. She could see more clearly than me how deeply you must have been affected by your father's death. Not being close to my parents, I hadn't realised the extent of it.'

'From the way you speak of your wife, I gather you had a good marriage,' she remarked. 'I'm glad I didn't turn you into a misogynist.'

He looked thoughtful. 'Yes, it was a good marriage. Carol was one of life's givers, a nurse and a very good one, too.' He looked at Bella sadly and shook his head. 'She never had what she wanted most in life, a child of her own. Lizzie is our adopted daughter.'

Bella was swamped with remorse. Oh God, she had deprived him of his only child. 'Was it a great disappointment to you, not having any of your own?' her conscience prompted her to ask.

'Not really. I'm more than content with Lizzie, and always think of her as my own.' He sipped his coffee meditatively. 'I suppose, like most men, I would have liked a son. But that's life, it wasn't meant to be.'

'It isn't too late,' she suggested hopefully. 'You might marry again.'

His mouth set in a grim line. 'I think not.'

They lapsed into silence, the atmosphere less strained but still fraught with emotion. Moving on, they walked by the River Seine, the city's illuminations reflected in its dark waters; *bateaux-mouches* gliding by like fireflies.

'Did you ever get my letter? I sent it to the prefab,' he said as they sat on a riverside bench.

'Yes.' The memory of it flooded painfully back.

'Why didn't you reply? I would have appreciated that.'

324

'By the time it reached me, I was already married to John. It seemed wisest to ignore it. I thought it would be easier for you to accept that it was over between us if you hated me,' she explained, remembering that terrible Saturday afternoon when she had received the letter as vividly as if it were yesterday. She spread her hands in a despairing gesture. 'I knew you would get to hear about my marriage through the grapevine. What else could I have done?'

'Why did you marry him?'

Her heart beat fast, her skin burned. 'I was still in shock after my father's death, and very confused,' she explained, aware that she was lying by omission. 'I suppose at that time John represented security to me.'

'And I didn't, I suppose!' All the old bitterness was there in his voice.

She didn't look at him, but concentrated on the patterns shining on the water. 'My father's death had a devastating effect on me. The hatred I felt for your father distorted my outlook. I wasn't myself for quite a while. By the time my head had cleared, it was too late. I was committed to John.'

'And you regretted it,' he suggested.

'I didn't allow myself to think about it,' she said evasively.

'Is it a successful marriage?' he asked.

'Excellent.'

'Excellent,' he echoed. 'What sort of an adjective is that? A good dinner is excellent, hotel service is excellent. But marriage ...'

'The word describes my marriage perfectly,' she said. 'It is comfortable and smooth. John and I have an excellent relationship.'

And then he unnerved her by saying, 'You, Bella, were the only woman for me.'

'We were young, Dezi, it seemed that way at the time, but we both found happiness elsewhere,' she reminded him shakily.

'Happiness and affection maybe, but not true love,' he said.

Still she dared not look at him. 'You loved Carol, I can hear it in your voice.'

'I was very fond of her, yes. I admired her, and what I felt for her was a kind of love. But it was never the *real* man–woman love I felt for you.'

'Ah well, it's all in the past now,' she said hurriedly, guilty at the pleasure his words had brought her. 'The intensity of youth is long gone. I'm a staid old married woman now.'

'What we had was very special,' he said, thrilling her despite herself. 'And it's still there, isn't it?'

'Don't let the romance of Paris turn your head, Dezi,' she urged, terrified now of what was happening to her. After all these years, she wanted him more than ever. 'You're free. I'm not. Whatever there was between us ended the day I got married.'

For the first time, he touched her. Just lightly on the arm, then tilted her face towards his. 'Don't lie to me, or to yourself. I can see the regret in your eyes, feel it like my own. Whatever has happened to us, however much we have changed over the years, we were meant for each other. It began when you were thirteen years old, and it exists outside our control. You know that as well as I do. I'll never get you out of my system and you will never be free of me. I knew it the moment I saw you this evening in the cocktail lounge. It happens sometimes to people.'

He was right. Bella remembered that night back in

1963 when she had dreamed he needed her. Two days later she had read of his wife's death, and had known it was some sort of telepathy. 'Yes, I'll admit that there is still something between us.' She shifted away from him and he took his hand from her arm. 'But it's hopeless. I'm married to someone else.' She stood up, shivering in the breeze from the river. 'Let's go back to the hotel. We'll need plenty of sleep. It's going to be a busy day tomorrow.'

'Yes, all right.'

Walking back to the hotel, their conversation was general, and Dezi wished her a terse goodnight at her door. Alone in her room Bella sank on to the bed with a mixture of relief and disappointment. She had almost forgotten how good it felt to be with him. No other feeling in the world matched it. Only in his company did she feel really alive.

Too restless to sleep, she wandered out on to her balcony and sat down, looking absently beyond the treetops of the square to the blazing sky beyond. The scents from the flower-beds below, enriched by nocturnal dew, wafted up to her deliciously. Everything seemed so vivid: the sights, the sounds, the smells. She had thought that this sort of sensitivity had faded with youth. Now she knew it had merely disappeared from her life along with Dezi.

Dezi stood on his balcony staring unseeingly at the city lights. His adrenaline was really flowing for the first time in sixteen years. He had been a good husband and father, a successful businessman. But as a human being he had been empty. The last few hours had proved that to him. He had felt happy with Carol, and would do anything in the world for Lizzie. But only with Bella did he feel truly complete. It had always been like that.

But she was right. No matter how emotionally tied they were, she was legally bound to another. Dezi had no wish to come between man and wife. He stood for a long time, deep in thought, then he went inside and placed an order with room service. Surely no one would begrudge him a little more of her company, after all these years.

When Bella heard the tap at the door, she knew it would be Dezi. He stood there, jacket and tie discarded, clutching a bottle of champagne and two glasses.

'Don't worry, I've no intention of getting you tiddly and dragging you off to bed,' he assured her lightly. 'But if you're not too tired, there's no one I'd rather share a bottle of bubbly with than you. It is a special occasion, after all, us meeting again like this.'

She felt as though she was glowing brighter than the Eiffel Tower when, against her better judgement, she said, 'What fun!'

As they sat on the balcony sipping champagne and talking softly, Bella felt such happiness it made her want to cry.

'Are you still as fond of the Thames as you used to be?' he asked her.

'Oh, yes. I still go to it when I'm feeling tense or worried,' she said.

The warm night was still young by Parisian standards. People walked through the square, music and laughter floated on the breeze. The joy of the moment was so great she couldn't keep it to herself. 'I am so happy, Dezi, so very happy.' She smiled at him, her cheeks flushed, hair shining in the light.

'So am I,' he said softly. 'It's just like it used to be. We were such friends, weren't we, as well as lovers?'

In that moment Bella accepted that whatever existed between them could not be destroyed by a lifetime of parting. They were born to be a couple. Other circumstances, even her marriage, counted for nothing beside that. She knew that she had not failed in her duty as a wife and mother, and she had done what her father had wanted of her and built Brown's into a fine business. As a woman, however, she had ceased to exist. She had lost herself in a dutiful existence, mistaking habit for contentment and pretending that the sisterly affection she felt for John was enough. Now, finally, she accepted that she and Dezi belonged together.

'I'm even more in love with you, if that's possible,' he said, taking her hand and putting it to his lips.

'And I with you,' she said tenderly.

Later, in the moments of profound peace after their glorious joining together, it was as though Bella had come home after a long absence. There were things to be said, decisions to be made. But not yet . . .

The next day seemed endless as she forced her mind to concentrate on business whilst her body still glowed from his touch. There were lectures and film shows and discussions. At lunch they managed only a brief word as Dezi's presence was once more required by the Craven management. She sat with Molly and co. who had been out on the town after the dance last night.

'You missed a good laugh,' said Brooks, yawning and turning first to Molly and then to Devon. 'Didn't she? We went to this terrific club.'

Bella noticed the palliness between Molly and Brooks with relief. That should prevent any further approaches in her own direction.

'We're thinking of booking for the Lido for tomorrow night,' Brooks said. 'Shall we count you in, Bella?'

Oh dear, how awkward, she thought, realising what a potentially cosy foursome they were. But after all these years she wasn't prepared to let a group of strangers stand between her and Dezi. 'I'm afraid not. I've met up with an old family friend, as it happens.' She glanced towards the Craven table. 'The chap from the Association, as a matter of fact. I've known him for years. He's got a few things planned for the evenings for me, I think.'

She guessed that she had given them cause for speculation, but it was worth it to remove the threat to her precious spare time.

Work for the day over at last, Bella and Dezi changed into casual clothes and took a bus to Montmartre. Hand in hand they wandered through the magical old streets, and ate ice cream sundaes in a pavement café in the Place du Tertre, while all around them the street artists were busy at work.

'This is my daughter's favourite place in all Paris. She has a talent for art, you see,' Dezi explained proudly. 'We've been here a few times together. She loves it.'

'Will she take up art seriously when she leaves school?' asked Bella.

'I shall certainly encourage her to.'

They strolled towards the Sacré Coeur and sat on the grass

by the steps of the exquisite domed building which enjoyed a breathtaking view of the city. The sun touched Bella's face in a benediction.

'Strange us meeting up again so far from home,' she said.

'It was meant to happen.' He tickled her chin with a strand of grass. 'You said something similar about our meeting in the Festival Gardens, long ago.'

'Fancy you remembering that.'

'Had you forgotten it then?'

'Not on your life.'

They didn't go back to the hotel for dinner, but dined in a bistro in Montmartre before walking under the stars, talking, laughing, teasing each other. It was as though they had been transported back in time to the carefree days before her father's death.

Bella learned that Dezi rarely saw his brother, and that his father's health was less good than it used to be, but very little else was said about his parents. It was as though talk of them would stir up too many unpleasant memories and break the spell. Back in Bella's room at the hotel the evening drew to a wonderful conclusion. Dezi crept back to his own bed at dawn.

The next two days passed in much the same way. At four o'clock each day they fled from the conference room like children from school. Greedy for their own company they avoided the famous Paris nightspots but did indulge in a nocturnal cruise of the Seine, enjoying a romantic candlelit dinner whilst viewing the floodlit sights.

And suddenly it was the last day and they were to be deprived of their evening alone together by the Craven Gala Dinner Dance. They were both gloomy that afternoon as they sat in the sunshine on a bench by the Seine.

'We can't possible get out of going, since you're to present the prizes and I am to receive one,' she said miserably.

But the arrangements for the evening were only the tip of the iceberg. They both knew it, although they were loath to say so.

'I can't let you go again, Bella,' he said. 'You must have realised that.'

Her misery seemed to blot out the sun, yet on the other side of the river the spires and towers of Notre Dame still shimmered in its light. She felt angry with the circumstances that had driven them apart. Now people must be hurt – John, Stevie. Oh God! She put her hands to her head despairingly. 'I can't let you go either,' she said, 'but I need time to think, time to work out how best to make the break.'

'Let's stay on for a few extra days,' he suggested. 'We need time together to work this thing out once and for all.'

Joy at the prospect was diminished by her strong sense of duty. 'What do you suggest I do?' she snapped. 'Telephone John and tell him that I'm staying on in Paris to spend the weekend with my lover?'

'Of course not,' he said sharply, anguish rendering him short-tempered. 'Just call him and tell him that you would like to stay on to see a few more of the sights. Surely he won't begrudge you that, if he's as good a bloke as you say he is. And it isn't as though your son's a baby. He won't even notice that you're not there.'

'What about Lizzie?'

'She's too wrapped up in her friends to worry whether I'm around or not. I have a resident housekeeper who spoils her rotten. I just have to call her,' Dezi explained.

'I feel so bad about deceiving John.'

'Someone has to be hurt in this mess, and it doesn't always

have to be me,' he told her. 'We need time to work things out properly. We can't possibly go back to London leaving things as they are.'

Back at the hotel she seemed almost to watch a deceitful woman who resembled herself pick up the telephone and say: 'John? Hello dear ... How are you ... Fine, that's good. And Stevie, he's not been too bad? Oh, wonderful ...Yes, it's all going very well here. Look, John dear, would you mind awfully if I stayed on for a few days ...?'

Had he been a rat, she might have hated herself less. But, John-style, he accepted everything she said without question and hoped she had a good weekend. Oh, the guilt!

But soon everything outside herself and Dezi faded in the joyful knowledge they would share a few more precious days together. Even the Gala dinner dance seemed endurable in the light of this new development. In fact, Bella positively sparkled throughout the evening. Stunning in a white, off the shoulder evening dress, she graciously accepted her award from Dezi, stating her intention to give the cheque to her favourite charity and place the silver plaque in a place of honour in the reception area of the garage.

Even Beastly Brooks was tolerated, albeit with gritted teeth and gratitude for the invention of distance dancing.

'How about us two slipping away afterwards?' said the bucketfuls of gin and tonic he had been sloshing down all evening, as he and Bella took the floor. 'We could go to a club, have a few drinks, a little smoochy dancing ... what do you say?'

Ugh, she thought, but said, 'Not for me, thanks. When this is over, I shall just about be ready for bed.'

'Would you like me to join you there,' he slurred, swinging

his hips to the music with all the grace of a drunken hippopotamus.

'Not if you were the last man left alive,' she told him bluntly. 'Anyway, I thought you and Molly had teamed up.'

'Variety is the spice of life,' he told her with a benign smile.

'Get lost', she said, leaving him to dance alone. He was too far gone to notice her going.

By mid morning the next day Bella and Dezi were all that remained of the Craven party. At last they were free from fear of observation. They retained their separate rooms, for the sake of appearances, but only Bella's was used. During the next two days they saw the sights and watched the world go by from the cafés of the Champs Elysées. They walked by the Seine, rode on the Metro, dined by candlelight and avoided talk of the future.

On the last evening they had dinner in their favourite bistro in Montmartre. They made a handsome couple: she in a flame-coloured sun dress with large matching earrings; he in white slacks and a black silk shirt. The night was warm and the meal superb: bouillabaisse, turkey cooked with pâté stuffing, and pineapple chartreuse. But the shadow of imminent departure hung over them and neither of them had much of an appetite. Over coffee, Dezi raised the subject uppermost in their minds.

'It's face the facts time, darling,' he said, reaching over the table to take her hand.

'Yes.'

'Would you like me to be with you when you tell John?'

She shook her head. 'No, that would make him feel worse.'

He squeezed her hand. 'I know it's hard, but he'll get over it.'

'Yes, I know,' she said again.

'And Stevie, will he live with us?'

'I hope so, but he may want to stay with John. They've always been very close.'

'Whatever you decide's best is okay with me. But the boy is very welcome to live with us.'

They thrashed out the practicalities further. They would live in Dezi's house in Putney for the time being and Stevie would be allowed to choose for himself whether or not he joined them. She would tell John as soon as she got back and move out right away. It was all settled. They both hoped the divorce wouldn't take too long.

Dezi ordered more champagne. 'To us,' he said, raising his glass. 'Together at last.'

'To us,' she said, smiling into his eyes.

But she lay awake long after Dezi had gone to sleep that night, agonising over her decision. Two men. One she loved as a man, the other as a friend. She wanted to hurt neither. She decided that it was too late to tell Dezi the truth about Stevie. Apart from the fact that Frank Bennett still lived, it would be too upsetting for Stevie, and cruel to John. In every way but biologically they were father and son, and always would be.

And as she lay still, listening to the pounding of her heart against Dezi's even breathing, she faced the truth. *She could not break up her family.* It was not a matter of love but of playing fair, something John had done with her all these years.

When Dezi awoke the next morning he found Bella sitting in an armchair beside the bed.

'I'm so sorry, Dezi,' she said sadly, 'I just can't do it. I can't leave John. It will destroy him.'

He flung himself out of bed and pulled on a dark blue

towelling robe. 'I see. So you can destroy good old Dezi again,' he said, pacing the room. 'I bleed, too, you know.'

'And so do I,' she said, her face as pale as her white satin robe. 'But it isn't in me to turn my back on my duty.'

'Duty!' he bawled, grey with despair. 'First to your father, now to your husband. What about duty to me, to our feelings for each other, don't they count for anything?'

'Of course they do.' She went to him, standing by the window with his back turned to her, and slipped her arms around him. 'You are the only man I will ever love. Please try to understand.'

Removing her arms roughly, he swung around. 'For God's sake don't add insult to injury by asking me to understand. I'm a man not a saint.'

Now *she* was angry. 'It's easy for you, you're free. Supposing this had happened when Carol was still alive, could you have left her?'

The question caught him unawares and he didn't reply at once. 'Don't drag the dead into it just to ease your conscience.' He stared at her coldly. 'I'll ask you once more: will you leave John for me?'

'No.' The word was torn from her.

'In that case, goodbye.' He gathered his clothes and marched to the door. 'Have a good life,' he said, and slammed it shut behind him.

She beat her fists against the door, sobbing violently. Still weeping, she bathed and dressed and packed her case. When she could trust herself to speak without breaking down, she telephoned home. Stevie answered the phone in one of his better moods. 'Hi, Mum, are you having a good time?'

'Yes, lovely. Everything all right there?'

'Fine.'

'I'm just calling to say that I'll be catching the one-thirty flight from Paris. I want to know if Dad's going to pick me up from the airport, or shall I get a taxi.'

'We're both coming to meet you,' he said in a rare moment of filial enthusiasm.

'Lovely,' she said, her eyes glistening with tears. 'I'll see you later.'

I was right, she thought tearfully, I've done the best thing for everyone. But beneath the smart, sophisticated exterior, a broken woman checked out of the hotel.

Dezi couldn't face going home that day and made the necessary arrangements to stay on another night.

'You old devil,' giggled Lizzie down the line. 'What's her name?'

'There isn't anyone,' he lied irritably. 'I'll see you tomorrow.'

Unable to face breakfast, he bathed and dressed and left the hotel. He had no plan and no purpose. He simply walked. Through boulevards and back streets, parks and gardens; past monuments and markets, fountains and flower beds. On and on, using up his energy, driving out the pain. At last he sat down at a pavement café in the Champs Elysées and ordered a cognac, followed almost immediately by another. Green and yellow umbrellas shaded the tables which were surrounded by wicker flower stands. The gaiety of the scene only depressed him further. What had he to do with sunlight filtering though the nearby trees, couples arm in arm, laughter, music, fun?

He drank the second cognac more slowly, engrossed in

thought. So immersed, in fact, that the woman sharing his table smiled at him several times before it registered.

'It sure is a lovely day,' she said in an American accent, forcing him into conversation.

'Yes, it is pleasant,' he said, surprised by her direct approach. She was an attractive woman of about thirty-five with shoulder-length red hair and deep blue eyes. Her exceptionally good figure was stylishly clad in a short close-fitting blue dress. Curiosity got the better of him. 'How did you know I would speak English?'

She laughed and waved her hand towards a copy of *The Times* on the table.

The cognac was beginning its work and Dezi smiled. 'Of course, I'd forgotten I had it with me.' He didn't remember buying it. He must have picked one up from the display of English papers in the foyer of the hotel.

'Isn't this the most fantastic city?' she said.

'Yes,' he agreed. 'Are you on holiday?'

Nodding, she said, 'I sure am. And you?'

'No, I'm here on business. I'm going back tomorrow.'

'Are you here alone?' she asked.

'Yes.' He noticed her flawless skin and sensual mouth.

'Me, too,' she confided wistfully. 'I lost my husband last year, and I'm still trying to get used to being a widow.' She sipped her coffee and shook her head. 'My God, but it's hard. I've never cared for too much of my own company.'

He found her frankness relaxing and warmed to her. 'Perhaps you'll marry again,' he suggested. 'After all, you're still young.'

She seemed flattered by this and smiled warmly. They made brief introductions. Her name was Elaine and she was from Los Angeles. 'How about you?' she asked. 'Are you married?'

'A widower.'

Her eyes brightened at this, and he asked her if she would like a drink.

Glancing at her watch, she said, 'Why, thank you, that's real sweet. A cognac would be lovely. It's a little early, but what the hell? I am on holiday.'

Dezi had lost all track of time. Looking at his watch, he noticed it was two-thirty in the afternoon. Cognac at this time of the day, no wonder I'm half cut, he thought, and ordered himself another double. An hour or so later, boozily benign, he leaned against the table listening to Elaine and thinking what a good-looking woman she was.

'Fortunately, my husband left me well provided for,' she was saying squiffily. 'So I booked a trip to Europe. Thought I might team up with someone, you know. But all the folks in the party are couples.'

'What a shame,' he sympathised woozily.

Eventually, they staggered on their way, she clinging to his arm, her perfume adding pleasantly to his mood.

'Would you like to come to my hotel for a drink?' she giggled. 'My suite is much too big for one.'

'Why not?' He felt jubilant and lightheaded, as though he was walking through a brightly lit fairground with cotton wool in his ears. The images and sounds of the colourful crowds roared around him, hectic but muffled. The foyer of her hotel was marble-floored and expensive. She squeezed his arm more tightly as they went up in the lift, then unlocked her door and ushered him into a luxurious suite decorated in shades of pink and cream.

'Make yourself comfortable,' she said, moving to the phone. 'I'll ring down for some drinks.'

'No, don't do that on my account,' he said as the gravity of the situation finally penetrated his addled brain. 'I'm sorry, but I can't stay.'

She frowned. 'Why not? We're having fun, aren't we?' Noticing the desperation in her voice, Dezi realised the depth of her loneliness.

'Yes, it's been great. I've enjoyed your company, but now I have to go.'

She moved back sharply and he knew that, drunk or sober, she was a woman of dignity. 'Sure,' she said.

He leaned over and kissed her cheek. 'Goodbye, Elaine. Enjoy Europe.'

'I will. Goodbye, Dezi,' she said, smiling bravely.

And then he was back out in the sunshine, still a little canned but in control now. He might be a broken man, but he was not yet reduced to having sex with a stranger as a means of revenge. As he walked back to his hotel, his muddled thoughts centred on Bella's last question: 'Supposing this had happened when Carol was still alive, could you have left her?'

His life with Carol came into focus suddenly. And the word Bella had used to describe *her* marriage now seemed the most suitable adjective for his. Excellent. Not earth shattering or particularly romantic but – excellent. He and Carol had built a loving and stable home for Lizzie. Could he have destroyed all that for Bella?

With a shock he realised probably not. It was not a matter of choice so much as of decency. Bella's decision did not mean that she loved him any the less, but that she was a deeply compassionate woman. Loving you hasn't changed her character, he told himself. Nor would you want it to.

He was filled with shame at his behaviour of this morning. You'd expect better from a teenager with no experience of life, he admonished himself. With a sense of urgency, he wondered if he might catch Bella before she left the hotel, to make his peace with her. But a glance at his watch revealed this to be a false hope. She would be back in London by now. He would write to her at Brown's, apologising for the way he had received her decision, he thought, in a sudden feverish desperation to have her know that he understood how it was for her.

But then he decided, just as Bella had done after receiving his letter all those years ago, that the kindest thing for both of them was to do nothing. He walked sadly back to his hotel, wishing he had not changed his flight. Home was where he wanted to be right now, at home with Lizzie.

Chapter Nineteen

A few months after her return from Paris, Bella received a telephone call at the office from a distressed Eve Bennett to tell her that Frank was seriously ill in hospital after a heart attack and was asking to see her. Naturally Bella was surprised. 'He wants to see me?' she said incredulously.

'Yes,' said Eve tearfully. 'I don't know why, and he's too ill to be questioned. Please say you'll come.'

'I'd rather not,' said Bella, unable to bear the thought of opening all the old wounds again. 'Please make my apologies.'

'He's very troubled,' Eve said, almost humble in her anguish. 'You wouldn't refuse to see a dying man would you, Bella?'

Typical of her to use emotional blackmail, Bella thought crossly. Was she never to be free of the Bennett clan? 'All right,' she agreed reluctantly, 'I'll come.'

Eve met Bella in the foyer of the private hospital and Bella was shocked at how the other woman had aged. She had lost a lot of weight and was thinner even than during the war, her eyes raw from weeping, her skin wrinkled and grey with tension.

'Thank you for coming,' she said, her voice barely audible.

And as her skinny hand rested shakily on Bella's arm, all dislike was forgotten in a powerful surge of compassion. 'That's all right,' she said kindly, taking the frail arm supportively. She glanced at Dezi and Peter, who were hovering behind their mother. 'It's a sad time for all of you.' She scanned the area. 'But where's Pearl?'

'She's at home,' said Peter, still boyishly slim though his hair was thinning slightly. 'A migraine. She's had to take to her bed.'

Her sister's friendship with Eve hadn't lasted then, Bella thought, but said, 'Oh dear. Poor Pearl.'

'It's good of you to come,' said Dezi.

'It's the least I could do,' she said, avoiding his eyes.

The two women entered the patient's room together, whereupon the nurse at the bedside left them, saying, 'I'll be just outside if you need me. Not too long now, or you'll tire him.'

Feeling nauseous and faint in the stuffy hospital atmosphere, Bella whispered hopefully, 'Shall I come back another time as he's sleeping?'

'He'll wake up in a minute, I expect,' said Eve softly.

It was strange to see the pompous and powerful Frank Bennett reduced to the vulnerability of a baby, his normally ruddy complexion now marble white with a bluish tinge, his ailing body assisted by an intravenous infusion. His alarming stillness reminded her of the time she had identified her father's body and she longed to escape. But Frank's eyes flickered open, settling first on Eve, then on Bella.

'Leave us please, Eve,' he said. And although his voice was physically weak, it still held authority.

'Yes dear,' she said, and crept from the room.

Bella waited, her heart beating fast, as she wondered if each breath might be his last.

'I was dragged up in the gutters of the East End,' he said, slowly and laboriously. 'I bullied and cheated my way to the top. I had it all. Success, money, power.'

All the old animosity flooded back and Bella stared at this sick man with hatred in her heart. She remained silent while he found the strength to continue.

'I couldn't stop. Even when I had more than I needed, I drove myself on. I became obsessed with your father's site. I didn't need it, but I couldn't bear the thought of him succeeding so close to my patch. Only now can I admit it to myself. It got out of hand. I went too far. I didn't intend to bring about his death when I arranged that spot of bother for him.'

At last it was out in the open. Under different circumstances she might have wanted to strike him. Instead she found herself willing him on to his next breath, which must have been some normal human instinct towards the dying.

'I know how much you hate me,' he continued breathlessly, 'but if it's any consolation to you I have had my comeuppance because Dezi hates me for what I did. I'd taken trouble to conceal it from Eve and him, but he made it his business to find out the truth, and forced me into a position where I could never make trouble for you or your family ever again. The love and respect of my eldest son was something I wanted more than anything. I thought that my financial success would automatically bring me that. Instead I lost it forever.'

He was very weak and Bella feared he had overtired himself. 'You ought to rest now, Mr Bennett,' she said.

'Let me finish,' he said irritably, with the firmness he had shown towards Eve. It was as though nature had given him this one last show of strength. 'One day, a long time ago, you warned me about my conscience. Well, you'll be pleased to know that you were right. There have been no peaceful nights for me, or days for that matter, since your father died. I haven't asked you to come here to beg your forgiveness. I know that isn't possible. I just want you to know, for what it's worth, that I'm sorry.'

Sorry now, with your Maker beckoning, she thought bitterly. But your being sorry isn't going to give me back my father, or my life with Dezi. She stared at the man, even now half expecting all this to be some sort of a trick. But for Frank Bennett the cheating was over. His plump hand lay still against the white sheet. Bella's slim fingers moved towards it, as though of their own volition, and clutched it.

His eyes rested on her for a moment, then moved away. Tears ran slowly down his pale cheeks. She leaned over and dabbed his face with her handkerchief. As her own tears began to fall she felt cleansed, free at last of hatred.

'You've made a success of the business. Your dad would be proud of you,' he said, and drifted off to sleep.

The next day she received a telephone call from Dezi telling her that his father had died shortly after she left. A few weeks later Eve called and invited her to tea at Ivy House. Bella accepted without hesitation. She had known that Eve would call.

It was a late October afternoon with hazy sunshine filtering from a low, steel-blue sky as Bella parked her car in a side street and made her way to Ivy House along the river bank. It was far too pleasant an afternoon to miss the chance of a walk.

Much of this stretch of the water had changed over the

years, she noticed. With the decline in the use of the river as a means of transport for raw materials and goods, the dock upstream at Brentford had closed and numerous boat-building and repair yards had been replaced by new warehousing and offices. As pleasure boats began to outnumber commercial craft, so new housing replaced many of the traditional riverside industries. Distantly, upstream, Bella could see the angular shapes of new blocks of flats contrasting with the dignified lines of more historic properties. That's progress, she sighed, grateful for the remaining areas of greenery, which included the riverside promenade where Ivy House was situated.

The landscape wasn't the only thing to have undergone a transition. Eve's attitude to Bella was unrecognisable. Robbed of her protector, Eve was as vulnerable as a frightened rabbit and almost deferential towards her guest. It was as though her pride and snobbishness had died with Frank.

Bella was in the superior position now. She had youth, strength and knowledge on her side, the latter being the reason for the invitation, she guessed. But she felt no sense of triumph, only pity. How would this sad little woman face the remaining years without her *raison d'être?* Bridge afternoons, evenings alone by the television . . .

'Make yourself comfortable,' Eve said, rising and greeting Bella who had been shown into the drawing room by the maid. 'We'll have tea now please, Mary.'

'Thank you,' said Bella, perching on the edge of a velvety green chair and noticing that the room had been refurbished luxuriously since she was last here.

'I suppose you're wondering why I want to see you,' Eve said, lighting a cigarette and sitting stiffly on the edge of her chair, looking paler than ever in her black woollen dress.

'You want to know why Frank asked to see me before he died,' Bella suggested.

'Naturally, I'm curious,' Eve said. 'We'd been married a long time, and we didn't have secrets.'

Maybe you didn't, but *he* certainly did, Bella thought, guessing that there was a lot more that Eve didn't know about her husband. How was she going to feel when she learned that she had been married to a cheap crook for all those years? Suitably humbled, Bella hoped.

But she heard herself saying. 'Oh, it was nothing of any consequence. He had drifted back in time and was brooding over the fact that he hadn't always been very kind to me when Dezi and I were together.' Well, the woman was as frail as a feather in the wind. And what purpose would be served by her knowing the truth now? 'He wanted to ease his conscience before he died by telling me that he was sorry, that was all.'

'So that was all it was?' said Eve, easily satisfied in her current state of defencelessness.

Bella hesitated for only a moment before offering her final assurance. 'Yes, that was all.'

'I see,' said Eve, her grey eyes resting thoughtfully on Bella, 'Perhaps we both could have been friendlier towards you.'

'I'll say you could,' agreed Bella, welcoming the opportunity to make a point. 'I've never forgotten your hostility towards me. It's a wonder it didn't scar me for life.'

Eve studied her bony hands. 'I didn't think you were right for Dezi,' she said feebly.

'*His* happiness didn't come into it,' Bella corrected forcibly, seeing no reason why Eve should be spared in every direction. 'I didn't fit the bill as your daughter-in-law. But it's water under the bridge now. We both survived.'

The older woman glossed over the awkward moment by saying, 'I understand that you've done more than just survive. A successful business woman, according to all reports.'

How anyone could equate business success with personal happiness was beyond Bella's comprehension, but respecting the older woman's age and current adversity, she just said, 'It has gone quite well, yes.'

'Well done,' said Eve.

A compliment to me? Bella thought incredulously. The old girl must be feeling desperate. 'Why, thank you,' she said graciously.

Later, Bella walked slowly back along the towpath, taking care not to slip on the fallen leaves. A smart cabin cruiser chugged by, followed by a streamlined diesel tug, so different to the grimy steam tugs of yesteryear. Times have changed, she thought again, standing on a grassy bank and looking at the river. Boats are smarter; tug boats rarer; the water cleaner.

Even Eve Bennett seemed to have changed for the better. But for how long? It wasn't in her nature to be pleasant permanently. Once she got over the shock of Frank's passing, she'd bounce back with all her old spite. And somehow the idea didn't displease Bella. People like Eve were like dust and bad weather – unpleasant, but a fact of life. A world without them wouldn't be quite the same.

'I just couldn't bring myself to tell Eve the truth about Frank,' Bella confided to John later. 'So I made up some story. I think she believed me.'

'You're too kind by half,' he said. 'She sounds like a right battleaxe to me.'

'She's that all right, but I didn't see any purpose in adding to her troubles right now,' Bella explained, 'I felt quite sorry for her.'

John listened with a heavy heart, wondering if Bella had seen Dezi at Ivy House. Just the mention of the name Bennett set alarm bells ringing in his head. But he didn't ask for fear that the answer would be yes. His relationship with Bella had been strained for a while after her Paris trip. She had been edgy, faraway, restless. And when she had rather too casually mentioned that Dezi Bennett had been at the conference, John, without actually questioning his wife's fidelity, had known that he lay behind this change in her. He did not question her but waited, dreading the worst, hoping it wouldn't come. And it hadn't. Bella had seemed to settle down, albeit with part of her missing. The danger had passed. But while Dezi Bennett lived, the threat remained.

'Sod the miners' strike,' cursed Pearl one afternoon in February 1972 having switched on the electric kettle to make some tea to find that the power had been turned off yet again. 'Sod the miners, sod the government, sod 'em all! Why should I have my life disrupted every time someone wants more money? Why can't Heath sort it out, isn't that what he's paid for? Sod Peter's argument that the government must not yield to union pressure. If it's going to get things back to normal, give the buggers their thirty per cent increase. It gets freezing in this house without the power. And if we're cut off again tonight, there'll be all the messy business of candles again. Oh, sod everything!'

Of course, Pearl was far too much of a lady nowadays to give vent to her feelings in such a vulgar way in company. This sort of outburst was strictly for when she was alone, which was a great deal of the time now that the children were off her hands. She lit a cigarette and perched on a stool by the radiator at the breakfast bar of her luxury kitchen, staring miserably out across the extensive gardens of her Surrey home. The power cuts were merely an excuse for her foul mood, not the reason. The truth was that she was bored and she was lonely.

Though why she should be was a mystery to her since she had everything she had ever wanted. A beautiful home in the best part of Weybridge, money to burn and, with Sandie away in Paris at a model school, Brett at boarding school and Peter out at work all day, she had more than her share of spare time. But what was there to do? Where could she go in her gleaming Mercedes? To the shops, to the hairdresser's, and that was about it.

Her circle of female friends was severely restricted because the women around here were jealous of her. Honestly, some people had no sense of humour! They were so possessive over their silly husbands that they couldn't bear to have them exposed to a little harmless flirting. And the few female acquaintances that she had managed to retain in stockbroker Surrey were all busy searching for their own identity now that the children were growing up. Those who didn't have part-time jobs (purely for the interest, my dear) were busy doing Open University courses, learning foreign languages, working for charity, or something equally tedious. Being poorly endowed with mental stamina, all Pearl's attempts at starting hobbies had petered out and a job was out of the question because the only thing she had ever been any good at was hairdressing, and now she was years out of date.

A major drawback of living among the moneyed classes, Pearl had found, was that many of the neighbouring women were better educated and more informed than she, which put her out of her depth conversationally. The sort of issues they discussed over morning coffee – world peace, rising unemployment and women's rights – all bored Pearl witless. She preferred the more interesting topics of last night's telly programmes, fashion, and who was screwing who locally.

And Peter was another clever dick who prattled on about things Pearl didn't understand, like the Common Market and Vietnam, would you believe? For God's sake, what had that do with them? It was miles away.

Pearl's marriage had been turbulent, with casual infidelity on both sides. Whilst Peter lived the life of a trendy executive with his E-type Jaguar and his golfing pals, Pearl was simply his glamorous wife with no interests of her own. But despite their explosive relationship, she wanted no other man on a permanent footing, any more than Peter wanted another woman. A little extramarital hanky panky now and then merely rejuvenated marital interest. But now, as Pearl hurtled towards forty, she knew that she was ready for something more than *just* marriage. Not independence, that was far too exhausting, but she did need some interest of her own. What, though, given her limited talents?

She wandered aimlessly around the kitchen, pressing the lightswitch to see if the power had returned. It hadn't. She mooched into the hall with its polished oak floor, and observing herself in the full-length mirror decided that she was still an attractive woman despite a few extra lines and pounds here and there. Hair short and blond, bleached to hide the grey, eyes bright and well made-up, lines covered with a generous coating of foundation.

Her thoughts turned to Bella. How had the advancing years

treated her? she wondered. She was older, of course. To think Pearl had envied her that at one time! In Pearl's early years of marriage she had been too busy promoting the image of glamorous young middle-class wife to wish to see her relatives, who knew her too well and would think nothing of cutting her down to size. A humble background was best forgotten by someone who could afford Yves St Laurent clothes and private education for her children.

But just lately, only God knew why, she had found herself increasingly tempted to renew contact with her sister. They had had little enough in common as children, there would probably be nothing at all for them to talk about now. But the urge was particularly strong today. Pearl sat down at the oak telephone seat, with its purpose-built shelves, and found Bella's home and office number, neatly filed in case of emergency in her pop-up personal directory. She hesitated, wondering if it was such a good idea because she didn't want Bella becoming too involved in her life again, disapproving and bossing her about. But if they met in town for lunch that would keep things nicely casual, and it was time Pearl had a shopping spree up West. She picked up the telephone and was surprised to find herself shaking with nervous excitement as she dialled the number.

They met in a restaurant near Marble Arch and found themselves breaking the ice by talking about the power cuts. But whilst Pearl complained bitterly about the disruption they caused on the domestic front, Bella seemed more concerned with the effect on the country as a whole. 'Terrible for the elderly and the sick,' she said passionately. 'And industry is crippled by the three-day week. With unemployment already over one million, that's about the last thing we need. I do hope the two sides come to an agreement soon, for everyone's sake.'

Oh no, not another smarty pants, thought Pearl, dredging her mind for some intelligent reply. 'Prices are rising, too,' she said hopefully. Inflation wasn't something that interested Pearl one iota, but people always seemed to be droning on about it so it must be fairly topical.

'Yes,' said Bella with a bemused smile.

They ordered roast lamb with all the trimmings and brought each other up to date on their respective family news. Whilst Bella thought that Pearl seemed far more concerned with the prestige her children were acquiring for their parents by their places of learning rather than the actual education, Pearl thought that the fact that Stevie was studying for a degree at a London college meant that he had grown up to be a boring bookworm. But each made the appropriate enthusiastic noises.

To Bella's surprise she was quite enjoying her sister's company. Pearl wasn't so bad really, if you disregarded the airs and graces. And Pearl thought that Bella was a good sort, if you could ignore the fact that she was a know-all and looked terrific. As slim as a reed and as dark as ever. It was so unfair. She obviously used a very good tint, but even so . . .

'What made you get in touch again, after all this time?' Bella asked finally.

'It seemed like a good idea,' said Pearl.

'*And*?' said Bella meaningfully.

'What makes you think there is an and,' asked Pearl innocently.

'I know you, that's why,' Bella informed her.

And to her amazement, Pearl found the fact comforting

rather than abhorrent to her. She told Bella all about her current predicament, relieved to be able to speak to someone on whom pretence was wasted. Bella knew that Pearl wasn't clever, she knew her age to be five years more than she admitted to in Surrey circles, she knew that she was the most terrible snob. It was such a relief to do away with pretence and speak freely.

Bella was relieved that her sister's marriage seemed to be hanging together, albeit tenuously. It was surprising to find that even now, after all that had happened, she still felt the same protective sisterly affection for Pearl. Involuntarily, she said, 'I'm sorry I was so horrid to you the day you got married. It was because I was so unhappy myself.'

Pearl looked mystified. 'That's okay. But why now, after all these years?'

'I thought it was about time I mentioned it, that's all,' explained Bella, and not wishing to pursue that subject further, turned her attention to the matter in hand. 'Why not try to find a job?' she suggested.

Pearl made a face. 'Doing what? I was only ever any good at hairdressing, and I've been out of the trade too long.'

'Take a refresher course.'

A flicker of interest lit Pearl's blue eyes, but quickly died away. 'And then what? Can you imagine me taking orders from some slip of a girl? I'm too long in the tooth for that.'

'Why not get Peter to finance you in a salon of your own?' said Bella enthusiastically.

'I couldn't take the responsibility,' Pearl admitted ruefully. 'I've no head for paperwork. Keeping books, doing wages and what have you, would terrify me. It was the actual hairdressing that was my thing.'

And Bella didn't argue with that. Pearl had been the best in West London in her day. She looked at her sister, wondering how someone who spent the earth on their appearance still managed to look like a barmaid in some sleazy pub. She was all bleach and bangles – her black woollen dress fitted like a vest and her hair was a most unsuitable bright yellow. But Bella didn't dwell on that. Her thoughts had raced ahead to something far more interesting. 'As it happens, I have a new project in mind,' she said thoughtfully. 'It's still very much at the embryo stage, but if you're prepared to do a refresher course in hairdressing, I might have just the proposition to suit you.'

A week later Bella drove the car along the bumpy lane towards Lakewood Manor, excited but fearful that it might have disappeared at the hands of some developer during the nine years since she had last been here. But there it was, exactly as she remembered it, dusty, decrepit, and very beautiful.

She stopped by the rusty metal gates. Despite the bitter February wind, she was delighted to find that the magic she had experienced on her first visit had not been a figment of her imagination. The place still drew her like a magnet. Right now, her plan was just an idea. Pearl had been told nothing more than to take a refresher course, and John had been told nothing at all. The only person she had spoken to about it was a local estate agent who had made some enquiries and an appointment for her to view the property. Bella had to be sure that the feeling was right before she made any further move.

The idea of buying Lakewood Manor and turning it into a country house hotel had been a fantasy that had teased her imagination frequently over the years, but only recently had it begun to take on any sort of credibility. She had always known that the day would dawn when she would wish to deflect her business interests from the garage, and now that time had come. She had fulfilled her obligations to her father. Brown's no longer offered her the challenge she needed to subdue the restlessness that had plagued her since the Paris trip, and which she had constantly striven to hide from John. Cutting Dezi out of her life for the second time was all very well in theory; in practice it was hell.

Since her plans for Lakewood necessitated her being resident in the property, she had not been in a position to make a move until recently, not wishing to uproot Stevie from his friends in Fulworth. But he had his own life now, happily settled in a flat in Hammersmith with three other students and deeply immersed in college life. The parental roof, from now on, would serve merely as an occasional haven.

Her sister's return to Bella's life seemed almost providential. Pearl was a pretentious bitch but she was family, and it had been their father's wish that Bella help her should the need arise. Maybe she would turn out to be an asset. Rich bitch or not, she was an excellent hairdresser.

There were still myriad obstacles standing between Bella and her goal, not least John's reaction to the idea ... But leaving her Mini outside the gates, for fear the metal would collapse altogether under the strain of use, she nipped through a gap in the hedge and walked briskly towards the house to confront the first possible obstacle.

She was ushered into a large, dank hall. She just had time to notice a wide stone staircase with a carved wooden balustrade, before she was shown into a spacious drawing room by

Colonel Dickie White and his wife, Dolly, a couple who looked to be in their mid-seventies. Of the four walls, three were painted in muddy beige and the fourth was wood-panelled. Hideous, bulky old furniture stood on a stained, balding Axminster through which the floorboards stared pitifully. A double bar electric fire burned incongruously in the expansive brick hearth beside an unlit oil heater, presumably put there for use in the current spate of power cuts. The efficacy of the little fire in this large area was rather like that of a single Swan Vesta in Wembley Stadium. It wasn't surprising that the elderly couple were huddled into their coats.

Although clean, the room was damp, dowdy and dispiriting, the cold, pale sunlight which filtered through the dusty windows emphasising the shabbiness. The lingering smell of paraffin hung suffocatingly in the air, and Bella could practically hear the woodworm chewing their way through the crumbling window frames. She adored every inch of it.

'I understand from the agent that you are interested in buying the property,' said the colonel, a thin, stooped man with sparse silver hair and watery blue eyes.

'Yes,' said Bella enthusiastically. 'The agent said you might consider selling even though the place is not officially on the market.'

'You might not be so keen after you've had a proper look around,' said Mrs White, a shaky, white-haired little woman with a bird-like face and worried blue eyes peering through winged spectacles. 'We only ever use this room and the one next door to sleep in. And the kitchen and ground-floor bathroom. The stairs are too much for us now.' She glanced at her husband almost furtively. 'The whole place is too much for us. Too big, too cold, too far from town, and too expensive to run.'

'Have you never thought of putting it on the market?' asked Bella, horrified by this picture of their life.

'We've thought about it, yes, but when it came to doing anything Dickie felt guilty about leaving, so we've never taken it further. It's been in his family for generations, you see.' She sighed and it was obvious that she desperately regretted the fact. 'But when we got the call from the agent, telling us of your interest, it did made us think again.'

The plight of the old people now took precedence over Bella's plans. 'Do you not have children who could maintain it for you?' she asked. 'I don't want to persuade you to sell if you'd rather stay, though I can see it isn't very comfortable for you, the way it is now.'

'We never had any children,' said Dolly White with a worried shake of her head. 'And we don't have the money to pay anyone to look after it for us. We're reliant on neighbours to take us into town for shopping. That was no problem when we had transport, but we can't afford to run our own car now.'

'The money has just dwindled away, maintaining the house over the years,' explained Dickie.

'If we sold this place, we could afford to buy one of those little retirement bungalows near the park in town,' said Dolly, her eyes lighting up at the thought. 'With a modern kitchen and central heating. Just think, I could walk to the shops.'

'And I could go and watch them playing bowls in the park,' said Dickie, warming more to the idea by the minute. 'We'd be able to afford outings again, too.'

Bella knew that this was true. Even allowing for the fact that Lakewood would be priced substantially lower than a similar property which had been well maintained, it would still fetch a much higher price than their dream bungalow.

The difference, properly invested, would be more than enough to keep the Whites in comfort for the rest of their lives. 'Well, perhaps I could have a look around then,' she suggested.

The property offered more in potential than usable space, since everything from the wiring to the woodwork needed renewing. On the first floor were five large rooms surrounding a galleried landing, with access to a further five from a short passage. This wing of the house was served by a secondary staircase which had originally been used by servants. Downstairs, there were six spacious reception rooms, including the drawing room, and a large kitchen whose only redeeming features were its red quarry-tiled floor, which Bella planned to keep intact, and spacious pantry and larder. The fixtures and fittings consisted of a cracked sink with a wooden draining board.

There were several ancient bathrooms on both floors and the house had both attic rooms and a cellar. The grounds proved to be more extensive than Bella had imagined with woodland on the far side of the lake.

'I love it,' she said, over a cup of tea in the drawing room. 'But before I proceed any further, I want to be perfectly honest with you about my plans for the property.'

They waited, eying her quizzically.

'I plan to turn Lakewood into a country house hotel,' she explained.

They both frowned and her spirits sank. But this wasn't just a building, it was their heritage, and if they disapproved of her plans she would look for another property.

'Do you mean a glorified holiday camp?' asked the colonel at last. 'With a funfair and hot dog stalls in the grounds.'

'And details of Dickie's family tree on sale,' suggested Mrs White anxiously. 'Oh dear, that would be awful.'

'No, nothing like that,' Bella assured them. 'I plan to make it into an hotel specialising in the traditionally English way of life. Obviously some modernisation is needed – central heating, bathrooms en suite, a new kitchen, etc. – and the whole house needs extensive redecoration, but I shall retain its original atmosphere as far as possible. I want guests to feel as though they are spending their holiday at a friend's country home rather than an hotel, though of course they will have such facilities as a restaurant and cocktail bar. We might put in an indoor swimming pool, given the unreliable British summer. It will be a commercial enterprise, but not run for profit alone. It will be my and my husband's home, too.'

'The Americans will love the view of the castle,' said Dolly White excitedly, a faint flush suffusing her faded cheeks. 'And the Kennedy Memorial at Runnymede is only a few minutes by car.'

'It's very well placed for the airport,' chimed in the colonel enthusiastically. 'And access to central London is good from here by car. And there's a short cut to the river across the fields.'

'You could have strawberry cream teas on the lawn,' suggested Dolly.

'There's a tennis court in the garden,' said Dickie. 'It's very overgrown but you could easily restore it.'

Bella smiled, knowing that she had just made two converts. 'If you're going to be living locally, you must join us for dinner whenever you feel like it. I'm hoping to persuade my aunt to take over the kitchen. She's a terrific cook.'

'We'd love to,' they beamed in unison.

'Well,' said Bella, rising and preparing to leave, 'I'll talk it over with my husband. Providing he agrees, I shall be in touch with the agent in the next couple of days.'

And leaving the couple twittering happily like a couple of sparrows at cake crumbs, she walked out into the freezing air. So far, so good. Now for the hard part – convincing that unadventurous husband of hers of the merits of the idea.

'But how do you propose to fund the scheme?' asked John predictably, after listening to her plan over dinner that evening. 'Knowing you, you'll have worked something out, I suppose.'

'I have, yes,' she assured him. 'I'll sell my interest in Brown's and with what I get for that, plus my half of the money we get for this house, I'll have most of it. And the deeds of Lakewood will stand me in good stead for any finance I need to borrow.'

'I notice you're saying you, not we,' he remarked.

'Well, yes, I don't expect you to give up your job at Brown's just because I want a change of direction. I feel guilty enough asking you to commute to Fulworth from Windsor every day.'

'That's no problem,' he said, brushing it aside in favour of more crucial matters. 'Do you intend to offer your Brown's shares to Trevor?'

'Only those that you don't want,' she said mysteriously. 'This is how it will work. You and I sell this house. My share goes into the Lakewood project; yours goes into buying enough shares from me to make you an equal partner with Trevor, since I'm sure he'll be keen to buy me out as well. He has more than enough collateral, with Brown's and his house, to raise a loan if he doesn't have enough capital to pay for them. This way everyone is happy. Both you and Trevor have promotion and half each of a very good business, and I get to do something of my own rather than something chosen for me by my father.

'Auntie Vi and Uncle Wilf are bored stiff with retirement,' she continued, sipping some white wine. 'And the house in Napley Road is only rented so I'm hoping they will come, too; Auntie to run the kitchen, Uncle to help look after the grounds. I don't think it will be too much for them, provided there are staff to do the donkey work. And to make it even more of a family concern, I'm going to ask Pearl to run the hairdressing salon I shall open for the guests' convenience.'

'Pearl?' he said doubtfully. 'Is that wise? Is she up to that sort of responsibility?'

'Her sole function will be as a hairdresser, for which she will receive a wage. I'll look after all the paper work and take all the responsibility. It will only be a small salon and she wouldn't need to work every day. From Wednesday to Saturday would probably be sufficient; it will merely be an additional service for the guests. She can have a junior to help her.' Bella paused and looked at him. 'What do you think of the idea as a whole?'

John hadn't seen her looking this animated in ages. She didn't just *want* this project, she *needed* it. And having watched her snatch Brown's from the brink of disaster and build it into the valuable establishment it was today, he had not the slightest doubt of her ability to succeed with the new venture. 'I think it's great,' he said with a smile.

'You do?' she whooped joyfully, leaping from her seat and flinging her arms around him. 'I'm so glad.'

'But there is one major alteration I insist on making to your carefully hatched plans,' he said ominously.

'Oh?' she said enquiringly, returning to her seat and facing him with a challenging light in her eye.

'I resign from Brown's, too. My half of the house cash goes

into Lakewood so you won't have to take a loan. We sell the whole of the rest of Brown's to Trevor. That way Brown's stays in the family, and you and I run Lakewood together. Any money we don't need from the sale of the shares, we can invest.'

This was something Bella hadn't expected and she was deeply concerned for John. 'I can't let you do that. The garage trade is in your blood. I can raise any extra cash I need without any sacrifice on your part.'

'No sacrifice, Bella,' he assured her ardently. 'It's time I had a change, too. And I really want to help you with Lakewood.'

'But if this did come about we'd be equal partners,' she said. 'So you wouldn't just be helping me.'

He smiled and shook his head. 'We both know that isn't true. You could run Lakewood, or any other project you set your mind to, without me. You've a natural talent for it. You are a leader. I am a follower. The idea of being an equal partner with Trevor terrifies me. My small area of responsibility at Brown's has always been more than enough for me. I would much rather spend my time working at Lakewood with you than worrying about the garage. With you in the driving seat, we'll make a good team. And later on Stevie may want to come into it with us on the management side. If not, at least he'll have somewhere nice to go for weekends. It's no distance by car.'

'Are you sure this is what you want?' Bella asked solemnly.

'Quite sure.'

'In that case, let's drink to it,' she said, raising her wine glass. 'To Lakewood Manor.'

'To Lakewood Manor,' he echoed, chinking her glass.

Chapter Twenty

It was Monday 19th June by the time the sale of the Sharpes' house and their purchase of Lakewood were finally completed. An oddly emotional day, when they found themselves pausing in the midst of personal excitement to count their blessings. And all because of an unexpected event the previous day ...

Although the property wasn't legally theirs until the Monday, the Whites were so co-operative about access, Bella and John made several trips to Lakewood during the preceding weekend, ferrying small items of sentimental value that they did not wish to abandon to the impersonal hands of the removal men: clothes, jewellery, china and glass.

Having safely delivered the last of these and joined the Whites for tea among the packing cases, they set off for Fulworth in the late afternoon, weary from endless clearing out and packing up.

'I could sleep for a week,' said Bella as they purred towards London along the outskirts of Staines.

'Me, too,' said John at the wheel of their estate car. 'But when we get home we've more sorting out to do.'

'Yuk, what a ghastly thought,' said Bella, yawning, her

muscles stiff and aching. 'When I suggested it, I'd forgotten what an exhausting business moving house is.'

She was staring idly ahead of her at some children peering from the back window of the car ahead. They waved at her and she smiled and returned the gesture, guessing that they were on their way home from an outing to Runnymede or Windsor which always drew the crowds on summer Sunday afternoons. The children's attention was drawn skywards, another popular attraction in these parts, too, as magnificent machines could clearly be seen ascending and descending from nearby Heathrow airport.

Absently following the children's pointing fingers with her eyes, she watched a plane flying as gracefully and steadily as a seagull.

'Looks like a Trident,' said John, whose interest in aircraft had lingered mildly since Stevie's plane-spotting days.

'I wonder where it's going,' said Bella casually. 'Somewhere exciting I bet. Oh, my God! Oh no, John!'

A monumental thump shook them to the bone, and before their horrified eyes they saw the tail break off and the plane drop out of the sky in front of them, disappearing from sight into the fields.

'Bloody 'ell,' gasped John, pulling into the side of the road, breathless with shock. But even as he spoke, though pale and shaking he was scrambling from the car. 'I'll go and see if I can help.'

'Me, too,' said Bella, leaping from the car with pounding heart and running in the direction of the accident. People seemed to come from nowhere and by the time Bella reached the scene there were crowds there, awestruck at the sight of the remains of a BEA Trident, just a pile of mangled metal, lying in a field. There were no cries for help coming from the wreckage. All was ominously silent. Bella turned and made her way back to the car, knowing that any offer of assistance would be more hindrance than help in this crush. Back at the car she shook uncontrollably and wanted to be sick. John joined her shortly afterwards and they sat together in silence, overwhelmed by grief, silently praying.

'I feel so helpless,' he said at last. 'The police have got everything under control. I'd just be in the way.'

'I know,' she said, taking his trembling hand. 'The best thing we can do to help is to get out of the way and leave the road clear for the ambulances.'

But that was easier said than done. There were cars and people everywhere, hurrying towards the field in groups, anxious for a glimpse of the disaster. The air screeched with sirens as fire engines and ambulances rushed to the scene.

'Trust some people to make a bleedin' picnic out of it,' said John in disgust as crowds tore past them.

It was some time before the traffic began flowing again and they listened to reports of the disaster on the car radio. The plane had been bound for Brussels and had crashed at 5.15, just minutes after take off from Heathrow. There were one hundred and eighteen passengers on board, just two of whom had been dragged out alive. It was estimated to be the worst disaster in British aviation history.

'It certainly puts things into perspective,' said Bella sadly. 'While we were moaning about the chaos of moving house, those poor people were about to die. Well, you won't get another complaint out of me for a while, no matter how fraught things get.'

'And I'll join you in that.'

Later that night when they heard that the two survivors had died, Bella wept, unable to distance herself from the news she had witnessed at first hand. They were both still very subdued the next day and managed not to break their resolution, despite a great deal of provocation, for that Monday heralded the start of six months' frantic and exhausting activity as they strived to transform Lakewood Manor from the shabby to the sumptuous.

Whilst employing an architect and a building firm, Bella and John also took a physical part in the proceedings themselves, living at first in dire discomfort in the rooms the Whites had used until their private attic apartment was ready, and later masterminding the whole operation from there.

Bella planned the decor and the landscaping of the grounds, attended a hotel management course, interviewed staff, worked out Lakewood's initial promotion, acted as gofer and general dogsbody to the builders, while John, with the help of some casual labour, took care of the painting and decorating. They thought it wise to hire a firm of landscape gardeners to establish some sort of order in the unruly gardens before handing them over to Uncle Wilf.

And so, as summer turned to autumn, and autumn to winter, damp dreary bedrooms blossomed prettily into inviting pastel-shaded retreats with lace-trimmed satin bedspreads and stylish en-suite bathrooms. The dreary conservatory at the back of the house was modelled into a sunny garden room, while outside was a swimming pool and paved terraces containing wicker tables and chairs.

All the wood panelling and solid oak doors were restored to their former richness, and the dank hall became an elegant reception area with a secluded hairdressing salon leading off.

The Whites' drawing room became a smart cocktail bar with expensive red-patterned carpet, soft leather furniture and tasteful wall lighting. The adjoining dining room was a vision in orange and cream, in which even the shade of the table napkins blended. Hygienic fitted units graced the kitchen in an abundance of cupboards, worktops, modern ovens, and all the latest gadgets. There were several luxuriously appointed lounges, and the entire property now benefited from under-floor heating.

Under Vi and Wilf's supervision, the derelict garden cottage became a cosy, comfortable home delightfully situated on the edge of the wood. They moved in the autumn, and while Wilf got busy planting bulbs and preparing the grounds for winter, Vi kept up the family's strength with her delicious home cooking. 'Gotta keep me 'and in for when I start work in the big kitchen,' she told them cheerfully.

Although Bella planned to make Lakewood so sought after as to eliminate any need for advertising, an initial promotion was necessary to secure those first bookings on which their reputation would rest. Advertisements were placed in various publications, and the opening was planned for Easter 1973. As the date hurtled towards them, seemingly at breakneck speed, they swung wildly between eager anticipation and blind panic as various unexpected hitches disrupted their schedule. Some bathroom fittings were suddenly unavailable; a cargo of light fittings was lost in transit; there were teething troubles with the central heating, and so on. But somehow all the hiccups were eventually overcome. Staff were engaged; menus prepared; food ordered. Right on schedule Lakewood Manor, elegant and inviting amid a riot of daffodils and tulips, was ready to offer the very best in hospitality.

The first guests on that pre-Easter Thursday, were warmly received by a slim, dark-eyed woman of forty-two, wearing an olive green suit with matching high-heeled shoes and pale lemon blouse. Her dark, shining hair was worn in a smooth bob around her attractive, modestly made up face. She was charming and confident and made the visitors feel that their comfort really was her concern. No one would have guessed that up until half an hour before she had had her sleeves rolled up in the kitchen helping her aunt, whose assistant had gone down with flu. Each new arrival received the same personal treatment from the proprietor and soon the building buzzed with the sound of happy people.

Vi's first public creation was simple and traditional and almost totally unaided by tin or packet. Homemade vegetable soup, followed by whiting in orange sauce, then roast beef and mouth-watering Yorkshire pudding, or roast pork with stuffing and apple, all served with a selection of fresh vegetables. A choice of desserts melted in the mouth: creamy trifle, apple crumble, or fruit salad. The meal was beautifully presented and served by carefully selected waiters. Pale orange candles glowed prettily over the small bowls of spring flowers gracing each table, and a pianist played softly in the background.

It was not easy to blend homeliness with style, and simple cuisine with luxurious surroundings, but the personal welcome and lovingly prepared fare were an unqualified success. Whilst Bella's praises were sung privately among the guests, their compliments to the chef were sent to the kitchen, via the waiters, in an effusive stream.

When the last guest had finally tottered off, replete and happy, and the staff had relaid the tables for breakfast and cleared up in the kitchen, everyone was invited up to the

Sharpes' apartment for a small celebration. It was a spacious home covering the whole attic area, consisting of a large open plan lounge with dining alcove, comfortably appointed with prettily-covered chairs, hand-made occasional furniture and a gorgeous antique fireplace which Bella had rescued from one of the bedrooms and had restored. There was also a streamlined kitchen, a bathroom and two bedrooms, the second of which was for Stevie's use whenever he wanted it. The attic had been the obvious choice for their living quarters since it meant that they saved the more valuable commercial space on the lower floors and were assured of more privacy than anywhere else in the house.

'Well, we did it,' said Bella, smiling happily when everyone had a full glass. 'Lakewood is finally underway. And I'd like to thank you all for the hard work you have put in to help our launch go smoothly. In particular, can you all join me in raising our glasses to Auntie Vi, who was in the hot seat and has undoubtedly got us off to a wonderful start with that superb meal.'

'Was it really orlright?' asked Vi, after the toast. 'I was afraid it might be too down to earth for such a posh place.'

When their denials had reached the rooftops, Bella said, 'With cooking like yours, not a chance. Anyway, simple home-cooked food is what we want to become known for.'

'Hear, hear,' said John.

And then, Bella was moved to tears by something Stevie did. Now a handsome young man of twenty with thick brown hair and smiling eyes, he was almost unrecognisable as the awful adolescent of five years ago. He had taken a great interest in Lakewood and was using his Easter vacation to help out.

'I'd like to propose a toast to my parents,' he said, making

Bella want to burst with pride at the sight of him, tall and casually dressed in jeans and a royal blue sweater. He raised his glass. 'To Mum, who masterminded this whole operation, and to Dad, who has worked so hard with her on the project. I'm sure tonight is just the first of many such successes, and this time next year we shall all be here again celebrating Lakewood's first terrific year.'

All eyes were on Bella, who rummaged in her bag in search of a Kleenex. Family relationships were rarely easy, with all their hidden undertones, but at moments like this there was nothing to match them. She embarrassed Stevie by giving him an emotional hug, repeated the process with John, who positively lapped it up, and that night went to bed a happy woman.

Stevie was right. That first night was the forerunner to many similar evenings as Lakewood went from strength to strength. They had a frantic summer season with a good proportion of foreign tourists, in particular Americans, and although residential bookings quietened slightly in the autumn, restaurant reservations flooded in as news of the Lakewood cuisine spread locally and beyond.

Winter residents were mostly foreign tourists taking an out of season vacation, or business people glad to escape from the impersonal nature of the large city hotels. Non-residential diners came from London and all over the South of England, many finishing their evening by booking a room for the night. By Christmas, they were booking three months ahead for Saturday evening dinner. And people were never hurried or encouraged to take coffee in the lounges, unless they wished to. Bella knew exactly how many people could be comfortably catered for in any one evening, taking the residents into consideration, and she was never tempted to overtax her staff or inconvenience her guests by exceeding that limit in the pursuit of profit.

Such was her determination to retain the human element within a commercial environment, she decided to dispense with profit altogether for two weeks each year by making Lakewood available, free of charge, to children of poor city families who would not otherwise have a holiday. LAKEWOOD FUN FORT-NIGHT, she called it, and arranged a packed programme of events, with a maximum stay of one week per child, to allow more youngsters to feel the benefit. With unemployment still rising, there was no shortage of applicants.

Vi's homemade scones and cakes made tea at Lakewood a popular event, too. It was served on the lawns in summer and in the log-fired lounges in winter. Vi and Wilf were in their element; she forever foraging in cookbooks for new ideas, he spending hours beyond the call of duty tending his gardens. And they loved the cottage. 'A proper little palace,' Auntie said. ''Oo would o' thought that our Bella could make our old age such fun.'

Trevor and Joan were regular visitors to Lakewood and rarely missed appearing for tea on a Sunday afternoon. Bella had insisted from the start that Auntie delegate to her assistant so that she could take time off to relax.

Even Pearl seemed moderately content, though Bella suspected that her sister enjoyed the company more than the actual work. Fortunately, she was able to indulge in non-stop conversation with her clients without spoiling the end result, and as she was on duty for only a limited number of hours, the arrangement worked quite well.

A year from the day of the opening, in the Easter of 1974,

Bella once again organised a party in the apartment. But this time the guest list also included Dickie and Dolly White, who now had a little car and were regular tea-time visitors to Lakewood, Trevor and family, Peter Bennett who came with Pearl, and an assortment of staff relatives and friends. It was a refined, elegant occasion with champagne flowing and Bella looking stunning in a red satin off-the-shoulder dress.

On this occasion, it was John who interrupted the general hilarity to say a few words. 'An average bloke,' he began, 'would probably laugh at his wife if she told him, out of the blue, that she wanted to buy an enormous relic of a place and turn it into an hotel.' He smiled at Bella and then at the gathering in general. 'But I knew better than to laugh when Bella said that to me. Because I know my wife to be a very determined woman who could make a Rolls Royce out of an old banger.' There was an outbreak of applause. He winked at Bella. 'A hard worker, I'm sure you'll all agree. A slave driver, perhaps.'

'Not arf,' laughed Vi, 'No one sleeps on duty in this establishment.'

There were gales of laughter and good-humoured agreement.

'But no one will deny the knack she has of making work seem like fun,' he continued to more cries of assent. 'She has given us all a new lease of life and I am very proud of her. So please, ladies and gentlemen, raise your glasses to the Lady of Lakewood Manor.'

Cries of 'speech' brought an emotional Bella to her feet and she said a few words, thanking John and Stevie for their support, and attributing her success to the close teamwork of the Lakewood staff and management. She was feeling deeply moved as the party continued. How lucky I am to have had this second chance, she thought, discounting the fact that, like most good fortune, hers was entirely self made.

A month later Stevie was on his way to a very different sort of party at the home of a college acquaintance in Chelsea. He could hear the muted strains of 'Tie a Yellow Ribbon' as he rang the bell, and when the door was opened the full blast of the music erupted into the street.

'Hi, Stevie,' said a lean, bearded young man with shoulder-length hair tumbling over the T-shirt he wore with bleached, flared jeans. 'Come on in, man.'

Stevie entered a smoky hall which was littered with young people sitting drinking on the stairs, or standing around talking. A benign communal 'Hi' was aimed in his direction. Through an open door he could see people dancing; through another door, as a guest emerged, he could just make out people sitting on the floor in a slightly darkened room. He guessed from the distinctive aroma in the air, that they were passing a joint around.

'Glad you could make it,' said his host, whose name was Guy, 'Come through to the kitchen and I'll fix you up with a drink.'

'Great,' said Stevie, and following him into the kitchen placed his statutory bottle of wine among the others on the worktop, which was also crowded with cans of beer and dishes of crisps and nuts.

The doorbell could just be heard above the clamour. 'Can you help yourself?' said Guy who shared this house with three other students, 'I'll just go to the door, then I'll take you round and introduce you to some people.'

Stevie snapped open a can of lager and drunk it straight from the tin. There was none of his usual crowd here and he barely knew Guy. He'd shared a table with him in the college dining room the other day and had accepted the invitation on the spur of the moment, as a welcome respite from months of intense swotting for his finals next month. But he'd known the minute he stepped through the door that it wasn't his scene. He'd stay for half an hour or so, then go back to Hammersmith and meet his flat-mates in their local.

A girl with long straight black hair, heavily made-up eyes and gigantic gold hooped earrings appeared, said 'Hi,' and helped herself to a glass of wine. She smelled of Indian perfume and was wearing a long, loose, printed cotton dress. She talked slow, gentle gibberish which seemed to be loosely related to the meaning of life and the universe. Her incoherent speech and general demeanour told him that she was smashed on more than alcohol.

He could hear people piling into the hall. A pretty blonde American girl came into the kitchen, said 'Hi,' filled two glasses with wine and left. More guests crowded into the kitchen, but Guy didn't reappear. Stevie and Earrings went into the other room and danced. Wearing a vacant smile, Earrings moved lazily and sensually in front of him, completely without inhibition.

When the music ended he decided to leave, and wandered off towards the hall, where several couples were now snogging against the wall. He pushed his way towards the kitchen to say goodbye to Guy, but there was still no sign of him, so he decided just to slip away. On his way to the front door, however, his attention was caught by a redhead standing by the door of the dancing room. She was singing with the record which had now been changed to 'Seasons in the Sun', and as she caught Stevie's eye she smiled.

'Hello,' he said. He wasn't going anywhere now.

'I love this song,' she said brightly.

'Do you?' The most striking blue eyes he had ever seen sparkled at him from a pretty, lightly freckled face which was surrounded by clouds of long red hair which curled loosely past her shoulders. She had the sweetest bowed lips and tiny nose. A green floral dress with a drawstring neck and full skirt enhanced her slim figure. She was fresh-looking, girlish, and incongruous among the other dope-eyed females.

'Have I grown another head or something?' she asked, and he realised that he had been staring at her for too long.

'I'm sorry,' he said. 'I was just admiring the scenery.' His head was spinning. This party was full of lusty males who would be only too eager to snap this beauty up once they noticed she was here. And that was another worry. Who had she come with?

'A girlfriend,' she said, when he asked her.

Thank goodness for that. He was tempted to ask her to leave with him now, but fearing that such a premature action might ruin his chances altogether, he asked her to dance first. Then, when the music ended, he said, 'Do you fancy getting out of here and going for a coffee somewhere?'

'I've only just arrived,' she pointed out.

'So have I, but most of this crowd are smashed.' he said. 'They're smoking pot in the other room.'

And fortune smiled on him because her smooth brow wrinkled into a frown and she said, 'Yes, I noticed that. This isn't really my scene to be honest, but I'll have to find my girlfriend and tell her I'm leaving. She might not be very pleased.'

But fortunately for Stevie, the girlfriend was far too preoccupied with a male science student to bother about her friend's arrangements. And ten minutes later, feeling ridiculously lighthearted, he studied his new companion across a table in the coffee bar at the end of the street. Her name was Elizabeth, though she told him she was known as Lizzie. She was twenty years old and at St Margaret's College of Art in central London. She shared a flat with two other girls not far from here.

'My home is in London, so I could have lived there through college, but I was keen to be independent,' she explained.

'Whereabouts in London do your parents live?' he asked conversationally.

'Putney. But there's only my father. Mother died some time ago,' she said.

'I was brought up on the other side of the river,' he informed her. 'In Fulworth.'

'Oh, that's a coincidence,' she said enthusiastically. 'My father has a business there. Bennett and Dent's Garage. Do you know it?'

'I know of it vaguely,' he said. 'But we lived the other side of town. My parents had a garage business there, too, funnily enough. But they're in the hotel trade now.'

Knowing nothing of his mother's connection with the Bennetts, Stevie turned eagerly to the more interesting matter of getting better acquainted with his new companion. After exchanging some personal details he told her that his college days were numbered.

'What are you going to do after graduation?' she asked. 'Do you have a job lined up?'

He nodded. 'Yes. I'm going into retail management with

the Hilbury Group,' he told her, 'conditional on my getting a good business studies degree.'

'Hilbury, the departmental store group?' she queried.

'Yes, that's right.'

'Will you be based in London?' she asked with interest.

'Initially, yes, I shall be working at their West End store. But when I have been trained they may want me to move around, either in this country or abroad, being a multinational company.'

'Did the fact that your parents are in business influence you in your career?' she asked, sipping her coffee and enjoying herself thoroughly. Stevie was much more fun than that awful party. And he really was rather gorgeous with his amazing brown eyes and thick wavy hair which he wore at a fashionable length just below his ears. He was tall and very macho in a striped blue and white shirt and jeans. She liked the clean-cut lines of his countenance, the well-shaped mouth, solid jaw, and proud nose.

'I suppose so,' he said thoughtfully. 'My mother is a superb businesswoman. I probably inherited my interest in it from her.'

'Will you eventually go into the family business?' she asked.

He shrugged. 'Who knows, one day maybe, but certainly not until I've gained some experience outside in a different field and at a much higher level. I want to make my own way, you see.'

'I can understand that, I'm just the same,' she said.

'What about you?' Stevie asked, observing her quizzically. 'Is it too early for you to think about your career? Are you going to paint masterpieces and starve while you get established?'

She roared with laughter, her cheeks flushing rosily. 'Oh

no, I'm much too fond of company and home comforts for that,' she told him unpretentiously. 'Anyway, my father would never allow me to starve. He's an absolute dear and would willingly support me forever if I wanted it. But I prefer to keep myself.'

'You must be a very good artist to have got in to St Margaret's. The competition is very strong there, so I've heard,' said Stevie.

'Ever since I was old enough to hold a pencil, I've drawn,' she explained modestly. 'It's the only thing I'm any good at. I really had to slog to get acceptable marks in the other subjects.'

'Andy Warhol had better watch out,' teased Stevie.

'Not yet,' she told him, smiling. 'First of all I hope to get a job in a design consultancy, creating the packaging for consumer goods – you know, chocolate boxes, greetings cards, that sort of thing. As well as giving me independence, it will be good experience and will help to develop my talent. Later, when I've matured a little, I might feel ready to explore the more individual side of art.'

'I'm sure you'll succeed in whatever you decide to do,' he said, ribbing her mildly. 'I recognise stubbornness when I see it.'

'And so do I,' she said, laughing heartily and eyeing him wickedly.

As they chuckled in unison, she seemed to Stevie to glow like a Christmas lantern, exuding warmth and cheer. Having by this time almost drowned in coffee, they mutually decided that it was time to leave.

'I'll walk you home, then get the tube back to Hammersmith,' he said.

'That will be nice,' she said as they clattered out into the warm May night, the scent of lilac blossom from some nearby green or garden prevailing over the traffic fumes and cooking smells from the local restaurants.

'Can I see you again?' asked Stevie as they walked arm in arm along the King's Road beneath a clear, star-sprinkled sky.

'Yes, please,' said Lizzie, looking up at him and smiling.

Chapter Twenty-one

'Stevie is bringing a girlfriend home to lunch on Sunday,' Bella told Pearl and Auntie Vi one afternoon in July, as the three women took tea and scones in the Sharpes' private garden at Lakewood. Pearl was between clients, Vi was having her afternoon break while her staff organised the teas, John was watching some horseracing on television, and Bella had been drawn outside by the sunshine. The Sharpes usually managed to grab some time to themselves on a weekday afternoon when the guests were either out or relaxing, though it was less likely on a summer Saturday when the place was hectic with arrivals and departures.

Although Bella still retained a great deal of personal contact with the guests, her previous years in business had taught her the value of allowing trained staff to take a certain amount of responsibility. Their shift-working receptionists and restaurant manager worked well without supervision, leaving her free to take care of the overall administration, while John was kept busy wherever he was needed, in the bar, in the garden, or on the maintenance of the property. Not desiring too much authority, he was perfectly happy for his enterprising wife to hold a more powerful position.

'Ah, bless 'im,' said Auntie Vi, who looked on Stevie more as a grandson than a great nephew. 'I 'ope 'e'll bring 'er over to the cottage to see us.'

'You bet he will,' said Bella. 'But I won't invite you to join us in the apartment for lunch on her first visit. She might be shy, and you know how daunting it can be visiting a boyfriend's parents for the first time.'

'I might just happen to be passing,' said Pearl wickedly. 'And pop in and have a dekko.'

'Don't you dare,' warned Bella jovially. 'We want to make her welcome, not suffocate her with relatives.'

'Just teasing,' laughed Pearl, 'I have enough of this place during the week without coming back at the weekend.'

'You can meet her another time,' said Bella, glancing idly across the sun-drenched lawns towards the lake, shimmering beneath the trees. This private garden was situated at the side of the property and was separated from the hotel grounds by shrubs, flourishing rose beds and a 'Private' sign, all the handiwork of Uncle Wilf. Whilst recognising the need for a refuge from the guests in summertime, Bella had found the idea of a fence too forbidding somehow. Flower borders seemed much more in keeping with Lakewood's friendliness, offering seclusion without isolation. And, apart from an occasional wandering child, the guests rarely intruded on them here.

While Pearl went to the kitchen for more milk, Auntie Vi asked, 'Has he said much about her?'

'Her name is Lizzie, she's an art student and Stevie seems smitten with her. That's all I know at the moment.'

The three women were having tea in the shade of the colourful sun umbrella fringed with white tassels which topped the marble-effect table. In the hotel grounds guests could be seen taking tea al fresco, or strolling by the lake. Thrushes rustled busily in the cherry trees nearby, and the sounds of conversation carried lightly on the breeze.

'I'd feel happier if my Sandie had a steady boyfriend,' said Pearl, returning and sipping her sea and surveying her companions through fashionable large sunglasses. 'But she seems to go through boyfriends quicker than pairs of tights, out there in Paris.'

Bella and Vi exchanged glances. 'No prizes for guessing who she takes after,' laughed Bella.

Pearl looked affronted. 'Well, perhaps I did like a bit of fun, but Peter was no saint.'

Did! That was a joke, thought Bella, who had had to warn her sister, only recently, about her flirtatious behaviour towards some of the married male guests. Pearl had said Bella was imagining things and Bella wondered if coquetry was more habit than hankering with Pearl after so many years.

From what Bella could make out, her sister's marriage had been a touch and go affair throughout, with both parties matching affair with affair as a sort of point scoring exercise. It was as though they needed the drama and intrigue to keep their adrenaline flowing. And age did not seem to have matured either of them. Yet, oddly enough, despite Bella's earlier doubts, she felt that they would not part for she had perceived that the relationship was an enduring one. Whether because of love, lust, hate or even habit she didn't know, but it did seem stable. Love has many faces, she thought.

'And young Brett is more interested in his pals than girls at the moment,' said Pearl mournfully.

'Make the most of it,' Bella said. 'They'll make you a granny soon enough. And I can't see you liking that very much.'

Bella didn't know Pearl's children at all. They had been to Lakewood once, briefly, with their mother about a year ago when Sandie was home on a visit. Bella had found them rather pretentious and spoiled. Brett had gone into the business with his father and Sandie was now modelling in Paris. Bella had often thought that it was a pity Stevie hadn't grown up closely with his cousins, as she had with hers. Being an only child they would have been company for him. But by the time she and Pearl had reunited, the children were all off on their own. Stevie had not been around the day they had called, so had never seen them.

'She'll be one of these glamorous grannies, won't yer, duck?' said Auntie, who was fond of her niece for all her faults.

'You bet. There'll be no grey hair and sensible shoes for me,' Pearl replied frankly. 'Not while I've got access to a bleach bottle and can still stagger about in stilettoes.'

There were gales of laughter from Bella and Vi.

'You can get away with it too, these days, things are changing for older women,' said Bella.

'And for the younger ones,' said Pearl sagely. 'They're not conditioned to see marriage as their only alternative, as we were. Sandie says she's not going to give up her career to have babies until she's good and ready. At that age all I wanted was to stay at home and be a housewife.'

'With unemployment rising at such a rate, many of them won't have any other choice,' Bella pointed out.

This sobering thought silenced them all for a while. Then Auntie said wistfully, 'It doesn't seem five minutes since you girls were courtin' an' off to meet yer boyfriends' folks. 'Ow does it feel to be on the other side of the coin, Bella?'

'I feel as though I am now officially a member of the older generation, while still remaining the same daft girl inside.' In being reminded of her own girlhood, it was not her first meeting with John's mother, dead these last two years, that filled her mind, but the woman who had so nearly been her mother-in-law. So long ago, yet that terrible tea party at Ivy House, when Dezi had introduced her so proudly as his girlfriend, still smarted as though it was yesterday. It was no bad thing to have recalled the incident because, in reminding her of the agonising sensitivity of youth, it made her vow that, suitable or otherwise, no girlfriend of Stevie's would be a victim of the sort of opposition she herself had received from Eve.

The resolution was easily kept, for Bella found Lizzie to be a charming young woman, so full of life and enthusiasm. And obviously very fond of Stevie.

'This is a wonderful place you have here,' the visitor said over lunch which was eaten late, due to various crises in the hotel, in the Sharpes' apartment. 'If I were Stevie I don't think I would want to leave home, ever.'

Bella beamed. She had been as nervous as a schoolgirl as the luncheon approached. The fact that this girl was obviously special to Stevie had made Bella feel excluded from his life for the first time, and she had been ashamed to experience some pangs of jealousy. But far from losing a son, she felt that she had gained a friend in Lizzie. 'Well, we all have to move on to make our own lives,' she said. 'It's the way of things. But I'm glad you like it. I hope you'll come again. You're welcome, any time.'

Stevie teased Lizzie affectionately. 'You would never be able to live in the country, you're far too much of a Londoner.'

Lizzie smiled prettily at him, her red hair swinging loosely over a fresh green summer dress printed with tiny white flowers. 'But Lakewood isn't too far out. And I just love the feel of it.' She looked around the room with its sloping beamed ceilings, and turned her glance towards the window where, in the distance, turrets and towers rose to the sky. 'What a superb view of the castle you have from here.'

'Yes, isn't it?' said Bella, glad that she had found the time to cook lunch herself, something she did all too rarely these days with well-cooked food always available. It was gratifying to know that she hadn't quite lost her touch with a traditional Sunday roast, as the empty plates proved.

'No one could have been more of a Londoner then Bella,' John said, pouring cream on to his apple pie. 'You could have knocked me down with a feather when she wanted to move out.'

'It was the house that appealed to me,' she said, turning to their guest. 'I fell in love with it at first sight. If it had been in Fulworth, or Hammersmith, or anywhere, I'd have wanted it just the same. And as you say, Lizzie, we are still close to town. The M4 takes you right into central London. Though I must say, I've grown quite fond of Windsor.'

'I know what you mean about the house,' said Lizzie, nodding sagely. 'It has a compelling quality to it.' She finished her second helping of apple pie. 'Stevie tells me that you are from Fulworth. I have loose connections with that area too.

My father was brought up there. My grandmother still lives there, as a matter of fact.'

Bella's eyes lit with interest. 'Does she really? Is she anywhere near Napley Road?'

'I don't know the area very well. My father moved to Putney before I was born and when I visit my grandmother we always stay in the house. She lives right on the river. Ivy House it's called, a big redbrick house with ivy growing on it, backing on to the towpath. Do you know it?'

Not much, Bella thought, her bones liquidising. Only every line and angle of the place. So, why didn't she just say so instead of muttering, 'I may have seen it, but there are several big houses along the towpath.'

'It's too big for Granny Bennett now that she's on her own, but she refuses to move into anything smaller. I suppose you can't blame her, all her memories are there,' said Lizzie kindly.

Bella's head was spinning and perspiration filmed her skin. The girl wasn't Peter's daughter, so she must be . . . Dezi's. Bella longed to steer the conversation away from the subject and pretend she'd not heard the name Bennett. She just couldn't face the implications. But how could she deny knowledge of the Bennett family when her own sister was married to one of them? But perhaps it was possible. After all, Stevie didn't know his cousins, and Bennett was a common enough name.

But to ignore the situation wouldn't change it. If Stevie married this girl he would be the son-in-law of his real father. There was nothing else for it. Bella would have to face up to things and work out what to do. Oh God, was she never to be free of that family? She looked at John and he smiled with his eyes to assure her he would take his lead from her.

Any lingering hopes that they had drawn the wrong conclusions faded as Lizzie said, 'Stevie mentioned something about your being in the garage trade in Fulworth. Funnily enough, my father has a branch there. He isn't based there now, but I think he used to be years ago. His name is Dezi Bennett. Perhaps you might have known him?'

In her anxiety to hide her real connection with Dezi, Bella gave a consummate performance. 'Well, isn't that the most amazing coincidence? My sister is married to your father's brother, Peter.' She raised her hands as though to emphasise her surprise. 'It rang a bell when you said Bennett, but I didn't think it was the same family until you said Dezi.' May God forgive you, Bella Sharpe!

Lizzie thought the connection was great fun. Her face glowed with pleasure. 'Does this mean that Sandie and Brett are Stevie's cousins too?'

'Yes, that's right,' said Bella.

Narrowing her eyes thoughtfully, Lizzie said, 'But Stevie and I are not related, are we?'

'No,' said Bella, thanking God for small mercies.

'My cousins are strangers to me,' said Stevie, looking rather bemused at the whole thing. 'Some family quarrel or something. Mum didn't see her sister for years.'

'I hardly know them either,' Lizzie said, directing her attention to Stevie. 'Daddy and his brother have never been close. They only see each other for business. So I've never seen much of Sandie and Brett. But that's no great loss, they're a spoilt couple of brats.' Her hand flew to her mouth. 'Oh, I'm sorry, Mrs Sharpe. I shouldn't be so rude about your sister's children.'

'Don't worry, my dear. I agree with you, as a matter of fact,' said Bella, managing to force out a smile.

'I don't share their blood though,' Lizzie announced cheerfully. And she went on to tell them something that Bella had known since her trip to Paris and had pushed to the back of her mind.

Bella remembered how tortured by guilt she had been, having deprived Dezi of his son, when he had told her that his only daughter was adopted. Now that same information filled her with relief. Maybe certain confessions were going to be necessary, but at least the romance could continue. But anxiety still prevailed and she longed for their visitor to leave so that she could gather her thoughts and assess the situation properly.

After lunch they took Lizzie for a walk in the grounds, a riot of colour and scent where pinks and pansies, sweet peas and stocks, bloomed brightly among the roses and rhododendrons. Tea was taken at the cottage with Auntie Vi and Trevor and his family, then the young couple headed off on their own towards the lake.

Watching them from the garden as they disappeared into the small wood, Bella closed her eyes and pressed her fingers to her temples as her head pounded with tension. A voice beside her said, 'You've nothing to worry about, you know. She's adopted so there's no biological or legal tie between them.'

She opened her eyes and turned to John, thankful for his deep understanding of her. 'I know, but it still seems wrong, somehow, with her legal father being Stevie's natural one.'

'A mere technicality,' John assured her, sitting down beside her and taking her hand comfortingly. 'I am Stevie's father in the same way as Dezi is hers. There is no need for anyone to know the truth.'

What a good and patient man he was. He made it all seem so simple. 'Yes, you're right,' she said. But still her doubts lingered.

'What do you think of my folks?' asked Stevie as he and Lizzie wandered through the foliage on the far side of the lake. 'Aren't they great?'

'Super,' agreed Lizzie wholeheartedly. 'Really super.'

But a frown hovered beneath her smile. She had indeed found the Sharpes to be a charming couple who had put her at her ease immediately. Such a warmhearted and glamorous mother with whom Lizzie had felt an instant rapport. But later Bella's attitude had changed. Oh, it was almost imperceptible, too slight for anyone else to have noticed. But Lizzie had felt Stevie's mother suddenly putting up barriers. Bewildered, the young woman had racked her brains to fathom exactly when the change had taken place, for she feared she might unknowingly have said something to cause offence. But having sifted through the conversation until her head ached, she could find no reason. It worried her. Stevie obviously adored his parents, and loving him as she did, Lizzie wanted to get along with them because she knew that would please him.

Now they stood under the trees beside the lake, watching some ducks glide by. Stevie turned to her and wrapped her in his arms. 'I love you,' he said.

It was the first time he had said it and she thrilled, melting against him. 'You've only known me a couple of months,' she reminded him.

'That's long enough,' he said.

'Yes. I think it is, too,' she said, kissing him with youthful disregard for some passers-by. 'Because I knew I loved you some time ago.'

'Well, I'll be blowed,' said Pearl, the next morning in response to Bella's news. 'My nephew from one side of the family, courting my niece from the other. Isn't that a turn up for the books? I vaguely remember hearing that Dezi's daughter was good at art, but I haven't seen the girl for years.'

Pearl didn't usually appear at the salon on a Monday. Today she had come in especially to attend to the thinning, octogenarian tresses of the grandmother of one of the cleaning staff, at the special reduced rate set by Bella for senior citizens. Being deprived of her Monday lie-in had soured Pearl's mood and she wished she'd not agreed to do the stupid woman's hair. It was all Bella's fault for making her feel guilty by wittering on about the poor soul having been in hospital and needing to look nice to go away on holiday with her son on Monday afternoon. Having settled her client under the dryer, she had escaped into Bella's office for coffee and a gossip. She lit a cigarette and lowered her voice confidentially.

'Lizzie isn't of Bennett blood, you know,' she said triumphantly. 'She's the love child of a garage mechanic and a typist.'

'So she was saying,' said Bella casually. Pick the bones out of that, you bitch.

'Oh!' Pearl was suitably deflated, 'Dezi told her, did he?'

'She was told some time ago, I think, before Dezi's wife died,' Bella informed her smoothly.

'Fancy telling *you* all her private business,' snorted Pearl, 'when she's only known you five minutes.'

'She's a very open sort of a girl, I think,' said Bella defensively.

'And why shouldn't she tell us? It's nothing to be ashamed of. Her adoption is all legal and above board.'

'Were you as frank with her?' asked Pearl nastily, striking terror into Bella's heart. Had her sister suspected the truth?

'What do you mean?' she asked, her cheeks burning brightly.

'Have you told them that her father is an old flame of yours?'

'No,' said Bella. 'Why should I?'

'Why not? It's nothing to be ashamed of.'

'It's all so long ago. Lizzie and Stevie are far too concerned with themselves to bother about what their parents did when young,' Bella said, calmer now there seemed to be no real danger from Pearl.

'I dunno so much. Kids like a juicy love story, and you were pretty keen on him,' Pearl pointed out.

'If they get serious, I suppose my friendship with Dezi might come up in conversation,' Bella said with feigned nonchalance. 'But I'd rather you didn't say anything for the moment. That sort of thing can undermine a parent's authority.' She moistened her parched mouth with coffee. 'Anyway, Stevie's too young to be considering a permanent relationship.'

'Yes,' said Pearl, feeling more amicable for her bitchy effusion. 'This time next week there might be another girl on the scene. Think how often Sandie changes partners.'

But there wasn't another girl. Not the next week, or the next month. Bella thought the couple might drift apart when Stevie began his career with the prestigious Hilbury Group and moved into a new social environment, but he and Lizzie seemed even closer when they came to Lakewood. She found her affection for Lizzie deepening, though feeling guilty at not having been honest with Stevie, Bella often subconsciously retreated into herself when they were around, functioning superficially, rather than from the heart.

In January 1975, Stevie telephoned to say that he was coming to Lakewood for the weekend, alone. Shamefully, Bella revelled in the thought that she and John would have their son to themselves for a change. But within minutes of his arrival she realised that she missed Lizzie dreadfully. The girl had become like a daughter to her. Stevie wasn't nearly so much fun without her. In fact, he seemed very tense.

Whilst suspecting that the romance was over, Bella and John kept diplomatically silent on the subject, allowing him to unburden himself in his own time. This development filled Bella with conflicting emotions. From a purely selfish point of view it would be simpler if they parted, for marriage would bring Dezi back into her life with constant reminders of the past and how she had deceived both him and Stevie. But deep in her heart she was depressed at the thought of a split, for Stevie's happiness must be her prime concern and she felt that this lay with Lizzie. Seldom had she seen a couple more right for each other.

On the Saturday evening, John had to make up a staff deficit in the bar as soon as they had finished dinner, leaving Bella and Stevie to have their coffee alone.

'We have several staff off with flu,' explained Bella as she and Stevie settled down by the log fire. She felt apprehensive, for she guessed that her son wished to speak to her confidentially. He would have offered to make up the staff shortage in place of John otherwise.

'I'll go downstairs and relieve Dad in the bar later,' he offered, 'but I'd like a few words with you alone first.'

Now that the end of his affair was about to be made

official, she could hardly bear it. She felt her fingers tensing around her cup. But the conversation didn't go as she expected.

'Do you like Liz?' he asked simply.

'Why, yes, of course, I'm very fond of her,' Bella said, flushing at the implication. 'Surely you know that.'

He looked sheepish. '*I* do yes, but she isn't so sure.' He raked his hair boyishly. 'You always make her welcome here and are friendly enough on the surface, but she says she often picks up bad vibes from you. She thinks she must have offended you in some way. And because she is so fond of you she would like to know what it is so that she can rectify the matter. She does want to be friends.'

Bella was stunned. Had she really been that transparent in the guilt that her son's romance perpetuated? Obviously she had, for Lizzie wouldn't invent a thing like that. 'Well, I've never meant to be cold,' she said, dry-mouthed and anxious. 'Perhaps I was preoccupied with business matters or something. I can assure you that Lizzie has never caused offence. On the contrary, she is a delight to have around.'

Stevie looked relieved. 'I knew she was worrying unnecessarily, but you know how sensitive these creative types are.'

'*She* asked you to speak to me about it, did she?' Bella asked in surprise, for Lizzie had always struck her as a very independent young woman.

He nodded. 'Yes, she thought you might be too embarrassed to tell her the truth if she had upset you in some way. She wanted me to clear the air before I told you about our plans.'

'Plans?'

He beamed. 'Yes, I've come to see you on my own to tell you that we are going to get engaged at Easter.'

'Engaged!'

'Well, don't sound so shocked,' he said, disappointment colouring his tone. 'Surely you must have been expecting it. Or did you think that we were going to be fashionable and live in sin together?'

'Well, no,' she said, putting her cup down with a shaky hand. 'I suppose I hadn't expected anything like this yet. You're still quite young, after all.' She didn't believe that. It was just an excuse to give credibility to her visible anxiety.

'I'm not all that young, I'll be twenty-two this year,' he pointed out.

'Yes, so you will. Are you planning a long engagement?' she asked, playing for time to accustom herself to the situation.

'We want to get married in the summer,' said Stevie.

'What! This summer?' Bella asked, taken aback by the speed with which things were happening.

'Yes, when Lizzie has finished at college.' He looked at his mother sharply, as though daring her to oppose him. 'We know that we're right for each other and we don't want to wait. If we were going to drift apart after college, we would have done so when I left.'

'How does her father feel about it?' Bella asked, her heart in her mouth.

'I don't know yet,' he admitted. 'She's spending the weekend with him to break the news. I doubt if he'll make any strong objections. She's almost twenty-one, after all, and I do have a job with good prospects.'

So they had both gone solo to parents to break the news. Rather touching, she thought. 'Well,' she said, rising and going over to his chair, 'since you have obviously thought this thing through, all that remains is for me to congratulate you.' As he rose she hugged him and kissed his cheek. 'Congratulations, son. I'm sure you'll both be very happy. Lizzie is a lovely girl.'

Stevie's face glowed like a lit window on a foggy day. Whatever personal difficulties this union might cause for Bella, she would willingly bear them just to see him as happy as he was at this moment.

'Now that it's official, we'll have to arrange for you and Dad to get together with Lizzie's father,' suggested Stevie.

'Yes, I'll look forward to that,' she said truthfully, for how could it be otherwise? But she felt as though she was sinking in quicksand.

Her son faced her in the firelight, so eager and intense, his tall, lean form clad in a navy blue fisherman's sweater over blue jeans, his thick brown hair flopping untidily on to his brow. How like his father he was. It might have been the young Dezi standing there, his rich brown eyes resting on her earnestly. But she must push all selfish thoughts from her mind for it wasn't right to let her past interfere with her son's future.

'In the meantime, we ought to put your dad in the picture,' she said, smiling.

'Yes, of course. He won't mind that I told you first, will he? I wanted to clear the other business up with you on your own and the rest just sort of slipped out,' he said, reminding her of his youthfulness.

'You know him better then that,' Bella said. 'He doesn't take offence at trivialities.'

'No, he's a good old stick,' said Stevie affectionately.

'Not so much of the "old",' Bella laughed. 'But let's go downstairs and you can tell him your news, and then we'll open a bottle of champagne to celebrate.'

'I'll give him a hand, too,' said Stevie. And mother and son went downstairs together, smiling.

'They took it really well,' Stevie said to Lizzie over his bedside extension later that night. 'Your dad was okay about it, too? Terrific ... And I love you, too ... Yes, I'll see you tomorrow ... No, I can't wait either. Goodnight, darling. Sleep well. Love you.'

He replaced the receiver and lay back against the pillow, weak with longing for her. It had been her idea for them to tell their parents separately. 'It's a big thing to them, especially with us both being only children,' she had said. 'We don't want them to feel as though they are going to be excluded from our lives. You tell yours and I'll tell mine. Make a bit of a fuss of them, you know.'

She really was the most thoughtful girl and weekends were too precious to spend away from her. He mulled over his parents' reaction to the news, wondering why his mother had been so devastated initially. Oh, she had soon recovered and put up a front, but there was no denying that first look of horror. Something was bothering her, Lizzie was right. Surely it couldn't be that she saw Lizzie as a rival for his affections; Mum just wasn't the possessive type. Love without suffocation was what he had grown up with. Oh well, whatever it was she was obviously going to keep it to herself, so the best thing he could do was to forget it. And he certainly wasn't going to upset Lizzie by mentioning it to her.

A rumbling in his stomach reminded him that, in all the excitement, he had eaten less than usual. Knowing that the gnawing ache would not let him sleep, he swung out of bed, slipped into his towelling robe and headed towards the kitchen in search of sustenance.

'You've got the whole thing out of proportion,' John told Bella firmly, distressed to see her so unnecessarily upset. 'As I said before, there's no moral or legal reason for Stevie and Lizzie not to marry. And no reason at all why Stevie should be told that Dezi Bennett is his real father.'

They were sitting either side of the smouldering fire in the apartment lounge, in their dressing gowns, drinking cocoa. Without Bella saying a word, John had known that Stevie's announcement earlier this evening had rocked her and he had suggested that they talk the thing through here, since their bedroom was a little too close to Stevie's for such a private conversation.

'You don't think he should know that his father-in-law will actually be his biological father?' she asked.

'No, I don't' he assured her forcefully. 'Stevie is a person in his own right. What does it matter who actually sired him? If I thought any good would come of us telling him, I'd insist that we do so.' He raised his hands emphatically, and watching the firelight flicker over his unusual pallor, she realised the strain this put on him, too. 'The only thing that will benefit from a confession is your conscience,' he told her bluntly.

She brushed a weary hand across her brow. 'Oh dear, am I really being that selfish?'

'Never that,' he told her. 'But in your anxiety to do the right thing, you could unwittingly cause a great deal of pain. It's too late for the truth. Both of us have done our best for

Stevie, and his future is set fair. Don't spoil it by burdening him with things that happened before he was born.'

Once again she felt calmed by John's down-to-earth logic. And this time she knew she must accept his advice once and for all. For he could so easily be hurt if she allowed her doubts to drive her to action.

'You're right,' she said, 'I'll put it out of my mind for good and all.' She yawned and noticed that she was nursing an empty cup. 'All this talking has made me thirsty. Would you like some more cocoa before we go to bed.'

'Yes please, if you're getting some for yourself,' he said.

On her way to the kitchen, she felt much more relaxed. Almost lighthearted, in fact. It was going to be such fun having a daughter-in-law and, later, grandchildren. Her a granny! What a ridiculous thought for a woman who still felt seventeen inside. She was smiling as she opened the door. But not for long. For standing outside was Stevie, ashen-faced and accusing. He had obviously heard everything.

'What a good job I decided to go to the kitchen to get something to eat,' he said coldly. 'Otherwise, I might never have discovered who I really am.'

She couldn't speak. When she reached out to him, he moved away as though fearing contamination.

John had heard Stevie's voice and was at her side. 'Come and sit down, Stevie,' he said shakily. 'We need to talk.'

He stumbled into the room as though in a daze and stood with his back to the fire, staring at his parents who were huddled together just inside the door.

'What is there to say?' he asked, looking from one to the other. 'I know that I am the product of some tacky affair with Lizzie's father, and that neither of you had the decency to tell me. Apart from that, nothing else matters.' He marched to the drinks cabinet and poured himself a brandy.

'It wasn't like that at all,' began Bella.

'My God, what hypocrites the older generation are,' he interrupted rudely, 'with your lectures about morality, and your disgust at today's sexually liberated society!' He gulped the brandy, grimacing because it wasn't a drink he was used to. 'And you call our generation irresponsible. I wouldn't call hiding someone's true identity a responsible action.' His eyes black with rage, he turned on his mother. 'Was it a one-night stand? Where did it happen? In the bushes, in the back of a car?'

The room resounded with the crack of John's hand across Stevie's cheek. 'Don't you dare speak to your mother like that,' he rasped, grey with temper. 'Don't you dare.'

But Stevie barely seemed to notice. He rubbed his cheek absently, eyes now flashing wildly at John. 'Why not?' he asked. 'She doesn't deserve my respect. Neither of you do. You've lied to me all these years.'

'Your mother deserves more than your respect,' John replied, his voice cracking with emotion. 'She deserves your admiration. A mother in a million she's been to you.'

'Just let me explain how it was,' Bella intervened desperately.

Down went Stevie's glass with a bang. 'Spare me the details,' he said, his voice wavering on the verge of tears. 'Isn't it enough that you've mucked up my life? I can't marry Lizzie now, knowing that I'm just the result of her father's wild oats.'

'Of course you can marry her, there's no blood tie between you,' John pointed out.

'There's more to life than biology,' Stevie snarled. 'There's such a thing as self-respect.' He turned to John. 'I suppose

I'm expected to be eternally grateful to you for saving me from being a bastard.' His eyes narrowed. 'Or did I actually go to your wedding outside of the womb?'

Now Bella was angry. There was no call for this boorish behaviour. 'Of course not, we were married long before. No one suspected anything ... John has been a wonderful father.'

'And that makes it all right, does it?' he interrupted bitterly. 'That the world has been fooled.'

'It was different in those days,' said Bella. 'I did what I thought was best for you at the time. There are things you don't know. Certain things happened ...'

Her words hung feebly in the air. Stevie seemed to have discounted any idea that he might have been the product of love, and before his mind could be opened to the facts, he said, 'I can't stay here a moment longer. I shall go back to London tonight.'

'You mustn't drive your car,' warned John. 'The wine you had with dinner added to the champagne will put you over the limit.'

'The car can stay here permanently. I don't want it,' he said bitterly.

His words struck like a knife to Bella's heart, for his MGBGT sports car had been his twenty-first birthday present from his parents. Her pain was magnified by the look of anguish on her husband's face.

'Don't be so childish,' she snapped. 'There are no buses or trains into London at this time of night.'

'Then I'll hitch or wait on the station platform 'til morning,' said Stevie with an insolent shrug. 'Anything is better than staying here.' And with that he marched from the room.

'Leave him,' said John, clapping a hand on Bella's arm to

restrain her as she made to go after him. 'He needs time to cool off. You won't get him to see sense at the moment.'

'Oh, John,' she cried miserably, taking refuge in the strong shelter of his arms. 'Whatever shall we do?'

'Nothing, right now,' he said sagely. 'He won't listen to the facts while he's in this mood. We'll have to wait until he's calmed down.'

Chapter Twenty-two

The sound of the door chimes echoing inside the sleeping house as he pressed his finger hard down on the bell button, gave Stevie a perverse sense of satisfaction. 'That'll get the bastard out of bed,' he snarled to himself. 'And I hope he breaks a leg on the way downstairs.'

It was a few hours since he'd stormed out of Lakewood. He was still so consumed by rage he barely noticed that, having hitched only part of the way to Putney and walked the rest, he was frozen to the bone and exhausted. It was a clear, bitter night, the moonlight on the frost producing a bright opalescence which illumined the shadows in front of this imposing, lattice-windowed house. Not that Stevie noticed the silvery stillness. He had too much on his mind.

A light appeared in the hall window and the door was opened by an irate, tousle-haired Dezi. 'Good God,' he said, his expression changing from annoyance to concern. 'It's you, Stevie. Whatever are you doing here? You'd better come in.'

Stevie's hurt and self-absorbtion didn't allow for sensitivity to the feelings of others. The explosion came even before the door was closed after him.

'You bastard!' he hissed vehemently. 'You rotten, stinking bastard.'

Dezi closed the door and pulled his dark blue robe more closely around him, shivering from the lingering draught. His expression was more of bewilderment than anger, though having been woken so abruptly his patience was not at its best. 'Well,' he said coldly, 'since you've woken me up at four o'clock in the morning to enlighten me on that fact, perhaps you'd have the decency to tell me how I come to qualify for the title.' He waved a hand towards the drawing room. 'Come in here. And keep your voice down. I don't want my daughter disturbed because of some brain storm of yours.'

But a startled voice from the stairs indicated that the damage was already done. 'Who was that at the door, Daddy?' asked Lizzie. 'Oh, Stevie, it's you. Whatever is going on?'

Even the presence of the woman he loved did not deter Stevie. 'Go back to bed, Lizzie,' he said coldly, sparing her only a glance as she peered over the banisters. 'This is between your father and me.'

Never a submissive type, she seemed about to retaliate but, reminding herself that this behaviour was quite contrary to Stevie's normal personality, she retreated silently up the stairs.

Behind closed doors it was Dezi's turn to expostulate. 'You've got a nerve, coming to my house, insulting me and upsetting my daughter!' he exclaimed furiously, standing with his back to the unlit hearth, his eyes heavy from interrupted sleep. 'Now say what you've got to say and get out.'

'I know everything, *Father*,' Stevie said sarcastically, and went on to relate the earlier events, selfishly unaware of the impact that this was having on the older man. 'I suppose she was an easy lay,' he concluded. 'And even easier to leave in the lurch.'

Dezi's reaction to this was identical to John's. 'Don't you dare speak about your mother like that,' he said, giving Stevie his second slap across the face that night. 'And don't you *dare* judge her for something you know nothing about.'

As it had been earlier, Stevie's reaction was minimal. He held his hand briefly to his cheek and continued to survey Dezi scornfully, his mind in turmoil. In his current confusion he did not blame Dezi more than Bella, or Bella more than John. They all seemed to be bound together in some sort of a conspiracy designed to ruin his life. He hated the lot of them. That he might be the product of love was the last thing on his mind. He saw himself only as some ghastly mistake.

An ashen Dezi walked shakily to a carved oak drinks cabinet and poured himself a whisky, without extending an invitation to his guest. He swallowed the liquid quickly, knowing that he must maintain his composure in front of this angry young man.

'The irony of it is,' continued Stevie, speaking without really considering how hurtful his words might be, 'that you turned your back on your own flesh and blood, yet you adopted Lizzie.'

Dezi stood with glass in hand surveying his son, who looked pale and monk-like with the hood of his dark anorak still covering his head. 'You probably won't believe this, given your current unreasoning frame of mind,' he said, 'but until a few moments ago I had no idea that you were my son.' He swallowed some whisky and shook his head as though this might help the revelation to register properly. 'No idea at all.'

'Oh!' This had not occurred to Stevie and he was taken aback. 'Surely you don't expect me to believe that?' he said scornfully at last.

'It's entirely up to you whether you believe it or not,' said Dezi, soured by Stevie's appalling behaviour. 'I don't have to justify myself to you. But I can assure you that it is true. I am as shocked as you by this news.'

And while his son seemed stunned into silence, Dezi sank into an armchair, weak with emotion. Even if Stevie's trauma had not rendered him incapable of viewing this situation from any other viewpoint but his own, he could never have known how deeply affected Dezi was by it. But above a plethora of confused emotions one sentiment reigned supreme, and that was sheer elation in the fact that Stevie, for all his present belligerence, was *his* natural son. How Dezi held back the joyful tears he never knew.

'Is it really true that you didn't know?' asked Stevie, slumping into a chair and eyeing Dezi warily.

'Why should I lie about it, knowing that you could easily check me out?' he asked. 'I'm sure that your mother would have told you of my ignorance of the matter, if you had given her the chance.'

'So Mum cheated on us both, is that what you're saying?' Stevie asked, bravado almost giving way to tears.

Wearily, Dezi accepted that his own personal feelings must be put aside for the moment. 'It isn't quite as simple as that,' he said.

'I hate her,' barked Stevie, 'and that man who calls himself my father. I never want to see either of them again.'

'You are being very childish, not to mention selfish,' Dezi pointed out. He paused, resting his eyes on the young man. 'Use your brain, boy. You are healthy and well educated. You have a good job with prospects. You have never known a moment's hardship in your life. Those things didn't happen of their own accord. Think yourself lucky that you have such caring parents and stop condemning them for things you know nothing about.' He raised his hands in a gesture of restraint as Stevie tried to interrupt. 'And whether you like it or not, John Sharpe *is* your father, both legally and emotionally. You and I are strangers. So go back home to them. Make your peace with them. Let them tell you how and why things are as they are.'

But Stevie was implacable. 'How can you take their side?' he asked, his mouth trembling slightly. 'Were you glad you didn't know about me? Is that it? Are you afraid that I might want you as a father now? Well, you've no need to worry . . .'

'I am very proud to have you as my son,' interrupted Dezi. Oh God, the boy didn't know the half of it! 'But I have no claim on you. Your mother and John have brought you up. Your loyalty lies with them. Whatever you feel for them at this moment, they have done their best for you and given you a good life. You know that, but you're too damned stubborn to admit it.'

'If you gave a tuppenny toss for me, you'd be outraged at being deprived of me all these years,' said Stevie. 'Why aren't you?'

Dezi sighed. Until now he had not realised just how much he had mellowed with age. If this news had come to him as a younger man, he'd probably have hot-footed it to Bella with murder in his heart. One of the bonuses of maturity was an increased quota of tolerance. Sure, he resented the fact that John Sharpe had taken his most precious gift. But he could live with that until he had put Stevie on the right lines. Then perhaps he could gather his own thoughts on the subject.

'Because of something that you will not understand until

you learn the whole story,' said Dezi. 'And that you must hear from your mother.' He paused, relieved to notice that Stevie's anger seemed to have subsided. The boy was silent suddenly, and very still. 'But right now you need some sleep, and to get warm. So you go and have a hot bath and I'll make up a bed for you in the spare room. Then I'll telephone your parents to let them know where you are. They'll be worried about you.'

Stevie didn't reply for a while. When he did, his spikiness had turned to an ominous calm. 'No thanks,' he said, rising. 'I'm going home to my own place. I don't need charity from any of you.'

'Don't be a fool, Stevie,' urged Dezi, stepping towards him anxiously. 'It's freezing outside. Just stay until the morning. We'll talk some more.'

But Stevie was already heading for the door, a ghostly pallor suffusing his face.

'*Stevie!*' Dezi tore to the front door after him.

Hearing the noise in the hall, Lizzie raced down the stairs, begging Stevie not to leave. But without another word he marched down the front path, his footsteps resounding in the slumbering avenue, while Dezi and Lizzie stood powerless at the front door.

'Don't worry, he'll come around,' Dezi assured his daughter, 'And in the meantime, I think I owe you an explanation.'

It was dawn before an enlightened Lizzie went back to bed and Dezi was alone at last with his chaotic thoughts. Huddled into an armchair, memories consumed him. In retrospect, it seemed clear to him that the blame for this emotional muddle lay at his father's door for initiating the events that had unbal-anced Bella's mind and impaired her judgement at such a crucial time. At least now Dezi knew why she had married John. Not for love, but to give the child a name. How it must have hurt her to keep it from him all these years! There was no anger left in him. Only sadness for everything he had missed.

Whatever the problems, however, nothing could diminish his pleasure in the glorious fact that Stevie *was* his natural son. He hoped that they could become friends when the boy had come to terms with the situation. For friendship was the most that Dezi could hope for. It was too late for a filial relationship, however much he might wish it. That belonged to John. Dezi could imagine how devastated he himself would be if Lizzie's natural parents suddenly appeared on the scene and vied with him for her affections.

Tiredness overcame him and he leaned back and closed his eyes. But then, remembering two other people who would not have slept tonight, he hauled himself to the telephone and dialled the Sharpes' number. He couldn't tell them that all was well, but at least he could put them up to date on Stevie's mood and movements.

Lizzie stared at Stevie in hurt astonishment. 'You are mad, Stevie Sharpe, absolutely bonkers.'

It was a few days later and they were in her room in the flat she shared in Chelsea. A modest student home with a bed, desk, drawing board, armchair, sofa, and a hi-fi on which Bob Dylan was singing at low volume. A variety of posters adorned the walls, a mixture of art and pop stars, and Lizzie's drawings lay untidily all around.

'Maybe I am, but that's the way I feel,' he said, still very pale, his eyes heavily shadowed.

She searched his face, finding those rich expressive eyes now blank and lacklustre, the mouth grim and unsmiling. 'Do you mean to tell me that you are going to wreck both our lives because of something that happened before we were born?' she asked desperately.

He nodded. 'I am ending our relationship, yes. I'm sorry, but I have no alternative.'

'I don't believe I'm hearing this!' exclaimed Lizzie, flopping down on the edge of the bed looking small and girlish in a white sweater and blue jeans, her hair tied back in a ponytail. 'I can understand your being shocked by this business with Daddy, but that has nothing to do with you and me. There is no genetic link between us, so it doesn't matter.'

'It's changed the way I feel. I'm not the same person now,' he growled.

'Don't you think you're being over-dramatic?' she said, staring up at him as he leaned mournfully against her desk. 'If you're going to dwell on the technicalities of your origin, I might as well dwell on mine and think of my father as a garage mechanic. Would that make you feel happier?'

He shrugged. 'Not really,' he said studying his shoes.

'I see,' she said with icy politeness as she realised he was deadly serious. 'This is all just an excuse because you don't want to get engaged.'

'Of course it isn't,' he denied.

'You either love me or you don't,' snapped Lizzie, feeling her world crumble around her. 'And you obviously don't or you wouldn't be doing this to me.'

'I'm all mixed up, Lizzie,' he explained, 'I want to get away from everyone, my parents, your father, the whole bloody lot.'

Two scarlet patches on Lizzie's cheeks stood out against her unnatural pallor. 'Me included,' she said miserably.

'Well, yes, I suppose that is what I mean,' he said, throwing her a sheepish look. 'But there's nothing lacking in you. It's the older generation who have screwed it up for us.'

Lizzie leapt to her feet and glared at him, her hands on her hips. 'Oh, don't pass the blame because you're too much of a coward to tell me the truth,' she said, fighting against tears. 'There is no earthly reason why we shouldn't continue with our plans except that you don't want to.'

'If you say so,' he said coldly.

'Please don't do this, Stevie.' She slipped her arms around him in a desperate attempt to change his mind. But feeling him flinch away from her she pulled back, and stared at him disbelievingly. How could this be happening when just a few days ago they had been so happy? 'Oh, get out of here,' she said. 'Go on, get out.'

She turned away and didn't move until she heard him close her door and thunder down the stairs. Then, she burst into tears.

Bella sank her hands into the pockets of her anorak as she walked along the riverbank near Lakewood, her face smarting from wind and rain on this grey January day. The rain gusted across the muddy waters and beat unevenly on the moored boats. This was a very different stretch of the river from the one that had soothed her as a girl. Here, there was no city smoke and grime, no factories or warehouses. Just expensive cruisers, smart pubs, fashionable restaurants and beautiful houses with private moorings. Here, riverside strollers wore Burberry raincoats and walked pedigree dogs. They went ski-ing in winter and owned villas in the sun. This was the land of stockbrokers and television stars.

The bitter wind in her face was positively welcome to Bella. She found it invigorating after so many sleepless nights. It was two weeks since the scene with Stevie and they had had no word from him. A telephone call to his flat and his office revealed that he had left both, giving no forwarding address. Bella and John had been forced to accept the fact that they would see Stevie again only when, and if, he wanted it. When Bella, in desperation, had suggested that they contact Hilbury again, for they would be sure to be asked for a reference by his new employer, John had been adamantly opposed to the idea. 'We'll drive him further away if we pursue him,' he'd said. 'The first move must come from him.' And, sadly, she had agreed.

Dezi had been wonderful, she thought. How good it was of him to visit them at Lakewood and assure John that he had no intention of trying to encroach on Stevie's affections. The meeting had been surprisingly civilised and without any harsh recriminations from Dezi. 'Naturally, I wish things had been different,' he'd said, 'but it's too late for hysterics, what's done is done.' It was as though Stevie's disappearance had diminished the importance of the bitter history behind it.

Now she shivered as the wind penetrated her clothes. Whilst she could see that Stevie had every right to be upset and angry with her, she could see no justification for his appalling treatment of John who had given him so much. The poor man was devastated. Stevie meant the world to him. Please get in touch, Stevie, she prayed into the wind, please get in touch.

★　★　★

'That sure was a lovely meal, Mrs Sharpe,' said Harry Baxter, a jovial American who was staying at Lakewood with his wife. 'Ain't that so, Alma?'

'It sure is,' agreed his wife readily, and turning to Bella added, 'I just *love* this house of yours. Just wait 'til we tell the folks back home that we stayed in a place with a castle in the backyard.'

'Well, not quite in the backyard,' said Bella, smiling at them across the reception desk. 'But I'm very glad you're comfortable.'

The Baxters were charming septuagenarians with all the warmth and effusiveness for which their race was known. Stylish in their bright clothes, which paid no deference to age, they breezed energetically through Lakewood, equipped with camera and tourist guides. Bella liked them very much. Indeed, she had found visitors from the USA to be the most enjoyable of guests. Naturally, given their own indigenous standards, they expected first-class service, but their gratitude was usually heartfelt.

'Did you get around to doing those couple of favours for us?' asked Harry.

Bella nodded and smiled her automatic public smile. 'Yes. I've ordered a car for you from the hire company and it will be here first thing in the morning. I've also booked you those seats you wanted for that West End show. The tickets will be at the booking office for you.' She handed a brochure to Harry. 'And here is a booklet about Windsor Castle. You'll find the visiting times inside.'

'Why, thank you,' said Harry. 'That's mighty nice of you.'

The couple looked through the literature while Bella answered the phone to a prospective guest, took an internal service call, assured a fraught understaffed barman on the intercom that help was on the way even if she came personally to assist him, and made polite conversation with chatty passing guests.

It was Easter Sunday evening and Lakewood had hummed with hectic activity all week, with every room booked and every table taken in the restaurant. It made life difficult enough having a barman and a receptionist taken sick at this busy start to the season, but with John being poorly too, things were practically impossible for Bella.

'Is your hubby still not well?' asked Alma, noticing the frantic pace at which Bella was functioning.

'He isn't too good, I'm afraid,' said Bella.

'Nothing serious, I hope,' said Harry in concern.

'Oh no, it's just a migraine, I think,' lied Bella brightly. 'He'll live.'

'Well, don't *you* kill yourself with work,' warned Harry kindly. 'You're a great little lady. We don't want you getting sick from too much rushing about.'

'Don't worry about me,' she said, his kindness added to the strain of these last few months making her feel dangerously close to tears. 'I thrive on hard work. It keeps me young.'

The Baxters shuffled off and Bella tore into the bar to help clear the rush there, knowing that she would have to dive back and forth to Reception until the night porter came on duty. Migraine, my eye! Malingering, more like. As if she didn't have enough on her plate with still no word from Stevie in over two months, John has to get an attack of lazyitis. It was most unlike him but there seemed to be nothing wrong with him apart from a sudden tendency to lie around in bed. No, he didn't feel ill, he assured her, and no he didn't need a doctor, he was just very tired. A reaction to the trouble with Stevie, she suspected.

Admittedly, Bella used perpetual activity as a friend and comforter to blot out the heartache of losing Stevie, but there was only so much that one pair of hands could do. If John didn't pull himself together soon, she would have to employ someone to take over his duties.

That night when she crawled up to the apartment, aching with tiredness and a splitting headache, to find John asleep on the sofa and the dishes, that she had not had time to wash that morning, still greasily waiting for attention in the sink, her irritation was tinged with concern. He obviously needed some sort of psychiatric help.

'You are going to see the doctor right after the Easter holiday,' she whispered wearily to the sleeping man. 'I am going to make sure of that.'

And so it was that at the end of April 1975 the Sharpes received their worst blow yet. Tests revealed not a psychological malady but a physical one. A terminal blood disease. A few months was all John had left.

Bella's initial reaction was rage against the Almighty for what seemed to her to be an appalling travesty of justice. Why John? What had he ever done to deserve such a fate? And why must everyone that she cared for be taken from her prematurely? Her mother, her cousin, her father, and now her husband. She had never felt more alone. For now she could not run to her husband's strong, safe arms. They were no longer strong or safe.

The period of self pity was quickly replaced by compassion for John and an uneasy conscience at having been impatient with him. He also went through a difficult period of adjustment after learning the truth about his illness, weeping a lot and losing interest in everything. But once that had worked its way through his system, he seemed to Bella to be unbearably brave, on better days almost like his old self.

But the strain took its toll on Bella. 'I feel so inadequate, Auntie,' she confessed one night in May when the kitchen staff had gone and she and her aunt were alone in the kitchen, checking the menus for the next day. 'I want to make John's last months happy, but I just don't think I can cope. I feel so afraid. I can't bear the pain of bereavement again.'

Auntie made a pot of tea and sat opposite her niece at the big working table, her wrinkled face full of concern. 'You'll cope, luv,' she said kindly but firmly. 'It's a case of havin' to, I'm afraid. An' you'll do it, believe me. Yer learned all about copin' at an early age when yer mother was taken. We all 'ave an inbuilt reserve of courage that doesn't surface 'til we need it, yer know. I learned that when Don died.'

'I feel as though I need John to help me through this, but of course it's him who needs me,' said Bella, sipping her tea. 'I *have* to be strong, especially as he gets weaker.'

'Take plenty of time orf to be with him,' Auntie suggested. 'The restaurant manager knows enough to hold the fort, an' we can take on someone to replace him in the restaurant. Wilf an' me will help out an' I'm sure the staff will rally round. No one is indispensable, yer know.'

'Yes, I'll do that, but if I give up work altogether John will feel he's a burden,' Bella pointed out. 'And I would probably go nuts. You know me, work has always been my salvation.'

'It's a shame Stevie ain't around,' said Auntie, who was fully informed as to the reason for the Sharpes' recent upheaval. 'If 'e came back, John would die an 'appy man. The boy ought to be told, yer know. An' yer could probably trace him through 'is last employer.'

'I've already thought of that,' said Bella, having mentioned this to her husband again in the light of their changed circumstances. 'But John is dead set against it. He says it would be emotional blackmail and would bring Stevie back out of duty not choice.'

'Duty or love, Stevie ought to be 'ere,' Auntie opined. ''E should be at 'is mother's side at a time like this. An' 'im an' John 'ave always been such pals, it wouldn't be right for his dad to go without things being patched up between them.'

'I agree,' said Bella. 'But it would be wrong of me to go against John's wishes.'

'I dunno so much about that,' said Auntie, her blue eyes resting shrewdly on her niece. 'People don't always know what's best for 'em.'

'Perhaps Stevie will come to his senses of his own accord in time,' she suggested hopefully, choking back the tears, 'I couldn't go against John, not now.'

'Yer must do what yer think best,' said Auntie, pouring them both another cup of tea.

And so, as the bleached spring leaves gave way to luxuriant summer greenery, Bella rose to the challenge, her biggest yet. John's condition fluctuated. On good days he was up and about and appreciative of every moment; other times he slept more or less continuously.

One good day in early August, Bella and John ambled slowly down to the river, now one of his favourite activities. Taking a gentle stroll upstream, they sat down on the bank in the sunshine amid the willows and hawthorns that sporadically edged the water in this remote spot. The trees twitched and twittered with birdlife; butterflies quivered delicately by; the water splashed softly against the bank.

But suddenly the peace was shattered by a streamlined cabin cruiser gliding sleekly past with a crowd of youngsters on board, the air ringing with the sound of youthful voices and pop music.

'I wonder how Stevie is,' said John wistfully, chewing a blade of grass. 'I hope he didn't harm his career by giving up his job just so that we couldn't contact him.'

'He was upset, but I don't think he'd have done anything stupid,' Bella said, clasping John's thin hand in a comforting gesture. 'He must have been fairly confident about getting another position. He does have quite an impressive CV, remember.'

'Yes, you're probably right,' he agreed. 'I do miss him, Bel, we were like best mates.'

'Why don't you let me try to find him?' she asked earnestly, searching her husband's pale face. 'It isn't as though we don't have a lead. I'm sure Hilbury's will be able to help.'

'And what will you do if you find him? Tell him to do his duty and come and see the old man before he pops off,' said John, staring down into water still choppy from the wash of the boat. 'No, Bel, that isn't what I want.'

'Don't you think he has a right to know?'

'He forfeited that when he stormed off without giving us a chance to explain,' he said, his hand trembling in hers. 'When I've gone, you can put Scotland Yard on to finding him if you like but I don't want him coming to see me out of pity. My health might have deserted me, but not my pride.'

Bella felt the passing of time beating through her body like the chimes of Big Ben. Another boat cruised by with a tanned man at the helm and a bronzed woman sunbathing on the deck in a white bikini. Bella experienced a moment of envy for their carefree life, and realised just how much she had taken for granted in those halcyon days of casual tomorrows.

'And on the subject of afterwards,' said John, 'I think you should consider remarrying.'

'Don't say such things,' she admonished.

'Why not?' he asked. 'We both know the score. And I'd hate to think of you spending the rest of your life alone. You're still quite a young woman with a lot to give. Don't waste your energy grieving for me.'

Bella listened quietly, realising that this was not just empty talk designed to evoke sympathy. He really did care about her future.

'Of course you'll be sad for a while, I know that,' he continued. 'I also know that you'll cope without me. You are a strong woman, a doer, you always have been. But everyone needs someone. We've had a good marriage, you and me. Not the romance of the century perhaps, I've always accepted that you didn't care for me in the same way as you did for Stevie's father. You married me because you needed someone and I just happened to be in the right place at the right time. But I could live with that. I've been happy to be the back-up man in your life. The worst part of being sick, for me, is not being able to give you that back-up support any more. When it's all over, I hope you'll find happiness with someone else. God knows you deserve it.'

'Don't you worry about me,' she urged him. 'I'll be all right.'

'One day, years ago,' he continued, his head bent towards the water meditatively, 'before you and me got together, I watched you and Dezi meet at the garage. I saw you light up

419

for each other. I've never seen two people so happy to be together. Of course, I was green with envy because I had already begun to fall in love with you.'

'It was all so long ago,' she said soothingly.

'When Dezi came to Lakewood to see us just after Stevie went away,' he continued as though she hadn't spoken, 'that light was still there between you. Oh, I doubt if either of you noticed it in the tension of the moment. But it was there, all right.'

'I'm so sorry if you were hurt by it,' she said, anxiously studying his tense profile.

'Don't be,' he said, and as he turned towards her he was smiling. 'I've always thought of Dezi Bennett as a threat, it's true, but that's all over now. I want you to grab your happiness, wherever it lies, with my blessing.'

'I don't even want to think about my life without you,' she said, close to tears.

'Just bear what I've said in mind when the time is right,' he urged her.

'I will.'

And as she conceded the issue, she knew that she must oppose his wishes on another matter. In his own best interests.

Chapter Twenty-three

Stevie washed the dishes after his solitary meal and, leaving them to drain, went into his poky living room, mopping the perspiration from his brow with a handkerchief on this stifling August evening, the hottest day in London for thirty-five years according to the media.

Flopping into an armchair, he stared thoughtfully at the telephone on a table beside him, his heart beating faster as the intention formed in his mind. The receiver felt slippery in his hand as he dialled his parents' number and his breathing was uncomfortably irregular as he heard the ringing tone at the other end. At the click of the downline receiver being picked up, he flew into a panic and replaced his with a trembling hand, filled with a sense of failure. This was a nightly ritual. The wondering how they were, the craving to talk to them, then the confusion, the anger, the shame, and the cop-out. What was the point of contacting them anyway, when he couldn't handle the way things were?

Taking some notes on the psychology of management from his briefcase, he leafed through them in preparation for a company exam he was to take at the end of the week. But

421

forced by lack of concentration to postpone his study until later, when it would be cooler, he rose and switched on the television. It was *Top of the Pops*, which he normally enjoyed. But the sight of crowds of exuberant teenagers being noisily ecstatic over their pop idols was acutely depressing to him in his melancholic mood, so he turned the television off and sat in the chair, staring idly around the room.

It was a tiny basement flat in Earls Court with just the basic facilities, a living room, a cupboard of a kitchen, a skimpy bathroom and a bedroom. One couldn't be choosy with the high price of accommodation in the metropolis, and his job offered more in potential than actual pounds at this early stage. He'd only managed to get this place through a friend of a friend he'd known at college. He had furnished it mostly through secondhand shops with a Sixties sofa, a pair of Fifties armchairs, and God knew which decade his cumbersome old dining table originated from. As long as he had a roof over his head, that was all that mattered to him. And the place was quite cosy really. The carpet was new and the Hockney and Blake prints on the wall added a personal touch.

He knew he had no right to be gloomy. After all, he had the world at his feet, career wise. He'd been told only the other day, by one of the hierarchy in the company, that they had great things in mind for him. He had been lucky to be given a second chance with another chain store firm. Leaving Hilbury's in mid contract could have been disastrous. But he had felt compelled to cut himself off from contact from his folks and start a new life. And Hilbury's had been very understanding. They had agreed to give him a reference, and had even hinted that there would be a place with them in the future, if he wanted it.

Currently on a management trainee course at his new company's head office in the West End, he would soon be ready to take up a position as assistant manager and which he would eventually progress to store manager, then area manager and beyond. But what was the point of getting to the top when you didn't have those you loved around you to share it?

When he'd stormed out of their lives seven months ago, full of righteous indignation, he had not realised just how much he would miss his family. In small everyday ways, like their guaranteed interest when he called for a chat, their certain welcome when he visited, their familiarity, their moral support.

And then there was Lizzie with the cornflower eyes and the red hair. Not a day passed that he wasn't tempted to call her, but didn't because she was all part of the muddle he wanted to forget.

The ring of the telephone startled him from his introspection. It was Mandy from Accounts. He'd got talking to her in the staff restaurant and they had gone for a meal together in a bistro in the West End last night. 'Hi, Stevie,' she chirped. 'I'm just calling to tell you that I had a great time last night.'

'So did I.'

'Are you busy tonight?' asked Mandy, a warm-hearted girl who made no pretence of being hard to get.

'I am, yes,' lied Stevie. He wasn't ready for a relationship.

'Oh, I see. Another time then.'

'Yes. I'll see you at work, we'll fix something up maybe.'

'Yeah, right.' She sounded hurt. Hurting people seemed to have become a speciality of his. 'I'll see you then.'

'Yeah, right. See you. 'Bye.'

The phone rang again almost immediately. This time it was his pal David from college. 'Fancy a game of squash? I've got a court booked, but the bloke I was due to partner cried off because of the heat.'

'I don't blame him, it's much too warm.'

'It will be cool at the courts,' David persuaded. 'And we'll have a couple of lagers afterwards. Come on, be a sport.'

'Okay, you've twisted my arm. What time?'

Play was fast and energetic and Stevie felt better for the exercise. But he was thrown back into turmoil in the showers afterwards when David said, 'I saw Lizzie Bennett at a party the other night.'

'Oh!' Stevie felt winded at hearing her name. 'How is she?'

'She starts work for a design agency next month,' David informed him.

Stevie was grateful for the flow of water over his face which hid his reaction. 'Good for her. I bet she's thrilled to bits.'

'Oh yes,' came David's voice from beneath the spray. 'She looks terrific, actually.'

Struggling unsuccessfully not to reveal his interest, Stevie asked, 'Was she with anyone in particular?'

'Yes, a chap she knew at college. A tall, bearded type.'

'Oh, I see.'

'I was surprised you two didn't make a go of it,' said David, stepping out of the shower and wrapping himself in a towel. 'You both seemed so keen.'

'We were never really right for each other,' lied Stevie with feigned nonchalance. He still felt shell-shocked when they arrived at the pub on the corner.

Bella parked her car in a metered space in a side street near the Strand and stood in the late afternoon sunshine, staring at a nearby office building, waiting for the glass doors to open and disgorge the hundreds of people who worked inside. The rush hour was already underway and the streets teemed with people. They poured towards the tube, queued for buses and jostled for taxis on this warm August afternoon. Yesterday the temperatures in London had soared to the highest for thirty-five years. Vehicle engines throbbed to a standstill, hooters blared in impatient staccato, traffic fumes hung suffocatingly in the air, and the sun burned the back of Bella's neck. Oh to be at Lakewood on a day like this.

They were beginning to come out, in dribs and drabs at first, then in a thick steady stream like gravy from a jug; secretaries in summer frocks, dark-suited executives, clerks, typists, accountants. Fearing that she might miss him in the crush, Bella screwed up her eyes in concentration, the reflection of the sun on glass making them smart. The rush was over, just stragglers now. She must have missed him. Or perhaps management finished later. Yes, that would be it. An hour passed. The building looked deserted. Oh well, she'd just have to contact the personnel department of these new employers tomorrow for his home address, something she had wanted to avoid out of deference to his privacy. It had been bad enough having to admit to Hilbury's that she didn't know where her son was.

But then he appeared. Despite the pain and anger that had driven her here, she was possessed with love and pride for this fine young man, smart in a business suit and carrying a briefcase. He was with a colleague and together they walked down the steps, then parted company oblivious of the woman waiting nearby. Bella pelted after Stevie who was about to disappear into the tube station. When she finally caught up with him, she tapped him on the shoulder.

'*Mum!*' A mixture of emotions registered in his eyes: shock, joy, sullenness. 'What are you doing here?'

'I must speak to you,' she said resolutely. 'My car is just around the corner. You can direct me to your place. What I have to say is best said in private.'

He stared at her silently for a few moments, his expression unreadable, then he said, 'I live at Earls Court.'

The atmosphere was unbearably tense on the journey which was lengthened by the heavy traffic. She was cool, he icily polite. He enquired after her health and John's and she answered vaguely, since this was not quite the moment to break the news.

'How did you find me?' he asked.

'Through Hilbury's. Your new employers asked them for a reference. They kept the details on file.'

'Oh, I see.'

'You seem to have landed on your feet,' she said crisply. 'I hope you realise how lucky you are. With unemployment rising it isn't as easy as it was, even for graduates.'

'I know.'

The conversation was formal, the generation gap exceptionally noticeable as she maintained the authoritative air necessary to the success of this meeting.

Inside Stevie's flat she accepted the offer of a cold drink, since she was parched, but declined food and dispensed with formalities. 'I'll come straight to the point.' Her tone was brisk. Having grown used to John's pallor and increasing weakness over the last weeks, Stevie's youth and robust health reminded her that he had so much, and John so little. Her anger was rekindled. Seeing no point in disguising the facts she said, 'Your father, and of course I mean John, is dying. He won't see Christmas this year.'

He flinched as though receiving a physical blow and turned ashen beneath his tan. 'What!' His voice was barely audible.

'I felt you ought to know,' she said, resisting the urge to fling her arms around him and comfort him as she had when he was a boy.

'Oh my God!' He cradled his head in his hands. 'What ... how ...?'

She gave him the basic facts, then continued, 'What I have to say might seem harsh coming on the heels of such news, but it must be said.'

He waited, wiping a handkerchief over his face which was shiny with sweat.

Her mouth felt arid as she began: 'You have seen fit to cut John and me out of your life. As a grown man that is your prerogative, I can't force you to change your mind. But I damn well *will* make you hear our side of the story, whether you like it or not.'

He didn't say a word, but sat pale and still as she told him the whole story. 'You cannot possibly equate today's attitudes with the way unmarried mothers were treated when you were born,' she concluded. 'I did what I thought was best for you at the time and I have always tried to be a good mother to you. Your rejection of me indicates your feelings on that matter, and of course you are perfectly entitled to your opinion.' She paused and sipped her drink, her face flushed with emotion. 'But John is a very different matter. I simply won't let you break his heart after all he has done for you. He didn't take you on out of a sense of duty but from love. Love for me which became love for you the moment you were born. He has given endlessly to you, of his time, of his patience and his energy. He has worked hard to give you a good standard of living.'

'I'll go and see him, of course,' said Stevie awkwardly, besieged by a crossfire of emotions.

'Just a visit won't be enough,' she explained firmly. 'Now it's your turn to give him your time and your patience. I want you to put things back to how they were between the two of you. And he must never know that I approached you. He wants you to go back to him of your own accord, but I am not prepared to risk him dying an unhappy man because of your selfishness.'

'Everyone has a right to know who they really are,' Stevie said defensively.

'Yes, and you do. You are Stevie Sharpe, a fine, healthy, intelligent young man with a lifetime ahead of you. What more could anyone ask? And what relevance does your biological origin have to your life now? None at all.'

'I should have been told,' he mumbled, his face red and blotchy. 'Supposing Lizzie had not been adopted?'

'Then I would have told you, but as she is it's irrelevant,' Bella reasoned. 'I wish to God you'd not overheard us talking. You've certainly not gained anything from it.'

'It was a shock,' he muttered, studying his polished shoes.

'Of course it was. But we all have those from time to time. And it was seven months ago. It's time you came to terms with it. I am sorry you're upset, but I refuse to get down on my knees and beg your forgiveness for doing what I thought was right,' she told him sternly.

He looked up and eyed her sheepishly. 'Did you really love my natural father?' he asked.

'Very much. And I still do,' she admitted frankly.

Stevie sucked in his breath, narrowing his eyes quizzically. 'So you've lived with . . .' he hesitated over the word ' . . . Dad all these years without loving him, just for my sake. Is that what you're saying?'

Shaking her head emphatically, she said, 'No, not at all. I love John but I've never been "in love" with him. He knows that. What I feel for him is something between the way I'd feel for a brother and a very dear friend. We've had a great many happy years together, but what I feel for Dezi is very special.'

'I don't understand,' said Stevie with a shake of his head.

'And you won't until you are a lot older,' she told him. 'You see, love is much more than just the magic you feel for Lizzie right now. As you mature you'll discover that for yourself.'

'Will I?'

'Oh yes,' she said, rising. 'Anyway, I must go. I don't like to be away from John for too long, things being as they are.' She picked up her bag and strung it over her shoulder. 'I hope to see you at Lakewood very soon. And not a word to John about this meeting.'

She walked to the door and turned. Stevie had risen and was standing stiffly in the centre of the room. They faced each other, mother and son, separated by the irreversible past.

And then he rushed towards her and they were hugging each other and weeping uncontrollably. 'I'm sorry, Mum. So sorry. I've missed you all so much. Last night I dialled your number, but I didn't have the courage to follow through. I've been so confused.'

'Shush,' she soothed. 'You've not been mature enough to cope. But I think perhaps you've grown up now.'

'There was some sort of a fog in my mind,' he confessed as they drew apart, smiling weakly with relief. 'I just couldn't see my way through it.'

'I know, son,' she said, remembering her own experience of long ago.

'Let's go and see Dad,' Stevie said, and Bella knew he wasn't referring to Dezi.

Bella swung on to the forecourt of Brown's one Saturday in September and parked her BMW in a corner out of the customers' way. It was nice to see standards being maintained here despite the strain of increased overheads caused by the continuing rise in petrol prices. Not to mention the worry brought about by fierce Japanese competition on the car sales' side. Indeed, the place looked a picture, with flower boxes dotted around the gleaming well-stocked showrooms, smart modern pumps and a bright garage shop selling everything from ice cream to anoraks.

'Wotcher, Bel,' said Trevor when she appeared in the office which had once been her own. He was portly and balding in middle age. 'Up from the sticks, are yer?'

'I want to take a wander down the High Street, and wondered if I could leave the car here,' she explained. 'I'll have the devil's own job finding a parking space on a Saturday afternoon.'

''Course yer can, luv,' Trevor assured her. 'No need to ask. 'Ow's things at my favourite country 'ouse? Glad to 'ear that the prodigal son has returned.'

She chatted to him for a while, giving him an update on the news at Lakewood, then strode off into the milling crowds of shoppers in the High Street. She quite often came to Fulworth for no other reason than to absorb the buoyant atmosphere she had grown up in. She would amble around the shops, call on a few old friends, take a walk by the river. Today she had felt irresistibly compelled to come. And with Stevie keeping John company, and the staff coping admirably without her, she was able to obey her compulsion.

Having purchased some of John's favourite homemade toffee from a shop in a side street, and bought an LP for Stevie, she headed for the river. The towpath was noticeably quiet after the bustle of the town centre and she felt the past embrace her like a living thing. Was that why she had needed to come here today, before John died? To force the past into focus, assimilate it and flush out any lingering resentment for all the years with Dezi she had lost.

She remembered the Paris trip and how she had almost hated John afterwards for her obligation to him which had separated her from Dezi. The late Sixties had been a delicate time for Bella and John. She had been distant, he edgy. They had stumbled warily from day to day, not daring to bring the problem into the open for fear that a careless word might be the beginning of the end. Gradually, with a great deal of diplomacy and a new challenge, they had become close again. Lakewood had been their salvation, there was no doubt about that. Now it was almost over for John, she knew she was going to miss him like hell.

Ivy House drew her like a magnet and she climbed the steps as though driven by some outside force. Butterflies gathered in her stomach as they always had at the prospect of meeting Eve. So why am I here? she asked herself. Am I a masochist or something?

If Bella had been expecting to see a frail old dear on her last legs, she was in for a surprise. Eve looked older, of course, but there was a new strength about her. She was thin but spry

431

and her white hair shone, as ever, in neat silvery blue waves around her pointed face. She was wearing a navy shirtwaister dress, and her watery eyes glared at Bella from behind a pair of blue-framed spectacles.

'Hello, Eve.'

The older woman leaned forward and peered at Bella as though through a mist. 'Bella Brown, as I live and breathe. You've come back to haunt me, have you? Well, you'd better come in.'

'Sharpe,' corrected Bella. 'I'm Bella Sharpe.'

'You'll always be Bella Brown to me,' Eve informed her categorically.

She led the way into the drawing room, now more brightly appointed with colourful cretonnes and pastel walls. Tea was ordered from the loyal Mary and as they settled into armchairs Eve asked with the forthrightness of age, 'Now then, Bella, what brings you here?'

'I don't really know,' she admitted. 'I just had this sudden urge to see you.'

'Wanted to see if there was still life in the old girl, did you?' Eve thanked the ageing Mary for the tea and began to pour.

'Not at all,' Bella said, taking a cup from her hostess and setting it down on a table beside her. 'But I can see that there is. Indeed, you're looking very well.'

'I'm surviving,' Eve said, sipping her tea. 'One has to when left alone, despite the creaking joints.'

'How do you fill your time these days?' asked Bella conversationally.

'Playing bridge mostly.'

'I suppose that gives you a social life.'

'Oh, yes,' said Eve, nibbling daintily on a custard cream. 'One meets such a *nice* class of person playing bridge.'

Bella smiled inwardly, relieved to note that Eve had reverted to type since the last time she had seen her. Bella had not believed that untypical burst of sweetness would last.

'You're not too lonely without Frank then?' she asked.

'Not now I've grown used to it,' Eve admitted. 'I quite enjoy myself actually. Frank never liked me to have friends of my own, and I must say I find it rather fun. It is important to be with people of the same social class, of course. I'm very careful about that.'

I'll bet you are, thought Bella, almost laughing out loud, but said, 'I'm glad you've managed to make a life for yourself.'

'Dezi is very good to me,' Eve continued. 'He calls in regularly to make sure that I'm all right. And my dear grand-daughter, Lizzie, is a frequent visitor. I don't see much of Peter. His children bother more about me than he does. Sandie writes to me often from Paris.'

Bella noticed the careful avoidance of Peter's wife's name. And she knew why. Pearl wouldn't go near 'the condescending old cow' if her life depended on it.

'I understand that Lizzie and your son have made it up,' said Eve.

'Yes.'

'Quite a coincidence, them getting together.'

'Yes. The two families do seem destined to be linked, one way or another.'

'If things had worked out for you and Dezi, our young lovers would be very different people,' said Eve.

Something in her tone made Bella wonder if she suspected

the truth about Stevie. Dezi would not have told her as he, John and Bella had decided to keep the matter to themselves. Maybe one day Stevie might want to tell his grandmother. That was his decision.

'Just as well it didn't, for their sakes,' said Bella lightly.

'Mmm,' said Eve, throwing Bella a knowing look which told her that her intuition had been correct.

Eve said no more on the subject, however, but moved on to other topics. 'How is this guesthouse of yours doing?'

'It isn't a guesthouse,' Bella informed her. 'It's a country house hotel.'

'Hotel – guest house – boarding house,' said Eve dismissively. 'What's the difference? You're still skivvying for people.'

'I do employ a considerable number of staff,' said Bella. 'And I don't think they consider themselves to be just skivvies.'

'Yes, yes,' said Eve irritably.

Now that the older woman's bitchiness could no longer hurt her, Bella found it quite entertaining. 'Lakewood is really rather lovely. You must come and visit us and see for yourself.'

'Oh!' Eve was clearly taken aback at Bella's offer of hospitality. 'Well, I don't know about that. It's miles out, isn't it?'

'It isn't far by car. Stevie can drive you down one weekend,' Bella said.

'No need to patronise me because I'm old,' Eve snapped.

That really would be a case of the biter bit, Bella thought, but said, 'I wasn't. I was only trying to be friendly.'

'You and I have never got on, so why change the habit of a lifetime?'

'Why not?' asked Bella rhetorically, but didn't press the matter. The first move had been hers, the second must be Eve's. Living so close to terminal illness had shown Bella the utter pointlessness of acrimony between people. Eve was a bitch but a lonely one, whether she cared to admit it or not.

Bella left without mentioning her own current crisis, knowing that Eve would get to hear about it eventually through Lizzie. And it was hardly the cheeriest of subjects for someone of advanced years. Outside in the sunshine Bella felt that the visit had had a cathartic effect on her. At last she was freed from the last shreds of resentment towards Eve Bennett. She also knew that she did not regret her marriage to John. It had been an inevitable part of the pattern of her life and she was a richer person for it.

The river was olive green in the sunlight as Bella walked back along the bank. The water carried many and varied passengers: a practising rowing team, a vessel clearing drift-wood, several pleasure crafts, ducks, swans, plastic detergent containers. Moored in the shade of an oak tree was a residential barge.

She didn't go directly back to collect her car, but strolled along the shady avenues of Upper Fulworth and onwards through the shabbier back streets to Napley Road. She stood outside number nine, now an owner-occupied house gleaming from fresh paint and new windows.

Flooded with memories, she was staring dreamily at its flagstoned path and postage stamp garden, when a boy of about nine emerged from the front door and gave her an accusing look.

'Do yer want summink, missus?' he asked.

'No, I don't want anything,' she said, guessing that she was suspected of lurking with intent.

'That's orlright then,' he said, but he still eyed her warily as he rode circles on his bicycle in the car-lined street.

Hawthorn Grove was her next port of call. The prefabs had long since been replaced by high-rise flats, and although the name remained, the hawthorn bushes themselves were the victims of progress – though madness was the word Bella would have used to describe the inspiration behind these cheerless tower blocks. But although the landscape was unrecognisable in this particular spot, the essence of the area as a whole lingered still, in the streets and in her heart. Although she loved Lakewood, this was her manor, this was home. She knew exactly why John wanted to be buried here. One day, when she was not tied to business, she would come back, maybe get a place on the river. But right now there were other calls on her time. She walked back to Brown's, collected her car and drove back to Lakewood to face her awesome responsibilities.

John's passing was quite peaceful. He slipped away one misty October afternoon in a nursing home in Windsor, with Bella and Stevie by his side. He never knew how his son's return to the fold had been engineered, and Stevie more than made up for his earlier immaturity by spending every spare moment at Lakewood. As well as a companion to John, he had also proved to be a tower of strength to Bella, both in a business and a personal sense. For as John deteriorated and Bella was able to give less and less of her time to the hotel, Stevie, having been around Lakewood long enough to be familiar with its administration, stepped into the breach as though born to it. It was a great help and consolation to her.

One Saturday afternoon a couple of weeks after the funeral, when they were having tea together in the apartment at

Lakewood, he gave his mother some surprising news. 'I'm thinking of resigning from my job,' he announced.

'Oh, not again, Stevie,' she cried in alarm, worried that another move really would damage his career prospects. 'What's the problem this time?'

'No problem. I've finally realised what it is I want to do,' he explained.

'That sounds ominous,' she said, buttering a crumpet. 'I hope you haven't decided to give it all up to become a hippy.'

'Nothing like that,' he laughed. 'I've decided that I'd like to run Lakewood with you, if you'll have me.'

'Oh, Stevie!' she gasped. This was her dearest wish, but was it the best thing for him? 'I would love it, but is it big enough for you? I thought you wanted to get to the top in a multi-national company. You mustn't let your protective instincts towards me colour your judgement. I can run this place single-handed.'

'I know all that,' he told her. 'And that's not the sort of role I have in mind for myself. In fact, I have plans for the business . . .'

'Like mother, like son,' Bella smiled. 'Come on, let's have the whole story.'

'During the time that I was away from you all,' he began, 'I realised that I wasn't getting the buzz I'd expected out of working for a huge corporation.'

'But you're only a trainee,' she pointed out, sipping her tea. 'The job will get more interesting as time goes on.'

'Yes, but that certain spark has to be there. And I have never had that, not really. The whole big company thing is too impersonal. I didn't know what it was that was lacking until I got really involved in Lakewood in the weeks before Dad died. Then I experienced the satisfaction of feeling personally involved in an operation. Ideas for expansion flooded in.'

'Expansion isn't in my plans,' said Bella, frowning. 'Lakewood's essentially a product of the "small is beautiful" maxim. Make it bigger and you lose that personal touch.'

'I quite agree,' Stevie assured her. 'I was thinking more in terms of opening other country house hotels run on the same principles as Lakewood. There are so many mansions throughout the country crumbling away through neglect.'

It was an exciting proposition, but was it the right thing for either of them? Since she was twenty-one, Bella's life had been ruled by business. Did she want the added worry of expansion at this stage when she had anticipated having more free time, not less? She expressed her doubts.

'I was coming to that,' he said. 'It's time you had more freedom, and with me at your side that should be possible. The amount of responsibility I take in the business will be entirely up to you. But this way at least you'll know that you can get away, confident that your interests are being taken care of.'

Bella's thoughts were racing. She didn't doubt that Stevie was more than capable of succeeding with this project, but there were still some points she needed to clear up.

'How can you be sure that hotel management is for you, after just a few weeks' experience?' she asked, determined her son was not going to act too hastily.

'You had even less than that when you started Lakewood,' he pointed out.

'I did a course,' she reminded him.

'And so will I, if necessary. And I do have a degree in business studies, remember.'

'Running your own business isn't like working for a company. There's no such thing as nine to five and a non-contributory pension,' she enlightened him.

'I'm prepared for that,' he assured her.

'And what does Lizzie think about all this?' asked Bella. 'You'll have to live at Lakewood initially. She may not want to commute into the West End to her job after you're married.'

'You know how Lizzie feels about Lakewood. Just try keeping her away.'

Bella rose and went to the window, looking out over gardens hazed with mist on this late October afternoon. Uncle Wilf, busy with his autumn schedule, pushed a wheelbarrow laden with garden debris across the lawn, happy and fulfilled in his work. Neither he nor Auntie Vi had showed any inclination to retire. It occurred to Bella that if she had stopped to consider the risk she was taking when she'd bought Lakewood, she'd probably never have got past the dreaming stage. And how much the poorer they would all have been.

Stevie must be given the chance that her daring had created for him. After all, he was older than she had been when she'd had a failing garage thrust upon her. She turned to him, smiling. 'As long as you're sure, son, I think it's a wonderful idea.'

Chapter Twenty-four

Bella sat on the hotel balcony looking down over the square and thinking that travel brochures did not exaggerate when they extolled the virtues of Paris in the spring. It was a fine sunny evening in April 1976, with a light breeze carrying that special scent which indicated that winter was over at last.

Dressed in a white trouser suit and red silk blouse, her hair worn loose, she looked smart but casual, appropriately dressed for a walk around the city followed by dinner in a small restaurant. She leaned back and closed her eyes against the pale sun, feeling completely relaxed. She remembered the traumatic events of her last visit to this very same hotel. So much had happened since then.

Life was good now. Very good. Maybe it was wrong to feel this happy just six months after John's death but she didn't think so, not when she considered his dying wish for her future. She tried not to remember her anguish at his death, but only the good years they had shared. A part of her heart would be forever his.

Lakewood flashed into her mind, bringing the usual

instinctive moment of anxiety. But it vanished almost as quickly. Stevie had shown himself a more than capable manager, worthy of equity in the firm, and she could only see him going from strength to strength when he got the expansion programme underway later this year. Though the next major event in his life was his marriage to Lizzie.

Although Bella was still very involved in Lakewood, she was grateful not to be a live-in manager any longer. She enjoyed her new house in Richmond, which had been chosen for its convenient location close to the hotel.

It was amazing how everything had worked out so well, she thought. Stevie and Lizzie together again, Dezi and Stevie becoming friends. Even Pearl had excelled herself by sticking to her job in the salon, albeit moodily at times.

Bella was so deep in thought, she didn't hear the door to the room open.

'Enjoying the sunshine?' asked Dezi, placing his hands on her shoulders.

'Yes, it's beautiful here.'

He sat down beside her, clasping her hand. He had been out for a stroll while she got ready to go out. 'Are you pleased that we came to the same hotel?'

'Very pleased. It's good to get away on our own for a few days.'

'Our next holiday will be a honeymoon, I hope.'

She turned and looked at him with love in her eyes. 'It will be, I promise you,' she told him earnestly. 'I feel I should wait just a little longer, out of respect for John.'

'I understand,' he said squeezing her hand. They sat together in thoughtful silence, until the past finally yielded to the present.

'What about our favourite bistro in Montmartre for dinner?' she suggested.

'I hoped you'd say that.'

And they went out into the Paris evening, hand in hand.